"I DON'T WANT TO BE FREE!"

"You are my wife. I want no other," Alex said.

Cameron stood dumbfounded. What sort of cruel trick was he setting her up for now?

"A bastard?" she screamed.

"Dinna swear at me. I'm wound so tight I dinna trust myself not to rape or kill you!"

"I wasna swearing," yelled Cameron. "I'm a bastard, Sir Alexander Sinclair – a bastard – a bastard! And you hate it!" she raged, pounding on his chest with her fists, unaware of the tears that raced down her cheeks. "How can a gentleman be married to a bastard? How can a gentleman love a bastard? Tell me. Tell me! I have no name. I canna be a fancy lady even if I wanted to be. Well, I don't want to be. I'd much rather be a proud bastard than one of your simpering, corseted, painted ladies!"

"Cameron, I love you," he said gently, but the girl ranted on, not hearing him. "Cameron!" he shouted, drowning out her screams so she fell silent, waiting for the blows to strike her.

Aleen Malcolm

The Taming

Macdonald Futura Publishers

A Troubadour Book

First published in Great Britain by
Macdonald Futura Publishers Ltd in 1981

ISBN 0 7107 3017 9
Printed and bound in Great Britain by
©ollins, Glasgow

Macdonald Futura Publishers Ltd
Paulton House, 8 Shepherdess Walk
London N1 7LW

Part One
Summer 1761

O Caledonia! stern and wild,
Meet nurse for a poetic child!
Land of brown heath and shaggy wood;
Land of the mountain and the flood!
Land of my sires! what mortal hand
Can e'er untie the filial band
That knits me to thy rugged strand?
—Sir Walter Scott

Chapter One

Alexander Sinclair cantered across the bleak heathered moors toward Cape Wrath, wondering what he was doing in such a godforsaken place. Overhead the sun shone brightly and yet the wind whistled and howled as if complaining of his presence in its treeless domain. Pulling his cloak around him Alexander laughed ironically, remembering his eagerness to leave Edinburgh far behind; now he longed for its loathsome clamor. What madness had made him ride the length of Scotland in answer to a curt message from a man he scarcely remembered meeting?

"Oh, to see one living soul!" He roared across the stark heath.

He rode on, his lean handsome face cynically set as he recalled the round of balls and assemblies he'd attended, where strident mothers paraded their young daughters like prize sheep, each hoping that one of the simpering lambs would catch his or any other unattached man's fancy. Even such a gathering, complete with the clashing colors of competing gowns and overwhelming perfumes that fought each other failing to cover the odors of tightly packed bodies, was preferable to this desolation. He sighed, not noticing the sweet, clean sharpness of the air.

It was midsummer and the heather and ling bloomed purple under the deep blue sky, where hawks soared seemingly idle, their wings outstretched and unmoving, allowing the air currents to sweep under them. Alex reined his horse as a large bird dropped swiftly before him, its talons spread to cruelly seize its prey. A shrill scream shattered the stillness and the hawk languidly beat its great wings and flew with the soft furry animal caught in taut claws. Alex was repelled yet fascinated and, feeling a quickening in his blood, urged his horse to gallop as an excitement stirred in him.

In the late afternoon he stopped and looked down the sweep of the rolling moor to a gray, crumbling castle poised on the tip of a cliff that fell straight to the sea. How often had his father described this place, and not even with his fine gift for words and exaggeration had he ever conjured up such awesome bleakness. The castle stood cold and unwelcoming, as natural as if the fortress had sprung out of the hard, pitiless rocks. Alex stared all around, there were no crofts, no sheep, not one sign of human life as far as the eye could see. What better place for Duncan Fraser to exile himself after the bloody massacre on Culloden Moor had dealt the coup de grace to the house of Stuart, extinguishing the last spark of hope in the proud Highlanders.

Sadness softened the chiseled features of the young man as he remembered his own father's self-exile, first to France and then to the promising New World. He pictured the tall proud man for whom he'd been named and saw himself as a small boy striding beside him, trying to match his steps, imitating his every gesture as he despaired of ever growing as strong and fearless. How close they had been, the two Sinclair men in a household of womenfolk, Alex believing his godlike father could conquer and cope with everything from dragons to the English. From the time of his first recollection until that nightmarish day at the age of twelve his father had been his hero, his world, the man he strove to be.

Alex's mind dwelled on that fateful voyage to North America, allowing the long-locked floodgate of grief, shock, and disillusionment to pour in. He remembered standing on the creaking, heaving deck as the tarpaulin-wrapped bodies of his mother and two sisters were committed forever to their watery grave, along with numerous anonymous others. He was twelve years old and had thought himself nearly a man but, as the waves closed over, leaving not a trace of the precious gifts that had just been swallowed, he'd felt unable to stand tall and straight. He had turned to burrow into the safety of his father's strong arms, only to see a pitiful, groveling man. He had turned his eyes back to the still-hungry, pitching sea, trying to block out the terrifying sight of the man beside him. He had locked his shaking knees to stand stiffly, ignoring the beloved hands that soon tore at his clothes seeking comfort. He had concentrated on the droning voice of the priest, refusing to hear the shattering cries of his father.

Alex had been loved and adored, protected and nurtured, as befits the only son of a proud Highland chief. He was totally unprepared for the crashing weight that fell on his half-grown shoulders as his father toppled from the high pedestal where his young mind had placed him. The terrible realization that a mere woman could have wrought the impossible feat of bringing such a mighty man to his knees, when the whole English army and the loss of his lands hadn't, tore into Alex, and he swore never to be so vulnerable.

His father had never recovered, but instead he shrank into a pitiful weeping shadow who had to be carried like a babe onto the shore of the brave New World, only to cry to be returned to his beloved Scotland to die. Numbly Alex became father to his own father, hating and despising him for the weakness of allowing his pride, dignity, and manliness to die with his wife. Silently he vowed never to let himself be so bound.

Ten years had passed since Alex had brought his father back to Scotland to die. It had taken three years of hard work in America to earn the fare, then ten long years of swallowing his pride as he claimed part of his family lands under English rule.

Now at the age of twenty-five the past with its pain and guilt rose up and flooded in as he stared at the cold fortress of his father's closest friend.

Alex rode into the courtyard, his horse's hooves clattering and echoing in the emptiness. It seemed deserted and he laughed hollowly, thinking he'd come so far on a wild goose chase. He looked up again, scanning the dark, haunted windows for some sign of habitation and was startled by a piercing cackle. A wild-haired crone stood in the doorway, clutching her hips with bony hands.

"Sir Duncan Fraser?" he inquired, leading his horse toward the strange woman.

"Do I look like a man?" screeched the hag, swinging her long gray strings of hair and pushing out her large sagging breasts.

"Does he live here?"

"Aye, what of it?" answered the crone, baring an ankle as if she were a saucy young girl.

"He sent for me."

"Did he now?"

"Aye. I'm Sir Alexander Sinclair," he stated coldly, his patience dwindling.

"I don't care if you're the pope hisself. Begone. He don't need anyone but me."

"I have ridden all the way from Edinburgh at his request and I will see him, my good woman."

"I am not your good woman!" she shrieked. "I know you fancy dandy lords, all after Mara's wee body. Well, you won't get it. 'Tis only for Sir Duncan, not for the likes of you."

Alex surveyed the old woman with disgust as she pranced and danced on her spindly legs, her heavy body flopping and heaving. He stood at a loss, not knowing what to do as she raged and ranted.

A bell sounded, its tinny noise seeming out of place in the massive stone castle. It belonged in a small tea parlor, thought Alex, hearing its persistent tinkle. Mara stopped her frantic prancing; she listened, cocking her head to the side and, picking up her filthy skirts, turned and ran into the darkness. Alex swiftly tied his horse and followed.

Through a center hall, where a fire blazed, and up wide stone steps he chased her, his booted feet echoing.

"He's mine, I tell you, mine," hissed the fleet-footed old crone ahead of him, coming to a door at the end of a long dark passage.

"Mara? Has Sinclair arrived?" asked a deep voice from within.

"Aye, 'tis Alex Sinclair," answered Alex.

"You'll kill him," whined the old woman, barring the door with her body.

"Come in lad, come in."

Alex gently but firmly lifted the old woman aside and opened the door. The setting sun poured through the slit of a window in a dusty stream, lighting the old man's bed with a reddish glow.

"Come nearer lad."

Alex stared down at Duncan Fraser, not knowing what to say.

"Put your face nearer." The old man's eyes stared into Alex's amber ones. "Aye, you've your father's whiskey eyes, lad."

Duncan Fraser was as gray as the stones he'd buried himself among. The iron-gray hair circled his head like a halo, and even his skin had a metallic pallor. Many sadnesses flowed through Alex in the few moments of silence as the old gray eyes probed his. This was the man his father loved as himself.

"Help me up, lad."

"You'll do no such thing. You'll kill him!" screamed Mara, pushing Alex aside and plumping and tucking the bed.

"Get out, you silly old coot." The strength in Duncan's voice belied his wasted body.

"You hush up and dinna fash yourself. I'll get rid of him," replied Mara. "You ken you must be still. I'm to die first, not you."

"I ken my time is near done, my strength near sapped, so don't drain the dregs from me, you old witch, or I'll leap out of this bed and die right now at your feet."

"I'm going, I'm going. I'm nearly gone," sniveled the old hag. She reached the door and turned back, tears streaming down her face.

"I'm near gone, but dinna go before me," she sobbed, and scurried out.

"I canna stand sniveling wet faces. Well, what are you a'waiting on, lad? I ain't got much time. Help me to the window. Oh, sick I am of staring at the walls and ceiling."

Alex hesitated and the old man chuckled. "Mind

your elders, son. 'Tis the privilege of the dying to have their last requests granted."

Alex wrapped the thin wasted body against the chill air, lifted him like a baby into his arms, and set him down in a chair by the window.

Outside the purples and grays of the heathered moors and rippling sea were reflected in the clouds that hung threateningly low, dipping toward the hard curves of the rolling hills.

"Like breasts they are today. Near full of sweetness ready to spill," chuckled Duncan, as he feasted his hungry eyes on his domain, miles and miles of windswept undulating desolation that fell abruptly to the sea in jagged cruel teeth.

"You need my help, sir?" ventured Alex.

"Wait. Wait. Youth is so impatient. You'll see. You'll see," hissed the old man, waving his clawlike hand as his eyes scanned the coastline.

Alex stared out at the deepening gray. So still, nothing moved. It all seemed to be waiting for the impending storm.

Was the old man senile? Was his own presence there just a dying fancy of Duncan's? Alex mused and smiled ruefully as he stared around the cheerless bedchamber, thinking of all the other bedchambers he could be in with much fairer companions than this brittle old man. What was he doing there? Was it some nostalgic sense of duty in the memory of his own dead father? How many times had his father entertained him with stories of his and Duncan's exploits? It was sad what age could do; it was hard to imagine this frail and wizened man as the redheaded warrior or the charming seducer of days past.

As though Duncan could read his thoughts, he said, "Oh, how the mighty have fallen, eh? Eh?" Even as he spoke, his eyes never left the coastline.

"Oh, once I was . . . Was is an empty word, isn't it now? Ah, but all things come to dust you know. I've had plenty of time to think. Too much time to think and not enough time to do. Too little time to undo. . . . His voice trailed off; his eyes, centered in a myriad of wrinkles, sharply raked the moorland. Searching, waiting, watching—for what?

Outside now the purples and grays had merged to a more ominous color, yet all was still. Not the whisper of a breeze nor the lap of a wave disturbed the heavy silence. Across the horizon was a bar of lilac light.

"'Tis nearly time," whispered Duncan, leaning forward, his face glowing with anticipation. Alex forced his eyes from the ancient features and stared out, expecting the storm to break, but saw nothing.

"There—there," breathed Duncan, pointing.

Across the frozen stillness something moved. Silhouetted against the horizon was a rider, a small figure on a giant horse, plaid streaming, kilt thrown up against the body, an enormous hound running alongside.

"There, there's my life. My reason, only reason for being. The only thing I will live on through. 'Tis yours now."

Alex, bewildered, stared down at the rider as the storm finally broke and the sea raged against the cliffs.

"I don't understand." The thunder drowned his words.

"You are your father's son. Spawn of a wild one that's why you're here. Not many of us left, mostly dead, their blood in the sunset or running in the heather."

Outside the storm raged in the growing darkness. The lightning rent the air, highlighting the rider who raced with the shrieking wind, seeming to dare the very violence of the elements. Alex watched with fascination as Duncan clutched his arm, the bony fingers digging through his sleeve into his flesh.

"See? See? Ever see such magnificence? 'Tis the spirit of true Scotland you are looking at. Wild and free but alas undisciplined, no direction. I was too selfish. Too bound up in my bitterness. 'Tis now for you to do. I give you my child, my bairn into your keeping."

As though all nature knew the sanctity of the old man's last earthly breath, the storm stopped abruptly and hung suspended. The rider turned and stared up at the window and, throwing arms out as though to embrace, screamed. The child was far away and yet the scream pierced the silence, echoing and spiraling into the darkness. As the anguished reverberation died away, the storm resumed with even greater ferocity.

Alex stared at the gnarled hand that still clutched him. Dead. Duncan Fraser was dead. How fitting, with all his father had told him, for Duncan Fraser to die at the peak of a storm and, in passing, silence it for so poignant a moment.

Gently untangling the hand from his sleeve Alex picked up the old man and laid him back on his bed. He stood looking down, wondering what sport his father and Duncan would be having in the afterlife, and then he remembered the child. What child? From all he'd heard, Duncan Fraser had never married, having had great disdain for women except to slake his desires. What would he do with a child? And a wild untamed one at that, judging from the display in the storm.

At that moment the door burst open, rudely shocking him from his jumbled thoughts, and the old crone leaped in. Alex opened his mouth to inform her gently of Duncan's death, but she threw herself upon the body and keaned loudly.

"You promised me, you promised I could die first. Gone are you my old man, my love, my life. Gone before me yet you promised I could go first. Never could trust you, never. Well, you'll not get rid of Mara so easy, my Jocko, I'm a'comin' too."

Before Alex realized what she was about, the old woman drew out a wicked-looking dirk from beneath her layers of rags.

"Aye, yer'll not rid yerself of me so easy, me old lad," she screeched, raising the dagger high with both sinewy hands, the blade pointing to her heart.

"What are you doing?" hissed Alex, springing out of his stunned inertia and wrestling the knife from her. "Take yer lecherous paws off me, yer filthy sassenach. Yer'll no stop me following the old reprobate to hell and back," she spat, trying to recover her lost weapon. Alex tossed it through the high window before letting go of the wild, clawing old woman, who sprang nimbly from him.

"I dinna need the dirk. I dinna need it. I can wait. I've waited long years enough, so a few more days I've patience for," she crowed, staring down at Duncan's still, gray face.

"Yer hear that, old man? Yer Mara's a'comin'. 'Twill not be long, yer lusty old rooster, and yer'll have me for all eternity, and that'll teach yer to keep yer promises. Twenty years and more yer've been a'promising to wed yer old Mara, but yer've always put it off, always putting me off, putting everything off except yer dying."

Alex stared in horrified amazement as she started stripping herself of her filthy clothes, baring her old dried-up breasts. The old woman froze, remembering Alex's presence, and then viciously stabbed a bony finger in his direction.

"Ooot! Ooot, I say, and take yer woman-hungering

eyes with yer, yer nappy-clad busybody! 'Tis a private time betwixt me and the old cockiedoodle. I'm just for him."

Alex stood outside the bedchamber door, unwilling to observe the old woman's mad ravings and scramblings. He gazed down the dark corridor to a warm light at the end and walked toward it, finding the stairs to the large central hall, where the fire blazed and a table was set with bread and drink. He called for servants but, getting no response, helped himself to whiskey and sat brooding by the fire. He felt totally unable to think logically. The touch of a cold wet nose broke his reverie, and he looked straight into the shaggy face of an enormous hound. He sat very still, allowing the giant beast to make up his mind as to his being friend, foe, or the next meal, and he sighed with relief at the animal's obvious approval of him.

"Well now, you big beastie, can you be telling me what in tarnation is going on here?" he asked, looking into the soulful brown eyes as he scratched behind one of the floppy ears.

A shrill whistle sounded, causing the great hound to bound away. Alex followed but soon returned to the sparse comfort of the fire, not wanting to get lost in the cold dark maze of passages that had spirited both whistler and hound away.

His body ached from the long grueling ride and hunger gnawed at his stomach. His tired brain strained to understand what had happened to him—what he was doing, why he was here. Had he somehow wanted to reach back through the years and find the strong father of his childhood through Duncan Fraser, his father's friend? Why? In atonement for the guilt of disloyalty and the disrespect he'd felt?

Unable to sit still Alex paced back and forth across the hard floor, his boots sharply cutting and echoing through the deathly stillness of the crumbling castle.

"Excuse me, sir?" A timid voice came from the shadows and two black-clothed people emerged.

"I'm Jeanette. I come here as maid. And here's Michael Grant from the stables." She clutched the arm of the young man beside her.

"Is there a room prepared for me?" barked Alex impatiently.

"Right away, sir. Sorry, sir, but we was off in Durness and we come home to find your horse, didn't we Michael?"

"Aye, sir, he's fed and rubbed down now in the stables. Sir Duncan's dead, sir. Or so crazy Mara screamed through the door when Jeanette here took up his supper."

"Aye, he's dead and he won't be coming alive again, even if I die of hunger and lack of sleep. So would you bring me some decent food and show me to my chamber?"

"Aye, sir, at once, sir, but Michael has to ride back to Durness to fetch the priest. He says the master dinna want no priest, though. He says he cursed the Catholic Church, sir." She hastily crossed herself before continuing. "But 'taint right, sir. Tell him he should go, sir."

Alex sighed wearily. "Is there no one else here to help you?"

"The master sent for his lawyer in Inverness last week and we've been expecting him these past days, sir," explained Michael Grant.

"Is there no one else here?" repeated Alex.

"Just Jeanette, crazy Mara, Dora, who come two weeks ago with Jeanette to help in the kitchen, and me, sir," stammered Michael.

"What of the child?"

"We's not to speak of it, sir. Sir Duncan asked us special when we got the jobs."

"Wish we never got the jobs, buried away in this dreary place," shivered the young maid.

Realizing his hopes of sleep were not to be answered yet, Alex turned to the young stableboy.

"Go to Durness, Michael, and bring women to lay him out. Bring who you think best. Jeanette, go and get me something hot to eat," said Alex, as he sat again in the hard uncomfortable chair by the fire.

No longer hungry but still unrested Alex plied the young maid with questions and got no answers.

"I don't know nothing, sir, nor does Dora. We only just come, and we was going to leave as soon as you and the lawyer come and went. 'Tis a strange place, sir."

"What of the child?" asked Alex again, but the thin shoulders just shrugged as she led him to a bedchamber and then scurried away silently in the darkness.

Fortunately Alex's weariness caused him to sleep as soon as his head touched the damp, mildewed pillow. He awoke in the morning, refreshed but disgusted at the filth he'd lain in all night. He stared around the cold, cobwebby room, his nostrils flaring at the musty, dank odor. The sooner he quit the place the better, he thought, as he slammed out of the room, determined to sleep on the open moors rather than in that filthy place again.

Where the rest of the day went, Alex had no recollection. It was as though he had joined the stones and walked, sat, and thought in a cold gray vacuum. He had strode behind the short funeral procession across the windy moor, his staring eyes glued to the black figures in front of him until the wailing of the pibroch awakened him, opening his heart with a sharp, sad aching. He had watched as Duncan Fraser's coffin was buried deep in the earth and the cairn piled high to mark the spot. Where was the elusive child? he thought, staring around at the few faces. Only the two maids and the groom stood stamping their cold feet and wrapping their bodies more tightly against the wind as they prepared to return home.

Back in the uncomfortable chair by the fire in the central hall Alex tried to recall the day. He remembered Mara's screams as the village women had pulled her naked from the dead man's room after she'd set fire to all Duncan's possessions. She'd run up the moor keaning and beating her bare breasts, but her shrillness hadn't penetrated the gray fog that surrounded Alex; only the pipe's lament had stirred him, and he sat now thinking of Duncan's last words.

"I give you my bairn . . . for your keeping," he murmured aloud. What sort of beloved son was this bairn who didn't even come to his father's burial? Legitimate issue or not, it was disrespectful, thought Alex, wondering what he was in for. He stared out of a high window at the sunset, hoping no English were near to hear the keaning of the outlawed pipes. The pibroch wailed and the piper, kilts tossed by the wind, strode toward the cairn followed by the large hound, stopping and letting the last note trail. Alex held his breath as he recognized the child, who then dropped the pipes and embraced the stones. He forced himself to keep watching, somehow unable to race out of the castle to finally confront the elusive, wild child.

It was a long time since Alex had seen anyone dressed in a tartan, and he wondered at the daring of the child, knowing it was punishable by death if the English saw. He smiled sadly, remembering how as a small boy he and his father had defied the English by striding bare with their britches on their heads, ridiculing the law which did not state *where* they were to be worn when the kilt had been outlawed.

How brave and rash they'd been, and had it been worth it? It was like looking at the past, seeing the small kilted figure stride proudly with the pipes. Alex shook his head to clear the feeling of nostalgia and looked objectively at the child. It was far, but he could see the long slender legs sticking out of the too-short kilt, a glint in the setting sunlight shining on a dirk tucked into a boot, and the child's hair, dark and glossy. He strained his eyes but could see no more. He debated going down but was loath to interrupt the child's private grieving, knowing also it would show a commitment he wasn't sure he wanted to make.

In fact he knew he didn't want the burden of a child. He enjoyed his independence and freedom too much to be weighed down with such responsibility. He eased his niggling conscience, having learned from the groom Michael that the lawyer from Inverness had arrived and the will was to be read the following day. Time enough then to meet Duncan's wild offspring, he told himself.

The next day found Alex seated at the end of a long table in an enormous banquet hall hung with the tattered banners of bygone glory, as a stout lawyer tried to add some levity to the dour proceedings. Not one of the stony faces so much as cracked a smile. Alex stared at the thin, gaunt, humorless features around him, skulls carved out of the harsh environment, closed and guarded, accustomed to isolation. Who were these people sitting around the table with him? he wondered, as they sat waiting, while the rotund lawyer droned on about his wife's vapors and his gout and finally sputtered into silence at the the lack of interest.

Alex drummed his fingers, assuming they were waiting for the elusive child, but the time dragged on until at last the rotund lawyer cleared his throat.

"Sir Alexander Sinclair?" he questioned, and the row of stony faces turned as one and stared at him. Alex looked at the expressionless facades and nodded slightly, acknowledging.

"I am Charles Hum, solicitor to the late Duncan Fraser, and these are the kind Christian people of Durness who are concerned with the welfare of the bairn," he gabbled, waving his hand.

"Aye, we'll have no more of that changeling turning our milk sour and weaving evil spells," hissed one of the women to her neighbor, who nodded, pursing her thin lips.

"Aye, 'tis evil itself riding that great devil of a horse with the great beastie of Satan a'flying beside," spat another.

"Spewed out of the sea at the full moon, I heard it tell, and many can bear witness to it," whispered another, and four black bonnets fervently bobbed up and down in agreement.

Seemingly oblivious to the sibilant gossiping Mr. Hum looked anxiously at his watch and the door, cleared his throat again, and read the last will and testament in a stentorian voice as he paced up and down on short fat legs.

Alex heard the pompous droning leaving all Duncan's worldly goods to one named Cameron. As Mr. Hum reached the part about legal guardianship there was a murmur of contentment and relief followed by a wild scream of rage. A small lithe figure in a swirling, green hunting plaid burst from behind the door and launched into the solicitor's belly, pushing him backward so he sat staring in fear as the will was torn into little pieces and thrown at him.

"Has the mark of the devil, all right," muttered a gray-haired woman, backing away and crossing herself hastily, along with her Christian friends, who hung onto their crucifixes for dear life.

Alex, amused at the turn of events, chastised himself on remembering his responsibility and eased his tall frame out of the chair to grab the wild Cameron, who proceeded to kick out at him wherever possible. This lad needs a lesson about fighting foul, thought Alex, as he avoided the jabbing legs. Tucking the wildly flailing child under his arm in such a way as to render the sharp feet and hands useless, Alex turned back to his companions at the table only to find them exiting as they tied their black bonnets and donned their black hats. Charles Hum scrambled to his feet, panting with exertion. Red-faced he handed Alex a copy of the will and scurried after the others, pausing for a brief second in the doorway.

"Well, I'm glad to see everything is to everyone's satisfaction. Good day." And ramming his hat on his bald head he left.

Alex stood in stupefaction, still holding the child in an effort to restrain him.

"To everyone's satisfaction except mine," he muttered, raising his eyes to the ceiling as he silently cursed his father for his friendship with Duncan Fraser. A stream of curses issued from his struggling charge and, mindful that he was not among his peers in a gaming house, Alex delivered a hard whack to the small wriggling behind. All struggling ceased and Alex found himself in possession of a dead weight.

"My God!" he groaned, not sure of how much force to use on a child, never having had occasion before to discipline one. He eased the child into a chair by the fire and as his arms relaxed, Cameron acted. One minute the small body was limp, the next it was coiled to spring with a dagger in hand. Alex saw the telltale glint and leaped aside in time, managing to wrest the weapon from his small assailant.

"Enough!" roared Alex, his temper aroused as he pinned Cameron against the table. Strange defiant green eyes stared into his, raven-black hair tangled across the panting little face. Alex swept the hair back roughly and held it in a painful grip as he scrutinized the rebellious face, struck by the delicately moulded features.

"I don't like it any more than you. We are stuck with each other whether we like it or not, until you reach your majority, and then you are welcome to this inhospitable pile of stones. But I'm warning you right now: You pull a knife or any other weapon on me again, I'll mark you with it, child or no child, you ken?"

The child neither answered nor looked away.

"Get your things together. And change your way of dressing, I don't fancy the English at my throat," he growled, unnerved by the wide-spaced green eyes staring at him. The child didn't move.

"Get your things packed. I've no desire to stay here longer than I must," Alex insisted, and still the child made no move to obey.

"Then take nothing. I'll strip and dress you on the way," Alex roared.

The defiance left Cameron's eyes and was replaced for a moment by fear, then quickly covered.

"Will you collect your things together?" asked Alex more gently, the fleeting moment of panic observed. The dark head nodded, and Cameron proudly walked to the door.

"And hurry."

As the door closed behind his ward, Alex poured himself a stiff drink and looked over the papers Mr. Hum had left. He was wet nurse to a snotty brat of unknown age, probably around twelve from the size and hairless cheek, he estimated, realizing to his dismay the years that stretched ahead before Cameron reached majority. Send him to a good school, and at sixteen or so into a good regiment, unless he's the studious type, Alex planned. Lost in thought Alex sat sipping his whiskey, not noticing the time pass.

"Excuse me, sir, but seeing as how we's off, I thought I should tell you," stammered Jeanette awkwardly, holding a large bundle. "I left food for your journey on the table."

"Where's Cameron?" asked Alex, getting to his feet.

"Rid off awhile back, sir, with that great savage beast."

"What? And nobody bothered to stop him or inform me?"

" 'Taint nobody's business, sir. Nobody dare tangle with that Cameron. 'Tis a changeling, witch's spawn, so crazy Mara says," explained Jeanette, backing hastily out of the room away from Alex's anger.

Alone in the dark cold castle Alex poured himself another drink.

"Well, I tried, didn't I?" he roared into the rafters. "You canna say I did not try, can you? But you canna expect me to go chasing over the Highlands after some wild changeling brat, can you now?"

He settled back in his chair and raised the glass to his lips only to fling it violently so that it smashed across the hard gray stones as he angrily rose and left the house.

Alex packed the prepared food and swung himself into the saddle. He cantered slowly up the moor toward Duncan's cairn, pausing to turn and stare down at the hollow-eyed fortress and the white-tipped waves that lashed the cliff. What would become of that stone monument now, he wondered. Would it be worn down little by little like the Scottish pride, eroding to dust, lost in the sands of time?

He swung his horse's head around and looked at Duncan's cairn, noticing the prints of a horse and hound in the damp, newly turned earth. So Cameron had come to bid his grandfather good-bye. Alex debated with himself whether to ignore the tracks and get himself to a warm comfortable inn in Durness, or to follow them. He felt a pang of unease remembering the "kind" Christian people of Durness's words of witch's spawn and changeling and knowing of the burnings that had taken place as Scots turned their fears and frustrations at each other. Reluctantly he put off the thought of a hot bath and comfortable bed and followed the tracks as they disappeared into the heather across the barren moor.

Chapter Two

What can I do? Where can I go? What can I do?
Where can I go, drummed the horse's hooves and
Cameron's thoughts, as they galloped over the darken-
ing moorland.

Cameron glanced down at the great hound who
loped beside and wondered fearfully if he could maintain the grueling pace.

The sun was setting into the sea behind them as
they raced toward the cover of a far-off valley. As beloved as the wild moors were, Cameron now cursed
them for their lack of safe arbors where they could
hide until the tall strong stranger had returned from
whence he came. Oh, that he had spoken truthfully
about disliking the situation, so they might go back to
the castle and live in peace.

Seeing a small pool reflecting the red sky in the
deep purple heather, Cameron stopped to allow the
great stallion Torquod to drink, and dismounting,
kneeled and stared into the reflection, for a moment
not recognizing the small, haunted-faced girl that
looked back at her. Bending closer and closer until the

faces merged, she plunged her hot, worried face into the crystal-clear water, but she could not allow herself to linger there. Remembering the possibility of pursuit Cameron threw herself on Torquod's high back and kicked with her heels, resuming the fast pace of before.

Finally Cameron slowed the horse to a trot, worried in the twilight of ruts and holes that could cause Torquod injury. Her mind dwelled on her predicament and panic flared. There was nobody now who cared whether she lived or died. She fought the panic, telling herself she needed no one. People weren't to be trusted anyway. Her grandfather knew that; that's why he'd hidden them both away from crofts and villages; that's why the servants stayed but a week or so, and left after robbing them blind. Even Mara, who'd been there forever, was not to be trusted.

Cameron's mind burned with the thought of Mara, whose insane jealousy and possessiveness had made life ofttimes unbearable, causing her to ride out on the moors for days and nights until her rage and pain had subsided. Mara's long nails, that had clawed and scratched, on hard sinewy hands that pulled hair and punched, were not as hurtful as her mouth, that screamed and spat terrible words.

"Witch's spawn, kelpie's kin, and your heart is black as sin." Terrible words that had been repeated by the people of Durness as they'd crossed themselves and herded their families protectively from her.

"Witch's spawn, kelpie's kin, and your heart is black as sin." The horse's hooves beat out the phrase that had been repeated and repeated, spiraling back through time to before Cameron's first rememberings.

Her first memories were hazy and nightmarish, as though a door stood barred and bolted in her mind, forbidding her from even the thought of knocking. Who was she? She had always known she was not of

Duncan's blood, although she called him Grandfather. How did she know? her mind had often puzzled futilely. She just knew, as though she were already a formed, reasoning child when she first met him, and yet there were no previous recollections.

After one particularly ugly encounter with Mara, when she'd been called the usual stream of names, one name had stuck out and been different. *Bastard.* The strangeness had hurt more than "changeling" and "witch's spawn." She'd found the word to mean "illegitimate," and on studying that incomprehensible word found it to mean unlawful issue, illegal, against the rules, not meant to be. At that time she'd carefully examined the dusty paintings of Duncan Fraser's ancestors, knowing as she looked that she'd find no sign of bright green eyes or ebony hair among the redheaded, gray-eyed Frasers.

When she had tried to speak to Duncan about it, he'd grown angry, telling her to ask no questions and she'd get no lies—nor death at the end of an English ax or gibbet. So she'd crept away to hide, knowing it must be true: She was a bastard and not supposed to be.

Cameron defended herself against Mara as best she could, clawing and kicking until they scrapped like two spiteful siblings, but each night it was Mara who was closeted with her grandfather, Mara chosen, and from a small child Cameron rode out in the dark to hide, knowing Duncan despised tears and tattling. As she grew older and saw the deer rut in the springtime, part of her understood the bond between the two old people, so she accepted her role in her grandfather's heart. She rode for him, hunted, read, wrote, swam, and dived, knowing Mara could not compete.

Cameron tossed her hair and the thoughts from her head. It was dark. She looked down to her hound, but he wasn't there. How long had she been rambling in a world of her own? She whistled but there was no answering bark or rustle in the heather.

"Torquil? Torquil?" she yelled, not caring now if anyone followed or heard her. She strained her eyes to see in the darkness. Turning her horse she walked him back the way she had come, whistling and calling, but there was no sight nor sound of him. The horse stamped impatiently and, lifting his head, joined his voice to hers.

"Dinna fret, Torquod. He's out looking for his supper." She patted the black stallion's neck, trying to reassure herself as well as him.

"We'll rest here and he'll come sniffing for us." Cameron dismounted and sat in the prickly heather, cursing her lack of foresight as she realized they'd have to make do without food or blankets. She whistled and strained her ears to hear a whine, some sign of her hound Torquil, but all she heard was the rustle of small rodents, the stamping of her horse, and the haunting call of owls in search of food.

That night was one of the longest Cameron had ever spent. Cold, hungry, and thirsty she dozed fitfully only to wake with her teeth chattering and a thousand fears preying on her mind.

As the first fingers of dawn striped the sky and blurred the hard line of the eastern horizon, Cameron rose stiffly, picking out the sharp spines of gorse from the wool of her kilt. She mounted her horse and scanned around.

"What shall I do, Torquod? Go back?" she asked of the horse, who blew in answer through dry thirsty lips.

Cameron knew she couldn't leave her hound and yet the thought of being caught by the strong stranger divided her mind. No, she couldn't leave the great shaggy friend who'd been her pillow ever since she could remember, who'd licked the guilty evidence of her salty tears from her cheeks, and who'd countless times grabbed Mara's beating arm to protect her.

"Oh, Torquil, be safe. I was so thinking of myself I dinna think of your old weary body," she cried aloud, as she resolutely turned her horse's head back toward the castle.

Cameron gave a hopeful whistle and, startled, heard a joyful answering bark as she urged Torquod to gallop up the slope toward the welcome sound. But when she reached the crest, her joy turned to horror as she saw her hound bounding to her alongside a tall figure on horseback.

She wanted to turn and run, hoping Torquil would follow, but remembering his old legs, and full of relief and happiness at seeing him, she flung herself off the horse and embraced him instead, burying her face into his shaggy softness.

Alex stared down at the ebony head nestled in the russet coat of the dog. If he hadn't spent such a damned uncomfortable night with a whining hound, he might have been touched by the devotion the large beast and the small child showed each other. As it was, all his tired aching eyes saw were two gross impositions that he had somehow gained responsibility for.

Cameron looked up at the tall stern figure. So cold and cruel, she thought, feeling at a decided disadvantage standing on the ground while he towered above on his horse. Many plans flashed through her mind before she decided to turn away, mount up, whistle for Torquil, and calmly ride off, hoping he'd not bother to follow.

Hiding her fear and apprehension she stared contemptuously at the rider and abruptly turned her back. She put one foot in the stirrup and swung herself easily onto her huge horse. Taking a breath she whistled for the dog, forcing herself to move slowly as she carefully turned her mount's head around.

"Now," Cameron exhaled, and she lifted her small heels to press Torquod into a swift gallop. The great black stallion leaped forward, only to be brought up short by Alex, who effortlessly reached out and grabbed the leather at Torquod's tender mouth. Cameron felt the reins torn out of her hands, and she clamped her legs to keep from being thrown as her horse reared.

"Attack, Torquil! Attack!" ordered Cameron, but the great hound just sat, his long freckled tongue hanging as he panted.

"Well at least you're not mute," drawled Alex languidly, his tone belying the anger he felt. Cameron reached to her boot for her dirk, but a strong hand held her wrist in a viselike grip.

Cameron felt such rage that her pulses raced and her heart felt near to bursting. She kicked and raged to no avail and found herself picked cleanly off her saddle and deposited with a thump across his, face down like a sack of grain. The wind knocked out of her she lay still in that humiliating position.

Alex cantered over the heather and Cameron felt as though her ribs were being broken. Lie still, she told herself; his grip will relax and slipping to the ground will be easy. Alex stared down at the small tousled bundle in front of him. He expected the boy to complain at the bruising pace, but he heard not a sound. He filled with fury at the stoicism and urged his horse to a gallop. He'd show the wild brat who was the stronger, he raged, as he thundered across the moor, Torquod and Torquil racing behind.

"What in God's name am I doing?" thought Alex, as his rage and need for dominance ebbed. He reined his horse and removed his hand from the small of Cameron's back. She lay still a moment and then slid to the ground, forcing her legs to support her, willing her stomach to stop heaving, willing the vomit to stay down. She was not going to show weakness by spilling her guts.

Alex stared down at the very white face. "Take some deep breaths, boy."

Cameron held her breath in rebellion, even though her lungs longed to gulp the air. So this pompous idiot didn't know! He thought she was a boy! Well and good, let him think it. She'd get rid of him one way or another. She took a few deep sobbing breaths.

Alex laughed, noting her capitulation, having seen her hold her breath in deliberate defiance before.

"Let's have a truce, lad?" he smiled, holding out his hand. Cameron turned away as a chill crept up her limbs, making her feel faint, and she shivered. She heard him dismount as the burning bile tore up her gullet and her stomach spasmed. She felt a broad hand on her forehead and another on the neck forcing her to bend.

"Don't fight it, let it out," said Alex gently, filled with guilt at his brutal treatment of the child. Cameron wretched and wretched, her stomach screaming at the dry heaves. The stranger sat her down gently and pushed her head between her knees.

"Rest awhile, 'twill pass," he growled, and Cameron was only too glad to obey and hide her face from those mocking amber eyes. She was humiliated; tears ached her nose. She chided herself with her grandfather's memory, knowing he'd turn the stones of his cairn in disappointment if she gave in to such weakness. How long she sat with her burning face buried in her arms she had no idea; it was as if she dropped off to sleep. She woke with a start and, remembering where she

was, furtively peeped out through strands of hair and
bent arms.

"Feel better?"

Cameron hid her face, fuming. This man saw everything.

"Let's start over. I'm Alex Sinclair," he said, resting
on his haunches beside her. Cameron threw her head
back, green eyes blazing with hatred as she spat full in
his face. Alex's hand flew out in a reflex action, striking her, but even though her head snapped back, her
eyes still stared uncompromisingly into his.

"I see your lesson wasn't learned," said Alex tersely,
pulling Cameron upright and pushing her toward her
horse. Cameron mounted silently, winding the reins
around her hands, but he jerked them from her and
led her as if she were a baby on her first ride.

Cameron was numb; nothing existed for her but the
hypnotic rhythm of her horse beneath her, yet it was
a beautiful, clear day, the air sweet and filled with the
busy buzzing of bees in the heather.

Alex felt an exhilaration. He found himself appreciating everything from the surprised deer that stood
curiously tense, their noses quivering, to the birds that
swooped and played, twittered and sang. Butterflies
flew lazily from flower to flower, alighting to stretch
their rainbow wings in the sunshine before disappearing into the colors around them. The deep blue above
and the rolling purples and pinks below soothed his
senses and he hummed happily, feeling at peace with
the world. He pulled himself up short seeing Cameron's closed, stubborn face. What had he to feel so
happy and carefree about, he thought, and laughed
cynically.

At noon they reached a ravine. Trees grew down the
steep banks and a mountain stream bubbled through

the center. Alex dismounted and led both horses to drink. Cameron sat silently, not stirring even when Torquod dropped his head into the water. She instinctively held the saddle to stop herself from sliding down his neck.

"Your horse needs rest even if you don't," growled Alex, slapping her boot, concerned at the child's blank expression and the wounded look in her eyes.

How dare that arrogant stranger tell her how to treat her horse, she fumed inwardly, as she slid from Torquod's high back and bent to drink.

"You'd better drink yourself," muttered Alex, his back turned to her as he took out bread and meat from his saddlebag.

Cameron stood shaking with rage. I'm about to drink and he tells me to. He'll not have the satisfaction, she raved to herself, and deliberately forced her eyes from the icy bubbling water as she walked away to sit on a fallen tree. She swallowed, feeling her parched throat prickle.

"Something to eat?" Alex called, holding the food out to her.

Cameron turned her back on him. She'd take nothing from him at all, she promised, wishing he'd eat and drink more quietly.

Finally Alex relaxed and lay back in the sunlight, closing his eyes. Cameron watched him, hoping he would fall asleep so she would have a chance to escape. This time her temper would not get the best of her. She'd take the food and his horse, making his following impossible. She waited, quietly edging herself closer, her eyes not leaving the seemingly sleeping man. His breathing was even and he didn't stir when she stood. Torquil lay snoozing, his shaggy head resting on Alex's thigh. Why had her dog taken such a liking to this cruel man? thought Cameron, not know-

ing how the two had shared a sleepless anxious night
drawn together by their mutual concern for her welfare. Satisfied that he slept, she crept away to the two
horses. Untying them and joining their reins together
she led them to an opening in the trees, planning to
creep back for Torquil and then fling herself on Torquod's back to gallop away. She stealthily crept back
to fetch her dog, not wanting to chance waking the
man by whistling. He still breathed steadily. Cameron
bent slowly, and as her hand touched Torquil's fur,
another hand grasped her foot forcefully, pulling her
down to sit with a thump beside the prone man, who
then rolled over, imprisoning her with his heavy arm
and leg.

"Now sleep," muttered Alex, pulling Cameron
closer and settling himself more comfortably.

Cameron lay stunned for an instant, feeling Alex's
warmth and scent envelop her. Then she fought like a
wildcat, but the man's heavy limbs seemed made of
iron.

"Rest easy or I'll tie you up," growled Alex. Cameron froze, realizing that there would be no escape if
she were tied. She lay rigidly, hearing his deep even
breaths until, despite herself, she relaxed with the
warmth of the body that held her and slept. It seemed
her eyes had just closed for a second before she was
shaken awake and deposited roughly on Torquod's
back, and the numb rhythm of riding started over
again.

For miles they jogged at an even pace, bearing
southeast Cameron judged, forcing her eyes to imprint
landmarks on her memory for her return journey. By
late afternoon the sky was overcast and the tops of the
grasses were whipped by a howling wind. Alex decided
to make for a line of trees he saw a mile or so ahead.

"Hurry before it breaks," he yelled, throwing Cam-

eron's reins to her and urging his horse to a canter.
Cameron grabbed her reins and her chance to escape
without thought. Whistling for Torquil she wheeled
her horse around and galloped back toward the valley
they'd passed through a mile or so back.

Racing with the howling wind Alex didn't realize
Cameron's treachery until halfway to his goal. He
turned to see how the child and dog were faring in
time to watch them disappear over the roll of moor
behind him.

Cameron reached the shelter of the trees as the first
flash of lightning lit the earth. She looked anxiously
around and sighed with relief at no sign of pursuit.
Torquil sat and panted, his long speckled tongue dangling.

"No time to rest," gasped Cameron, riding in and
out of the trees. Torquil whined, looking for Alex,
and then followed down a steep sandy slope to a
wildly rushing stream, swollen by the rains in the
mountains. Cameron urged her horse into the seething
torrent as Torquil protested furiously.

"'Tis a wee drop of wet, you misery. Shame on you
making friends with the enemy and now turning
weak," she hissed, riding her horse into the foaming
water. The dog refused to follow as he dashed forward
and back along the bank, whining and barking as the
lightning and thunder flashed and crashed.

Torquod picked his way carefully, his hooves skit-
tering on the smooth slippery pebbles. He pranced
backward trying to maintain balance against the surging current. Cameron gave him her full attention as
the raging water broke against his chest and dashed
against her face. She felt his fear and, knowing how
she'd feel battling the current with an added burden
upon her back, wound the reins around her hand and
slipped off his broad back into the turbulence. The

raging current caught her body, forcing it downstream as the panic-stricken horse desperately tried to drag her to the other side. Cameron's body screamed at the torturous tug of war as the water thundered around her head, cracking her with broken branches and other debris. She tried frantically to free her hand from the wet tightened leather, but her efforts were in vain.

What seemed an eternity later the horse Torquod pranced up the slippery bank, dragging his battered, choking young mistress to safety. She lay half-conscious and near drowned, still imprisoned by the reins. Dimly she heard the frenzied cries of the hound stranded across the thundering raging water, but the strains of the previous night, along with the grief-filled days before it, had taken their toll, and it was nearly an hour later that Torquil's frantic baying penetrated her dazed brain. She forced herself to stand on aching legs, despite the heaviness of her sodden woolen garments, and wrestle with the cutting leather. Freeing herself she cupped her hands to call for her dog.

"We'll walk this side, you that, until we find a place to cross," she yelled, as the thunder and lightning roared, drowning out her words. She stood, taking Torquod's bridle to demonstrate, but the huge hound barked furiously, running up the steep slope on the other side of the river, returning in the direction from which they'd come.

"No! No! Come back!" screamed Cameron, but the dog disappeared among the trees.

For over an hour Cameron waited for his return. The storm rolled away until just soft rumbles could be heard in the distance and the night blanketed everything. Cameron was wet and bitterly cold. She could see nothing and only heard the steady rushing of the angry stream.

"Torquod?" she cried out anxiously, and was heartened to feel a strong nudging as he bent his head and butted her gently. Feeling for the stirrup she hoisted her tired aching body onto the horse's back and leaned forward, hugging his neck. The exhausted horse slowly picked his way through the dark forest, until the trees became too dense and his hooves too heavy to pick up.

Somewhere deep in her aching head Cameron felt the steady jolting beneath her stop, and her body slid to the ground. She wanted to curl up and sleep, and yet a feverish urgency beat within her—don't stop, mustna stop, dinna stop. She tried to stand, forcing her screaming eyelids to open. Her eyeballs seemed on fire as she tried to focus. Everything was black as pitch. She willed the panic away as she groped and felt the safe, firm side of her horse. She buried her face into his warmth to take a breath for the effort needed to remount his high back and slowly sank to the ground, unconscious.

Through thick layers Cameron heard mocking laughter. She opened her eyes and stared at the sky sifting through the firred branches overhead, blurring and dancing as she tried to focus. Again the chilling laughter and a frightened whinny. Cameron tried to move her head and a pain shot through her.

"'Taint dead but 'taint no use to this fine beast," rasped a voice very near, and a hard boot kicked her. She lay still, her heart pounding as she heard their feet move away. She propped herself on her elbow and stared feverishly at the legs of two burly men who examined the contents of her saddlebag. Discovering a well-worn book they riffled the pages as if looking for something.

Her book, the existence of which she'd forgotten for weeks at a time, had always been with her, as had her horse Torquod and hound Torquil. Her book, as familiar and unquestioned as her fingers and toes, always a part of her and yet filled with a strange undecipherable hand. As well as its familiarity and comfort there was also a fear. Duncan's voice pierced through the thunder in her head and she remembered watching his mouth as he'd raged and ranted, wondering when she'd understand the multitude of words that poured out. She'd backed away, understanding only his extreme displeasure and the words "death" and "destruction."

"Dinna touch, 'tis mine," she croaked, her voice sounding far away to her own ears. She felt another kick to her head, and she lay fighting the blinding agony that rang in her skull. Her pounding head felt the vibrations of Torquod's hooves as one of the men mounted him. She pursed her hot stiff lips and whistled, hardly blowing any air, but the horse heard and obeyed, flinging the man through the air into the hard trunk of a tree and he lay still.

Summoning up all her energy she picked up a piece of heavy wood and, bracing herself against a tree, stood. The other man held the screaming horse, cruelly pulling at his mouth. Cameron struck out blindly, hitting the man behind the knees so he staggered, not loosening his vicious grip. Miraculously Cameron managed to claw her way onto Torquod's high back and, stabbing her heels into his heaving sides, she begged him to run. The proud animal tried to obey but screamed at the agony of the man's merciless hold. Cameron kicked out wildly, not hearing her own screams as she tried to loosen the inhuman hand. The first man sat stunned, watching the battle. He wiped the blood from his eyes and laughed maniacally as he reached for a long leather whip.

"Stand away. I'll teach 'em both a lesson," he snarled, cracking the leather.

"Dinna mark the horse, 'twill fetch a fair price," answered the second, letting go with relief and backing off quickly. Cameron tried to back Torquod away from the snapping leather, but they were hemmed in by trees. The horse's eyes flashed white in fear, eyeballs rolling, bloody foam from his torn mouth bubbling as he bared his teeth, still screaming. The first man cracked the whip again and Cameron felt a searing pain flash across her face and chest. Torquod reared and Cameron urged him forward, digging her small feet into the heavy sweaty belly. Again the whip, but Cameron didn't feel the stinging cut; all she saw was red, all she heard was the thunderous roll of her own blood. She was deaf to the unearthly sounds of her own, and her horse's, pain. Again she forced Torquod up, forward and up, not heeding the whip that lashed the air. Forward and up, and down and up, until she felt his hooves strike soft flesh, and another scream joined the chorus. Up and down, screaming, screaming, everything red, up and down, screaming, barking and red darkness, the screams dying to strange moans, and silence.

Chapter Three

Alex once again spent a damnably uncomfortable night, wet and cold with a whining hound for a bed companion.

There was no point in looking for the child once darkness had closed in on them, Alex reasoned, feeling Cameron couldn't get very far. He made camp for the night and tried to sleep, reassuring himself that the dog would track down his young master the following day. Sleep being somehow impossible he sat by his fire watching the pine needles hiss and spark, the heavy shaggy head on his leg.

"What are you trying to tell me, big beastie?" he asked, feeling ill at ease as the soulful eyes stared at him.

The enormous hound had bounded to him through the raging storm, frantically barking and pulling at his clothes. Alex knew Torquil wanted him to follow, but the fury of the wind and sheets of rain made it impossible to see, let alone stand upright. He had waited out the storm, trying to calm the nervous animal, only to have darkness detain him further.

"You're a strange one, aren't you? A person would think you wanted your young master caught," he crooned, scratching behind the floppy ears that hung damp and dismally on each side of the sorrowful face. The dog whined dolefully.

"Seems almost like betrayal, old dog. Now why would you be wanting to do that?"

The hound only howled in answer, and kept it up most of the night.

At the first signs of daylight Torquil barked loudly and tore at Alex's clothes, snarling and pummeling with his massive paws. Sensing speed was needed Alex hastily saddled up and galloped after the hound that bounded ahead into the gray mist. Reaching the valley where Cameron had sought asylum the night before, he slowed his horse and picked his way through the maze of trees, hearing the rush of the racing stream that foamed high up the sandy banks. Alex rode carefully down the steep, slippery side, avoiding the treacherous roots exposed by the continuous erosion. Over the roar of water he heard the blood-chilling screams of child, horse, and man.

Torquil leaped into the furious waters and Alex watched helplessly as the huge, shaggy body was picked up and tossed downstream as though a mere twig. He fought the instinct to plunge in after the valiant animal as the horrific screams continued. His heart sad at seeing the waters devour the hound, leaving no trace, he urged his frightened horse into the maelstrom.

He entered upstream of the screams, reasoning that he'd use the current to his own advantage. Gently and firmly he guided his terrified mount forward, soothing and crooning to him like a nurse to a child, until the horse felt firm ground through the shallow water and sprang onto the safety of dry land.

Still the blood-curdling screams continued, and Alex kicked his steed savagely, urging him through the thick growth toward the source.

Rounding a tall pine Alex's blood chilled to the very marrow of his bones at the sight that met his eyes, a sight unequaled on any battlefield he'd been on or heard of.

The child Cameron, raven hair wild, rode the horse Torquod, mane streaming, bloody foaming mouth screaming, rearing, rearing, and beneath his flailing hooves what was once a man. Again and again before Alex's horrified eyes the horse reared, iron hooves smashing the once-living creature.

The moment seemed frozen in time as Alex, stunned by the violence, sat on his horse unable to comprehend the nightmare before him.

"'Tis from the devil, the devil," whined a voice, and Alex stared blankly at the ragged man who was flattened against a tree, crossing himself and praying madly.

The horrible screams slowed and quietened. Torquod sank to his knees heavily and, summoning all his energy, gave one last unearthly cry before rolling over, dead, and flinging the limp rider to the ground.

Alex shook his head to free himself from the numbing paralysis.

"Didn't mean no harm, just a wee spot of fun," babbled the grizzly ragged man. "'Taint natural, 'tis evil spirits, there's them that should be fetched!" And with that he ran into the forest as though Hecuba and all her coven were after him.

Alex looked at the three still figures: the small child lying like a discarded rag doll, the bloody pulp of un-recognizable man, and the black stallion stiff in death. He dismounted and bent over Cameron, checking her limbs carefully for breaks, and was reassured. The child was whole but a fever raged, the skin so white and yet so hot, the breathing labored and rattling in the chest.

Alex removed the saddle and blanket from the valiant Torquod and, wrapping the child, mounted his horse, cradling her in his arms as he prayed he'd find a croft or house nearby.

He followed the stream for miles seeing no one nor even a sign of human life. His unfogged brain now wondered if it was a blessing or not, as the ragged man's words came back to haunt him: ". . . evil spirits . . . should be fetched." In the process of seeking help for Cameron he could also be delivering the boy into the hands of fervent witch-hunters, he thought.

"The lad is burning enough without the stake," he said out loud, staring down at the small flushed face that whistled in breath through flaring nostrils.

Alex rode slowly and steadily, his mind in turmoil. In just over a week his whole life had been disrupted. His life—comfortable, rhythmic, and without stress— had been just as he wanted it: his country estate to tend and run, his townhouse in Edinburgh when the country's serenity bored him and he needed amusement, his mistress Fiona. At the thought of Fiona he smiled, hearing her earthy chuckle at the idea of him being nursemaid to a halfling child. Comfortable, rhythmic Fiona. Unpossessive and undemanding, independent and as fervently against the strings of commitment as he was. He congratulated himself on obtaining Fiona from under the noses of the other men who flocked for her favors.

What was he, Sir Alex Sinclair, doing? What was this small defiant scrap of humanity to him? What was he doing with this child?

"Oh, well," he sighed aloud. "This will teach me to complain of boredom and complacency."

Alex let his horse drink and, balancing his charge, reached into his saddlebag for some bread. He ate, letting the horse forage among the tender green by the stream. He looked down at the dry, hot face, still surprised and shocked by the livid weals of the whip, and urged his horse on.

For over an hour he rode slowly, his eyes scanning the stream for signs of the great hound. The water still flowed swiftly, but it had run much of its fury out.

"Does no one live anywhere in this savage country?" he muttered.

He plodded on slowly, his arm aching from the weight of the child, who looked so small but now seemed so heavy. Just as he was deciding to stop and make camp, he saw a pile of logs stacked neatly up the bank out of water's reach. Not freshly hewn by the lichen and moss that covered them, but chopped by human hand, no less. Riding up the bank he came in sight of a small stone house. He slid from his horse's back, still holding Cameron, and knocked at the door. Getting no answer, and noting that the windows were shuttered, he put down his young burden and opened the door.

The stone floor was dusty and strewn with the evidence of many small rodents, who had also sought refuge from the inhospitality of the wilderness outside. The air was musty and dank. A large fireplace dominated the only room; in competition stood a large wooden bed covered with a straw-filled pallet. A quick search of two shelves and a small cupboard unearthed several pots, a bucket, and some rags.

Alex hauled the straw mattress off the bed and out the door where he shook it free of dust and any creatures that might have made their nests in it. He left it to air while he checked Cameron. She still lay inert, but her breathing now railed and rasped loudly.

After poking a nursery of crows and their home out of the chimney he speedily built a fire and filled two large pots with water from the stream, hanging them to boil.

He worked quickly and efficiently, cleaning the dust from the small room, knowing Cameron's laboring lungs could not survive the particles. Devising a makeshift broom from pine boughs he swept the floor, sprinkling water over it, and then, tightly refastening the shutters, he let the water boil to fill the room with steam. Setting the mattress back on the bed he pulled it nearer to the fire. He surveyed his handiwork before carrying Cameron in.

Alex laid the child on the bed, cursing to himself as he unwrapped the blanket to find the thick woolen garments sodden.

"I have to get him out of these damp things, if it isn't already too late," he muttered, pulling off Cameron's riding boots.

Cameron stirred restlessly and began to thrash and scream. Alex held the wildly writhing child, rocking and soothing until the cries ebbed to soft whimpers and the child drifted back to uneasy sleep.

Gently Alex eased the leather jerkin from the thin shoulders and unbuttoned the shirt. The whip marks glared angrily out of the white flesh, the blood oozing and sticking the linen to the skin. He wet a rag and dampening, pulled off the cloth carefully. He was so absorbed in his task, he didn't realize what he had uncovered.

Alex stared in stupefaction at the small firm breasts the lash of the whip crisscrossed symmetrically between, almost by design.

Cameron was no boy! He was saddled with a *girl* and if now a child she would not be one much longer. He estimated her age to be somewhere around thirteen.

or fourteen, not having experience with unfledged
females.

Cameron moaned and tossed, forcing Alex to put his
troubled thoughts aside and proceed to remove the
rest of her damp clothing.

He flung off his own jacket in the heat of the fire
and steam and stared down at the small naked girl
lying still, her breath rasping.

A fine-boned little beauty, he thought, as his eyes
traveled down from the mass of raven tangles, past the
perfect uptilted breasts marked ironically with Saint
Andrew's cross, along the flat firm belly to a triangle of
blue-black hair, and down the slim legs to her dirty
little feet. Never before had he looked at a naked female
with such objectivity. He was surprised. He felt no
stirring of his maleness, just the stirring of compassion
for this small near-woman who had fought with more
courage than most men he knew.

He dabbed the open weals with whiskey, cleaned the
many abrasions on her legs and arms, and, lifting her
head, poured some of the spirits into her mouth.

For the third night in a row Alex had no sleep. He
nursed the raving girl as she deliriously tossed and
threw the blankets off her. Alex was determined to
break the fever as he added another blanket, his heavy
cape, and lay across her, joining his own body's heat to
hers. As morning broke, the sweat beaded on her face
and she slept quietly.

Alex left the closeness of the steamy room and
stepped outside into the chill morning air. He
breathed deeply, appreciating the crystal freshness. His
poor neglected horse still stood patiently beneath the
trees. Finding a crude lean-to behind the house he led
his horse in, rubbed him down, and, filling an old
trough with water, left the animal content.

He checked Cameron, but she still slept, her forehead now damp and hot. After feeding the fire and refilling the steaming pots he went out and sat in the sun by the stream.

What a mess, he thought, stuck out in the middle of nowhere with a sick girl who couldn't be moved, no food, no one to help for miles around. He laughed, thinking of the poachers who often helped themselves to game from his estate. The old rascals were better equipped to survive than he was. He remembered his father boasting that he could tickle a trout and, thinking to himself that if his father could do it he certainly should give it a try, stared into the clear water.

The current ran swiftly between water-smoothed rocks, making deep clear pools and miniature rapids over shining pebbles. Green weeds streamed with the flow and the sun on the water made seeing difficult. Alex lay on his stomach, scanning the stream, and caught sight of a large speckled fish gently moving its fins to keep still in the water. Slowly he dipped his hands into the icy cold. The fish started and darted away, but stopped and gently waved his fins again. Alex inched his hands closer, wriggling his body over the bank. He now was only a few inches away from the languidly waving fish. Nearer and nearer and one finger touched, and Alex fought to keep his balance but fell in face first, submerging his head and upper torso in the sparkling water.

To hell with tickling, he vowed, he'd make a rod, pulling off his dripping clothes and jogging briskly to the stone house.

Cameron still slept, her breath whistling up painfully from her lungs. Alex hung his wet shirt and vest to dry and donned dry clothes from his pack. He set about looking for something from which to fashion a fishing rod, finding a trim piece of sapling, a bent pin, but no line. He spent an hour unraveling some linen, only to find that it snapped as soon as he tugged on it. Furious he threw it from him. I've grown so soft, he raged. What good is a man if he can't even nourish himself? He had bread and cheese left in his bag, but he was reluctant to touch the last remaining food. All that day his stomach growled as he tried to make a fishing net from Cameron's shirt.

Occasionally he checked his charge, lifting her tousled head to drip water into her mouth and lay cooling cloths on her head. He kept the fire burning and the pots steaming, and the cloying heat drove him outside into the cool clear evening. He sat watching the red sun dip below the trees and peek out in sudden flashes as he moved his head. He sat unthinking and unfeeling as darkness descended and the moon rose and reflected on the water that rippled and danced, fragmented, and came together. His whole body ached with weariness.

Suddenly he realized how he could make the fishing line.

"That's it!" He cried out loud. He'd take hair from his horse's tail or mane. He laughed, remembering his hopelessness that afternoon, thinking that they would die of starvation because of a lack of twine. His whole world had collapsed, his manhood, his pride, his very life, because he had no twine and couldn't think of a substitute. The worries of the day fell off him and he walked up to the stone house feeling chilly but perfectly happy.

Alex entered the stifling heat of the room. It really looked welcoming, he thought yawning sleepily, as he observed the firelight playing on the walls and turning the cold stones to warm colors. He needed sleep, but where? The floor was hard; he looked at the bed, his sense of propriety battling with his tired body. His

tired body won as his weary brain reasoned that he'd
be better prepared to help her if he was closer at hand.
He lay down carefully beside Cameron and was sound
asleep before his tawny head touched the straw pallet.

Chapter Four

Cameron tossed restlessly. She was running, running.
She had to get away. From what? She didn't know. She
just had to. The harder she ran, the more she stayed in
the same place, as the ground rolled back toward her.
Unearthly laughter cackled above, from holes in the
low sky where green witches clawed at her, pulling at
her clothes so she ran naked. She tried to veer to the
side but giant strings pulled her back on the treadmill.
She tried to stop the clawed hands pinching her body,
but her arms were pulled away and outstretched like a
marionette's.

Suddenly she found herself on a barren plain, the
earth scorched and cracked into giant irregular pav-
ings. Torquod and Torquil were with her. They
walked and the earth began to move, the cracks opening until they stood on one flake of ground, spinning
in a void of nothingness. Scabs whittled off the piece

of ground making it smaller and smaller, and she clutched her horse and dog close to her as she grew larger and larger, her animals like toys in her arms. Spinning, spinning, spinning until they fell down a deep black hole.

Cameron landed on her feet lightly, like a butterfly. The sun shone and the birds sang. She looked into her arms that embraced her loved ones and found she had strangled them to death. She screamed and the witches laughed. She was back in the futile, frustrating race on the treadmill, her arms outstretched, her body being clawed and pinched.

Alex distantly felt the thrashing in the bed beside him, and he fought to rouse himself but succumbed to the seduction of sleep. The rhythm of Cameron's pounding heels became the pounding of the waves beneath the creaking hull of the boat. Her anguished screams and cries became those of his two sisters and mother, as he and his father fought to stem the tide of cholera that swept their lives away.

Alex sat up sharply at the piercing scream. He gazed around in puzzlement at his surroundings before his eyes lit on the writhing figure beside him. Cameron's legs drummed on the straw pallet, her arms flung wide, her breathing rapid and even as she moaned and cried. The covers had been kicked off and the fire burned low. Alex swore as he covered Cameron and leaped off the bed to tend the fire. The sun was high in the sky, meaning he'd slept longer than he had meant to.

Cameron continued tossing, throwing the covers off, her movements strange and jerky. Like a puppet's, thought Alex, watching one hand and then the other strike her breast. Alex felt her brow, expecting the resumption of the dry fever, but her brow was cooler than it had been before. At the touch of his hand

Cameron opened her eyes, and Alex involuntarily stepped back when he saw the depth of the pain and fear in them.

"Hurt, don't hurt," she whimpered, rubbing her hand and crying out sharply as she tore the healing skin off the weals. Alex wet a rag and laid it on her, and she was still, staring at him.

"Torquil? Torquil?" she cried hoarsely, moments later.

Damnation, swore Alex, how can I tell her that the poor valiant creature is dead? Maybe 'tis best to lie to her until she has more strength.

He didn't answer, searching for the words.

"I killed them. I killed them," howled Cameron. "They are dead. I killed them.

"I fell down the deepest hole, I tried to save them, but I was too strong and squeezed them to death with my love," sobbed Cameron, tears pouring down her face. Alex, distracted by her nakedness, quietly covered her as she sobbed out her dream in incoherent sentences.

The girl really is a witch or has second sight, thought Alex, knowing there was no way on earth the girl could have seen their deaths. She stopped talking and, wiping the tears from her eyes, looked at Alex and recognized him as her pursuer.

He watched the green eyes widen in shock and then harden with hatred. Hurt and angry he turned and marched out of the house.

Cameron knew that he had left her before, going in and out numerous times, bringing wood and water. He had sat swearing, trying to tie something to a sapling, then had thrown it across the room in a fit of temper. She wished that now he would not come back. She was extremely uncomfortable and needed to slip into the woods for privacy. Each time he had left she had waited, listening, but he'd returned in too short a time. Twice she had managed to swing her legs over the side of the bed and, fighting the dizziness, tried to stand, only to lie back as waves of blackness engulfed her.

Cameron lay swallowing hard to stop the coughs that threatened to make her lose her self-control. She crossed her legs and thought frantically. She would get up and go outside to relieve herself. She had to. She had lost too much pride already to the hard stranger, she felt she'd die if she lost any more. As she pulled herself up, Alex strode in again.

"Glad to see you sitting. You must be better. I'll be gone awhile to get food. The fire's banked and pots filled. So stay still and rest. I need you strong for the long journey ahead," he said, looking at Cameron, who didn't make any sign that she'd heard him.

He left the house apprehensively. The silly chit hadn't the strength to run; besides he'd taken the precaution of hiding her clothes on one of his trips for firewood, but just in case he positioned himself on a large flat rock in sight of the stone house.

Cameron breathed with relief as he left. She looked for her clothes hanging by the fire, but they had disappeared. She shrugged. She'd been naked before, running over the moors and the beach to swim. She only wore clothes for warmth and to protect herself from Mara's pinchings, and it was quite warm and there was no Mara here, she thought, sitting on the side of the bed. She stood up gingerly. Her legs felt watery and weak and the room spun around alarmingly. She took some deep breaths and, holding on to the wall, she made her way slowly to the door.

Alex held his breath as the fat lazy fish came teasingly close to his hook. Come on, come on, his mind urged, and the fish moved a fraction closer. Just then

there was a loud crash as the door of the house swun
open and banged against the outside wall. Alex's arr
jerked up in a reflex action and the fish darted away

"What the hell!" he roared, looking up to the hous
where the naked girl swayed in the open doorway.

"What the hell do you think you're doing?" h
cried, dropping his fishing rod and racing up th
bank. Cameron stared at him, her eyes wide with em
barrassment, a flush creeping up her face from he
neck. Don't let him look down, she prayed, trying t
hold his amber eyes with hers, but Alex did look dow
and his anger gave way to mirth.

Cameron stood clutching the door as his open laugh
ter burned into her. She had no pride left, and th
shaming tears ran down her face at her own weakness

Alex stopped laughing as the humiliated girl shiv
ered. He stared at the wet face and the wet ground an
chided himself for his stupidity. It had not occurred t
him—and here he was thinking he had thought of ev
erything.

He raged inwardly at himself for his thoughtless
ness. Surely he had wanted to crack the child's wil
arrogance, but not that way. What was the matte
with him anyway? It had never occurred to him tha
woman had to answer the call of Nature as well a
man. Of course he knew they had to, but it wasn'
something a man was disposed to thinking about
Good thing she must have the bladder of a came
thought Alex, three days was a very long time.

Cameron stood in her puddle, her legs and feet sting
ing in the warmth of her own water. Alex picked her u
and put her back on the bed, wondering if she had fin
ished and what to do about it.

"If you're holding in more, tell me," he muttered
embarrassed himself. Cameron didn't answer. She wa

ot ever going to speak to him again, or ask for any-
hing from him.

He filled a bowl with warm water and, rummaging
hrough his pack, found soap and a clean nightshirt of
is own. Time she wore some clothes, he thought,
ot used to celibacy or sleeping so close to a young
irl.

"Why don't you clean yourself up while I catch
ome supper," he said roughly, turning to leave the
ouse.

As he neared the stream he saw a great thrashing in
he water. He stopped, puzzled by the angry churning.
His line so carelessly dropped in the weeds had se-
urely hooked a large salmon who fought futilely to
ree itself, winding the strong horsehair around its
vrithing body. With a whoop of triumph Alex waded
oward the battling fish who whipped its tail in pro-
est against Alex's groping hands and slithered, slip-
ing away, to continue its struggles against the tight-
ning line. Alex grabbed his makeshift net made from
Cameron's shirt and scooped it up. He felt pure, un-
rammeled joy at his catch. It symbolized a man able
o provide.

Alex entered the house whistling merrily and was
lisappointed that Cameron slept and was unable to
pplaud his triumph. He stood staring down at her,
oping the brilliant green eyes would open, but she
lept soundly. His brow furrowed with concern as he
ealized the washing water stood untouched and her
ace still showed the tear lines of her previous humilia-
ion. He was unaware of the great tenderness that
illed him.

He gently bathed her, enjoying her passivity, de-
ighting in the feel of her firm, young body beneath
is soapy hands. Cameron didn't stir, even when he
ulled the too-large nightshirt over her head and

brushed the tangled hair from her face. He lowered her back onto the mattress and she gave a small cry of protest and nestled back into his arms.

Strange turn of events, thought Alex, staring down at the raven-haired beauty who cuddled into him. He sat, oddly content, until her breathing was even and then gently slipped his arms from her and, humming happily, went to cook their supper.

Cameron awoke to the savory smell of cooking salmon, mixed with lavender. She frowned, puzzled, and sniffed her hands, looked at her arms and down the length of her. She was dressed in a linen nightshirt. She felt clean and cozy. She stared bewildered at Alex's broad back as he squatted by the fire, gently turning the spitted fish. He hummed softly to himself. Feeling Cameron's eyes, he turned.

"So you are awake, my fine lady, in time for a feast fit for a queen." His mischievous amber eyes glowed warmly above his tanned high cheekbones. Cameron felt even more confused.

Alex carefully transferred his catch to a slab of wood covered with chestnut leaves and carried it to the stool by the bed. Alongside it he put a pot of sparkling spring water, which he proclaimed was nectar from the gods, as he tried to get a smile from the solemn girl who lay on the bed.

Cameron, used to veiling her feelings from the spiteful Mara, fought to bury the liking she felt for the man. She hated him and yet when he had bathed her half-conscious body she had felt safe and cared for, hearing the steady, strong beat of his heart under her cheek. She had wanted to stay in the circle of his arms, as it somehow fed an aching void in her. Cameron had never known tenderness or comforting arms. Her grandfather, with all his love, had reveled in her wild fearlessness, despising weakness and pampering.

Cameron was afraid. She stared at Alex, tense, her hands tightly holding the blanket. She didn't need anyone but herself. All she needed was her freedom to run on the moors with her horse and hound. Where were they? She hadn't seen them. The few times in her life she had been sick, Torquil had never left her side. She peered over the side of the bed. He wasn't on the floor. Guilt flared up in her. Why hadn't she thought of him before?

Alex watched the girl frantically look around the room. He'd carefully boned her portion of fish and now held it out to her, fragrant and steaming.

"Here. Eat it up." But Cameron's wildly flailing arms knocked it from his grip.

"What did you do that for?" he roared. Food was precious enough without that blasted brat—

"My dog? Where's my dog?" Cameron screamed. Alex froze for a moment. So she *doesn't* know.

"Saints preserve us, would you eat? Look at the mess you've made," he grumbled softly, not willing to broach the subject before his young charge showed more strength. He scooped the fish back on the layer of leaves he'd fashioned into a plate, and held it out again to her.

"Where's Torquil?"

"I refuse to say a word till you've eaten," returned Alex sternly.

"I want my dog," insisted Cameron stubbornly, but Alex, true to his word, did not answer. He ate, relishing the freshness, satisfying the gnawing hunger that had tormented his belly for the past two days.

"I said I want my dog," screamed Cameron. Alex ate with more relish, his eating noises exaggerated to drown out the girl's voice.

"I won't eat till you tell me."

Still Alex ignored her, concentrating on the juice that ran down his hand. He licked it up.

Cameron attacked him with her fists, pummeling his back, but he calmly went on eating as if she were a gnat. Blind rage took over as Cameron snatched his meal and threw it against the wall.

"I said I want my dog!" she screeched.

Alex fought the fury that raged in him, demanding release. He counted in his head, breathing deeply before he stood to retrieve the precious fish. As he worked, he whistled, forcing the pressure of his anger out in short sharp sounds, totally ignoring the wild tantrum that Cameron was having, as she spat and screamed out every hurtful thing she'd learned from Mara's spiteful mouth.

She can't go on forever, reasoned Alex, as he salvaged the last of the fish and put it out of harm's way. He then opened the door and, grabbing one of the pots of cold water, deliberated whether to throw it on the hysterical child. Instead he dashed it onto the greasy floor and savagely swept the muddy mess outside.

As he filled the empty pots in the stream, he heard Cameron's voice echoing furiously from the house, so he took his time and checked the make-shift salmon net, then walked through the forest smelling the sweetness.

Cameron raged and raged until, exhausted, she lay sobbing for her dog, hiccuping his name over and over. Alex paused with his pots outside the door and then, hardening his heart, he strode in.

"Ready to eat?" he asked curtly, crashing the iron pots angrily.

Cameron stifled her tears and turned her face into the mattress, her thin body jerking with spasms.

"Ready or not you'll eat. I'm sick of being nurse-maid to a whining brat."

Cameron's body stiffened with rage. What was the matter with her? Why all this blubbering and crying? What would her grandfather say if he saw her now? She buried her face deeper into the straw pallet as she heard his heavy boots coming to the bed, and then the mattress sagged as he sat upon it. She held her breath hearing a thud of something being placed roughly on the stool, and two strong hands gripped her shoulders and forced her over. She fought him but he easily pinned her down.

"Look at me," he commanded, and cursed himself as the green eyes closed firmly. He should have told her not to stare and then she would have.

"You will eat even if I have to force it down your throat. It's up to you."

Cameron opened her eyes and glowered at him. "You can force me to eat, but I can force it up."

"And I'll just force it back down your throat." They stared at each other, the hard amber eyes and the flashing green ones.

"I want my dog," she hissed between clenched teeth.

"You'll eat first."

"Why won't you tell me?"

"I'll tell you when you're done," answered Alex firmly, handing her the food. "And chew it slowly. You have not eaten in a few days." Cameron stared sullenly at the fish, knowing that he would ram it down her throat if she didn't eat it willingly. She put a small piece in her mouth.

"Keep eating and listen. You'll not be very strong for a few days, so anything you need, ask it. Nature calls us all, you know." Alex smiled warmly at her. Cameron's jaws stopped chewing and she froze. Why did this despicable man have to remind her of that?

Right now it was true she was nearly helpless, but she'd get strong and gain her freedom *and* her revenge. She went on eating with her head lowered, seemingly obedient as she finished.

Alex tossed the leaves that had sufficed as a dish into the fire and watched the flames spitting their appreciation as he played for time, not wanting to hasten the girl's grief. He wet a rag and handed it to her so she could wipe her hands and face.

"Life is hard, isn't it, Cameron?" The girl didn't answer.

"How old are you?" She still didn't answer.

"You are near grown it seems. Childhood has to go, and we must face things like death and go on living," Alex said gently.

"You are saying Torquil is dead?" Cameron's green eyes probed him painfully.

"Aye."

"How?"

"Trying to save you. Drowned in the storm, swept downstream by the current." Alex found himself angry and unable to stop as he continued. "Same with that proud stallion of yours."

"Torquod?" Cameron whispered.

"Aye. Dead. Killed himself saving you from yourself, used all his strength, gave his life for yours. So use your life wisely or they died for nothing." Alex flung the words at the small tortured girl and strode out, slamming the door.

Chapter Five

Long after Alex had left, slamming the door, Cameron lay trying to numb her mind to his harsh words. The memory of Torquil, whining at the edge of the rushing water as she cajoled him to cross, kept flashing through her mind. She fought a larger panic, not wanting to remember, but the sound of her horse's unearthly screams touched the edges of her memory. She didn't want to hear, somehow knowing if she let the memory in, she would split into a million howling pieces. Her body started to move rhythmically forward and back, forward and back, faster and faster, until once again she rode the rearing horse, urging him, urging him, up and down, up and down, smashing the ragged man into the ground. She sat, her eyes staring vacantly as she gently traced the marks of the whip down her face and across her breasts, her body now still as she remembered.

Alex walked along the banks of the stream in awe of the strength that Cameron seemed to possess. Weak from illness her temper was formidable; what would it be like when she was back to full capacity? As he walked he worried if they were safe from pursuit, remembering the ragged man's threat to come after Cameron. He decided to return to the scene of Torquod's tragic death to see if anything had been disturbed, reasoning that by the time Cameron's rage was spent she'd have no energy left but to sleep. He picked his way carefully, looking for signs, and was relieved to see none until he neared the glade where the body of the black stallion still lay. There he found several makeshift crosses to ward off witchcraft surrounding the great horse. Ascertaining that no one was about he felt compelled to bury the animal, wondering at his sentimentality as he scratched at the earth with his bare hands and piled leaves and branches. Waste of good horseflesh, he thought savagely.

The man's mutilated corpse had been removed and, noting the presence of the crosses and many footprints in the soft earth Alex began to worry. It was fortunate he'd kept to the stream on his way to the stone house, making tracking difficult, but he wondered how long it would be before someone came looking for them. Cameron's distinctive coloring had surely been marked and, when she was fit, traveling would have to be done avoiding roads and villages, for even in the sparsely populated Highlands news spread like wildfire, sparking and building in its intensity. Deep in thought Alex made his way back to the stone house, being careful to leave no tracks.

Cameron watched him approach from a great distance. It didn't matter. Nothing mattered. She felt nothing.

Alex banked the low fire and, wrapping the remaining fish in some wet leaves, speared the bundle and squatted on his haunches toasting it in the flames.

"How do you feel?" he asked gruffly, without turn-

ng. Cameron heard the deep voice but didn't relate it
to herself. Sulky spoiled brat, Alex thought, as he
turned the fish. Well, at least she isn't screaming and
spitting, draining the energy she needs for recovery.
He poked the rolled leaves onto the slab of wood,
burning his fingers, and unwrapped the steaming
salmon.

"Here's your food."

Cameron lay still, her eyes open and unblinking.
Worried, Alex put down the offered meal and waved
his hand in front of her eyes. She didn't even blink.

"Another game," he breathed with irritation, sitting
to eat, wondering how long she'd be able to keep it up.
He ate slowly, watching her. There was something disturbing about the way she lay there so still. He remembered seeing young soldiers without a mark of
battle lying just so; their minds, unable to withstand
the torment of war, had blocked out life itself.

For more than an hour Alex sat watching for one
single movement before the startling realization
dawned on him. He leaped up with a groan and
grasped her by the shoulders, shaking her and shaking
her, trying to shock her out of the dreadful inertia.

"Cameron? Cameron?" he yelled, but the blank eyes
didn't move and her head, neck, and shoulders remained stiff and rigid under his violent hands.

Alex let her fall back onto the mattress and paced
the room, cursing himself for the brutality of his
words that blamed her for the deaths of her pets. He
put himself in her place, raised on that lonely promon-
tory, in that cold stone fortress that shut out warmth
and companionship. Raised with Duncan Fraser whose
hate and bitterness toward the English and much of
his own fellow Scots had taught the girl to distrust and
fear. Raised with crazy Mara who, from the little Alex
had seen, could not have been much joy to a growing

child. All the girl had to love was her horse and hound, the storms, moors, and the sea.

"What has the poor bairn left to love?" cried Alex aloud, as his mind tried to grasp some understanding of his new responsibility. If she hadn't been defiant and wild, would she have survived? What other way did he expect her to react to an arrogant stranger who came out of nowhere to take the reins of her life? He remembered his own pain and confusion at fifteen, finding himself alone in the world. Even at twelve, without mother and sisters, trying to make his way in a strange land had made him want to find a quiet place to die. It had been the responsibility of taking care of his father that had somehow made him find the strength to go on living. At twelve he had to become father to the broken man, but even that had not prepared him to be an orphan three years later.

He had buried his father on his native soil and joined the army—the Union army—fighting the useless wars on the continent, as he hardened his body and heart, reasoning that Scottish nationalism only meant sure death. Better to live and prosper. So with that in mind he served the English until his family homes and lands were back in his possession. He fought his guilt with logic, telling himself that if Scotland was to rise again, some Scots had to be left, not just the spilt blood, broken bones, and ashes of pride she had now. He remembered Duncan's words about Cameron being Scotland, wild and free but undisciplined with no direction.

Alex gazed at the staring, still girl, knowing somehow he had to break through the barrier he had helped to erect. He wondered how he could reach into her tortured mind. He sat talking to her for hours, apologizing for his cruel words, telling her about his life and sorrows, but he got no reaction.

As Alex talked to the girl, his own protective shell softened and the words poured out, releasing all the pent-up emotions he had hidden for years. Things he had never spoken aloud—feelings, fears, memories— everything streamed out in a torrent until he sat spent and wondering at himself for spilling his soul to an unfledged girl who couldn't even hear him.

Cameron heard his words from far away, heard his voice droning, but it seemed she was wrapped from head to toe in thick unspun wool, her senses bound and muted. She was aware yet unaware when Alex sat beside her on the bed.

He lay on his back watching the reflection of the flames licking the stone walls and casting shadows on the rafters. He decided to be patient, hoping her wild youth would free her troubled mind and bring back the spirit of before. But how long to be patient was a problem. The witch-hunters might already have found the buried black horse, and even though he'd kept to the stream, they could be tracking them down. Even if this was just a vain fear, winter would be coming and would mean sure death if they were imprisoned in the small stone house. He decided to give her twenty-four hours to rest her mind and then he would try to break through somehow. The "how" still churned in his brain as he drifted off to sleep.

Alex slept late and the sun was already high above the treetops when he opened the door and stretched his body in the clean fresh air. Cameron still lay as she had the night before. Had those green eyes closed at all in the night? wondered Alex.

He walked down to the stream and, feeling stale and grimy, shucked his clothes and ducked himself in the icy water. He enjoyed the rush of the current as it eased the tension from his muscles, and he let the stream carry him, feeling an exhilaration at somehow being a part of nature, until a sharp rock cracked the small of his back. He leaped out of the water and jogged along the bank, slapping his arms against his body and shaking the water out of his hair to warm and dry himself. He checked his empty net, and his dangling horsehair line. No breakfast.

"Why didn't I bring my gun?" he swore, staring at a flock of noisy crows. "Even I could eat crow in times like these."

Pulling on his clothes Alex walked back to the house, feeling more alive and aware than he had for years, despite his worry about Cameron and the prospect of no breakfast. If was as though a sleeping part of him had suddenly awakened. His skin tingled, each pore. His nose smelled the freshness of nature, and his eyes saw more brightly, as though a numbing layer of film had been removed from his senses.

Alex stood in the doorway. The girl still had not moved. He watched her thoughtfully.

Shock had hidden her away; maybe shock would bring her back. He turned and looked down at the stream to a flat outcropping of rock baking in the sun. He smiled, nodding his head, and decisively hung a blanket around his neck and picked up the stiff girl. He put her down on the warm flat rock in the sun and with much difficulty removed his nightshirt from her awkward rigid body. He removed his own clothes and, picking her up in his arms, walked carefully into the water, searching for a deep pool without jutting rocks.

Cameron felt the shock of the icy water as Alex lowered her gently. She threw her arms about his neck and arched her body upward, away from the cold, and whimpered.

She stared up into the amber eyes, awareness overtaking her. She saw his worried face burst into a grin of pure delight and felt her body pressed against his warm bare chest. Fighting the strange sensations she felt she loosed her arms and pushed her body from him. Alex, unprepared, over-balanced backward with a splash as Cameron felt the icy water close over her. She came up choking to see him sitting waist-high in the stream, laughing with untrammeled joy. Furious she splashed water into his face, but he laughed and splashed her back. Cameron's rage built and built as she whipped and kicked and flailed until, exhausted, her movements slowed.

"I surrender," laughed Alex, standing with his hands raised high in mock defeat. Cameron gazed at his naked body with open interest.

"Come on, you'll get a chill," he said gruffly, not used to females who stared so frankly. He scooped her up in his arms and waded to the flat rock where he deposited her on the blanket and wrapped her warmly. Cameron still stared with fascination at his nakedness, never having seen a bared male before.

"Didn't anyone ever tell you it is rude to stare?" barked Alex, turning away and pulling on his pants.

"No," replied Cameron.

"Well, it is," retorted Alex tersely, wondering what was the matter with him. He actually felt *desire* for the unfledged girl. He longed to lie with her in the sun, his face buried in the tangled raven hair, his hands exploring and caressing.

"Why is it?"

"Why is what?" he said hoarsely, his loins aching.

"What you said."

"What did I say?" replied Alex, unwilling to turn to her until his desire had ebbed.

"That it is rude to stare."

"Because it is. It just is, that's all."

"Doesna make one bit of sense to me. I like to look

at things," muttered Cameron, feeling cheated that hi
body was now hidden from her. She had liked the fee
of his strong arms holding her, of her naked breast
pushed flat against his.

"Well, I'm not a thing," said Alex, thrusting hi
arms into the sleeves of his shirt.

Cameron shrugged and lay back on the rock, closin
her eyes. The sun felt warm upon her face. She flun
the blanket off her and let the sun soak into her skin
Seeing the warm red and orange colors dance beneath
her eyelids, she felt at peace for the first time since th
death of her grandfather.

Alex, in control of himself, turned around. H
stared down at the relaxed naked girl, noting the smile
of contentment on her face. He stifled a groan and
clenched his hands that longed to cup the two nearl
grown breasts, that longed to run down the youn
firm belly to the saucy hair that sprang so tantaliz
ingly. He reached his hands toward her and, graspin
the blanket, pulled it around her.

"Don't do that!" said Cameron indignantly, throw
ing the cover off her.

"You should be back in bed."

"Nay, the sun will heal, has always done. Anyway
feel good," protested Cameron, stretching her bod
like a cat in the sun.

"Be that as it may, there are things to be done,"
hissed Alex, between stiff lips that ached to kiss he
petulant mouth.

"Like what?" purred Cameron, her eyes closed.

"Eating," retorted Alex curtly, wanting to nibbl
her small, pink nipples. "So put the nightshirt on and
go back to bed while I catch some breakfast."

"Can I watch?" asked Cameron, turning on he
stomach and looking eagerly at him.

"If you get dressed," answered Alex, tempted by the round, pink buttocks that teased him.

Cameron frowned, puzzled, and then stood up in all her wild naked beauty. Alex resisted the urge to pull her to him and flung her the nightshirt as he turned away to walk down the bank, muttering to himself.

Cameron pulled the large shirt over her head and ran after him, watching as he checked the empty net and line.

"Never catch anything that way," she clucked.

"Did before," answered Alex.

"Must have been chance," replied Cameron saucily.

"All right, little miss know-it-all. You catch something," challenged Alex.

"I need a knife."

Alex debated the sense in giving her a knife, feeling she might not hesitate to use it on him. He stared at her thoughtfully, not believing the wide-eyed innocence written on her face. She's too mercurial, he thought, not knowing what was going on in that busy ticking brain.

"So I'll tickle one," said Cameron, shrugging off his silent staring, and the too-large nightshirt fell down her arms and slid to her feet. She stood naked, gurgling with laughter. It was the first time Alex had heard her laugh, a bubbling free sound, like the tripping of a mountain brook, that lit up her bright green eyes and opened her face. Still laughing, Cameron stooped and shimmied the shirt up her body. She rolled the sleeves up past her elbows and walked along the bank, silently scanning the water. Suddenly she froze, and putting a finger to her lips she sank quietly her knees on the bank and her toes caught in the hem of the garment. She wriggled back from the water's edge and pulled the shirt off, throwing it behind her.

Cameron lay naked, flat on the bank, her hands in the water. I'm saddled with a wood nymph, thought Alex, his eyes glued to the speckled trout which Cameron softly stroked. His desire rose again, watching the small hand tickle the silver belly, so gently and artfully, seducing, until with one deft move she tossed the salmon from the water onto the high bank.

"What did you need the knife for?" asked Alex an hour later, as they returned to the house with four good-sized fish.

"To whittle a stick. 'Tis quicker than tickling," replied Cameron, tripping over the nightshirt that Alex had insisted she wear for warmth. He cursed himself for his own stupidity in not thinking of so simple a device as a spear.

Alex insisted Cameron get straight into bed while he cooked the fish, telling her she'd been up enough for her first day, but really feeling the temptation of her body close to him while he cooked would be too much of a distraction.

Saving two of the fish for supper they ate every morsel of the two Alex cooked, sucking the bones and eating the last hard piece of bread. Cameron, full and relaxed, fell fast asleep, so Alex sat outside whittling sharp spears out of long straight sticks.

He had to talk to Cameron about their trip south. If he could somehow calm her fears, telling her what to expect, and what their relationship was, he could avoid a lot of strife, he felt. The problem was how to explain it to her without marring the happiness that was now emerging from Cameron.

Cameron woke up and smiled sleepily around the room. Alex wasn't there. She leaped off the bed, remembering the water. She wanted to swim with him again and feel their soft nakedness together. Dashing out of the door she shed the cumbersome nightshirt.

"Come on," she cried joyously, seeing him whittling. Alex, startled out of his thoughts, stared up at her.

"Cameron, I have to talk to you."

"Later. 'Twill soon be night and I want to swim with you."

Alex looked away, wrestling with himself, loath to strain his self-control and yet not wanting to cast a cloud on Cameron's sunny disposition. He smiled and stood as the impatient girl hopped up and down, pulling at his arm.

"All right. One quick swim."

Cameron raced down the bank like a young deer as Alex strode behind, wondering whether to keep his britches on.

"Hurry," called Cameron impatiently, as Alex stripped off his shirt and sat removing his boots.

"I'll race you in," he challenged, standing in his buckskins."

"You have your breeks on," laughed Cameron.

"Aye," answered Alex dryly.

"They'll be all wet."

"Aye."

"You'll swim in them?" asked Cameron puzzled.

"Aye."

"Why?" questioned Cameron. "That's silly."

Alex laughed suddenly and tore his britches off, wondering why should he not have some pleasure after all he'd been put through. A madness surged through him and a need to press that teasing young body against his.

Cameron swam like an otter in the deep pool. She took a breath and dove under the water.

Alex, swimming above, watched her small white bottom break the water and the graceful straight legs follow as she disappeared. He laughed, seeing her swimming under him, seeing her hand come out as she reached closer to stroke his underside. He felt her small hand close about him and even the cold water didn't stop the fire that surged through his body. She let go and emerged laughing to take a breath. Alex tried to catch her but she dodged away and lay on her back kicking the water into his face. Cameron wanted him to catch her but delighted also in the chase. He dived under her and she, seeing, eluded him again. The hunger to press against her drove Alex wild. She was like a slippery fish darting away as soon as she was within his grasp. Finally common sense told him it was just as well, and he climbed onto the bank and with difficulty pulled on his leather britches over his wet skin.

"Time to cook the supper," he called out, turning toward the stone house, boots and shirt in hand. Cameron was angry and splashed the water, feeling cheated.

They ate supper quietly, the air charged with tension. Later Cameron lay in bed, wondering at the unknown and unseen friction and tautness she felt. Alex brooded, angry with himself for spoiling what had been a beautiful day with his carnal desires. But he was thankful in one sense for the unfulfillment as it made his position of guardianship much less complicated.

He broached the subject of their journey gently, aware that Cameron could change into a spitting wildcat at one thoughtless word. He explained patiently that he was her guardian, like a father (he underlined more for himself than the girl), but only until she was twenty-one.

"Why twenty-one?" asked Cameron.

And Alex explained that that was when she was legally of age under her grandfather's will. Cameron didn't understand, so Alex explained about law.

"Whose? The English?" she snapped, and Alex let it ride as he went on to describe his own estate and Mackie, his old nurse. Just like Mara, thought Cameron, but she kept her mouth shut.

"There's a little problem of your clothes," said Alex tentatively.

"You mean *your* clothes," retorted Cameron, pulling at the hated nightshirt.

"Your kilt and plaid."

"Because they're to be worn by boys?"

"Because it's forbidden to wear the tartan," explained Alex gently.

"By the English!" snarled Cameron.

"Aye."

"Then I'll wear it!" shouted the girl.

"And what use will you be dead or deported to some strange land the other side of the earth?"

Cameron couldn't find an answer, and while her furious brain fought for one, Alex pressed home his point.

"Don't you think I'd like to wear the Sinclair plaid?" he asked softly.

"Then why don't you, you coward?"

"There's a world of difference between a fool and a hero," countered Alex. "To put your neck in a noose for pride that should be in your heart, not on your body, 'tis foolish and just drains Scotland of more of her blood."

" 'Tis the noblest thing to die for one's country," challenged Cameron.

"Aye, fine and noble, I'm sure, not having then to hear the death cries or see the pain anymore. How will the country rise again if all are dead? Who is left to teach the new bairns the history and tales? Who will instill the pride of their heritage in their hearts? The English?" hammered Alex.

"But we should be fighting the English," cried Cameron, confused by the sense Alex made.

"How? Tell me how, silly child? Scotland is weak. Her best warriors slain or dispersed to the colonies. Did you know there are even lairds selling their clansmen as bonded slaves so the English can build their empire? Scotland is sapped, Cameron. She must rest as you must and build her strength so she can spawn strong proud people who will fight to free her."

"When?"

"Maybe not this generation, or the next, but we must build for a future beyond our life span," explained Alex gently, knowing it sounded inconceivable to the little rebel's mind. "I know it's hard to ken, 'twas hard for me, but think on it," he murmured, still finding the fact hard to accept himself. He threw the leaves into the fire and turned back to the bed. Cameron slept, her body curled like a baby's, one small hand raised by her pink-tinged cheeks and her breathing soft and even.

Alex watched her and heaved a sigh of relief. He'd surmounted the first hurdle; she was alive and still near him.

Chapter Six

Alex decided to wait for three days before setting out on their journey to the south. Time, he felt, would strengthen Cameron and, hopefully, the bond of trust and understanding. In the cool of the morning his decision had seemed rational and of good sense, but as the day burnt on, he questioned his sanity.

The morning after his talk with Cameron he'd awakened early with the child curled enticingly into him. He'd summoned up his control and rolled carefully away, leaving the house for a private cooling swim. The sun was only just rising and he lay on his back in the water, drifting with the current as he marveled at the changes in the sky as dawn subtly tinted the clouds.

He was rudely jolted from his reverie by a sudden force to his belly, dunking him under the water, as Cameron leaped on him from the bank. He sank, clutching the firm satiny body, not realizing for a moment what he held. His arms wrapped around her back, pushing her breasts into his.

Their bellies pressed together and below excitement

flared as she realized what touched her. For a moment suspended in the water, suspended in a delicious moment in time, she was still, feeling the waves lap through her and over her. She thrust her hips forward, feeling the fires streak through her. Then the moment was fragmented into cold icy shards as Alex's head broke the surface of the water, allowing the cold, clear light of reason to flood in. He thrust her from him, roughly pushing her backward into the crystalline stream. She came up laughing, eager to play until she saw him mounting the bank and climbing into his clothes. Feeling strangely bereft she watched him walk away.

For three days Alex paid sore penance for Cameron's healthy lust for life. The more joyful she became, the more tense and irritable he grew. He was awed by her freedom and her ability to survive. Not only could she tickle fish, but they ate grouse and partridge and venison, seasoned with wild herbs. He sat back as she supported him, angry at her ability that threatened his maleness as much as his continence. He had nearly starved them and she, still weak from illness and not full-grown, could provide easily and naturally.

If Alex felt he paid penance by day, he went through torture at night. He had tried to sleep on the floor, propped against the wall, and even outside without successfully blocking out the thought of her young desirable body stretched on the bed.

Each night Cameron went to sleep in a state of confusion, her thoughts and emotions jumbled. She felt lonely and shut out, and wondered why Alex didn't sleep on the bed anymore. But why did she feel that way? she asked herself. He was taking her freedom, taking her to unnamed and unknown terrors, and yet he made her feel safe, filling an undefinable ache inside her.

On the morning of the third day both were awakened by a whining and scratching. Alex was asleep on the hard cold floor, as the rain had forced him in. Cameron heard the noise through the muffled warmth of her dreams, and she closed her ears to the beloved sound, not wanting to relive the pain by thinking of Torquil.

Finally Alex sprang up and opened the door, falling to his knees before the big shaggy beast.

"Cameron? Cameron! Wake up, you've a visitor," he cried joyfully.

She lay still. Suppose it was a cruel dream, she thought fearfully, her heart beating triple time. The bed shuddered under the weight of the large dog as he sprang up to welcome his mistress and lick the tears of joy that coursed down her face.

Alex watched Cameron nestle her face into the tawny matted fur as she spoke words of endearment. He found his mouth stretched to a wide grin and, wondering how long he'd stood with the inane expression, pried his lips from his teeth and prepared breakfast for the three of them.

After Alex and Cameron had examined Torquil for cuts and breaks and found the animal exhausted but whole, Alex walked off alone into the forest, leaving the two to their private reunion. He was thinking, wondering whether to put off their departure for a day so the dog could rest. They were ready to leave that morning, their two saddlebags packed with smoked meat, and he had cut down a set of his own clothes for Cameron to wear. He'd not found the courage or inclination to show her the garments, deciding to wait until the very last minute. She'd look like a boy once again, which was better than brandishing her rebellion against the English by wearing her Fraser kilt.

He returned to the stone house in time to see Cameron splashing in the stream with Torquil. He watched them unnoticed before entering the house. They would leave early the following day, he decided. The trip would be rough and hard with only one horse between them, and having to avoid the more populated areas where tales of Cameron's "witchery" might already have spread, they would be forced to take the more difficult roads.

That night Alex slept upon the bed, figuring the large hound that lay between them, much like a bundling bolster, was adequate protection. Alex stared up at the rafters and found himself feeling sad at their imminent departure. You'll be glad to get out of this godforsaken place back to civilization, he told himself savagely.

"Are you sleeping?" whispered Cameron, interrupting his thoughts.

Alex turned his head and stared into the wide green eyes. With her head on Torquil, Cameron stared at him as he gazed into the bright green depths, wishing he'd pretended to be asleep. He was mesmerized by the color, thinking they were the most beautiful eyes he'd ever encountered.

"'Tis rude to stare," Cameron teased softly.

"Aye, 'tis so," he murmured, hopelessly lost in the green depths. "But I've never seen eyes so green before in all my born days."

"And I'd never seen a man as naked as the day he was born before," countered Cameron dreamily.

"And what did you think?" asked Alex, dimly wondering why he was having the tantalizing conversation.

"First 'twas strange to me, like when my own body started to grow, I was excited but afraid."

"Why?"

Cameron seemed to ponder for a moment, her small face serious as she contemplated.

"'Tis difficult to say, never having talked about it before. 'Tis like everything about me had always been just there, like the sky and the sea and the moors, just there, familiar like, and then it wasn't anymore. It seemed to change each day, so I dinna know myself. Mara said it 'twas a sin."

"What 'twas a sin?" asked Alex softly, delighting in the way her mind flowed freely.

"Looking at my body in the glass. Was that what you meant the other day about not staring?"

"No, 'twas not that," Alex replied, hoping his answer would suffice, not willing at that time or any other to have to explain the facts of life between a man and a woman.

"Dinna seem a sin at all seeing my body was mine, except it didn't seem to belong to me much, changing the way it did."

"Did you talk to Duncan about it?" queried Alex, interested to know the extent of the bond they shared.

"Goodness, no! He dinna hold with woman things. He'd had a craw full of females, crying and pulling on him."

"What of your parents? Did he talk to you of them?" asked Alex.

Cameron shook her head.

"Did you not ask?"

"Aye, but he'd get angry and shout," Cameron said quietly, remembering.

"Your father was his son?"

"I think not," whispered Cameron.

"Nor your mother his daughter?" asked Alex, eager to know all he could.

"No, he said all women were sent by the Devil to tempt man."

Alex laughed softly at his own temptation by the near-woman lying near him.

"And what did Duncan say about you one day becoming a woman?"

"I said we dinna talk of such things. You dinna ken, I was just Cameron to him, just Cameron. Crazy Mara was his Lilith, stayed in his room and tempted him. He rutted her, I think," said Cameron thoughtfully.

"What!" he gasped, unprepared for such knowledge or frankness.

"They rutted like the deer and the seals, I think, from what I heard sometimes at night."

"Oh?" Alex wasn't sure how to respond. "Was there no one else besides Duncan and Mara?"

"No, dinna need no one 'cept servants, but they came and went. Mara chased them away. She dinna like the way Duncan looked at them."

"How did he look at them?"

"Like he was full of springtime," said Cameron, smiling sadly, remembering.

"But I thought he dinna hold with women?" Alex teased gently.

"He dinna hold with them don't mean he dinna like to strut before them, like the cock pheasant," said Cameron drowsily, as her thick lashes drooped to her cheek. Alex realized he was stroking her hair softly and he wondered how long he'd been doing it. He withdrew his hand but she grabbed it, placing it back among the curls.

"I like the feel of your hand. Do it more," she murmured sleepily.

Alex stroked the waves of ebony long into the night, the responsibility of Cameron weighing heavy on his heart.

Chapter Seven

Alex rose as the sun did and quietly eased himself from the bed, careful not to rouse Cameron. He laid the cut-down clothes across the bed, hoping Cameron would don them later without fuss, and tiptoed out of the house with Torquil padding by his side.

He led his horse down to the stream to drink and, after splashing water on his face and torso, lay back on the flat rock watching the sky brighten into a clear new day. The large hound sat by his side as Alex played idly with his floppy ears. Who had built the little house, wondered Alex, so carefully and painstakingly, stone by stone? Whose dreams were built in it? What had happened that it stood deserted after such loving labor? They couldn't have left without regret—an idyllic spot tucked cozily into the pines, the bank gently sloping from the door to the crystal water.

"Time we were on our way, Torquil," said Alex, feeling a pang as he realized this would probably be his last moment of peace for a great while.

"Your young mistress isn't going to take kindly to civilization. How about you?" he asked the dog as he sat up. Cameron was as untamed and natural as any wild animal, he thought, and he shuddered. What if she were to tear off her clothes to swim whenever she felt like it? Or even worse challenge the English soldiers they were sure to meet as they traveled southward? What was he going to do with her upon reaching home? He'd have to hire a governess and a chaperon to stop wagging tongues—and to protect her from his desires. Better yet he'd send her to a good strict school for young ladies. Alex stifled a chuckle at the thought of her sewing samplers and tinkling away on the harpsichord in a polite, pink parlor. He'd have to smooth away some rough edges before a school would accept her, he thought, smiling.

"Oh, well, Torquil, it's first things first. Getting safely home is our first priority."

Alex led the horse up the bank and tied it to a tree near the house. Going inside he saw that Cameron was awake but not dressed. She sat crosslegged and cross-armed on the bed, scowling ominously. Oh, no, groaned Alex inwardly, realizing his trials were to start sooner than he imagined. He forced a cheery smile.

"Good morning."

"I'm not going," stated Cameron.

"You scared?" he challenged, relieved it wasn't a battle over the clothes that was to follow.

"I'm not scared of anything."

"Prove it, then," said Alex tersely, throwing his cut-down garments into her lap.

Cameron stared at them, puzzled, before picking them up with disdain.

"What in God's name are these?"

"Watch your mouth and put them on. We need a good start this morning."

"I want my own clothes."

"We've been through that."

"Where are they?" she demanded.

Alex debated lying to her, telling her that he'd burned them when in fact he'd folded them neatly and hidden them in the saddlebags. It had been against his better judgment to keep them, as any search by the English would uncover them, and both their necks would be stretched. Yet if he told her they were destroyed, he'd have her uncontrolled temper to deal with and the morning was too sweet.

"Safe," he muttered, and Cameron eyed him with distrust.

"Where?"

"Packed, outside. Torquil and the poor horse are raring to be off while you sit here like some wee bairn who canna dress herself in her clothes," he challenged.

"They're not my clothes," she argued.

"Nay, they're mine and mighty fond I was of them too. Now look at this," said Alex, as he picked up his britches and held them against him, the trouser legs barely reaching his knees. Despite herself Cameron grinned.

"That's a better face to start off the morning," he said, tossing them to her and striding out, praying there'd be no more resistance to her dressing.

Alex saddled the horse and sat outside waiting. He was just about to see what was taking her so long when the door opened and Cameron stood in the doorway, holding up the trews, her face alive with mischief.

"Look," she ordered, and threw her arms in the air. The trews fell promptly to the ground.

"Thank the Lord the shirt is too long," chuckled Alex, joining her laughter.

"Why?"

"Never mind. Here's a kilt pin; turn around," he said, and Cameron obediently shuffled her feet so she didn't trip on the trews that were still around her ankles.

"Pull them up," he ordered. She bent obediently, saucily exposing her bare bottom.

Alex took a wide tuck, tightening them around her tiny waist.

"There now, turn around."

Cameron faced him, her hands feeling her back.

"That's fine," said Alex, satisfied.

"But there's a big lump behind like a tail," she complained.

"What's wrong with a tail? Torquil has one, don't you, boy?"

"Aye, and so do you from what I've seen," answered Cameron wickedly.

How was he ever going to teach her to curb her forthright tongue? he wondered, turning to his horse.

"Put your boots on, Cameron, you're holding us up. And your vest's by the fire."

The girl turned back into the house only to shout out a moment later. "I canna find my boots."

"They're under the bed," he called back, thinking that no matter what age, women could never dress in a hurry.

"No they're not," Cameron sang out. Alex knew they were there, having placed them himself. "They're there," he thundered.

"Not," she spat as he strode in.

They weren't under the bed. Where had the little nuisance hidden them? raged Alex to himself.

"You'll have to go barefoot then. I'll not play nanny to a twelve-year-old that canna dress herself," he shouted, throwing her leather jerkin at her.

"I'm fifteen! . . . I think."

"Don't you know?" Alex asked, a bit taken aback at her thinking herself older than he had anticipated.

"Of course I know," raged Cameron. "I'm fifteen."

"Then that's all the more reason for you to be acting your age. Now find the boots or start walking as you are."

Cameron sulkily pulled her boots from under the mattress and, taking her time, put them on.

Not as good a departure as he'd hoped, mused Alex, as they finally set off, but not nearly as bad as it could have been either. He congratulated himself on managing to keep his temper and holding her in check from one of her uncontrollable tantrums. He led the horse that Cameron rode as Torquil bounded ahead, sniffing the thick bracken that grew on the banks of the stream they followed. Alex judged them to be somewhere between Ben Hea and Ben Klibreck and was glad to see that the water flowed joyfully south toward Loch Shin and not east to the town of Altnamarra, preferring to avoid people altogether for as long as possible. He judged the time to be about seven and hoped they could travel without stopping for four or five hours.

They traveled in silence for the first hour, until Cameron broke into his thoughts.

"I'm hungry," she declared.

Alex silently handed her a piece of meat and bit into one himself. Cameron stared at the meat and looked at the back of Alex's tawny hair, blowing in the breeze, ruffling like a lion's mane. He walked, munching, lost in his own thoughts.

Cameron, who usually liked silence, was piqued. She wondered why he was angry with her. An hour had gone by before she complained about her hunger, even though she'd promised herself she wouldn't talk to him unless he spoke first. She cursed herself for weakening, letting her anger cover the fear that bit into her belly as they made their way south toward all the evils her grandfather had fled from. She'd never seen any English and she wondered what they'd look like. "Animals!" Duncan had roared. What sort of animals, she wondered, knowing she preferred animals to people.

"Aren't you going to eat it?" asked Alex, seeing the meat held in her hand.

Cameron stared into his eyes. Suddenly she wasn't hungry. Fear gnawed inside her and she shook her head and handed the food back. Alex wondered if she was going on another hunger strike, but curbed his concern, reasoning she'd eaten well in the past four days and going without breakfast wouldn't hurt.

For three more hours they traveled, both lost in their own thoughts, Alex relieved in the silence, Cameron afraid of it. She longed to ask where they were going but feared what she might hear. This time she'd keep the promise to herself and not talk to him. Her back ached and she longed to stretch her legs; it seemed they'd been traveling all day, but the sun stood overhead in the sky above the pine-tree tops. She'd just made up her mind to slip from the horse's back when Alex veered down the bank to the water.

The stream had widened to a pool the size of a small mountain tarn that, at the far end, poured down six feet or so in a small waterfall. Seeing it, Cameron forgot her promise and her anger.

"I'll race you in," she shouted, sliding off the horse's back and tearing off her shirt and jerkin. Before Alex could collect himself, her boots joined the other clothes and she stood bare-breasted trying to undo the pin behind her to release the britches.

"Whoa there. There may be people about."

Cameron cocked her head and frowned. "What if there are? Oh, you mean like the English?"

"Cameron, young ladies dinna go about throwing off their clothes at the first sign of water. You dinna see Duncan Fraser running about in the alltogether, did you now?" Alex asked, thinking it was as good a time as any.

"Mara did, but Grandfather had a bit of rheumatics," explained Cameron, trying to loose the pin.

"You have to learn 'tis not done in polite society."

"But there's no one here but you!"

"Cameron, you must understand and learn not to."

"But you do," retorted Cameron, frustrated by the stiff and stubborn pin.

"Not anymore, except if I'm alone," said Alex firmly.

"But we are alone."

"I mean really alone. Without you. Or you without me," he struggled.

"Why?"

"Because I say so. Now get dressed and let's eat."

"I want to swim," said Cameron defiantly, hands on her hips, green eyes flashing.

"All right, but 'tis the last time." Alex turned away, leading the horse to drink.

"But I canna get the pin undone."

"If you want to swim, you do it yourself."

"But you did it up. Won't you help?"

"No!"

"You bloody bastard!" Cameron screamed.

Alex only turned away, ignoring her. One lesson at a time, he thought. He'd curb her language another time.

Cameron twisted her body this way and that, trying to undo the tuck in her trews, but her usually nimble fingers were unable to free the stiff kilt pin.

"I canna do it."

"Then you canna swim," replied Alex tersely.

"And what about the call of nature? You expect me to wet my breeks like a baby?"

"Then you'd better learn, as you're the one th
wears them," called Alex, resting his back against
tree as he watched with amusement the half-nak
girl's antics to free herself. Her face was a picture
concentration, her black hair tossing this way a
that, her breasts pushed forward as her arms thru
back trying to work the metal pin. He ate slowly a
leisurely.

"Better eat; we have to be on our way soon." Ca
eron turned and spat such a filthy stream of langua
at him that Alex forgot his vow to keep his temper
check. He leaped up and, picking her up by the seat
the pants and her tangled hair, shook her until h
teeth rattled.

"Guard your filthy tongue! You'll not speak to n
or anyone else like that again, you ken?" he roare
holding her face just inches from his own. She star
back in white-lipped rage.

"Do you ken?" he repeated.

Cameron spat full in his face and Alex, fearing
would strangle her or beat her to death, threw her in
the pool.

"That should clean your filthy mouth!"

All through the encounter Torquil had whined, u
easy but somehow knowing that Alex meant his you
mistress no harm. Breathing deeply to control his ra
Alex stared into the water, watching for Cameror
head to emerge. He froze, not seeing it, and waite
cursing himself for his own lack of control. What
she'd hit her head on a hidden rock?"

Swearing, Alex dived into the pool fully clothed
search for Cameron. The water was clear and deep, th
bottom sandy with no large rocks that could ha
caused her injury. He swam underwater, looking un
his lungs nearly burst, then came up for air and sa
Cameron on the bank, casually eating with one ar

round the large hound. He felt like an idiot being
taken in by the simplest of tricks and decided to cool
his heels and his temper by floating on his back, even
though his riding boots made that very difficult.
He'd not give the brat satisfaction by storming up and
continuing the battle she seemed to want.

Minutes later Alex swam strongly to shore and, sitting on a rock, he merrily whistled as he emptied the
water out of his boots. He pretended a happy noncha-
lance he didn't feel, secretly hoping they'd soon be
able to strike out across the moors in the sunshine so
he could dry off. Still whistling he packed the food
away and led the horse up the bank. Cameron pulled
on her shirt and boots and watched him leave. Torquil
pulled at her sleeve, whining for her to follow.

Why should she follow him like some stupid sheep,
she thought rebelliously. She didn't want to go anyway. She tried to shake her dog off her arm but he
whimpered and pulled at the fabric, tearing the sleeve.

Alex stood high on the bank watching. He was sick
of being tested; his patience and understanding were
wearing thin. He strode down the bank and picked
her up, depositing her unceremoniously on the horse.

Cameron sat and fumed, not realizing her rage hid
the panic that beat frantically inside. For two hours
they plodded through the pine forest until it met the
moors, where it trickled thinly through the heather.
Alex recognized they were nearing the road that ran
between Scourie in the west and Lairg southeast and,
knowing they had to cross it to reach Loch Shin, he
scrutinized Cameron carefully. How could she pass for
a boy? he wondered, with her fine features and distinctive coloring? She had fooled him before but now,
knowing, it was difficult for him to realize. He pulled
out the tail of his shirt and tore a strip of linen off

and, taking the girl from the horse, tied her wil
mane of shoulder-length hair back in a ponytail.

"There are people we might meet who'll ask que
tions. You'll say nary a word, you ken?" he growled.

Cameron was silent and Alex curbed his rising ten
per.

"That's the way," he said sarcastically. "Remember
it because it means your neck. And better keep you
clothes on too while you're about it," he added, sur
veying her critically and noting that his fine tailore
trousers and linen shirt were well disguised with mu
and grass stains. He looked down at himself and sav
that he looked rather disreputable himself. His usuall
gleaming boots were soggy and wet, the leather luster
less and scuffed. Hopefully they'd be taken for an
poor Scots making their way to the central lowland
for work in the mines or spinning factories.

Leaving the scrubby shelter of the stunted trees the
entered open moorland. Cameron longed to dig he
heels into the round firm girth of her mount and ga
lop. But it wasn't Torquod beneath her and she rod
the numb slow rhythm remembering her black sta
lion, unable to believe she'd never see or ride hir
again.

In the late afternoon they reached the beaten trac
that was the main thoroughfare northwest, and Ale
anxiously scanned the road before crossing to th
shore of Loch Shin. Cameron was confused as the
traveled northwest when their direction had seeme
southeast, not knowing that Alex had chosen to make
wide detour around the town of Lairg, which lay on th
eastern tip of the loch.

His legs were weary, aching from the grueling wal
and, wanting to travel as far as possible, he mounte
behind Cameron as they rode beside the still wate
Cameron had never seen a large body of inland wate

nd she wondered if it was an arm of the sea, but there
vere no gulls or salt smell.

Alex let the horse drink and Cameron realized the
vater was sweet, as she gratefully slid her aching body
rom the high back and plunged her face and head
nto the freshness. She drank her fill and then, stretch-
ng her cramped limbs, rolled on her back in the fra-
rant grass and closed her eyes. Alex, discovering they
ad traveled farther east than he meant to, was impa-
ent to keep moving, knowing they were dangerously
ear the busy crossroads outside Lairg. He picked up
ameron without ceremony and tossed her into the
addle, mounting behind her. He urged his horse west
long the banks of Loch Shin, not daring to traverse
ie shorter but more popular route east.

The sun was low in the sky as they rounded the end
f the loch: The dying rays burned bloody strips
cross the sky, staining the heather and the summit of
en More Assynt in the distance. Alex headed for the
ountain.

It was night and still they traveled, in the pitch
lack, the horse picking his way slowly through the
orse and heather. Cameron thought they'd never stop,
ut she said nothing, as Alex didn't speak first. Now
nd again she felt her body relax against his as her
yelids drooped, but then she jerked herself awake.
lex, on seeing the red sunset, had decided to travel
l night and sleep the following day away, as he had
ssumed the sky would be clear and the moon nearly
ull. To his irritation there was no such light and he
ad to keep going until they reached cover, as sleeping
xposed on the barren moor was too dangerous.

The rolling moor seemed endless and he was con-
used, knowing they should have reached the scrub-
and at the foothills of Ben More Assynt. He felt the
eariness of his horse beneath him, and the arm that

held Cameron ached unbearably, but he was afraid to dismount for fear the nodding girl would fall sound asleep and lose her balance. Torquil plodded stoically behind, his heavy head lowered and his proud tail drooping with fatigue.

Just as Alex decided they could go no farther, the moon sailed out from behind a cloud and ahead Alex saw the treeline they had been aiming for. The moon was very high and he estimated they'd been traveling most of the night. He kicked his tired mount to a faster pace as they headed for the trees, fearing the moonlight would again disappear.

Every muscle in Cameron's body screamed. Each jolt of the horse's new rhythm jarred her and she wanted to bite the strong arms that cradled her like a baby. She wanted to resist but welcomed the sensations. What were they? Her befogged mind tried to reason but sank into oblivion instead.

Alex laid the sleeping girl beneath a tree. He looked around for Torquil and, not seeing him, whistled. The huge hound bounded up and licked his hand with an icy tongue, his shaggy face wet and cold.

"So you've been drinking, have you, old lad? Well, show me," said Alex, taking the horse's reins and following the dog through the trees to a small stream that ribboned its way through the fallen needles. It was so tiny it crept without a sound and Alex had to pat the ground until he felt it. Leaving the horse to drink he surveyed the terrain. The moonlight hardly broke through the thick branches overhead. He patiently let his weary eyes accustom to the dimness. A large conifer stood, its branches dipping low, making a shelter like the make-believe houses he and his sisters had played in as children. He turned, sniffing the air for smoke as he scanned all around him looking for the unwelcome signs of human life. The air was resinous and the tree trunks stood stiff and still, like soldiers, on their carpet of soft needles.

"We'll take the chance, old dog," he growled to Torquil as he returned to fetch Cameron.

"Thank God she weighs no more than a bairn," he panted aloud, as he lifted her in his aching arms and carried her to the shelter. Pushing the pine boughs aside with his back so they didn't snap back into the sleeping girl's face, he entered and laid her down. She whimpered softly and tried to clutch him to her as his arms left her. Alex left her to unsaddle his horse and, tethering him, he lay down on the fragrant carpet and drank from the stream. The water was bitter and resinous but still thirst-quenching. He sat chewing some smoked meat as he listened to the noises of the night.

Chapter Eight

Alex did not ever want to wake; he felt he'd never slept so deeply or soundly. There was a completeness about him. Memories buzzed in his brain, the perfume of the pine, the softness in his arms. He opened his protesting eyes, seeing the lacy pattern of the sunlight flickering through deep green, and then down at the warm bundle that lay cuddled and curled to his belly. He savored the moment, watching her—the gentle swell of her breathing, the caress of her ebony hair against his cheek, her small bottom thrust into him, her knees bent, and the small hand holding his encircling arm.

In sleep Cameron turned toward him, pressing her body closer. Alex felt his passion flare and bent to the soft parted lips, meaning just to gently taste. His mouth lightly touched hers and with a groan he felt it open to him. It had been too long. Nearly three weeks without a woman and here was a lovely female body pressing up to him. Alex tried to reason with himself, but his surging excitement took over.

Cameron, half-awake, felt a stirring in her body and, in turning toward the warmth against her back, experienced a rush of excitement as her pelvis met a hardness. She felt her mouth enclosed by Alex's and opened to him, poking her tongue and sucking the hard probing of his. She pressed her pelvis rhythmically against him.

Alex thrust back, his hand opening the buttons of her shirt to cup her breasts. He wrenched his mouth from hers and bent to suck her hard nipples. Cameron writhed, trying to connect her pelvis back against his hardness, whimpering and panting. Out of his head with passion Alex tried to lower her britches but they wouldn't budge. He frantically kissed her breasts and neck as he again found her mouth. His manhood strained painfully against the confining material of his tight trousers.

He groaned, wanting to enter the warmth of her as she increased her movements. Realizing what was happening Alex used all his willpower to hold himself back. He lay still, willing himself to reason. What in hell am I doing? She's just a child!—yet often girls are wed much younger. Some at twelve or thirteen, eleven even, and many times to men much older than I, came a traitorous thought. But I am her guardian, his censoring mind railed.

He lay still, closing his mouth firmly, but Cameron, stirred to fever pitch, kept kissing and trying to pry his lips open with her small tongue, all the while rhythmically rubbing and thrusting against him, faster and faster, until she froze, hips pressed forward, straining into him. Her sensations culminated in an explosion that throbbed through her as she whimpered and arched her back.

Alex lay stiffly with his eyes closed, feigning sleep, his loins aching unbearably. He wished he could gain relief as easily as she.

Cameron was watching him, puzzled that he slept. She looked down toward the place that had given her such pleasure and noticed the front of his trews was different. She gently traced the hard outline, squeezing the pulsing firmness curiously. Inquisitively she stroked and tried to grasp him through the tautness of his britches, but giving a sleepy groan Alex rolled onto his stomach, thwarting her exploring hand.

Cameron stared at his broad, still back and around at her surroundings. She sat hugging her knees, smelling the sweetness, and then she crawled out from the low-hanging branches. Where were they? A narrow stream of water trickled, winding through the roots of the trees, whose hairy trunks stood stiff and erect on a brown carpet of soft pine needles. Torquil bounded up, bidding her good morning as she wrestled with the kilt pin behind her back.

Alex, still pretending to sleep, lay pressing himself against the ground, wishing they had made camp on the shores of Loch Shin, so he could cool himself off. Then he wryly realized he'd probably have had to contend with her nakedness there. Finally the aching ebbed, leaving him feeling bruised and sore. He swept the branches back and looked out at Cameron wrestling with the tuck in her trews. Thank God for that blasted pin, he thought, knowing well what would have happened if it hadn't frustrated his progress. Seeing him Cameron debated whether to ask for assistance but, remembering the day before, bit her lip and tried until her fingers hurt and her twisted shoulders ached.

"Hold still," Alex growled, finally taking pity on her, seeing her crossed legs. The blasted pin had buried its head and tangled itself in the torn cloth. Alex worked until he had loosened it.

"There, now you can unlock it yourself," he muttered, as he strode behind some trees. Cameron pulled the pin out and, holding her trousers up, went behind other bushes. She longed to ask Alex about the sensations that had made her body throb and tick deep inside her, but she remembered that she wasn't speaking to him.

And Alex, although he longed to take Cameron to task on her unladylike behavior and wantonness, berated himself instead for his own ungentlemanly conduct. Not knowing how to broach the subject without rearousing himself or igniting her fierce temper, he said nothing. They ate in silence, each lost in his own tumultuous thoughts.

Alex judged the time to be late afternoon. He stared over the stretch of land they'd traversed the night before, noticing that they had somehow traveled east parallel to the mountains instead of the short distance straight south. In a way it was better, having made more distance, but it left a stretch of rolling, treeless moorland ahead of them. He gazed a long time toward Loch Shin, knowing it was a miracle that the horse hadn't tripped or broken a leg in the treacherous crevices that were hidden beneath the heather. Someone must be looking down on them, he thought ironically, and so He'd better after the coil that He had wound him in. He wondered wryly if Duncan Fraser could see down and, if so, whether he and Alex's father were enjoying a rare chuckle.

They set off an hour before sunset and Alex broke their customary silence. He debated his wording an hour before speaking.

"We'll be meeting people soon and I want to explain to you that there's a code of behavior and speaking." He stopped, hoping Cameron would continue by asking what the code was, but she kept her head averted and her mouth closed.

"I've told you before, so it'll come as no shock. You're to curb your tongue—no cursing or foulness—and keep your body covered." He droned on about being circumspect, reticent, and demure and having to wear dresses and ride sidesaddle. Cameron didn't understand half of what he was saying, but she would have bitten out her tongue sooner than admit her ignorance. Alex skirted the real issue he wanted to set her right about. Not that he in any way really *wanted* to, but he felt he had to. Cameron's sensuous nature troubled and confused him. Most young ladies of his acquaintance showed no sign that they knew or experienced anything of a sexual nature. There were women of course who were in the business of prostitution, but even they seemed to show no enjoyment. His mistress Fiona was worldly and experienced, but still she was the essence of propriety except in bed, and even then the light was doused or subtly dimmed. How was he to deal with Cameron? Was she destined to be a harlot? What if she behaved as she had with any male she bumped against? puzzled Alex, as he rambled on about what was expected from a civilized young lady.

All night he walked, until he mounted behind Cameron to ease his sore legs. As the first gray light peeked over the horizon, they reached the road that ran from Lochinvea to Carbisdale. There was a thick mist and Alex was surprised to see people loom out of the fog. The first human beings they had seen since the ragged men. He debated heading back to the wilderness but, fearing for his horse on the rugged terrain hampered by the mist, he kept to the road.

The sun rose, clearing the day to brightness. Many people walked alongside of them, carrying baskets, driving goats and sheep. The delicious aromas of fresh-baked pies and breads hung in the air. Cameron stared in amazement, never in her life having seen so many people. Pony carts full of children. Chickens, ducks, and geese quacking, honking, and hissing. Small boys poking grunting hogs. Girls in bright dresses and bonnets. Men in their Sunday best, striding painfully in shining shoes. Happy music playing from squeeze boxes and reed pipes. It was a parade of color, smells, music, and people.

At first Cameron was afraid, but then her fascination took over as she feasted her eyes, relating the sights to those she'd read about in her grandfather's books, reading having been one of her few escapes in the freezing winter months on Cape Wrath. Torquil plodded beside her, ignoring the barking prancing dogs that teased and goaded him for attention. I wonder what he thinks of all this? thought Cameron, watching his great shaggy head. Two small boys, thinking Torquil a Shetland pony, tried to leap on his back and, before Alex realized what was happening, Cameron slid off the horse and ran to protect her pet. Just in time she remembered she was not to utter a word, so she picked up stones and started flinging them at the boys, frightening sheep, ducks, and the like before Alex hauled her back up by the big tuck in the back of her pants. He then dismounted and led the horse, keeping his hand on Torquil's head.

Alex flowed with the crowd to the Carbisdale market, reasoning they were fairly well protected by the surge of people—that was if Cameron could behave herself, having already caused a small stampede and some bad feelings on the way.

Cameron's head whirled at the sights and smells. It was more than she ever could have imagined. The colors, the laughter, the hustle and bustle. Was this a city? she wondered, staring around in awe at the small market town that had been the scene of a bloody siege more than one hundred years before, when Cromwell defeated the Scots.

Alex kept a tight rein on Cameron as they roamed around looking at the sights, both their mouths watering at the appetizing aromas. Seeing a stall boasting hot steaming meat pies and dark ale Alex succumbed, buying some of each. Cameron savored her pie slowly, not ever wanting it to end and Alex, feeling much the same, bought a dozen more. He gave two to Torquil and another to Cameron and himself before storing the rest away for their journey. Cameron drank the warm bitter ale thirstily and was furious when Alex, on recollecting his guardianship, whisked her second mug away and downed it himself. Feeling guilty at her unhappy face he bought her a wedge of blackberry pie as a substitute. Cameron had never seen money exchanged for wares before and wondered where one acquired the coins.

Her mouth had feasted and now her eyes devoured all she saw. Seeing a knife-throwing game she pulled on Alex's arm impatiently, dragging him over and holding out her hand for a coin. Alex laughed and waved at the redheaded proprietor.

"He be a mute?" asked the burly man sadly, staring at Cameron who mimed urgently to Alex that she wanted to play.

"Aye," Alex replied, handing him a coin as he thought at least Cameron obeyed him to the word by not uttering one. He scanned the course. At the far end a robust, scantily dressed woman was lewdly painted with arms spread, fifteen feet from the line where Cameron stood, clutching ten throwing knives. The nipples on each grotesque breast were painted with a number too small for Alex to discern, and at crucial parts of the anatomy—navel, crotch, and eyes—were more microscopic numbers amounting to ten as they traveled to less lurid spots on her knees and big toes.

Cameron threw the first knife, hitting the left eye, and a gasp went up from the few spectators.

"The lad hit the one!"

" 'Twas luck," growled another.

Cameron waited until the people were quiet and, concentrating, threw the second knife. Alex expected the second eye to be penetrated but instead the dagger quivered into the left big toe.

"He got two!" gasped some of the crowd that pressed, peering closely, at the painted, pierced wench.

"Stand back afore he gets you too," shouted the red-haired proprietor.

Cameron threw the third knife, hitting the left knee, as the crowd increased and grew wild, calling out to passersby to watch the wee lad throw.

The fourth knife hit the right eye, the fifth the right knee, and the sixth the right toe.

The child must have the eyes of a hawk, thought Alex, awed as much as the milling crowd by Cameron's dexterity. Bets were being placed fast and furiously, as the crowd tripled, pushing to witness Cameron's prowess. Once again Cameron waited until the mob had quieted. People hushed each other until a pin could be heard to drop, and then the small bundle of ragged clothes raised her arm and threw the seventh knife, hitting the right nipple dead center. The crowd roared with excitement.

The eighth knife flew straight and true to the navel, the ninth to the left breast, and the tenth quivered in the crotch.

The noise was deafening and Cameron, exhausted from a lack of sleep and the demanding concentration, felt terror as the mob surged toward her. Torquil, sensing her fear, growled menacingly to hold them back and Cameron sank to her knees, blocking her ears and burying her face in the dog's russet coat.

" 'Twas fixed!" screamed a graceless loser.

"Aye, crooked," chorused more of the same.

"Stand back!" roared the redhaired giant. "Dinna squash our young hero; 'tis a braw Scots lad from the good old days."

"Let him prove it then," yelled some angry men, loath to hand over their scarce money to smiling winners who stood, palms outstretched.

"Aye, and double the bets," shouted another voice that was greeted by a chorus of delighted assent.

Alex stood still, his mind racing to figure out how to get them out of the pressing mass of people. Here was Cameron making them the center of attention when they were meant to be as inconspicuous as possible, he fumed unfairly.

"He proved his worth already," bellowed the redhaired owner of the game, "and he deserves his reward," he added, stooping and pressing a warm coin into Cameron's hand.

"They're in it together," screeched an irate woman.

"Aye," chorused others, waving fists and sticks. Cameron looked up into Alex's worried eyes and to the dirks in the redhaired man's hands. She stood unsteadily and indicated she wanted the knives.

The redhaired man looked compassionately into Cameron's bright green eyes.

"The puir wee lad don't have to prove hisself no more. You should be shamed picking on the bairn. He's mute."

Cameron silently held out her hand.

"Witch's spawn! Look at that devil's hair and his eyes unnatural green," screamed a haglike crone, the spit hissing through her sparse yellow teeth.

Alex's blood froze remembering the witch-burning at Dornock, less than ten miles from where they stood. Nothing much had changed in the Highlands since that excruciating execution in 1722, thirty-nine years before, except an escalation of the frustration that English oppression and repression caused, making Scot turn against Scot to somehow ease the futile violence that writhed within.

It was a terrible tangle, for if Cameron threw again, straight and true, it would convince some that the allegations of the hag were true, and if she missed her targets, the rest would feel there was cheating of them being done.

"Give back the money, Cameron," he murmured, but the child's determined face turned from him as she took the knives from the redhaired man.

"We'll choose the target," shouted the mob.

"His pa," yelled a voice, setting up a chant.

"His pa—his pa—his pa."

Alex looked at the screaming crowd of demanding

faces and, knowing how quickly the mob could surge upon them, walked silently to the wall and stood against it.

Cameron looked at Alex standing, fifteen feet away, against the painted lady. In each hand he held a thin piece of grass. His head was twisted to the side so she saw his profile, a tiny twig protruding from his mouth.

Alex's heart beat like a lead hammer in his chest. He was really at Cameron's mercy now. He knew the child wanted her freedom more than anything else, and now she had her chance. As he stood waiting, he wondered why she hadn't used her knife so deftly in their first encounter that seemed years ago, instead of about a fortnight.

Cameron waited for silence and, concentrating, threw the knife, pinning one dried stalk of grass to the wall. Alex, eyes closed, steeled himself, expecting to feel pain, but his head rebounded at the sharp thud. A gasp went up from the crowd and he opened his eyes and saw the lethal weapon still shaking less than a sixteenth of an inch from his closed finger and thumb. He let go the straw and dropped his hand as people rushed to see.

When all was quiet, Alex stood still, not knowing which of the two targets he held were being aimed at. He felt the whistling and the deadly thud, opened his eyes, and saw nothing. He took a breath and dropped his outstretched arm and again a gasp of disbelief surged through the mob.

This is it, Alex thought, perspiration beading and trickling down his itchy face. A severed finger was one thing, but a dagger in the eye or face could mean blindness or death. His temple throbbed, a fly tickled his nostril, and he steeled himself to be still. He tried to keep his mind from what was happening, and at the same time he wished Cameron would hurry and throw so the painful anticipation would be over.

The crowd was hushed and Alex waited in the terrifying silence for an eternity, half of him wishing he could see her, the other half glad that he couldn't.

Cameron aimed but couldn't throw the knife. For a moment she felt a surge of power, knowing Alex was at her mercy. She'd wanted to break his arrogance, reversing their positions. She wanted him to sweat and had deliberately left the hardest target for last. She wanted to punish him and have her revenge. Now her arm shook as she aimed. She dropped it to her side and flexed it as Torquil whined softly. What was the matter with her? She could do it. Hadn't she done it thousands of times before? But what if she missed? her frantic mind wondered. The crowd grew restless.

"Dinna rush the lad. Give him time," barked the red-haired man.

Alex's body was in excruciating pain, every muscle knotted and screaming, his kneecaps jumping in spasms. He forced himself to breathe shallowly, afraid of making even the slightest movement. His teeth ached as he bit on the tiny twig and panic flared as the clenching caused a numbness and he could no longer feel the small target. Had he dropped it? Or worse still, made it smaller?

Again the crowd grew silent as Cameron raised her arm and aimed the dagger. She drew it back, but the knife dropped out of her lifeless fingers and stood quivering in the earth at her feet. She stood staring at her own hand that seemed to do its own bidding, and then fell to her knees, burying her face in Torquil's fur.

Alex, upon hearing the clamoring crowd and the absence of the deadly thud, dared open his eyes and swivel his stiff neck. Cameron knelt with her dog as the crowd dispersed, chattering among themselves. He relaxed his body and leaned back against the painted lady, shaking his head at Cameron's ingenuity. She had brilliantly disentangled them from the mess, he thought, seeing the third knife still in the ground.

Cameron was unaware that she had inadvertently done the only thing possible to appease the crowd. She only felt shame and confusion at her inability to throw the last dagger.

Alex strolled calmly to the redhaired proprietor who slapped him heartily on the back.

"Some fine lad you have there. Bet he could have done it but he a'feared hurting you. That's some fine loving bairn. No man could ask for more, mute or otherwise," he said.

Alex wanted to get far away as quickly as possible, knowing as the word spread about Cameron's strange eyes and raven hair, it might couple with more stories from further north, but the heavy, jovial arm around his shoulders, accompanied by the redhaired giant's obvious desire to talk, made leaving impossible.

"Time's hard, but there's room for the two of ye with me. Living's fair to middling, country fairs, and in the wintertime the city's warm and some of the gentry generous," he offered.

"How 'bout it, lad? 'Tis a rare, free life traveling the length and breadth of Scotland from fair to fair, market to market. We'll put your name up and have everyone flocking to see that fancy throwing of your'n." He stooped, talking to Cameron, who kept her face hidden in Torquil's warm fur.

"Do he hear me?" asked the redhaired man of Alex. Alex smiled sadly and shook his head as he pulled the girl to her feet. Cameron's shamed green eyes met his inquiring amber ones. Then she looked into the light blue eyes beneath the thatch of red hair, her mind racing. She wanted to go. She wanted a rare, free life. As though Alex could read her mind, his hard fingers dug into the soft flesh of her shoulders and he steered her to his horse.

"Think on it. I'll be here till the morrow and then on to Tain. The name's Ben," the proprietor shouted after them, and Alex lifted his hand in acknowledgment.

As they rode through the fair, Alex spied a stall with plain homespun dresses. It would be better for Cameron to wear one as they neared his home, he thought. He also saw a straw farmer's hat that would hide her telltale mop of hair. Dragging her with him he stopped and bought the hat, cramming it on her head as he inquired the price of a green- and oatmeal-checked dress.

"Is it the right size?" asked the woman.

"I'm not sure," Alex answered, the thought not having occurred to him.

"For your wife, is it?"

"Daughter," he improvised quickly.

"How big?"

"Well, she's much the same as her brother here," replied Alex, keeping his hand firmly on the top of Cameron's hat, so it stayed crammed on her head covering most of her face.

"Twins, are they?"

"Nay, she's older, but skinny and scrawny for her age," he laughed, mischievously, hoping for some spirit from Cameron, but the girl didn't react. She was lost in her own thoughts about escaping Alex and finding the man called Ben. Funny kind of name for a person to be having. Ben sounded like a mountain, but then the man had been very large, she thought, as the jolly round woman held the dress against her. Cameron stared at her in surprise.

"Oh, my, look at those eyes on him! Green as the spring grass. Does the girl have the same?" she chattered.

"Aye. I'll take that one," growled Alex, eager to be gone.

"Matches, don't it? The green of the frock sets off them eyes really pretty. Like a cat's. Ain't never seen such green on a bairn before," she rambled, as she wrapped the dress.

"Anything else you'd be needing? Petticoat? Drawers?" Alex, about to turn away, stopped. He hadn't thought of what Cameron should wear under her clothes.

"Aye, give me two of each, same size. 'Tis her birthday soon," he stammered.

"Well? What do you think of our purchases?" Alex asked, as they cantered away from the noisy hive of people. Cameron didn't answer.

"Wake up! What do you think of all your new finery?" he repeated.

Cameron stared at him blankly. What finery? Her head was too full planning how she could escape and double back to join the knife-throwing game.

Chapter Nine

Fearing they'd be followed, Alex reluctantly took to the mountains. They had not slept for twenty-four hours, though, so he made camp before sunset.

" 'Tis all right to talk now," said Alex gently, unpacking the meat pies he'd bought at the fair. Still Cameron didn't answer.

"Did you enjoy yourself?" he probed, and still getting no answer, added, "Have you been to a fair before?"

"You know I haven't, and don't be so unkind. I want to forget it," she retorted, turning away.

"Did you not like your success and attention? And if it weren't for your quick thinking we'd really be in a mess," said Alex, confused.

"What success? I dinna throw the last dirk. I dinna finish what I started!" shouted Cameron hotly.

"You meant to?"

"I feel shamed enough, so leave it be," yelled Cameron.

"There's nothing to feel shamed about," exclaimed Alex, thinking her shame very misplaced for so wanon a girl. "You fair took my breath away, and everybody else's too. Where did you learn to throw like that?"

Cameron sat eating her pie, refusing to answer.

"Cameron, would that redhaired fellow have wanted you to join with him if you were shameful?" asked Alex, who then silently asked himself what he thought he was saying. Here he was trying to get her to be a civilized young lady and yet he was applauding her knife-throwing.

"Why didn't you throw the last knife?" he asked roughly.

"None of your concern."

"Well, let's forget it if you'd rather. But the rest of the market? Did you not like that? The food and the music? All the people?" he asked, having noticed her wide-eyed fascination.

"Aye, 'twas strange like a dream. I dinna ken there was so many people alive," she smiled, remembering the rest of the day.

Alex, pleased that he'd got her talking at last, handed her the bundles.

"Here's your presents."

"What for?"

"Pretend it's your birthday."

Cameron looked puzzled. "My what?"

"Birthday," repeated Alex.

"Oh," said Cameron, not knowing what on earth he was talking about and not wanting to show her ignorance.

"Well, aren't you going to open them?" Alex asked.

Cameron tore the paper off and looked at the dress.

"Pity you canna see the pretty green by the firelight," he murmured, as Cameron stood slowly and held the dress against her. Her thoughts were in turmoil. She had felt awkward and clumsy around the gaily dressed girls at the fair. She dropped the dress and, sitting, opened the other package.

"What is it?" she said, holding up the pantalettes.

"To wear under the dress."

"Why?"

"Because 'tis done. That's what ladies wear, like men wear britches," explained Alex patiently.

"But there's nothing in the middle," complained Cameron, thrusting her hand through.

"That's how they're made. 'Tis for convenience."

"I dinna ken," replied Cameron, throwing them aside and picking up the petticoat.

" 'Tis a nightshirt?"

"Nay, a petticoat."

"A coat?" frowned Cameron, turning it the other way up.

"A chemise, a petticoat to wear under the dress," struggled Alex.

"Why is everything to be worn under the frock where it canna be seen?" puzzled Cameron, beginning to feel she was being teased.

"It's just what's done. Now why don't you try them on while I water the horse," said Alex, making his escape.

Cameron sat and stared at the clothes. Part of her wanted to put them on and dance around like the girls she had seen at the fair. The other part of her rebelled against change. I won't know who I am anymore, she thought, remembering her grandfather's vehement rages against silly frilly females. She threw the clothes aside and bit into her meat pie, wondering what she'd look like in the dress. She had noticed how the women and girls had reacted to Alex, fluttering their eyelashes and smiling as they purposely brushed against him. She had felt rage when Alex smiled, his amber eyes twinkling appreciatively at them.

"Are you ready to show me?" Alex's deep voice came through the dark.

Cameron stuffed the last morsel of pie in her mouth and rolled on her belly pretending to sleep.

She lay there hearing the fire crackling and Alex wrapping her clothes. Planning her escape she fought the sleep that tried to claim her, watching through her eyelashes for Alex to go to sleep himself.

He sat by the fire carelessly stroking her dog. Why wouldn't he leave Torquil alone? Why wouldn't he go to sleep? her impatient mind raged. Why didn't she resist eating the pie so she had it for her journey back? The angry questions kept popping into her mind as she tried to keep awake.

Finally Alex stretched out to sleep across the fire from her. She waited until his breathing became even and quietly rose. She'd take his horse and both saddlebags. That way she'd get the food without having to rummage through and by chance wake him. She didn't need to saddle the horse, preferring to ride the bare back and needing to be quickly on her way. Torquil sat up, watching her movements. She patted her leg to get him to come to her. He whined and looked at the sleeping man but came, wagging his tail hesitantly.

Placing both saddlebags across the horse's shoulders, she untied him, stood on a rock, and leaped on his broad back.

Alex heard the horse snort and felt the vibrations of hooves pound through the ground to his head. He sat up.

"Horse thieves," he muttered, and gave a shrill whistle.

To Cameron's dismay her mount turned around and started back toward the fire. She pulled frantically trying to turn his head, as her feet dug into his muscled sides. The reins were whipped out of her hand and she sat miserably staring at Alex, silhouetted by the red of the fire. He was just a large black shape, but she could see the ticking of one cheek.

"Get down," he said curtly.

Cameron's mind rebelled against the order and thought of taking him by surprise and urging the horse to gallop straight at him, loosening his hands from the leather.

But as she planned, she was roughly hauled off the horse and held in a viselike grip.

He thinks I'm a sheep to be led around, fumed Cameron, as he dragged her with him to retie the horse.

Each time I think I'm making progress with her she makes a fool of me, raged Alex. I should have bought stout rope at the market, he seethed, feeling Cameron deserved to be hogtied. Instead, he threw her down next to him by the fire, still keeping hold of her arm. He fought the sleep his exhausted body needed, not trusting Cameron's need to escape or her need to somehow rub as close to him as she could.

Both of them lay rigid, angrily fighting sleep. Alex held her at arm's length so there was a space between them. He watched the fire slowly die down, feeling the jerks of Cameron's body as she fought the sleep that weighed her lids. He debated relaxing his grip but was determined not to spend the night in pursuit of the girl. His mind raced most of the night. Why was he so bound to take care of the unruly little heathen? Many reasons flooded him, but none rang true as he carefully avoided thinking he cared for or even admired the little savage. He managed to stay awake the entire night and when the first gray fingers of dawn touched the sky, he quietly rose.

Five hours later, as he wearily led the horse across the eastern slopes of Ben Wyvis, he longed to close his eyes as he stumbled and put one heavy foot in front of the other. He resisted mounting behind the girl, afraid the hypnotic motion of the horse would lull him to sleep. Once again the hostile silence came between them; not one word had been spoken since he'd dragged her off his horse in the night.

Cameron watched the back of his tawny head and thought of his body lying close and yet apart from hers the previous night. She didn't understand her feelings, loving to lie so close to him and yet wanting to free herself from his hateful presence. Why hadn't she thrown the knife to his head? Why did she care if she hit him or not? She could have won her freedom. Right now she could have been on her way home to Cape Wrath or traveling with Ben's knife-throwing act.

Alex gave the town of Strathpeffer a wide berth and, crossing the Inverness Road, carefully headed for Beauly, staying close to the mountains. Cameron wished something would happen to break the oppressing silence that lay between them, weighing her down and feeding her fear of the unknown. She wanted to scream and scream, do anything to shatter the tension and apprehension. Where were they going? How would she ever get back to what she knew?

The day seemed endless as they trudged through the breathtakingly beautiful countryside, both blind, wrapped deeply in themselves. Alex knew if he stopped he'd never get back on his feet, so he strode mercilessly, not stopping for anything, past Beauly, until they reached the wilds to the northeast of Loch Ness. They arrived in sight of the loch at sundown, and he tiredly led the horse to the water's edge and faced the girl, his face gray with fatigue.

"You have me in a bind, my girl. I've had no rest now for two nights and three days. I've had no sleep and I'm afraid to close my eyes lest you get some fool notion to run away. Cameron, you killed a man with your horse. They're looking for a small person with hair as black as coal and green eyes like a cat. You. You ken?" he said, forcing her to meet his eyes. She didn't answer and looked away, but he roughly grabbed her small chin and held her face straight to his.

"They think you're from the Devil, my lass, and sometimes I think they might be truer than they know. You know what they do to what they dinna ken, don't you? They burn them alive!" he cried out, satisfied to see a spark of fear flash in her eyes. "And dinna think of ripping off your clothes to swim in that water unless you want the monster to eat you."

" 'Tis Loch Ness then?" asked Cameron excitedly, forgetting all else.

"Aye, 'tis," replied Alex, taken aback by the sudden change in Cameron's mood. He watched her eyes glow as she gazed over the glistening waters that didn't seem the least murky or mysterious.

" 'Tis where my grandfather spent his growing," she whispered aloud but to herself.

Of course, thought Alex, they were in Fraser country.

"What is your whole name?" he asked.

Cameron looked at him, frowning. "Cameron, of course. You know that."

"Cameron what? Or something Cameron?" questioned Alex, and, seeing her puzzlement increase, added gently, "My name is Alexander Sinclair. Two names."

"*Sir* Alexander Sinclair," she corrected.

"Aye. But what are your two names?"

"What does it matter?" bridled Cameron defensively, as she felt he was deliberately trying to make her feel stupid. Alex shrugged, not knowing how to explain that most people had a family name and a given name.

"No one called me anything but Cameron. Why should they? They had no cause to," she spat.

"I suppose not," replied Alex tersely, wondering why she flared at the least provocation.

"So Culloden Moor is near?" she asked eagerly, swinging back to her exuberance. " 'Tis said no animals will live there until Scotland is free."

"Aye," he answered, noncommittally, not wanting to give away any direction in case she got it into her rebellious head to pay a pilgrimage to the bloody spot.

" 'Twas the year I was born," offered Cameron, and at his bewildered look explained, "Culloden Moor."

Alex's tired brain tried to keep up and it took a moment for him to realize she was therefore born in 1746.

"Then you are fourteen years old, not fifteen."

"Does it matter?" shrugged Cameron.

Unless she was born earlier in the year and she could therefore be fifteen, his foggy brain figured.

"You could be fifteen," he mused.

"Why does age matter so much? Why do names matter so much?"

Alex shook his muddled head and turned to get the food from the saddlebag he'd thrown down.

"Which way is Culloden Moor?" Cameron asked.

Alex pretended not to hear as he rummaged for the pies.

"Is it near?" pressed Cameron.

" 'Ways a bit," he growled, handing her food and filling his own mouth.

"Why won't you tell me?"

"Because I don't trust you not to go running off."

"So then it is near?" she crowed.

"Dinna say that."

"Aye, you did too, in some way," smiled Cameron,

taking a bite of her pastie and talking excitedly with her mouth full, which Alex noted as yet another habit he would have to break her of.

"My grandfather told me all about his close kinsman Simon Fraser. The English took him to London after Culloden and chopped off his head. He was laird of all this," she stated, waving her hands around.

Alex nodded as he ate, thinking of all he had heard about the infamous Lord Lovat. Maybe Cameron was sprung from Fraser loins, if half he'd heard rumored about the infamous Simon was true. The man had delighted in mixing culture with barbarity, had tried to marry his own niece to gain possession of the lands they now rested upon, and when that had failed, had raped her mother, his own widowed sister-in-law, to force her into marriage, causing a feud with her clansmen, the Murrays of Atholl. The consequence of it was that he was tried and sentenced to death but won a pardon from King William, and was only charged with rape. When he refused to stand trial, he was outlawed.

"He founded the Jacobite Association," said Cameron proudly, and was confused as Alex laughed ironically.

"Aye, and played one side against the other, turning coat whenever it was to his advantage."

"He did no such thing! Why do you tell such lies?" Cameron raged. "He gave his life for the Stuart cause."

"And betrayed it more than once," retorted Alex.

"Nay, 'twas not like that. He just pretended loyalty to the English Crown for information. He was braver than most," protested Cameron.

"Seems from what I've heard he was more mercenary than most, selling his soul and Scotland to be laird of all this."

"If 'twere so, why then did the English kill him?" challenged Cameron.

Alex sighed. He was too weary to get into a political discussion, knowing if he told Cameron of Simon's selling of information for the dropping of the rape charges and liferent of the Fraser estate, he'd have to contend with a tantrum.

"Aye, maybe you're right," he said, raising his hands in mock surrender.

"Aye, there's no maybe. 'Tis the truth," stated Cameron angrily.

Alex didn't much care whether Simon Fraser was guilty or innocent. The man was dead, executed thirteen years before. Life was for the living now.

"Time to be moving again," said Alex, stretching.

"Thought you were tired?"

"I am, but there's still some light," he noted, holding the horse steady for her to mount.

"I prefer to walk."

Alex shrugged and mounted alone, riding along the banks of Loch Ness with Cameron and Torquil trailing behind.

Chapter Ten

For three grueling days they traveled southeast through the Grampians, each silent, at first because of fear and anger and then because there was nothing to say as they succumbed to the aching, plodding rhythm.

Alex welcomed the sight of farms as they descended to the mid-Lowlands, knowing they could be housed at night, not having to fear the superstitions of isolated people. Cameron stared in amazement at the neat patchwork of fields below them, wondering what she looked upon as she'd never seen the like before. She was hypnotized as the horse wearily swayed down the hillside and the neat pattern became foreshortened until each patch ran together and disappeared into hedgerow or stone wall.

Entering the town of Perth, panic flared through Cameron and terror beat in her throat and chest. As far as she could see were buildings clumped together into a smoky sprawling mass, the sun setting and reddening the roofs and cobblestones. Nothing looked soft and natural—just hard and impenetrable. Men, women, children, cats, and dogs bustled, screeching nd yelping as they went about the business of their everyday lives. Cameron was appalled and offended by he clamor, filth, and smells. Except for the sunset, which itself seemed somehow tainted, everything was arsh and gray, as though an ugly suppressed violence omehow pervaded. Did people choose to live on top f each other in such an inhospitable place? her terrified mind wondered, as she closed her eyes against the ght, just feeling the sharp hooves clatter on the cobblestones and jar through her body.

Cameron dozed and was jerked awake as the horse opped and loud, raucous voices sang and bellowed ith laughter. She opened her eyes to bright lights in he darkness and the stale smell of ale. They were outde an inn and Alex held out his hand for her to discount.

He had purposely picked an inn in the squalid secon of Perth, not wanting to be recognized by any iends or acquaintances. Cameron sat still, staring at s outstretched hand in fear. She couldn't go into that oisy place with all those people. Alex gave her his ual impatient glare as he hauled her unceremonusly off his horse and pushed her in front of him ward the building. A large robust woman roared and rew a man out the door so he fell flat on his face nd sobbed drunkenly in the dirt. Cameron stepped ack in horror, but Alex relentlessly pushed her forard.

Cameron had felt the Carbisdale market held all the eople in existence but now, in the smothering heat of e room, they all seemed crammed one on top of each her. Burly redfaced men banging their boots and sts as they drank, amply bosomed women who gigled and squawked, toothless old crones who dribbled nd cackled, all whirling together with noise, color, nd clatter, their voices blending to a giant roar.

Keeping tight hold on his charge Alex ordered a whiskey and, tossing it down, tried to make himself heard.

"Have you a room for the night?"

The heavy woman bustled up to him, pushing against the mass of people, separating them. She saw a tall, well-muscled but lean young man, handsome, with tawny hair and a two weeks' growth of beard, holding up a small ragged child in a large hat.

"Can ye pay?" she barked.

"Aye," replied Alex wearily, feeling the whiskey burn his throat and increase his fatigue. "How much?" he countered, not willing for her to raise the price when she saw how much he carried.

She named a ridiculously high amount and he replied with what he thought was fair. The bargain struck, she led them out of the close noisy barroom to the stairs at the back of the house. Alex's weary brain remembered the horse and dog.

"Is there a stable?"

"Aye, but 'tis extra," retorted the landlady greedily. Too tired to haggle Alex tossed her another coin.

"There's also a hound."

"It'll have to stay with the nag. I'll not have any flea-bitten curs in my clean house."

Alex nodded as he followed her up the stairs, virtually carrying Cameron, who kept tripping as her feet felt too heavy to lift.

"Need a hot bath and supper," said Alex, already feeling in his pocket, anticipating the woman's open hand.

Cameron stood swaying by a steamy bath that had been placed in front of the fire.

"I'm going to tend the horse and Torquil. You'll lock the door after and not let a soul in while you bathe. You ken? You'd better because down there are

eople who'll cut your hair from your skull to make a
rig for the English gentry. When I return I'll knock
ke this," Alex softly tapped his finger twice, paused,
nd tapped again three times.

"You ken?" he whispered.

Cameron didn't answer.

"I'm going to look after your hound, get him some
upper and see he's warm and safe for the night. And I
von't do that unless you tell me you have heard and
nderstood," threatened Alex quietly.

Cameron nodded.

"How will I knock?"

Cameron tapped softly the way he'd done.

"Right. Now lock the door after me and have your
ath." With that Alex left and Cameron heard him
vaiting for her to shoot the heavy bolt. Then his foot-
teps faded into the raucous noise from the saloon be-
ow.

Cameron felt very much alone and frightened. She
vished Torquil was with her, as she looked around the
oom. It was really quite cheap and dreary, but to
Cameron it was the most comfort she'd ever seen, her
wn home being nothing but gray stone and mostly
alling to rack and ruin. Everything here was warm
vood, even the mantelpiece over the cheerfully blazing
re. There was a table and two chairs, a washstand, and
large bed with a fluffy eiderdown quilt. She hauled
erself up and sat on the bed, her legs dangling. She felt
er bottom sink into the softness as she hunched for-
vard with her elbows on her knees. Alex had said she
houldn't remove her clothes at the sight of water, but
he could not figure out how to bathe fully clothed, and
er drowsy mind, not wishing to incur his wrath, could
ot figure out how to bathe, except to bend over the
ub and dip and dab. This seemed too much effort so
he lay back thinking and promptly fell asleep. A loud

rapping at the door awakened her and she sat up, her heart pounding with fear. The knock was repeated.

"Here's your vittles!" bellowed a voice.

Cameron froze, not knowing what to do, and was relieved to hear Alex's deep voice.

"I'll take the tray. Thank you. That'll be all. Good night."

When the staccato footsteps had faded, Alex knocked in the arranged way. Cameron dragged her protesting body from the bed and her aching arms drew back the bolt.

Alex put the tray on the table and relocked the door.

"Why haven't you bathed? I waited damn near half an hour in the perishing cold wanting my supper and rest. Why the hell can't you learn to do as you're told?" he hissed, not wanting to be overheard by curious ears. His anger woke up the rebellious spirit in Cameron.

"I try to do as you say: Dinna talk, do talk, dinna talk. Keep your clothes on, you say. I dinna ken how to keep my clothes on and wash my body. I'm not a civilized lady. I dinna ken how to!" Cameron yelled, and to her own horror burst into tears.

Alex stared at her in amazement. She did listen. She once again had tried to obey him too literally. He stifled a laugh at how apt her statement about bathing with all her clothes on like a civilized lady was. Most of the upper crust he knew were very "crusty" indeed, as that's exactly what they did, relying on an unsubtle covering of perfume, wigs, and fine clothes to mask their filth.

How ever much Alex tried to stifle his amusement, Cameron saw it and the hurt flared in her tear-filled eyes.

"I'm not laughing at you, you silly bairn. I'm laugh-

 g at the stupid fool I am. Of course you must take
ur clothes off to bathe," he reassured her.

"But you're not alone. I mean *I'm* not, and I don't
ant to be alone," she trailed off as a loud guffaw of
ughter echoed from the room below. Her eyes wid-
ed in panic and Alex chided himself for filling her
ead with terrifying thoughts she couldn't possibly
eal with.

"Tell you what. 'Tis a shame to have the bath and
pper grow cold. You hop into the water and you'll
t in the tub. Have you ever done that?"

"You'll not leave me here?" asked Cameron anx-
usly.

"I'll stay right here," said Alex, thinking his weari-
ss was her protection.

She looked at him doubtfully, her face white and
awn. Alex poured a glass of rough red wine and
nded it to her. She took it, sniffed it, and then
ank it thirstily as if it were water.

"'Tis to be sipped," laughed Alex, as Cameron
oked and sputtered, too busy to show the embarrass-
ent she felt at having once again done something ig-
rant.

She slowly undressed, dropping her filthy clothes
to the floor, and climbed into the tub. Alex sat with
s back to her, eating and drinking. He'd placed her
pper of roast mutton, carrots, potatoes, and bread on
chair by the bath where she could reach it. The food
as greasy and unappetizing, but it was food neverthe-
ss, he thought, as he ate hungrily. He heard the wa-
r swishing behind him as Cameron knelt, submerg-
g her head. Her hands wrestled with the strip of
nen he had tied around her hair. Some water
lashed on his leg and he turned, witnessing the
range sight. What was the girl trying to do? Drown
erself? He pulled her head up out of the water.

"'Tis all knotted," cried Cameron, frustratedly tugging at the ribbon.

"You'll drown yourself. Let me," he said, busy with the tight wet knot until he released her hair. Cameron lay back and sank into the warm water.

"I wouldna mind drowning myself in here. It feels so good," she murmured, her heavy eyes closing sleepily. Alex realized she was exhausted and not able to scrub herself unless he were to nag and bully her, and not having that energy nor wanting a cold bath himself when she was finally through, he resignedly picked up the soap.

"If my friends could see me now," Alex muttered, as he lathered her hair.

"Stand up," he ordered briskly, and like a zombie Cameron obeyed, swaying as he lathered her body as familiarly as he did his own.

"Sit."

Cameron sat promptly on his command, giggling as the water drenched him.

"Duck under," he snapped, and she submerged, rinsing the soap off her so the bubbles sat in clouds on top of the water.

"Step out."

She stepped out to be embraced by the fire-warmed towel Alex held. She stood in front of the fire like a docile obedient child as Alex dried her hair and body with the coarse towel. Never before had she felt so safe. There had never been tender mother's hands for her and, without her understanding why, Alex's ministrations fed a hunger that Cameron didn't know she had.

Efficiently Alex deposited her in the bed, a towel wrapped around her wet hair, and handed her the plate of food. Propped by a bolster and pillows and snug under the feathery eiderdown Cameron ate and

tched Alex strip and sink with a moan of pleasure
o the not-so-clean soapy water. He was still for a
nute, feeling the warmth, and then reached for his
finished supper and commenced eating.

The stringy greasy mutton tasted like ambrosia as
ey both ate ravenously, until each plate was wiped
an with the last crusts of hard bread.

Alex idly drank red wine in the fast-chilling water,
iting for Cameron to sleep. Seeing she lay with eyes
sed, the empty plate balanced precariously on her
sed knees, he rose and soaped himself all over. Rin-
g himself off he looked around for a towel and real-
d the only one they had was still twisted around
meron's hair. Stepping out of the tub he tiptoed to
e bed, his flesh goose-bumped by the chill as the fire
d died down. He gently unwound the towel from
e sleeping girl's head and briskly rubbed himself.
e landlady was pretty miserly with her firewood, he
ught, as he put the last thin log on and warmed
nself in the small blaze. Where to sleep was his di-
ma and, reasoning that they were both utterly
ined and exhausted, he tucked himself into the
ge soft bed and slept before his damp hair touched
e pillow by Cameron's raven curls.

Cameron was so very comfortable, her skin tingly
d glowing. She snuggled deeper into the softness of
e bed, curling her knees up and pushing her back
ainst Alex's safe satiny strength. She turned to bur-
w further into the sanctuary of the warm hard body,
en in sleep somehow aware of the security of the
own arms that encircled her.

Alex thought he was dreaming and he never wanted
wake as his hands explored the fantasy he held. He
und a warm yielding mouth that kissed him sweetly
d then hotly, an eager tongue that ran along his
eth and gently raped his mouth with sharp strong

thrusts. He thrust back against the softness as his excitement grew, feeling small curious hands exploring
his own body. He sucked sweet breasts as he felt the
tentative touching of his manhood, and he rose his
hips, seeking firmer pressure. How infinitely pleasurable was this seductive dream. He held his body still,
feeling the small hand grasp him gently, and his own
hands felt the tickle of curls at the base of the flat
belly and explored as wonderingly as she.

Slowly and deliciously the excitement grew. Waves
of aching pleasure gently lapped and increased until
they surged against each other, thrusting and grinding.
Alex rolled her over and positioned himself between
the parted legs as Cameron's tensed hips arched up toward the pressure she hungered for.

Alex, preparing to thrust into the warmth he
yearned for, opened his eyes to the stark reality of
Cameron writhing below him. Fully aroused himself
he tried to push her from him, but as soon as his
hands touched her soft shoulders, she ground against
him and he savagely grasped both her small buttocks
and pressed her to him as his mouth angrily closed on
hers.

"Please, please," whimpered Cameron urgently between the brutal kissing and writhing. Please what?
She wasn't sure, but her young thrusting body knew.

Alex longed to penetrate and explode inside her,
but he feared for her youth and knew he'd not be able
to face her or himself if he did. He fought for control
as he told himself that in less than two days they
would be home and Fiona would be available to him.
Forcing himself he rolled over on his back, but Cameron frantically straddled him, her hair wild and her
breasts seeming larger as she bent to kiss him. Alex
tried to pull the covers up to hide his rearing passion,
but the girl sat astride his thighs making it impossible.

He debated overpowering her but feared her wild raging would awaken the landlady, causing a terrible scene.

"Please," begged Cameron, rubbing her erect nipples against his chest.

Alex grasped her two slender wrists in one of his large hands and, putting the other hand over her mouth, forced her off him and back against the pillows.

"Now listen. You scream and I'll hit you hard. I've had enough," he said roughly, as her body arched, trying to connect to his.

"Cameron, you're but a child. You've a whole life ahead. 'Twould be foolish," he whispered, as Cameron wrapped a leg around his and rubbed her pelvis against his thigh. Alex tried to twist his body away but got his feet tangled in the covers. Cameron bit his hand and with a muffled curse he removed it.

"Please touch me," whispered Cameron.

"Oh, Cameron," he groaned, " 'tis no way for a young lady to behave." And then, on a hopeful afterthought added, "Have you before?"

"Have I what?"

"Lain with a man?"

"Just with you. Please."

"Before me?" questioned Alex.

"Nay."

"What is it you want me to do?" asked Alex, his voice hoarse.

"Touch me more, and more, I want more. It aches in me for something."

"What?"

"Like before when I saw a stag with a doe."

Alex wished his own passion would ebb instead of being fanned by Cameron's words.

"I saw his male part, like Torquil's and Torquod's,

and yours," she said, reaching for him, and under his mesmerized eyes she grabbed and held it firmly. "It grew like yours too, and so did the ache in me."

Alex lay back, seduced by her hands as she gently touched the tip, sighing with excitement. Then coming to his senses he firmly removed her hands and, picking her up, deposited her in the cold tub of water.

Cameron sat, too shocked to speak, as he pulled on his breeches, muttering to himself about how he should be the one cooling off in the tepid water. Cameron gave out a loud scream of rage and beat at the foam that still floated on top, splashing the water all over the floor as a flood of abuse poured out of her mouth. With a curse he clapped a rough hand over her mouth and hauled her out, throwing her on the bed where he pinned her down as he tried to mop the enormous puddle of water with the rough towel.

"What the hell's going on in there?" yelled a voice accompanied by a violent banging on the door and many footsteps.

"Nothing. 'Twas just a bad dream," answered Alex, indicating to the now-silent wide-eyed girl to get under the covers.

" 'Taint all right. I have water dripping through the ceiling."

"I kicked into the bath in the dark," he improvised.

"Open the door and let me get it out of there," the voice insisted.

"There's no need," returned Alex.

" 'Tis my ceiling you're ruining, so open up a'fore I get some men and break it down."

Cameron heard the muffled whispers of many people outside.

"I'm opening it," said Alex, waving a clenched fist at Cameron's white face which just showed above the enormous eiderdown. He slid back the heavy bolt and the landlady strode in accompanied by three burly men. The narrow corridor behind was filled with curious lodgers in an odd assortment of sleeping wear.

"I'm sorry to disturb you—" Alex tried to apologize but trailed off as the landlady looked around the room suspiciously with her oil lamp.

"Where's the woman?"

"What woman?" asked Alex innocently.

"The woman I heard," stated the large lady emphatically.

"There's some mistake, there's just the boy and myself," he lied.

The woman turned to the audience in the corridor that pushed and clustered around the door curiously.

"Did you hear?" she demanded.

There was a chorus of assent and nods.

"Aye, you'd have to be deaf not to. Sounded like some whore off the docks, it did, and this is a clean respectable hostel," she informed him, standing with both hands on her ample hips and staring at the lump under the eiderdown where Cameron hid.

"I assure you," Alex began, but froze as the aggressive woman ripped the covers back from the bed to expose the naked terrified girl. A gasp went up from the onlookers as they pressed further into the room.

"Oh ho ho ho! Will you look at that!" roared the landlady, turning and pointing dramatically at Cameron. "That is the *boy* he come with," she declared, as the nightgowned people snickered and smirked.

Alex stood shaking his head at his dilemma when, to his amazement, Cameron leaped up in all her naked glory and stood with both hands defiantly on her slim hips.

"How dare you!" Cameron thundered magnificently, tossing back her ebony mane. "How dare you come bursting in on a husband and wife!" Alex was too busy wishing she'd have some modesty and cover herself from the lecherous eyes of the men who licked their lips as they stared at her, to realize what she had said.

"So you're husband and wife are you?" sneered the landlady.

"Aye," stated Cameron boldly.

Alex's mind churned, knowing that by Scottish law a public declaration of marriage in front of witnesses was binding, unless of course the other party denied it.

"Well?" said the ominous voice of the landlady, cutting through his jumbled thoughts. He looked, stunned, into her bulldoglike face.

"Well what?" he countered, playing for time, trying to find some solution.

"Is she your wife?"

"What business is it of yours?"

"It's plenty of my business. 'Tis my roof you're fornicating under and the lass looks a might too young for a braw man like you," she shouted, and the crowd agreed.

Now I'll be jailed for child molesting too, for who would believe that the child had molested me? he thought.

"So you deny she's your wife?"

"Of course she's my wife," Alex breathed, finding the words hard to form.

"Well, if she wasn't before, she certainly is now," chuckled the woman, her triple chins quaking as she indicated to two men to remove the bathtub. The nosy snickering onlookers slowly trickled out.

"Keep a tight hold on him, lass," chortled the landlady to the still-standing, naked Cameron as she shut the door.

Cameron stood smiling triumphantly on the bed.

"There now, aren't you proud of me?" she crowed.

Alex, still staring at the closed door in a fog, turned to her, his face furious. Cameron's delight turned to confusion and she stepped back from his obvious rage and sat down hard on the pillow.

"You ken what you've done?" he roared, approaching slowly like a large animal stalking its prey. Cameron shook her black hair silently.

"You are now my wife whether I want you or not!"

"'Twas just pretend," she whispered, inching back.

"And legally binding, said in front of witnesses. You are now my lawful wedded wife!" The words rumbled dangerously from Alex's throat.

"Whose law? The English?" spat Cameron, still backing as he neared the bed.

"Nay, the Scot's!" Alex bellowed, his fists clenched, wanting to beat her black and blue.

"Oh!" The little explosion popped out of Cameron's mouth as Alex towered above, and she pressed herself against the wall that stopped her escape.

A sudden violent hammering at the door saved Cameron from Alex's black rage.

"Lassie, if you need help just give a yell. The brute will not beat a poor defenseless girl under my roof. That'll teach you, laddie, that'll teach you." The landlady's fat gurgles of laughter punctuated her words.

Cursing, Alex strode to the window wondering what he would have done to Cameron if the landlady's knock hadn't interrupted. He stared out at the dark night feeling helpless; the frail-looking child had somehow come to manipulate his whole life.

Cameron still pressed against the cold wall, staring at him as she hugged her knees.

"They dinna know your name. We'll not see them again, so who's to know?" she said to his broad back. The same thoughts had been passing through Alex's brain. He didn't answer, he just stared out into the night as the sky lightened to gray. Cameron sat shivering, watching him, afraid to wrap herself in the covers, feeling that any movement would cause him to turn on her and release the fury that charged the space between them.

Coming to a sudden decision Alex turned sharply and picked up one of the saddlebags. He wrenched the parcels of underwear and the green and oatmeal frock out roughly and threw them at her.

"Put them on."

Cameron shivered as the cold steely voice continued, "And try some modesty. I'm sick of you flaunting your body at every Tom, Dick, and Harry. What in hell am I saddled with? A harlot? Standing there on the bed letting all those greedy lechers feast their filthy eyes on everything that you were born with!" he raged bitingly.

Cameron, trying without much success to dress herself in the strange garments, looked at him in surprise.

"Haven't they much the same? 'Cept for the men who are like you. Don't they know anyway?"

Her honest puzzlement fanned the flames of his wrath until he stood blind to the beauty of the wild-haired girl, whose tiny nose crinkled in consternation at her dressing predicament and his obvious fury. All his fixed, flashing eyes saw was a larger-than-life woman who, despite her outwardly small size, had made him lose his pride, dignity, and freedom. How dare she show her naked body to all eyes and now pretend to be a naïve innocent? Who did she think he was, a callow youth to be taken in by that guise of bewilderment? She was a witch all right, could even manage to weave a spell to make herself appear innocent and vulnerable.

"You are impossible! Ignorant, ill-bred, wanton— and impossible. You can't even dress yourself," he sneered, as she struggled with each garment, not knowing the front or back.

"Doesn't even know her own name! Doesn't know how old she is! Doesn't even know her parentage! Or what a birthday is! Acts like a bitch in heat! There she is, everybody, my wife, *Lady* Sinclair. Has no table manners, talks with her mouth full of food, oh, but she can swear like any barroom trollop and throw a knife better than any cutthroat scum."

Cameron tried to block the cruel stream of words and tried desperately to prove him wrong by dressing herself.

"Need help, *Lady* Sinclair?" he asked mockingly.

Cameron shook her head, afraid to speak in case the tears burst out in a wail. She closed her mouth firmly and struggled to dress, not knowing what tied to what, or which button went where.

"As you wish, my lady," sneered Alex, enjoying the vicious relief from his pent-up rage and frustrations.

"There," said Cameron defiantly, having managed to get all three items on her person. She stood with the dress backward and the petticoat hanging out of the neck. She knew something was wrong, as she felt strangely constricted, but being unused to wearing such clothes she hoped it was the way they were meant to feel. As she stood boldly before him, covering her apprehension, her pantalettes dropped to the floor around her ankles. Alex tilted back in his chair and roared with laughter.

"Which one is your wife, Lord Sinclair? Oh, the one who drops her drawers," he cried, tears streaming down his face as his mirth renewed, so he did not hear the rapping at the door. His laughter died abruptly as the landlady poked her face into the room.

"Glad to hear you're happy. We have a little surprise for you. Reverend Wilson?" she called as she opened the door wide to admit a small wiry man in a clerical collar. Alex's plans for making an early escape were thwarted. He nearly fell back off his already-tilted chair.

"Good morning, good morning. So you are the lucky man," chirped the little sparrow of a man.

"Reverend, why dinna you take the lad downstairs while I help the puir wee bride to dress. So nervous she is, seems she needs a bit of help," purred the landlady, frowning at Cameron's drawers.

Alex was borne off by the energetic man who flapped his arms and cheeped out words a mile a minute, while the tough buxom landlady chattered like an adolescent as she helped Cameron get her garments on straight and firm.

"I love a wedding, I do. Never had one myself, but had the bad done to me just like you. Took an oath I did, told myself, 'Mabel,' I said, 'if you see any puir wee young lass being taken advantage of by a brute of a man, you make sure she gets what is coming to her. A ring on the right finger and a name for her and her bairns.' There now. Turn around. Pretty little thing, ain't you? A wee bit bony, but he looks lusty enough and will be taking care of that soon if he ain't already. You have a bonnet?"

Cameron shook her head, staring at herself in the glass.

"I have the very thing," gushed the landlady, rushing out with surprising lightness for so large a person.

Cameron stared at her image in awe. It didn't look like herself at all. It didn't look like other girls either, she thought, remembering the girls at the fair with their rosy cheeks and light hair.

"You look a bonny treat," cooed the landlady, appearing next to her in the glass. "Hold yourself still now," she added, tying a white scarf under Cameron's chin.

Cameron stood awkwardly in the parlor of the inn as the Reverend Wilson lectured them on the sins of the flesh and the landlady clapped her enormous hands together enthusiastically after each chirped-out sentence. Her three burly henchmen stood threateningly behind Alex and several spectators from the night before clustered as witnesses.

The reverend joined them in holy matrimony after asking if there was any just cause why they should not be joined, and Alex felt a sharp object pressed into his back, making him hold his peace. As the final pronouncement was made, the enormous woman burst into tears, sobbing that she always cried at weddings, as she heartily slapped Alex on the back and held open her hand for payment for the use of her parlor.

"Well, lass, I've made an honest woman of you," she sniffed, taking the white scarf roughly from Cameron's head.

Chapter Eleven

Perched sideways on the slippery leather, Cameron clung desperately to keep herself from sliding off the horse as Alex trudged silently leading. It had been six hours since they had been married and the only words he had spoken were his roars when she had tried to pass one of her legs to the other side so she could ride more comfortably astride.

"You'll sit as you are and pretend to be the lady that you aren't!"

Cameron, her legs hopelessly entangled in the full skirts of the dress and petticoat, had frozen at his unconcealed hatred. Now the aching of her back from the unnatural precarious position awoke the rebel in her. She eased her stiff cold hands off the saddle and slid to the ground. She'd rather walk, she fumed, and promptly fell flat on her face. If Alex knew, he made no sign and kept a steady pace. After tripping a number of times so the dress was muddied and ripped at the hem, she picked the cumbersome skirts up above her knees and resolutely trailed after the plodding horse.

Alex walked mechanically, his head a jumble of thoughts. What to do? Should he take Cameron to his country estate of Glen Aucht and try the seemingly impossible task of making her somehow presentable to society? Should he hide the fact that she was his wife and tuck her away in some seminary for young ladies, hoping that they could teach her the basics of propriety? Should he go straight to his townhouse in Edinburgh, acknowledge her as his wife, and let her sink or swim? What *should* he do? Why hadn't he let the girl have her freedom? He owed her nothing, so why had he been so bloody cavalier?

Cameron, muddy and tattered, trudged behind his stern broad back. The countryside was flat and the road well traversed as Alex headed for the town of Kinross, not realizing that by breaking from the Stirling Road he'd made a decision.

Cameron's smaller strides made it hard for her to keep up and the distance between them widened. People came and went, staring at her curiously as she held her dress high, exposing her legs to the middle of her thighs as she walked alongside the enormous hound. Cameron's face burned with their stares, not understanding the lewd comments called out to her. She trudged on, feeling very small and lost, wishing she could grab Torquil and run free, back to the isolation of Cape Wrath. There she felt graceful and light; here she felt awkward and clumsy, weighed down by the unfamiliar clothes. Why did women have to be imprisoned in such tight constriction? she puzzled, trying to ignore the staring passersby. Her breasts were pressed painfully flat by the tight bodice of the dress and petticoat. The pantalettes chafed and rode up until they pinched the flesh behind her knees. She longed to rip off the binding garments and feel the sun and wind on her body and breathe deeply, expanding her ribs to their fullest.

Alex looked sharply around. Hearing provocative jeers and catcalls and, seeing his empty saddle, he wondered how long Cameron had been missing. As he looked ahead and saw Ogilvie Castle, he realized he'd been lost in thought for a great while. He stared back along the track and was infuriated by the sight of Cameron exposing her limbs, a group of enthusiastic young bucks cantering beside her.

"Damn her!" He swore aloud as he threw himself onto his horse and galloped the hundred yards or so back to her, dispersing the disappointed riders. Lost in her own agony Cameron had hardly noticed the young men and she kept on trudging, unaware of Alex staring down at her as he took in her soiled appearance.

"Drop your skirts," he hissed violently. Startled, Cameron straightened her shoulders and lifted the skirts even higher as she kept walking, not hearing his words but assuming his anger was at her inability to keep up with him. Alex sprang off his horse, all too conscious of the curious eyes focused on them, and pulled her skirts from her clenched hands. She stood still, gazing in bewilderment at him as he glared at her, refusing to see her weariness or confusion. He took her arm roughly and pulled her off the road into a small copse. Her feet tangled in the dress and she fell as he dragged her, making her even muddier.

He leaned against a tree surveying her. This was his wife! This wanton strumpet was his wife! This wild-haired wench who couldn't even keep herself clean for half a day was his wife! He compelled himself to check his rage, lest he should show her all too clearly the force of his anger.

Alex opened the saddlebags and drew out bread and

cheese. He cut two portions of each and held hers out silently. Cameron stood and, taking the few steps toward him, trying to walk sedately, tangled her legs and tripped flat on her face. She lay with her face in the dirt waiting for his cruel laugh, but it didn't come. Alex felt his anger ebb and a curious detachment came over him, as if Cameron was someone he'd only just met, and seeing the small face lift from the ground, streaked by tears and dirt, the green eyes wide and afraid, he wanted to pick her up and cradle her to him. Cameron hid her face again, feeling the stiff grass and sharp stones scratch her face. She tensed, waiting for the cold anger she had seen on his face to erupt.

Chiding herself for her fear and subservience Cameron summoned the courage to rebelliously raise her head. She sat back on her heels and watched Alex casually eating his meal, indifferent to her. It was worse than his jeering laughter, she brooded.

But Alex felt anything *but* indifference, much to his self-disgust. He had caught himself with knees bent and arms outstretched to her, but just in time an image of his broken father flashed through his mind, reminding him of just how powerful a woman could be, and he had straightened and stared at her coldly before turning away.

He wanted to reach the town of Glenrothes by nightfall. It was the nearest fair-sized town to his estates, and from there he could hire a carriage for the rest of the journey to Glen Aucht; he'd decided to leave Cameron there and go to Edinburgh alone to rest and wrestle with his problem.

He threw Cameron into the saddle, sideways, and mounting behind her urged his horse on. He was not letting Cameron make an idiot of him again by strolling behind and flaunting herself. Once in Glenrothes he'd check them into the Golden Pheasant, where he was well known, and introduce Cameron as his ward. On the morrow he'd see her equipped with clothes and luggage. She'd be well provided to spend however long it took for him to decide what to do with her. At Glen Aucht she would be under the eye of Mrs. MacDonald, his old nurse and housekeeper. He wondered what Mackie would think of all this, and smiled despite himself. Oh, if Fergus MacDonald knew the half of it, he'd crack his leathery face in two. He chuckled thinking of Mackie's husband, who'd known him since he was born.

Alex tried to cheer himself by thinking of Edinburgh, where he would be within a few days, but found it somehow depressed him. He tried to conjure up Fiona's sensuous face and irritation flowed through him. To hell with this ragged chit, he thought angrily, feeling she'd soured his whole life. Well, he'd not allow it, the wanton wench would not disturb his life anymore.

"No one is to know that we are married," he stated firmly out of the blue. Cameron didn't answer.

"Did you hear?"

"Aye," Cameron nodded.

"You are my ward, that's all," he pursued.

"Aye," she nodded.

He wanted to strike her cool nodding head off her shoulders, but he breathed deeply, clamped his jaws together, and urged his horse to quicken his pace.

In the late afternoon they reached the outskirts of Glenrothes. It had been drizzling for a number of hours, but Cameron stayed still and said not a word, uncomfortable in her sideways position, her hair and skirts plastered wetly to her. Alex had tried to wrap his cloak around her, but she had silently shaken it off. Now nearing the respectable inn where they would spend the night, he grew apprehensive at her sullen silence. He turned her face roughly to his, his hard fingers pressing into her thin cheeks. For a moment he saw fright in her green eyes, fanning his guilt, but he covered his concern with harshness.

"We are nearly there. You will be circumspect, you ken?"

Cameron hadn't the slightest idea what circumspect meant and she stared defiantly back at him without answering.

"If you shame me or yourself I won't be responsible for what I do to you!" he bellowed.

Cameron couldn't answer, as her teeth were tightly clenched to stop them from chattering. She nodded, not knowing what she was agreeing to.

"Aye, 'tis better to keep your treacherous tongue stilled," growled Alex, releasing her face and noting the marks his fingers made.

Word travels fast, so it's best to stay the night in style, openly, so it seems there is nothing to hide, Alex reasoned, as they arrived at the Golden Pheasant. He handed the reins of the horse to an ostler and lifted Cameron down, feeling the iciness of her hands. He frowned.

"Should I take the dog, sir?" asked the ostler.

"Nay, he stays with my ward," answered Alex gruffly, seeing the telltale panic flicker for a split second in the green eyes.

"I'd like separate, nonconnecting rooms and baths sent up to each."

"Aye, Sir Alex," replied the landlord.

"And have you a maid to see to my ward's needs?"

"Aye, that I have, sir," he said, ringing a bell. "From the looks of the poor wee thing we'd better hurry. She looks chilled to the very marrow," added the landlord, looking at the blue-lipped girl. Alex was furious with himself for being so wrapped up in his own thoughts that he'd nearly frozen Cameron. He was even angrier at her for not complaining and making him look like a monster.

"Jeannie, see that a hot bath is taken up to number four. And you'll be seeing to the young lady's needs for the night," said the landlord to a rosy-faced girl a few years older than Cameron.

"Aye, sir, right away, sir," smiled the girl, bobbing a curtsy with each "sir."

Ten minutes later Cameron lay in a copper bath feeling the cold melt out of her as Jeannie washed her hair, casting apprehensive glances at the enormous hound who lay exhausted, drying himself off in front of a blazing fire.

"He's a big wicked beastie, ain't he now? Do he bite?" asked Jeannie, lathering Cameron's hair. Cameron remembered Alex's warning and shook her head, smiling. She whistled and Torquil reluctantly left his comfortable spot and ambled over. Jeannie gave a shrill scream.

"He's big enough to eat me all up with one gulp."

Cameron laughed and offered her face to Torquil who licked it lovingly, getting soap bubbles on his furry chin. The two girls laughed merrily.

Never before had Cameron been with anyone near her own age, and she wished she was allowed to talk, as she had a great many questions to ask. She contented herself with listening to Jeannie's steady stream of chatter.

"Here. Lord Sinclair says you're to drink every drop while it's still steaming," declared Jeannie, handing a mug of hot toddy to Cameron, who still sat in the bath. Cameron sipped the whiskey and honey as Jeannie told her about her family of eight brothers and sisters, with another one on the way.

Later, wrapped in an enormous soft towel and sit-

ing on a cozy armchair by the fire, Cameron was
erved a delicious meal of broth, tender young lamb
vith tiny potatoes, and peas, while Torquil chewed
10isily on a huge bone. Cameron refused the fish, pie,
ind cheese, already sated and drowsy. She watched
leepily as the bathwater was removed and an extra cot
et up in the room.

"I'm to sleep here with you tonight!" said Jeannie
xcitedly. "The master says to give you this nightgown. It must be terrible to lose all you own in an
iwful storm, but you'll be fine, mark my words. That
Lord Sinclair is a right proper gentleman, he is.
Handsome too, ain't he? All the fancy ladies are after
iim to marry their daughters. And tomorrow we's to
go to all the fancy shops and buy all new things for
you—beautiful clothes and the like—and ride in a
ancy carriage to Glen Aucht. I'm to go with you and
be your lady's maid, if you like me. Do you like me?"
isked Jeannie, stopping her explosive chatter and star-
ng at Cameron questioningly.

Cameron smiled and nodded, and Jeannie ecstatic-
lly jumped up and down.

"Just fancy me a proper lady's maid! I gotta tell the
girls in the kitchen. Oh, they'll be livid I can tell
you!"

Cameron stared into the fire sadly as Jeannie
pounded out of the room. How could Jeannie be a proper lady's maid when she wasn't a proper lady?

Alex relaxed in a hot bath, feeling the whiskey burn
his innards. Lucky thing, he thought, being able to
get the girl Jeannie. He was sick of playing nursemaid
and yet felt somehow bereft, alone in his room.
His mind kept flashing to bedchamber four, and he
envisioned Cameron in the bath, her green eyes flashing and her hair curling riotously in the steam. Every-

thing must be so strange to her. This luxurious inn with its thick warm carpets and elegant furnishings compared to the pile of cold stones she was used to at Cape Wrath. Outside was the sweet gentle roll of verdant land, not the harsh barren moor. Everything was as different as night is to day. How would she adapt to the restrictions of society, having to trot sedately on a tight rein? For a moment Alex closed his eyes to recapture the image of Cameron galloping freely, ebony hair streaming, lithe legs hugging the shining black of her stallion as she raced with the storm and brought life to the bleak stillness of the moor.

Alex washed furiously, trying to free himself of her unwanted presence in his thoughts. Why the hell should he care if she suffered or not, or was bewildered or not? He savagely toweled his hair, attempting to erase the flashing image of her haunted eyes from his mind. He began to wish he had clean clothes to change into so he could drown his thoughts with the merry mob below in the public rooms.

He ate an enormous five-course meal with two jugs of red wine and tasted nothing. He climbed into bed at an indecently early hour, and felt, to his intense irritation, lonely at the cold emptiness beside him. Sleep eluded him, chased away by thoughts of Cameron; cursing he sat up and forced his mind to plan each waking moment of the following day, determined to arrive at his estate by early afternoon.

He reached for the bell to summon the valet. He had to send word to Mackie to prepare for his arrival, and to warn her of his ward. How would Mackie find Cameron? he wondered, and grinned as he thought of Fergus's noncommittal face when he saw the girl ride. His reverie was broken by the valet answering his call.

As the door closed after the servant who was to send someone immediately to Glen Aucht, Alex realized

that he had left Edinburgh three weeks before for
Cape Wrath without informing the MacDonalds of his
departure. He lay down ruefully, anticipating the
scolding he'd get from Mackie.

Cameron slept very late, disturbing Alex's exact
plans. The girl, Jeannie, awakened at six, though, and
crept out of the room and down to the kitchen, where
she mended and ironed Cameron's freshly laundered
dress. Alex sent for her.

"You'll accompany me to the shops, as you'll know
better what a young girl needs," he said curtly, not
knowing how to deal with the bobbing maid in front
of him.

"Yes, sir. Oh, but sir, won't the young miss be disappointed, sir?"

"Then she'll be disappointed," he shot back, irritated at the girl's impertinence.

"Yes, sir. Sorry, sir," she replied submissively. Alex
was angry with himself. He was no snob, so why was
he so irritated? It had to be his long abstinence, he
thought, highly unnatural for a healthy man of
twenty-five. The sooner he got to Edinburgh the better.

"Better bring the dress along for measurements," he
said roughly, hating himself still more when he saw
Jeannie's youthful exuberance replaced by blank
subservience.

"Yes, sir."

Four grueling hours later, trailed by Jeannie and
five men laden with packages, Alex returned to the
inn. He sent another man off to buy a large trunk,
realizing he had nothing to put his purchases in.

"Jeannie, run and see if your mistress is awake,"
said Alex, pleased to see the girl bound up the stairs,
her usual verve restored. Jeannie stopped on the landing as she remembered she hadn't bobbed her curtsy.

"Sorry, sir. Yes, sir. Right away, sir," she babbled, bobbing after each "sir." Alex shook his head and waved her toward Cameron's room.

Jeannie burst in, forgetting to knock, and Torquil bounded up and growled menacingly as he was rudely awakened.

"Aah!" Jeannie froze, skidding to a halt, and Cameron laughed and whistled for her hound.

"Master sent me up, miss," she stammered, her eyes not leaving Torquil. Remembering not to speak Cameron motioned the girl to come closer as she patted Torquil's head to show Jeannie he wouldn't bite. She approached cautiously and Cameron caught her arm, pulling her down next to her on the rug. The great dog licked Jeannie gently, as if he knew she was afraid, and Cameron took the frightened girl's hand and put it on the great shaggy head. Soon they played happily with the enormous dog who lay on his back enjoying the attention as they giggled at his antics.

"I trust you slept well," rumbled Alex's deep voice from the open door. Jeannie hastily leaped to her feet and stood hanging her head in shame. Cameron looked at her, not understanding, and stared inquiringly at Alex, then caught her breath.

How fine he looked, so tall and handsome. Their eyes caught and held. She had missed him. Just one night alone and she had felt disjointed and incomplete. Similar thoughts surged through Alex as his eyes were held captive by hers. He freed his gaze abruptly and threw some packages on the bed.

"Bring the rest in," he ordered, almost barking, and a line of men entered from the hall.

Cameron stared at the mountain of parcels.

"Jeannie, see that your mistress is dressed in the green traveling suit."

"Yes, sir. Very good, sir," bobbed Jeannie.

"And when the trunk arrives, get it packed. Luncheon will be in half an hour, and then we set off."

Cameron shuddered as the door closed after him, feeling shut out and lost, but Jeannie once again became the chattering joyful girl.

"Just wait and see! Your eyes will pop. He must have spent a hundred crowns. No, more—five hundred crowns! Look at this and this and this and . . . oh, my, isn't that a sight? Hold it against you; matches your eyes, it does," gushed the maid, as she tore off the wrappings, showing Cameron dresses and nightdresses, underclothes, riding habits, corsets, capes, dressing gowns, shoes, boots, brushes, combs, and a hundred more strange and incomprehensible items. Cameron looked with horror at the enormous pile. It would smother her so she could not breathe. Panic pricked into her like a million stinging bees, and her skin crawled. She fought to control herself as Jeannie crowed with delight, holding up the possessions one by one as she danced in front of the mirror.

Cameron forced herself to take deep breaths and stood stiff and unfeeling as she allowed Jeannie to dress her in a dark green suit. She looked at herself in the mirror and wanted to smash the glass.

"Hold still, here's the finishing touch," said Jeannie, placing a ridiculous hat on Cameron's head. For a moment Cameron thought she was back at the inn being dressed for her wedding, and she gave a cry and tore the hat off her head, flinging it violently from her. Jeannie froze.

Cameron was weighed down by the heavy clothes; she couldn't breathe. She backed to the bed still staring at herself. Her feet hurt, imprisoned in the tight high-heeled shoes. She couldn't walk properly; her ankles turned. Trying to stop the dreadful panic that threatened to topple her into insanity, she sat down, taking in gulps of air.

"You look beautiful, miss," stammered Jeannie, not certain of what was happening. "Don't you like what you see?" she added, nodding her head toward Cameron's image in the mirror. Cameron shook her head slowly.

"We've got to go downstairs now, miss. The master said special we shouldna be late."

Cameron shook her head.

"Don't you want your luncheon?" asked Jeannie, feeling very hungry herself. Again Cameron shook her head and the maid backed to the door, frowning.

"Well, I'll just go see what the master says, all right?"

Cameron stood in the empty room, afraid to take a step in case she fell and broke her ankles. She wanted to run and yet where could she go? How could she ever run again when she couldn't breathe, move her legs, or bend her feet? She was bound and tied up more tightly than if it were with rope.

Her mind raced. Life was so different here. Coins exchanged for what she had always freely picked or hunted; coins meant the difference between survival and death. She had one coin from her knife-throwing, but what could she exchange it for? Cameron felt ignorant and ill-equipped to live in such a place. She could not stay, yet she could not go. At Cape Wrath life had been simple and straightforward. There had been no mass of people to guard oneself against—just Mara, and that was in the open and one to one. No shops, society, or coins, just the three of them and the servants who came and went like anonymous shadows. She had to get home, but how? She had lost all sense of time and had been so weary and confused that she hadn't kept track of the landmarks that could lead her back to Cape Wrath. Lost in thought she stared blindly into the glass.

"They'll be plenty of time for self-admiration when we get home," Alex said curtly from the door. *Home?* questioned Cameron's mind as Alex stooped and picked up the ridiculous hat.

"We must leave, so put on your hat."

The sight of the silly feathered thing triggered Cameron's fears.

"I canna. I canna!" she cried, frantically pushing the hat away. "And I canna wear these!" She tore furiously at her clothes. "I canna breathe. I canna walk. I canna run!"

Alex grabbed her hands so they didn't rip the material.

"You can wear them and you will," he growled, pulling her to the door remorselessly. Cameron's legs tangled in the skirts as her ankles turned and knocked against each other.

"I canna. I canna. I canna breathe!" she sobbed. Seeing her hysteria mount, Alex slammed the door to avoid a public spectacle and, lifting her, sat her firmly on the bed.

"Listen to me, Cameron. Listen to me," he ordered sternly, feeling if he could somehow calm her until they got into the carriage, she then could scream as much as she pleased.

"Cameron, I'll give you a few minutes to compose yourself and then we are going downstairs quietly to get into the carriage. Do you ken?"

"To where?" she whispered, shaking her head.

Alex then realized he'd not told Cameron of his plans and he cursed his forgetting so important a point.

"To my country home of Glen Aucht. You'll like it. 'Tis near the mouth of the great Firth of Forth. I'll tell you more as we travel, as I don't want to arrive too late."

"Who's there?"

"I'll answer all your questions, I promise, when we are on our way," said Alex firmly as he rose to answer a tap at the door.

Cameron sat there trying to control her panic as Alex showed the man her new trunk, her feet busily trying to remove the pinching, crippling shoes by pulling at the heel of one with the toe of the other. The first shoe fell with a thud and she stopped, but Alex hadn't noticed, so she resumed her efforts and rid herself of the other, furtively kicking them under the bed. At least now her feet could breathe.

"Ready?" asked Alex, holding out his hand.

"Aye, but I'll not wear that thing on my head," she said defiantly, and was relieved when Alex nodded. She took Alex's hand and stood on her stockinged feet, wishing she'd had time to remove them too, as the garters pinched and seemed to drive the blood from her legs. Without her shoes the dress dragged along the ground and Alex, noting the fact, figured the rest of the measurements had been rather accurate, so he couldn't really complain about the length.

Cameron felt the blood redden her cheeks as she descended the stairs, clutching Alex's arm tightly. She raised her head proudly to hide her terror upon seeing the people milling around the vestibule, and she unfocused her eyes as she trod the stairs, thankful for Alex's strong arm.

"Well, Alex where have you been hiding yourself?" called out a merry voice.

"Ian, 'tis good to see you," Alex returned, genuinely delighted, and Cameron swayed as she felt his strong arm leave her to embrace his friend. She clutched at the newel post, relieved that they had reached the last step.

"Who's the proud little starling?"

" 'Tis a long story, Ian, that can wait in the telling. Miss Cameron Fraser, I'd like you to meet Sir Ian Drummond." Cameron looked into the open pleasant face and then down at his outstretched hand. My God, thought Alex, she doesn't even know to offer her hand.

"Miss Fraser is my ward, Ian, and she's very fatigued and not quite herself, so I'm anxious to get her to Glen Aucht and into Mackie's capable hands, but I'll ride over to see you tomorrow," said Alex hurriedly.

"Aye, you'd better. You'll have no secrets from me, old friend. A ward have you now? You'll have to mend your ways some and set a good example," chuckled Ian merrily, and he raised his hat and bowed to Cameron, who looked very confused.

"Till the morrow then."

Alex walked Cameron to the coach and handed her in, but her foot stepped on the hem of her gown and she tripped. With an exasperated sound Alex put his hands around her waist and lifted her inside.

They rode in silence for a mile, Cameron wishing she sat on top in the air with Jeannie and the driver instead of closeted in the dark suffocating space. She stared out of the window watching the rolling green countryside as they headed for the town of Leven.

Once again she had done something shameful. She had been ignorant in some way with Alex's friend Sir Ian Drummond. She had seen it in the embarrassment in both men's faces; but what had she done? And then to trip with all those staring eyes! She, who had been so fleet and nimble, was now as clumsy and ugly as a toad or fish, or a seal denied water.

"Now what is it you want to know?" asked Alex,

interrupting her thoughts, but Cameron just stared at him blankly, her heart hammering painfully at the thought of their impending arrival at his unknown home. A thousand fearful questions rose in her head, becoming one loud droning noise. Alex let her be but watched her anxious face peer out at the passing countryside. He wondered what was going on in her mind, and to his surprise found himself wanting to take her in his arms and soothe her. It would not help either of them, he chided himself, and would even be crueler in the long run. She had to learn, but she was bright and would adapt when she wanted to. *If* she wanted to.

"You asked me who you'd be meeting at Glen Aucht," Alex said, after several miles, but Cameron just stared out at the waters of the firth.

"Cameron, look at me. I dinna like talking to the back of your head." Cameron hesitated. As much as she wanted to know what to expect, she also feared knowing, as it might trigger the panic she held down so tightly inside.

"I will have obedience!" said Alex coldly, turning her to him. But seeing the fear fluttering like a wild bird in her eyes, his hard hands loosened their grip and he wrapped her in his arms and held her so close he felt the terrible pounding of her heart.

"Cameron, Cameron, there's nothing to fear. There's Mrs. MacDonald, Mackie we call her. I think she knew Duncan Fraser. And she changed my breeks when I was a wee baby. And there's her husband, Fergus, who manages the stables and helps Mackie manage the other servants, and helps me manage Mackie when she gets out of hand," he crooned softly.

Cameron held herself stiffly, knowing if she relaxed in his arms she would fall into the yawning panic inside herself, not ever to come up. She would not be weak; she needed no one. She would not cry, she told herself, as the warmth of his arms and the scent of him seduced her to relax. She pushed her hands on his chest to free herself and stared once more out of the window.

Alex was furious at the rejection and at himself for weakening. She needed discipline and a taut rein, not pampering.

Within a mile of their destination Alex noticed that Cameron was shoeless.

"Where the devil are your shoes?" he demanded.

"Under the bed," she replied, tucking her bare feet away so he wouldn't see she was also stockingless, having removed them and furtively dropped them out the window a few miles back.

"You mean under the seat?" snapped Alex impatiently, bending to look, but just finding Torquil.

"Under the bed."

"What bed?"

"At the place," shrugged Cameron, not knowing what to call it.

"Why?" he asked, unable to comprehend.

"I canna walk in them."

Alex took a deep breath and stared out the opposite window over the firth toward Edinburgh. I canna wait to get there, he thought savagely, and comforted himself with the knowledge that in less than an hour he could turn her over to Mackie, lock himself in his study, and get drunk.

Part Two
Autumn

A fig for those by law protected!
Liberty's glorious feast!
Courts for cowards were erected,
Churches built to please the priest!

What is title? What is treasure?
What is reputation's care?
If we lead a life of pleasure,
Tis no matter how or where!

Does the train attended carriage
Thro' the country lighter rove?
Does the sober bed of marriage
Witness brighter scenes of love?

Life is all a variorum,
We regard not how it goes;
Let them cant about decorum,
Who have characters to lose.
                              —Robert Burns

Chapter Twelve

The carriage stopped in front of heavy iron gates and Alex got out to speak to a large burly man who came out of the stone gatehouse. 'Tis a prison, Cameron thought, looking with horror at the black iron palings that went on as far as her eyes could see. And that man is a gaoler. Alex and the man looked toward Cameron and she withdrew her head and hid back in the shadows.

"Oh, Torquil, he's telling the man not to let me out ever again," she whispered fearfully to the large dog who sat unconcerned, his freckled tongue hanging.

Alex reentered and the carriage moved slowly through the gates, which decisively clanged shut, causing a knot to form in Cameron's stomach. She stared around frantically at the green manicured lawns that rolled by on each side of the driveway. It was fascinating and yet frightening in an indescribable way. It was as though nature itself had been confined and molded by man, harnessed and civilized, leaving nothing to chance. She saw the coastline of the firth silhouetted against water and thought sadly of her horse Torquod, who lay dead and alone.

Cameron froze suddenly as the movement of the carriage stopped and the door was opened by a thin old man.

"Good to see you, Fergus," smiled Alex.

"Aye," replied Fergus dryly.

"Master Alex, you had us fair fretting. Three weeks and not a word from you! Fergus was looking for you the length of Edinburgh," scolded another voice.

"Mackie, Mackie, here I am safe and sound," grumbled Alex, swinging a short round woman in his arms.

"Put me down, you scalawag. 'Taint fitting!" puffed Mackie, indicating Jeannie's wide eyes.

"Who's the lass up there?"

"I'm Jeannie, mum, lady's maid to Miss . . ." said Jeannie, trying to curtsy from her high perch.

Seeing her chance Cameron silently opened the door on her side and leaped out, heading for the woods she saw across the lawn.

"I went to Cape Wrath at Duncan Fraser's bidding," explained Alex.

"So that's where the old devil hid himself is it?" clucked Mackie. "And what did he want of you?"

Alex smiled wickedly at her. "You'll see. Cameron? Cameron?" Receiving no answer he poked his head into the carriage.

"That what you're looking for?" asked Fergus, indicating the running girl and large hound streaking across the lawn.

"Christ!" swore Alex.

"Ah ha, Master Alex," said Mackie disapprovingly, but Alex was racing after Cameron and Torquil.

"Where is that boy off to? And who's that he's after?" asked Mackie, looking disgusted at the amount of bare legs Cameron exhibited as she held her skirts high.

"His ward, mum," offered Jeannie. Fergus watched the girl and dog disappear into the trees, well ahead of Alex. He chuckled.

"And what are you finding so amusing, Mr. MacDonald?" snapped Mackie, but she got no answer from her taciturn husband.

"And who might his ward be?" she asked sharply.

"Miss Cameron, mum."

"And her other name?"

"I don't know, mum."

"I need a cup of tea with all this dither. Fergus, get some lads to take that trunk in. Let the boy handle whatever it is he's handling. Stop gawking, girl, and get in the house," ordered Mackie.

"Aye, mum," said Jeannie curtsying.

"Stop that bobbing and stuff. You're making my old knees ache."

"Yes, mum. Oops, sorry, mum."

Cameron ran frantically, cutting her feet on sharp sticks and stones as she plunged into the woods. Looking behind her for signs of pursuit, she fell headlong down a small bank, landing in a dense blackberry bush, the sharp barbs tearing at her face and legs. She was firmly trapped by the brambles that wrenched her hair and wrapped around her clothes, but she fought furiously to free herself, ignoring the pain as the thorns scratched and tore.

"I should leave you there all tangled up. 'Twould maybe teach you a lesson, but I doubt it," panted Alex, coming up behind her. Cameron made no sign of hearing him, as she worked to free herself, sobbing for breath and with frustration. Horrified, Alex watched the blood flow out of the long scratches on her small determined face. Her hands flailed at the thorny branches which clawed and raked her back. What a place to have one of her wild rages, Alex thought, in the middle of a briar patch! Knowing there was nothing he could do until she calmed down, as he certainly was not disposed to fighting her and thereby entangling himself in the cruel barbs, Alex stepped back and waited.

Cameron slowly tired until she stood quietly and defiantly, even more entangled in her patch of thorns.

"Are you ready to behave now?" he asked curtly, hiding his concern for the damage she had caused herself. He took her stony silence as assent and worked calmly and methodically until he'd freed her from her prickly prison.

Silently they walked back through the woods but, at the edge, facing the large house across the sloping lawn, Cameron stopped. Alex, keeping hold, kept walking, dragging the unwilling girl who refused to move her feet at all. With a snort of fury he picked her up and threw her over his shoulder like a sack, not noticing that the hand that held her legs reddened with her blood.

Alex walked up the front steps and through the main door followed by Torquil, past the astonished footman.

"Mackie? Mackie?" he shouted, his voice echoing in the spacious entrance hall.

Mrs. MacDonald scurried in, wiping her hands on her apron. She stared at his tousled bundle for a moment and then down at Torquil.

"That's a rare big beastie."

"Aye," nodded Fergus, coming up behind her.

"Aren't you two going to ask who this is?" laughed Alex, slapping Cameron's rear end.

"Guess you'll tell us when you're ready," retorted

Mackie, frowning at the lacerations on the girl's legs.

"This is Cameron," stated Alex, hauling her down so she stood barefoot and bedraggled in front of them.

Humiliated, Cameron was glad that her hair covered her face so she couldn't see the eyes of the strangers.

Alex savagely grabbed her hair and pulled it aside, at the same time tugging her head back. Cameron's rage flared at his treatment and he laughed harshly at her useless defiance.

Mackie's kind face frowned at Alex's behavior, and Fergus silently turned on his heel.

"Well, Fergus, what do you think of my ward? Real young lady, isn't she now?" shouted Alex, angry with his own behavior but somehow unable to stop.

"Aye," replied Fergus curtly, unable to stay and watch the young girl's tormented eyes. He went out of the house, his heart bleeding for the poor wild-haired child.

Mrs. MacDonald had never seen Alex so cold and cruel before. There had been times after the death of his family, but never so shaming as what he was doing now to the poor torn bairn.

"Get to the kitchen!" she snapped at the ogling footman, not knowing how to deal with the situation. She reminded herself that she was a servant.

"Well, Sir Alex, if there's nothing you're needing from me, I've my work to be doing."

Alex felt her censure but didn't know what to do.

"Mackie, this is Cameron *Fraser*, old Duncan's grandchild," he stated, feeling convention required her to be given a surname.

"But the old goat never married. Oh!" Mrs. MacDonald retorted without thinking, and then recollected herself as her concerned face creased with vexation at her loose tongue.

"Duncan's dead, leaving me guardian to the girl."

"May his soul rest in peace now. The good Lord knows he never allowed himself any in life," prayed Mackie, staring at the bright green eyes kindly. Where had she seen such eyes before? The elusive memory teased her mind.

"Would you like a nice hot cup of tea and some scones?" she asked Cameron, trying to soothe the tense child.

Cameron didn't answer.

"Would you like some tea and scones?" repeated Alex, and still hearing no answer he shook her rigid shoulders.

"Cameron, I'll have no ill manners here. You will be courteous and answer when you are spoken to," he roared.

Mrs. MacDonald held her tongue, watching Alex's harshness with consternation. This was her lad? The man she had seen enter the world, nursing and caring for him as she would have done if he had come from her own belly? The lad she'd seen grown from suckling babe to man? She knew he had changed in those awful five years after Culloden Moor, those five years when she did not see him as the Sinclairs fled to France and on to the savage New World that had killed his gentle mother and the two lassies. He had returned to her and Fergus bitter and closed, scarcely fifteen, but already his eyes old and his brow furrowed. She had comforted and soothed him until his face opened and he was young again. She had wept at the pain she could not heal and shuddered at the cutting cynicism he sometimes resorted to, but that was in the past. Time had healed; but had it? Looking now at his closed, bitter face, Mackie fretted.

"I'll bring tea and scones and you can eat or not. And I think you be needing something stronger, Sir Alex," muttered Mackie.

"We'll have it in the drawing room," said Alex, pushing Cameron in that direction.

Mackie trotted off, unwilling to watch the cold anger pulsate between the small girl and tall cruel stranger she didn't recognize as her lad.

Alex wrenched his eyes from Cameron's and stared into the fire. Now the wild heathen was disturbing his home. Mackie usually called him Master Alex, and only when she was furious did she revert to "Sir," as she alluded scornfully to their different stations in life.

"That woman Mrs. MacDonald is a warm loving soul, and I'll not have you uncivil to her, do you ken?" he roared. "I'll not have you hurting her with your selfish ways."

Cameron had no intention of hurting anyone and for a moment forgot their battle of wills.

"I didna mean to hurt her," she whispered.

"Then answer when you are spoken to," retorted Alex lamely, wondering why with all the other problems he had to pick on such pettiness to thunder about.

Mrs. MacDonald came bustling in with a tea trolley, followed by Jeannie carrying water and towels. Alex noted the bowl.

"This is no place to freshen up. She has to learn to do it in the proper place, her own bedchamber."

"Aye, but the puir wee lass is tuckered out. Must all seem strange to her after being stuck away up north," chirped Mackie, undaunted by Alex's anger.

"I'll be in my study," snorted Alex, quitting the room.

Mackie heaved a sigh of relief as the door slammed after him, and she took the bowl of water from Jeannie.

"Jeannie, run along and make yourself useful hang-

ng up Miss Cameron's clothes. Then see if cook needs
help in the kitchen. I'll tend to these cuts."

Jeannie left the warm room reluctantly, as Mackie
pulled up a stool and sat beside the girl, bathing her
arms.

"You don't have to do that, 'tis but a few scratches,"
said Cameron, drawing her arms away.

"I know I don't have to, but I want to, so keep still.
'Tis a long time since I've had a bairn to mother, so
you give in to an old woman's fancy." Her sharp
Gaelic speech reminded Cameron of her grandfather,
and her eyes welled with tears; she held her arms obe-
liently still. She stared into the fire trying to control
herself and Mackie noticed but made no comment.

"Give me them puir wee feet and legs now," Mackie
muttered and clucked at the scatches and cuts.

"Here, put those poor feet in the bowl, 'twill ease
them," she said, rubbing ointment into the last of the
abrasions. "And here's your tea. Drink it all down, as
I've put a little something in to soothe you. 'Tis
strange to you, is it not?"

Cameron nodded.

"Then take it minute by minute lass, so it'll not all
tear into your poor head all at once. I best be off to
my work now, but if you need something, you just give
a tug on that," Mackie said, heaving herself onto her
feet and indicating a thick bell cord. She left the room
mumbling and shaking her head.

Alex sat in his study with a bottle of whiskey, feeling isolated and closed off. It was what he had longed
for the whole day and now that he had attained it, he
was dissatisfied. What the hell was the matter with
him? What was making him behave in this churlish
and cruel way? He thought of Cameron torn and tired
and found himself wishing that it was he bathing the

scratches. That's ridiculous! He'd had enough of playing nanny and nurse to last him a lifetime.

What had made her run away this time? As he realized she had only done the expected, he grew angrier. Why couldn't he forget her? Just close his mind, relax, and forget her? How could he have allowed her to lodge herself so firmly in his heart and mind? He laughed ironically and took a long punishing drink as he avoided his real feelings and grew steadily angrier. He had been with the trollop too long with no other females to divert him, and that would soon be remedied. He would leave for Edinburgh as soon as possible.

Cameron awoke with a start. Where was she? The fire blazed and Torquil lay snoring softly before it.

She remembered and looked down to see that the bowl had been removed and a soft blanket tucked around her. The room was dark, lit only by the burning logs. She wanted to look out of the window but worried that it might be somehow uncivil and disobedient. She sat awhile and then threw off the blanket and padded on her sore feet to the window. She stood looking out at the moonlit lawn.

"I see you've decided to wake."

Cameron started like a wild deer and tensed, poised for flight.

"Och now, there's nothing to scare you, little goose. Come, I'll show you your room," said Mrs. MacDonald, and she led the girl out to the central hall.

"'Tis a pretty room," she continued, her eyes clouding as she remembered Alex's two little sisters, who played and sang there. With a sharp jerk she thrust the memory of their soft pink cheeks and golden curls from her. "Does that big beastie follow you everywhere?" she asked as Torquil padded up the wide stairs after them. Cameron nodded.

"Well, I hope he knows how to behave respectable in the house."

Cameron was confused, not knowing if Mrs. Mac-Donald was talking about her or Torquil.

"If he makes a mess, he'll have to sleep in the stable," Mackie panted, winded after the climb.

Cameron's bedchamber was beautiful. The walls and curtains were covered with tiny rosebuds, the materials soft and light. It was all so delicate and pretty that Cameron felt like an ugly clumsy giant.

Mrs. MacDonald watched the girl's face and the love that she felt for the two golden-haired little girls was given to the tiny raven-haired one who stood looking like a lost wild thing in the middle of the room. Where had she seen such eyes and hair before?

"I'll send that rattlebrained girl of yours up to help you change for dinner."

Cameron looked at Mackie with bewilderment. Change for dinner? What did that mean?

"Something the matter?" asked Mackie, seeing the girl's confusion.

Cameron shook her head, afraid to admit her ignorance.

"I'll send that Jeannie up to you then," said Mrs. MacDonald, bustling out.

Cameron stared out of the window across the moonlit lawn that sloped to the firth. She could hear the sound of the tide and she ached to run in it. Jeannie skipped in, chattering.

"Isn't it a fine place? I have my own room. Dinna have to share it, seeing as how I'm a lady's maid. I'm higher up than the others. I've never been higher up than anyone before. Oh, it's so exciting! What'll you be wearing for dinner? How about this light green one?" she suggested, pulling out a filmy dress sewn with tiny flowers.

Cameron shrugged and Jeannie, talking a mile a minute, helped her remove the hated, heavy suit. But she was struck dumb when Cameron refused to wear the tight underbodice, stays, petticoat, pantalettes, stockings, garters, and shoes.

"You canna go to dinner like that. It ain't decent!" Jeannie managed to gasp, looking at Cameron in the nearly transparent dress.

"Who'll look under to know?" retorted Cameron.

"They dinna have to look under—can see right through."

Cameron bent down to see through her own skirt.

"I canna see a thing; and what if I could? We're all alike anyway."

"Stand in front of the fire. Now look."

"I won't stand in front of the fire, but it all seems silly."

"You're a strange one, you are. And look at your naked toes too," said Jeannie, shaking her head.

"I'll just bend my knees a wee bit, see?" Cameron walked around the room, hiding her toes, and Jeannie giggled nervously.

"But you can't, Miss Cameron. You're near naked."

"But I have a dress on."

" 'Taint right," protested Jeannie.

"Why?"

"It just ain't," shrugged the unhappy maid, wondering if her precious job hung in the balance.

Cameron pushed the worries aside. She felt unrestricted. The material caressed her skin like a soft breeze. She wouldn't stand near the fire, so who was to know? She'd be very careful to keep her toes hidden beneath the long skirt.

A bell sounded.

"Must be the call to dinner," informed Jeannie, rushing out. Cameron followed her to the stairs.

"Go before me and see if anyone is there," ordered Cameron, and the maid nervously scampered down the stairs, looking both ways, and then beckoned.

Cameron picked up the filmy skirt and raced down in her bare feet, coming to a sudden halt as she saw a footman standing there grinning. She dropped the skirt and pushed her head back arrogantly.

"Where do I go now?" she whispered to her maid.

"I dinna ken, just about know the way to the kitchen myself," Jeannie replied, scurrying off down a long passageway. Cameron started to follow, her hand braced on Torquil's head, when the footman stepped forward and opened a door.

"This way, miss."

Cameron jumped and stared apprehensively at him as he opened a door. She looked in, seeing flickering candles reflecting on the polished wood of a long table. Was she meant to go inside?

"Come in, Cameron. You're causing a draft," Alex said sarcastically.

Cameron stepped into the room and the heavy door shut behind her. She was glad Alex sat far away at the end of the long table, the reflection of the fire playing on his high chiseled cheekbones. He tilted back in his chair, a drink in his hand, and stared at her. A place was laid beside him at the table, but Cameron just stood avoiding his gaze as she looked at the thirty heavy chairs that lined the shiny table.

"Sit down, Cameron," sighed Alex impatiently, standing and pulling out the chair next to his.

Cameron walked the long distance toward him, keeping her knees slightly bent and her head raised so she captured his eyes.

"That dress is very becoming. Stand straighter and

let me see," ordered Alex, but Cameron reached the chair and quickly sat, hiding her feet under the table. Alex's hands clenched the back of her chair, and an angry tic worked in his cheek. He took a deep breath and sat down, deciding to let it go until they'd eaten. He rang a small bell and two footmen brought in soup and bread.

"We'll serve ourselves," he said, waving them away after they had set the tureen and board on the table.

Alex ladled the soup, wondering if he was being deliberately cruel by insisting that Cameron dine formally with him. The knives, forks, and spoons were lined correctly in front of her, and he held his breath waiting to see if she used the right one. But Cameron, looking at the neat rows of cutlery before her, waited to see which Alex picked up.

"You don't want soup?" he asked with a grin, knowing very well why she hesitated. Knowing that he knew, Cameron took a chance and grasped the round-headed spoon that lay on her right by three knives. She bent her head to eat, expecting to be mocked for her mistake and was surprised to hear him commence eating without a word. Fish was brought in and once again Cameron was faced with the dilemma. She noticed that the strangely shaped knife and fork had a finlike design and picked them up confidently, much to Alex's surprise. As the meal continued, she realized that if she worked from the outside in, she would know which of the cutlery to use, but the whole meal took such concentration that she tasted nothing.

Alex leaned back in his chair, satisfied that she handled her knife and fork deftly and ate prettily. His stomach full of food, he surveyed the fruit and cheese.

"No cheese and fruit?"

Cameron shook her head.

"I don't hear you," he growled.

"No, thank you, Sir Alex," retorted Cameron, exaggerating her enunciation.

Alex stifled a smile.

"Stand up," he ordered.

Cameron hesitated, painfully aware of the bright fire and her bare feet.

"I want to see you in your new finery. Stand up."

Cameron reached for an apple and bit into it quickly.

"A young lady cuts her apple to delicate slices," informed Alex, grabbing her wrist and taking the fruit from her.

"Why, if she has strong teeth?" retorted Cameron with her mouth full, hoping to avoid the subject of her dress.

"A young lady does not talk with her mouth full!" Cameron swallowed quickly, feeling the hard apple scrape her throat. Alex still held her wrist.

"Stand up," he ordered as he stood.

Cameron took a deep breath and stood defiantly as Alex held her at arm's length.

"Turn around," he said, releasing her and standing back.

Cameron stared at him with her hands on her hips and then spun around, the skirt whirling.

Alex gazed, seeing the budding lines of her lithe body silhouetted through the filmy material. So young and vulnerable, yet so worldly and wanton. He sat and leaned back in his chair, still watching her, his eyes tracing each curve so blatantly that Cameron grew restless and her defiance became embarrassment. She felt like she was being judged for mating or slaughter, like a hog or a sheep and, unable to bear his burning eyes any longer, she tossed her head and flared her nostrils as she spun away, heading for the nearest door.

"I did not give you leave to . . ." thundered Alex,

reaching out to stop her in one fluid movement. But Cameron fleetly eluded him and dashed through the door into the kitchen.

Fergus, Mackie, Jeannie, and an assortment of other servants sat eating at the large, scrubbed, kitchen table. They stared in amazement, forks raised and mouths open, as Cameron burst in, barefoot, holding up her skirt to her midthigh. Her hair streamed behind her and her eyes flashed with fury. The look of rage on Alex's face stopped Mackie's motherly cluckings. She resumed eating and motioned the others to do the same.

Cameron felt trapped. She stood behind Fergus at the head of the table, Alex behind Mackie at the foot. Cameron reached forward and grabbed a long bread knife.

"Nay, lassie," growled Fergus, wresting it from her as Alex's hands closed about her. She fought, kicking and screaming abuse as she was carried out of the room.

"That one sure gives the master a run for his money," chuckled a voice, as the door swung shut, and the apprehensive silence broke into loud chatter.

By God, 'tis time I taught her a lesson she'll not forget, Alex fumed, as he entered the study, his ears burning from the stream of words that poured out of Cameron's mouth. How dare she make him a laughing stock in front of his staff? How dare she take up a knife to him again? He had never felt so violent in his life. Kicking his study door shut behind them he roughly deposited her in the nearest chair and strode to the window, putting distance between them as he fought to control his rage.

Cameron felt herself unceremoniously dumped and her already-ignited fury exploded. She leaped to her feet, still spitting out every insult she could think of.

Her frustration grew as she got no reaction from the broad stiff back. The insufferable man just stood there, staring out the window as though she wasn't there.

Alex leaped aside as a crystal humidor crashed through the window, and he ducked just in time to avoid his ebony pipe rack complete with pipes.

"You English-loving bastard!" screamed Cameron, letting fly more missiles as her eyes lit on a large, lethal-looking claymore. Alex, following her gaze, read her mind and grabbed her just as she was reaching for the heavy sword. Feeling his hands she kicked backward.

"Bastard! Bastard!" she yelled, totally out of control.

"Enough!" roared Alex, shaking her to no avail as she continued kicking, her fury giving her surprising strength and courage. Alex slapped her hard across the face, but Cameron didn't recoil, just slapped him back and kicked out toward his groin.

"Stop!" thundered Alex, but Cameron fought with even more vigor, as though her very life depended on it.

"Bastard. Bastard. Bastard!"

Alex picked her up, imprisoning her wildly flailing fists and feet. Rage thundered in his ears as he pinned her across his lap and brought his broad, strong hand down hard across her buttocks.

"Stop!"

"Bastard! Bastard!" screamed Cameron, refusing to ackowledge the blow. It was as though she thought that if she kept shouting and fighting it would stop the fear and panic from consuming her.

Alex hit Cameron. He rained slap after heavy slap as she lay imprisoned across his knees. At first the feel of her young body pressed to him made his passion flare, but that only increased his rage, so he hit her as much to beat the passion from himself as to punish her. He derived tremendous satisfaction from the first stinging slap but, to his frustration, Cameron did not stop struggling or admit defeat. He hit again and again with the same reaction. Cameron kept up her stream of struggles and insults, and the thunder roared in Alex's ears. He lost count of the times his hand descended.

As Alex's rage ebbed, the pounding of blood no longer echoing in his ears, he became aware of a frantic scratching and howling at the door. He stared down in horror at the prone girl across his lap.

What have I done? What is the matter with me? The shock of his own lack of control and brutality shook him to his very core. He sat still, not knowing what to do or how to undo the hurt he had afflicted.

Cameron lay half-conscious, her buttocks and the back of her thighs burning and throbbing. She felt her skin stretched to bursting. She heard her dog's frantic barks and whimpers.

"Torquil?" she whispered and tried to roll off Alex's knees, but his hands pulled her toward him. Cameron looked into his face and, summoning up all her energy, spat. Alex stared blankly as the girl pushed herself from him and stood.

He'll not get the satisfaction thinking I'm hurt, she swore, as the room spun and the pain surged. But her quaking legs collapsed beneath her.

Alex picked up the unconscious girl and laid her face down on the couch. Torquil was beside himself, howling and throwing himself against the heavy wood door of the study.

Would be my just desserts if that great hound devoured me, Alex thought, as he opened the door and Torquil leaped in to lick Cameron's still face. Mackie and Fergus stood outside, their faces set and worried. The other servants peered curiously and wide-eyed from the kitchen. Alex beckoned to the MacDonalds, waving away the others.

"I need cold water and cloths," he said quietly.

"Aye," answered Mackie flatly and, looking up at his anguished face, her disapproval softened.

"I'll fetch them," growled Fergus, turning to the kitchen.

"I heard your blows."

"Aye," answered Alex.

"Aye. You've done bad, real bad, to a puir wee wild thing. She needs gentling, not skelping," said Mackie softly.

"Will you see to her?"

"Nay, you clean up what you started. You did the hurting, now you do the healing. I'm shamed with you, right shamed. Dinna teach you right. What's lying in your heart that you're not feeling?" Mackie hissed, her eyes full of tears.

Fergus silently held the bowl out to Alex and again turned away.

Closing the study door behind Alex, Mackie dashed the tears angrily from her eyes and bustled back to the kitchen, yelling at all the nosy parkers who had nothing better to do than gawk and flap their ears and tongues.

Alex stared down at Cameron. He gently lifted her skirt and stared down at her naked back and legs, his own large hand imprinted on her flesh many times, the fingermarks raised and angry. My God! he thought, how many times had he struck her? Twenty? Fifty? There was not an inch of flesh from the small of her back to the back of her knees not angry at his abuse. He wet the thick cloths in cold water and placed them on her. He did not know what else to do

except to change them as soon as they warmed from
her burning skin.

"How is she?" Mackie's concerned face popped i
the door.

"See for yourself," he answered moodily, as Macki
closed the door behind her.

Scandalized, she stared at Cameron who was nake
from the waist down.

"What are you doing?" she quavered indignantly.

"Healing her as you told me to do."

"And how was I to know that's where you beat th
poor child?"

"Where was I meant to hit her?" he snapped, out c
patience with Mackie's prudery.

"Where are her underclothes?"

"She will not wear any."

"Then out you go, I'll tend the lass. 'Tis not decen
you being a full-grown man," clucked Mackie, wring
ing out cloths.

"Dinna fash yourself, Mackie, I've seen her all man
times."

"Oh, you have, have you? And what is she to you?
Alex longed to tell Mackie the truth but bit the word
back.

"I was alone with her in the wilds for over tw
weeks. She was attacked, sick, and there was only m
to play nursemaid. What would you have me do? Eh
Leave her to die?"

"Well, you're not in the wilderness now, so off wit
you."

"Nay, I'll stay!" said Alex firmly.

Mackie looked at him and, recognizing the resolu
tion in his eyes, nodded, shrugged resignedly, an
peeped under the compresses.

"Oh, my heavens! Oh, my Lord! What have yo
done? The puir child willna sit for a week," she u

ered, whipping off the other cloths to see the bruised, wollen back.

"What got into you, Alex Sinclair? The Devil? What is eating into you that could cause you to strike anyone, let alone a bairn, like that?"

Alex didn't answer, just stared into the fire feeling his eyeballs burn.

"Poor, sweet, innocent thing," crooned Mackie, wiping the sleeping girl's face.

"Not as innocent as you think," retorted Alex.

"And what is that suppose to mean?" snapped Mackie.

" 'Tis a long story."

"Which you better now be telling me, seeing there is no more to be done until the puir battered bairn wakens. We both need a drink and it's been a long time since we had a chat," she said, seating herself firmly in a chair by the fire and fixing her eyes on him. Alex looked at her round homely figure, remembering how as a small boy he'd buried his face in her ample breasts as her dimpled arms rocked and soothed him. Oh, to be a child again, he thought.

"Come along. Cough it up. 'Taint just bairns that need to talk to their nannies, you know," she urged, as reading his wishes.

Alex handed her a glass of whiskey.

"A man has to stand by himself, that's what you taught me," he teased.

"Aye, and it's true, not just a man, woman too. No one can breathe for you but you, nor die for you neither. That's just a fact that is, but it doesna mean we don't share the good and the bad."

Alex turned from her, pacing the room, his nose itching and eyes burning.

"What ails you, my bonny boy? Tell Mackie what hurts? You're like a keg of ale, all shook up and ready to burst the barrel slats. Look what happens: You blow the cork and beat the bairn, vent your spleen and let the gases out."

"Dinna keep harping! I know I hurt her. I know it," raged Alex with pain.

"And why did you hurt her?" insisted Mackie, knowing he soon would explode again, this time, she hoped, with words.

Alex kept pacing. He recounted his trip to Cape Wrath, trying to edit and summarize, but soon the words bubbled out as they used to so long before in the nursery, when guilts and indecision dug into him. Mackie listened quietly, not saying a word until he was done, hearing behind the words what Alex would not admit to himself.

"So the bairn's your wife?" she said when he had finished.

"Aye, curse her to hell!" he spat savagely, furious at himself for having spilled his guts like some puling child.

"Well, 'tis tit for tat," chuckled Mackie.

"Meaning?"

"Meaning you took her freedom, now she's took yours."

"I didna ask to be her guardian."

"And she didna ask to be your ward. Most times a girl doesna ask to be a wife."

"That's neither here nor there. I'll be going to Edinburgh for the winter, and she stays here. See if you can civilize her for me. And Mackie, 'tis a secret. I don't want a wife. No one is to know of the marriage," he stated firmly. "No one!"

"Puir wee thing," said Mackie, changing the compresses.

"Live with her awhile and then *you'll* be feeling like the puir wee thing," he hissed, resuming his pac-

ing. "I'll be leaving first thing in the morning, so have
my things taken care of."

"Yes, your lordship," answered Mackie scornfully.
Alex gave her a long hard look and slammed out of
the room.

Chapter Thirteen

Cameron lay in the bed in the pretty delicate room,
staring at the rosebuds on the walls. She was glad to be
lying on her back after three days flat on her stomach;
she was glad to be hidden away from the house of
strangers whose curious eyes made her feel awkward
and ashamed.

Jeannie skipped in and out, chattering enthusiastically about handsome stableboys and footmen as she
brought meals and brushed Cameron's hair.

Mrs. MacDonald bustled in and out, shooing Jeannie off to work in the kitchen so Cameron could rest.
Cameron felt drawn to the kind woman but drew
back, afraid of her own desire to be loved and comforted. Mackie realized this and did not press the girl,
although her own heart longed to mother and gentle
Cameron into trusting her.

Now Cameron was bored. The sun poured in through the window. She tiptoed over to it and flung it open, breathing deeply of the sweet air as her eyes devoured the autumn colors. There were no trees to watch at Cape Wrath, so this seemed a magical unreality. Reds, golds, yellows, and oranges blazed in the crisp clean sunlight and were reflected in the mirror-still waters of the firth. Her eyes filled with tears as she thought of Torquod. How he would have loved to race along the green rolling coast.

"'Tis good to see you on your feet again," said Mackie, after watching the girl for a few minutes, noting the tears that clung to the long curling eyelashes and marveling at the delicate profile.

Cameron turned, brushing her hands across her eyes to hide her weakness.

"I'm thinking you'd like to be out there running wild with your hound."

Cameron smiled tremulously and then her face fell as she thought of what she might have to wear.

"I'll send your chattering Jeannie up to you, but first put some meat on those skinny shanks of yours." Mrs. MacDonald indicated a tray by the bed.

As Cameron sat eating, Jeannie burst in.

"Mrs. MacDonald says as how you were needing me, that you're getting up and going out for a spell. What do you want to wear?" Jeannie asked, throwing open the armoire and indicating the array of clothes. Cameron stared at the hated garments and thought of her kilt and plaid, wondering where they were. She couldn't run free wearing any of the confining cumbersome clothes she surveyed.

"Jeannie, sit down here a moment." Cameron patted the bed beside her and Jeannie sat gratefully.

"My feet are worn down to the very bones," she confided. "That Mrs. MacDonald is a slave driver. Up and down, up and down. Do this. Do that. Don't she know that a lady's maid ain't supposed to work in the kitchen and scullery?"

"Jeannie, I need some trews and a shirt."

"For what?" exclaimed Jeannie, her mouth hanging open, and then tightening to a small round o. "Oooh! Oooh! No, Miss Cameron, you'll not be getting up to any more of your scandalizing. Didn't I tell you before? Didn't I? And look what happened to you then, all colors of the rainbow was your poor arse. I ain't never seen nothing like it before."

Cameron shook her gently.

"I canna wear those things, Jeannie. I canna run or feel free. It's just for a little while, and no one will see," Cameron urged.

"I'd give my eye teeth for any of them pretty things," said Jeannie, staring at the full wardrobe.

"And you'll have them all if you'll just get me a kilt."

"A kilt! You really are mad. They'd hang you! 'Tis against the law, and besides, even if it weren't, 'taint decent for a lass to wear, showing off her legs. They be men's clothes."

"And what's wrong with legs? Ain't we all got them?" retorted Cameron.

"Oh, aye, but just fallen women show them off."

"You mean when a woman falls off her horse? It's no wonder, having to ride all twisted and sideways," snorted Cameron.

"Don't you even know what a fallen woman is? Why, 'tis a whore and a harlot," crowed Jeannie.

Cameron grew angry at Jeannie's remarking on her ignorance. "You'll get me the trews," she ordered.

"I cain't, I cain't. I'll lose my job."

"You'll lose it if you don't get them. I'll say I don't like you anymore."

"But where would I get them?" Jeannie whined, tears pouring down her face.

"What about the stable lads you keep telling me about?"

Jeannie stared at Cameron in dismay. "But I canna take their breeks, I'm a good girl. I'm a good girl and now I'm going to lose my position—" and she wailed loudly.

"I thought a lady's maid had to serve her. Do what her mistress asks?" said Cameron coldly.

"Aye, but 'tis Lord Sinclair what pays me," sniffed Jeannie.

Cameron looked at the other girl's wet unhappy face, hearing the truth of the words, crashing her hopes. The two girls sat side by side on the bed, their shoulders slumped dejectedly, both faces the picture of gloom.

"And what have we here on this beautiful day?" asked Mackie, and at her warm voice Jeannie broke into wails and sobs as she hiccuped her words a mile a minute.

"Ooooh, mum. Ooooh, mum. It weren't my fault, truly it weren't. I tried to dress her, mum, really I did, mum, but she wants to wear the kilt, yes, the kilt, mum, said to get her trews too, mum, you know, breeks, and I canna . . ."

Mackie firmly ushered the wailing bobbing girl out of the room.

"Hush up your noise, Jeannie, and go down and tell cook to give you a spot of tea. And if I hear any gossiping about this, I'll turn you out without a good word. You ken?"

"Ooooh, mum. I wouldna say a word to a living soul, mum. I likes Miss Cameron; but I dinna ken her."

"'Tis not for you to understand. Now scoot, you silly wench."

Mrs. MacDonald shut the door after Jeannie and looked at Cameron, who sat with her face set and closed.

"Kilts? Trews?" she said, raising an eyebrow at each word.

"Look at yourself. Go on, look," urged Mackie, pulling the girl to her feet and pointing at her image in the glass. "You are a lass, and a rare bonny one at that. Look at yourself and be proud of what the good Lord made."

Cameron stared dispassionately at herself and wrenched free of Mackie's hands. She picked up a cup from her breakfast tray and hurled it at the mirror.

"No! No, I hate it!" she screamed, and then attacked the clothes that hung in the armoire, tearing them out and throwing them on the floor, trying to rip the materials, destroy them any way she could.

"I'll not wear those English clothes! They torture my body, cut off my breathing, bind me so I canna move! They choke me, they'll kill me! I hate them! I hate them!"

Later Mrs. MacDonald sat in her parlor talking with Fergus.

"What could I do? What would you have had me do? I know 'twas not seemly."

"Same as you done. I'm right proud of you," he growled, patting her dimpled hand with his thin leathery one. Mackie's face flushed with pleasure and then fell.

"I don't think Master Alex will agree."

"He ain't here."

"Could just pop in."

"Aye, he could. Maybe he's back to his senses. He

ain't in his right mind, Mackie. Worries me. He ha
the gentlest hands of any man. I seen him breaking i
many a young horse without breaking the spirit or th
mouth."

"Miss Cameron is not a horse, Fergus," said Macki
sharply.

"She's a little wild filly, and he's trying to break he
with a tight rein and a saddle. He'll break her bacl
mounting her," Fergus rumbled angrily.

"Fergus MacDonald! I dinna ken what you're talk
ing about, and it don't seem decent neither. Mountin;
indeed!"

"Bet 'tis why the lad's itching, 'cause he wants to
and maybe loving is how she'll be tamed," said Fergus

Mackie clucked indignantly and poked him witl
her elbow.

"Not that sort of loving, *gentle* loving."

"Aye," answered Fergus, grinning at her warmly
"That dark little filly is under his skin, all right."

"But he don't know it."

"He don't want to know it," corrected Fergus.

"The poor lad. Loving can hurt the heart."

"Aye, but he's out of knee britches and I've no pa
tience with him," snapped Fergus.

"Funny thing about heart pain: You can remember
it so sharply, not like body pain that you just remem
ber you had but canna recall," said Mackie wistfully
thinking of the long years after Culloden when sh
and Fergus were separated.

"So you put her in trews and let her run?" said Fer
gus gently.

"Aye, and let's hope Master Alex stays put in Edin
burgh. Fergus, you should have seen the poor bairn'
body. Not just the bruised back, but her wee chest i
scarred with whip marks. Looks like Saint Andrew'
cross."

"You don't think the lad did it?" frowned Fergus.

"I hope not, I dearly hope not," murmured Mackie, relaxing in Fergus's arms. "Mr. MacDonald?"

"Aye," he replied, staring down fondly at his wife's neat bun.

"That coal black hair and green eyes . . ." she mused.

"Aye? What about them?"

"It teases my mind. I canna think where . . . But he doesn't look like any Fraser I've seen."

"She's a throwback to some Roman or Spaniard who sowed his oats in the Highlands, no doubt. There's many a black-haired Scot."

"Aye, but Duncan Fraser never married, so what's this about a grandchild?"

"Och ye old innocent. Ain't you ever heard of a by-blow?"

"Get away with you now!" said Mackie, pushing herself away from him. "'Tis time the lass was back. Hope she don't take no notion into her head to run away, or they'll be the Devil to pay."

"Nay, the lass is fine," said Fergus, staring out of the second-story window at Cameron sitting on a bluff with Torquil, staring over the water.

"They look like two lost souls," sniffed Mackie, seeing the great dog's head top Cameron's.

"Aye, looking toward another lost soul," replied Fergus dryly, indicating Edinburgh across the water.

Alex strolled down Princes Street oblivious to the bustle and noise of the traffic. Now that he was back in the city, he didn't know what to do with himself. He was not used to being fashionably idle; he sat alone in his townhouse, loath to call on any of his numerous friends. He found he didn't even want to see Fiona. He had been in Edinburgh for a week and this

was his first emergence, already having tried to drive
Cameron out of his mind by reading, drinking, and
yelling at his staff. Everything irritated him—the
noise, the dirt, the business, the efficiency of his hovering staff as they tried to please him, but most of all
his own thoughts, which plagued him. He was now determined to force himself into the social swing, even
though the thought of crowded and exaggeratedly gay
parties with overpainted women clashed horrifically
with the small, green-eyed face that tormented his
mind.

A cheerful voice called his name a few times. He
dimly heard but did not turn until his arm was
grasped.

"Where have you been hiding yourself, Sinclair?"
Alex stared a moment before recognizing the man.

"Fiona is in a rare state. She'll be pleased to know
you're back. I hope you've a good story ready,"
laughed the young man.

Fiona, thought Alex. It seemed like years since last
he'd seen her instead of less than a month. So much
was on his mind that even her name sounded like
something from another life. Fiona? He couldn't even
picture her face.

"You all right?" asked his friend, perplexed at Alex's blank silence.

"Aye, let's have a drink, Peter," said Alex, taking his
arm and forcing himself to be friendly.

Many drinks later in the warm noisy tavern Alex
blearily surveyed the faces of his friends about him.
Who were all those people? All those people with shining teeth and shrill voices? Of what use were they?
Who *were* they? Oh, he knew their names, but what
was the point in any of them being alive? What was
the point in even being born, when everyone had to
die anyway? He sat musing drunkenly as his so-called

friends planned a welcome-home party for him. Any excuse to have a party! Any excuse to fill up the marching days before they all died, he thought morbidly, feeling detached from them.

He heard his friends swearing each other to secrecy and became belligerent when he concluded they kept their secret from him.

"What secret?" he demanded, banging the table.

"Oh, boy, are you drunk!" slurred a friend.

"The secret is not to tell Lady Fiona Hurst that her protector is back in Edinburgh, and we're to have a party uniting them," explained another, carefully trying to control his sliding tongue.

"Why?" swayed Alex.

"Because it's a secret."

"Oh. Who's her whatever-you-said?" asked Alex.

"I don't know. How should I know? You are the one who gets in the lady's bed."

"What lady?" shouted Alex, his head reeling.

"Better get him home."

Alex dimly remembered swinging his fists as his sotted friends drove him home.

He awoke the following morning with a foul hangover. He lay, his head pounding, as fragments of the night before danced heavily in his brain.

Fiona? Oh, dear Christ! There was to be a party with him and Fiona as the guests of honor, but she wasn't to know he was back in town. Fiona, his mistress of two years standing; quite a joke in his circle, where mistresses were cast aside after a few months play. He'd had many other women in those two years, and he suspected that Fiona had also had other men, but they both were discreet and the license to see others had made the two years of the affair possible.

Fiona was fiercely independent, running her own gaming parlor, her tall voluptuous body sweeping regally between the tables, her flaming red head held proudly. Fiona, the sixth daughter of an impoverished laird married off at thirteen to an eighty-year-old English lord.

"Thank God he was eighty. A year in bed with me killed him off," Fiona had chuckled. As a rich young widow in the English court Fiona could have her pick of any, and she did, but not for marrying. She left the court at twenty years of age, with a terrible reputation and a terribly large amount of money, to return to her native Scotland where she found her infamy had preceded her. The dour society matrons had barred the doors of the respectable assemblies to her.

Alex's friends envied him Fiona, as they had to support and maintain houses for their mistresses, keeping them in clothes, jewelry, and servants for fear of losing them. Alex refused to pay for his women, as there were so many offering their favors freely, and Fiona refused to allow him to support her, not wanting to be tied to any man again. Which suited Alex perfectly.

He wondered why he was so reluctant to meet Fiona again. He tried to arouse himself, imagining her as he had so often seen her, naked, her full ripe breasts available to him, but all he felt was distaste. He blamed it on his queasy stomach and aching head.

He slept the day away and by early evening, after a hot bath, he felt more able to face the party that loomed ahead. He dressed, rationalizing and convincing himself that Fiona was just the diversion he needed. With a stiff drink in hand he surveyed himself, the tight breeches and the gleaming high boots, the snowy-white shirt and perfectly tied cravat that fell in casual folds. He tried to look in the mirror and see himself as another would. What did she see? What was it that made the flicker of fear flash through her green eyes? He knew he was passably handsome, that women often fell over themselves to get his attention. His own amber eyes stared back. Was his face cruel? Did his thin mouth have a cynical twist?

"Well, are you beautiful enough?" teased a cheerful voice, and Alex turned to see three grinning friends lolling in chairs; he'd been so intent on thoughts of Cameron, he'd not heard his servant announce the men's arrival.

"Aye, I guess I'll do," he laughed, forcing the cobwebs from his mind. "What do you think, will Fiona approve?"

His three friends turned to each other faking indecision as they frowned, walked around him, and bit their lips.

"Do you think he'll do?"

"I'll not be sure."

"Aye, she's been in a terrible taking."

"Aye, that she has, biting customers' heads off."

"A veritable shrew."

"Who? Fiona?" asked Alex, laughing.

"Aye, wouldn't like to be in your boots, me lad."

"Stop exaggerating. Fiona's not like that," Alex protested, refusing to take them seriously.

"Any woman is like that if you take off for a month without a leave or word."

"Aye, but Fiona and I leave each other free to do as we please."

Alex brooded as they rode to the house where the party was to be held. It was true that they left each other free to do as they pleased, but he usually informed her when he left the city; sometimes weeks went by when he was busy overseeing the sowing or the harvest at Glen Aucht, but she always knew where he was.

The four of them clattered along on horseback through the streets of Edinburgh, three chattering and laughing while the fourth set his face in a frown as he wondered why he'd decided to go to the party at all.

The room was full of smoke and about twenty young, noisy bucks.

"Where's the ladies? By jove, this ain't stag, is it?" yelled one.

"Wait until the show's over at the corps de ballet," shouted another.

Alex groaned and decided to have a lot to drink before the screaming, fawning, overperfumed, painted sirens descended. He wondered at his sanity for agreeing to such an escapade, knowing Fiona despised such women. He sat with his legs stretched in front of him, nursing a large brandy, smiling ironically at the thought that Fiona seemed to hate other women in general. She never exhibited any jealousy, not even at his frequent dalliances. She just hated the women of the upper circles that shut her out, and she hated the women of the lower class, and she hated women who stretched their youth and beauty, desperately clinging to paint and other artifices, and she hated women who didn't.

He was forced out of his reverie to shake hands and converse civilly with friends. He answered their questions reservedly about his absence, saying nothing except he'd been north to visit an old friend of his father's. His eyes opened wider as Ian Drummond strolled in and winked conspiratorially at him. Ian was bursting with curiosity, but he controlled it humorously until they stood alone.

"I waited for your promised visit but you didn't show," chided Ian. "So I rode over and found you had left for these parts, and Mackie barred me from seeing your black-haired you-know-what."

Alex frowned at him.

"Sorry, business," he answered shortly.

"Aye. Have you seen the fair Fiona since you've been back?" pressed Ian wickedly.

"Looks as though you know the answer to that one," sparred Alex.

"Better not tell her you've been back a week. Nearly let it slip myself, but seeing the raging mood she was in I preferred to hold my tongue."

"This doesn't seem to be your cup of tea," said Alex, indicating the party.

"Yours neither, but as for myself I couldna resist a fireworks display."

"Ian, I'm trusting you not to breathe a word of Cameron."

"Aye, I'll not say a word of your ward," he whispered roguishly.

The deep rumble of male voices gradually faded and Alex turned to see Fiona standing at the entrance to the room, her eyes staring at him. She stood breathtaking in her majesty. A tall statuesque woman with a mane of red hair, who knew both how to dress and pose herself to her best advantage. Alex watched her objectively, admiring her ability to stand so regally, so imperiously, seemingly unaware of the attention she was receiving. Every pair of eyes in the room flickered back and forth between them until Fiona broke the stillness by tossing her wrap off in one magnificent, dramatic movement and glided archly in the opposite direction, pointedly ignoring Alex.

"That told you," chuckled Ian.

"Aye," breathed Alex tersely, turning his back on the rest of the room and looking into his friend's honest eyes that brimmed with suppressed mirth.

"There's many a man here wanting it to be over between you two," said Ian.

"Aye."

"Maybe 'tis time?"

"Maybe."

"She's a bit older than you and 'tis time you settled, had an heir."

"You sound like Mackie. And what of you? If I remember we are of an age," laughed Alex.

"You have four months on me, old man," retorted Ian merrily, but his face dropped as he stared over Alex's broad shoulder. "I think I'll mingle now and make sure I get a front row seat. The fair Fiona doth approach and methinks she's full of wrath," murmured Ian, hastily bowing to Fiona and giving Alex a wicked look as he excused himself.

Alex was aware of every eye riveted on them.

"So, my lord?" said Fiona stiffly, as he touched his lip to her glove. Alex looked at her quizzically, not knowing what to say.

"So you've returned?" she commented between clenched teeth, her lips turned up in a false smile.

"Aye," he answered tersely, noting she had used some artifices of rouge, lip paint, and something about the eyes. Not a lot but a trace. He noticed the fine lines that she had somehow made more noticeable with powder, and wondered how long they'd been there.

Fiona stared at the arrogant face that seemed to be detachedly and impersonally assessing her. How dare he, she seethed, longing to strike his face, but she curbed the impulse with a sickeningly sweet smile. Alex noted the clenched, gloved hand.

"You'll not give them satisfaction, I hope?" he said dryly, indicating the staring room. Fiona glared at his beloved face. How she had missed him, and how she hated him. For two years she had lived just for the few times they were together, keeping busy in between so the lapses didn't yawn achingly before her. Never before had he gone without a word for four whole, long weeks. Her heart beat frantically beneath her cool exterior. Even now she wouldn't let him know how much she loved him.

"I'll not give you the satisfaction, Alexander Sinclair," she said quietly, her soft words belying the raging violence she felt. Alex noted the hardness in her blue eyes and wondered what his next line should be.

"May I get you a cool drink?" he inquired politely.

"Damn you to hell!" she hissed, her mouth smiling civilly for the benefit of the onlookers.

"Why?" asked Alex innocently, enjoying the mastery he felt.

"Why? Why?" sputtered Fiona.

"Careful, madam, you'll make a vulgar display of yourself," he chided, signaling to a footman for a drink. Fiona swallowed the gall that rose and smiled sweetly as she took a proffered drink.

"I'll see you later, madam, away from this circus," said Alex, and Fiona forgot her anger and smiled seductively at him.

"Now let us mingle and give our audience relief," he said, offering her his arm and congratulating himself. Fiona rose to the occasion, smiling brightly among the guests, in her element in the all-male company.

The meal was served at an enormous banquet table. Alex presided at one end and way in the distance, at the other end, was Fiona. At least fifty young men lined each side. Alex watched her critically, a queen surrounded by her admirers. She felt his eyes on her and noted the cynical humor in them when he silently raised his glass to her. A pang went through her.

A sumptuous repast was served, course upon course of excellently prepared food, throughout which Alex kept his cold gaze on Fiona. She was uncomfortable and insecure, and she vent her feelings by flirting outrageously with the young men around her. She listened attentively, not really hearing a word as the flustered, embarrassed young men interrupted each other to get her attention. She bent forward, exposing her cleavage to their greedy eyes, teasing them until their appetite for the luscious food was gone and they longed to devour the ripe breasts that hung temptingly in front of them.

At thirty-two Fiona felt she neared middle age, and Alex's long unexplained absence had caused her to examine herself more closely in the mirror, seeing to her horror that the ravages of age were inexorably etched. She saw them not as faint lines but noticeably deep crevices, as her fear exaggerated each unfavorable trace. The terror of the too-quickly passing years clawed into her and she was afraid that she was ugly and no longer desirable.

All around her the young men sang praises to her beauty, feasting their eyes on her sensuous body, but Fiona was not gratified or reassured. She derived nothing from the clamorous infatuation around her; all she wanted was Alex. He sat at the distant end facing her, silently staring, goading her, it seemed, to redouble her efforts to make him jealous. She drank glass after glass of wine to blot out the cold gnawing fear.

Through the hazy hum of deep male conversation Fiona saw the door burst open to admit a colorful, shrieking swarm of scantily dressed whores, and all attention left her. She fought the dizzying effects of the wine and cursed herself for declining the delectable dishes that had been placed before her.

Alex was a long way from the busy scene around him. His eyes seemed to stare at Fiona, whose usual unruffled exterior now bristled with ill-disguised fury at the orgy that was unfolding around her, but he was miles away, back at the quiet stone house with Cameron.

Fiona seethed as his cool gaze seemed to mock her. He treats me like a worn-out whore, inviting me to be a party to such depravity, she raged, seeing that around her the very men who had hung on to her every word now groped and sucked inviting flesh. She laughed viciously as her searching eyes saw women older than she, but a small cry issued from her mouth as a pink-feathered doxy dropped herself on Alex's lap. Fiona frantically scanned the room for an unavailable male to pretend to prefer, but all were taken. Despite her pain and disgust Fiona found herself aroused by the blatant sexuality displayed around her as the men and women entwined, many spread upon the table as though they were desserts.

Alex felt his own passion rise as he thought of himself with Cameron in the clear clean mountain stream. He stared down and discovered a plump, pink-feathered girl greedily rubbing her hands up his thighs. He stood abruptly, dumping her to the ground, and surveyed the thrusting and rutting around him.

Fiona summoned all her energy to rise coolly and sweep with dignity from the room. But the room seemed to spin, kaleidoscoping the mass of writhing flesh. She closed her eyes and clung to the back of her chair, not knowing if her legs could support her. A strong arm encircled her and she looked up into Alex's amber eyes.

"I wish to go home," she stated, desperately trying to be haughty and cool amid the hot snorts and pantings.

Alex steered her to the door and ordered her carriage to be sent around.

"It's later," swayed Fiona, reminding him of his promise of before. "There's no circus now."

Alex helped her into the coach and slid in beside her, feeling Fiona's heaviness against him. Thank

heavens she seemed to be falling asleep, he thought
relieved that he would avoid a painful scene. He
stared out of the window thinking of Cameron. Was
she happy? What was she doing?

Fiona's hand rubbed against his chest demanding
his attention, as her red hair tickled his chin irritat-
ingly.

"Kiss me, Alex, 'tis been a long, long time," she
murmured. Alex bent his head, meaning to give a per-
functory peck but as his lips touched hers, a surge of
fury burst through him. He roughly pulled her hair,
forcing her head back, and bruised her mouth with
his, not heeding her whimpers. His hands tore at her
gown, releasing her heavy breasts, only to recapture
them savagely, pinching and kneading, as passionate
rage flooded through him.

"Alex, please," protested Fiona, preferring a softer
approach, but he threw her back and prepared to
mount her. He wanted to stab into her again and
again, hammer at her, drive at her, pound her to a
pulp. Mercifully the coach came to a sudden halt,
bringing him to his senses.

"My, you're certainly hungry," gasped Fiona, adjust-
ing her torn bodice and wrapping her cape around
her.

Alex silently adjusted his own clothes and they
walked sedately into Fiona's townhouse and up the
too-familiar stairs to her boudoir.

They made love violently, both trying to relieve the
frustrations that trapped them. Fiona, testing and
clawing, trying to possess, Alex silently pounding, wiping his brain to nonthinking numbness in the cres-
cendoing inexorable rhythm.

Not quite awake, Alex felt soft hands caressing him.
He kept his eyes closed, seeing Cameron's small face in
his mind. He relaxed, allowing the seduction to con-

tinue as knowing hands rekindled his passion. Waves of pleasure flowed through him as the wet warmth of a greedy mouth trailed down his body toward his straining manhood and encompassed him. He opened his eyes, ill-prepared for the shocking mass of red hair against his belly, then closed them recalling Cameron, and allowed himself to be manipulated and tucked inside Fiona's heat.

The patterns never changed, he thought later, as he sat beside Fiona in bed, balancing a breakfast tray on his knees and listening to her maid coo trite phrases about young lovers. They never change.

Chapter Fourteen

Cameron galloped through the storm beside the raging waters of the Firth of Forth. Three weeks had passed, yet to Mackie and Fergus's dismay she still clung to the shirt and trews of the stableboy. Each morning she rose with the sun to ride freely with Torquil for hours on end, returning to eat in the kitchen only to ride out again. The MacDonalds knew not to expect her back until long after dark, when she'd return glowing and happy, her hair wet even in the driest of weather.

Mackie fretted herself into a dither the first time the girl rode off into a storm. Cameron had been lying on the floor by the kitchen fire reading a book when the first low rumble of thunder vibrated through the air. The green eyes had lit up and she dashed out, followed by the great hound. Mrs. MacDonald trotted after, trying to stop her as Cameron ordered a horse saddled. Her order refused, Cameron just opened the door of a stall and leaped on the bare back of one of the horses, galloping off into the raging night. Fergus had come, hearing Mackie's frightened cries and shouts.

"You did what you could. The wee un knows. She's more at home with the forces of nature than cooped up in a fancy house," he had said, comforting his distressed wife. The two old people had watched Cameron that night from their second-story parlor, as she dared the storm and defied the elements. There were no words to describe the awe they felt; they just held each other tightly, keeping their eyes glued to the small figure, somehow knowing Cameron needed the release.

"I love that wild bairn," growled Fergus, his usually impassive face choked with emotion.

"Aye, so do I. But what of Master Alex?" answered Mackie.

"Aye," he sighed, and shook his head.

At the first peal of thunder Mackie now insisted Cameron wear a leather jerkin and warm cape for protection from the cold rain. As was their wont, Mackie and Fergus watched the girl ride the storm, each fascinated and afraid lest she be thrown. That stormy night three weeks after Alex's departure as they stood marveling at her graceful speed and worrying about Alex, Fergus saw a parade of carriages snaking up the long driveway, the outriders' heads bent against the violent wind.

"I'm a'thinking 'tis now out of our hands," he growled.

"Lord have mercy," breathed Mackie, and she followed her husband down the stairs as he barked sharp orders to the servants.

Mackie reached the kitchen out of breath.

"Put down the knitting and hop to it," she told the cook. "The master's back with a houseful of guests, it seems."

Suddenly the large kitchen was a beehive of activity, as maids seemed to come out of the woodwork with armloads of linens, pots and pans, fish and fowl. Servants ran right and left as Mrs. MacDonald directed them.

In the front carriage Alex sat cursing the storm and thinking ruefully of Mackie's consternation at a houseful of guests descending without warning.

" 'Tis going to be wonderful," murmured Fiona, snuggling into his heavy cape as the thunder rolled and the lightning flashed.

Alex frowned in the darkness. What was he doing? Why was he bringing Fiona and all these others to his home? What rashness had induced him to invite them for shooting? *He* should be shot, he thought savagely.

"At last I'm going to see your family home," said Fiona, her blue eyes alive, anticipating a proposal of marriage. "Oh, Alex!" she gasped, as the carriage rounded a curve and the magnificent mansion came into view. Alex noted each window was ablaze with light and servants stood ready to hand guests from the coaches. "That Mackie has second sight," he chuckled.

The servants stood at attention in the hall, prepared to take dripping capes and show each guest his bedchamber. Mackie stared at the bevy of young men and her eyes rounded in disapproval at the only female, who clung to Alex, her painted face sparkling greedily as she looked around. Mrs. MacDonald's usually fair mind saw no beauty about Fiona, so closed and clouded was it by anger. How dare that lad bring a doxy home to his family home? She seethed inwardly as she saw that all the guests were taken to their separate rooms and she made very sure that the painted hussy was put not only at the opposite end of the house but also on a different floor from Alex's suite of rooms. After warm water had been sent up so the travelers could wash away their grime, Mackie saw to it that a light repast was laid out in the largest drawing room, as dinner would be unfashionably late.

The storm raged on, and as Mackie bustled about she prayed that Cameron would notice that the house was ablaze with light and steal in through the servants' way, out of Alex's sight. Surely if she didn't see the lights she would notice that the stable was full of strange horses, Mackie thought, trying to calm her nervous fretting.

The guests, dressed in their formal dinner clothes, stood around talking jovially as they sipped drinks and ate the hastily prepared snacks. Several young men stood idly chatting and staring out at the raging storm that whipped the waves of the firth to a frenzy. Mackie wanted to close the curtains but froze as she overheard an excited exchange.

"By jove, look at that!"

"What?"

"Someone's riding like the bloody Devil!"

"Where?"

"My God, the bloody idiot!"

Alex turned and fixed his eyes on Mackie, who stood as if paralyzed, her eyes glued to his face. She turned and scurried to the door. Alex disentangled himself from Fiona's clutching and followed her into the hall.

"I want to see you in my study," he ordered tersely. Mackie looked around anxiously for Fergus as she trotted before Alex, and, not seeing him, hoped he waited at the stables for Cameron.

" 'Tis Cameron?" Alex asked, as soon as the study door was closed behind them.

"Aye, 'tis the lass, your wife," added Mackie, her anger at Fiona's presence rekindled.

Alex stared into the eyes of his old nurse as the blood pounded furiously in his ears.

" 'Tis not your place to be impertinent to me," he answered bitingly.

"Is the truth impertinent?" she parried.

Alex swung on his heel and gazed out into the stormy night. Mackie panted, her breasts heaving.

"That woman is Lady Fiona Hurst?" she ventured, and, taking his silence as assent, added, "Aye, I've heard of her. Even the debauchery of the English court was offended, as I've been told. I'm shamed that you'd bring your fancy piece to soil your family home. 'Tis well your mother and wee sisters are dead." And Mackie burst into tears and ran out of the room.

"You let a *servant* talk about me in that disgusting way?"

Alex turned sharply to see Fiona standing at the door, her eyes flashing. How long had she been there? What had she heard besides the insults to herself?

"Calling me a fancy piece, saying I soil your family home! And you just stand and let her? She should be whipped and thrown out!" spat Fiona.

"Fiona, join the others," barked Alex, relieved that she had not heard about Cameron.

"I will not be talked about in that way by low-class scum. How dare you allow it!" Fiona raged.

"Leave me, woman!" he roared.

Fiona's eyes widened at his vehemence. "I'll play the hostess in our gracious host's absence. After all, dear heart, we mustn't be rude to our guests," she purred.

Cameron felt exhilarated and, as the storm abated and the soft rain gently misted down, she turned the exhausted horse toward the house, feeling cleansed and purged of all her troubles. She rode slowly, savoring the feel of the sweet rainwater that washed her upturned face. She breathed deeply, filling her lungs with the freshness of the wet earth, her eyes closed, feeling the steady rhythm of the horse beneath her as she pretended she was home on the moors. Everything was right and as it should be. She felt complete, unaware of the eyes that peered curiously at her.

Alex entered the drawing room to find his guests clustered at the windows.

" 'Tis a child!"

"Aye," chorused awed voices.

"No doubt some stable brat," interjected Fiona, piqued that the attention was not on her.

"Whoever 'tis can ride like the very dickens."

"Would it be a ward?" whispered Ian roguishly in Alex's ear.

"I'd like to meet the lad who can sit a horse that well. He has a promising career."

"Watch out, Alex, or your young jockey will be stolen from you," laughed another voice.

"You have a secret young protégé?" asked another.

"You could be saying that, couldn't you now, Alex?" said Ian wickedly, out loud.

"All this fuss over some ragged brat!" Fiona complained. Her biting, bitchy voice grated on Alex's nerves, and before he gave himself time to stop and think, he flung open the doors to the garden and gave a piercing whistle. Seconds later Torquil bounded in, shaking his drenched coat as Fiona screamed, alarmed at the enormous animal.

At the sound of the whistle Cameron's mount changed directions and headed after the dog. She opened her eyes as they galloped toward the house which was ablaze with light and filled with excited voices. Cameron pulled frantically on the reins, trying to head him back toward the stable. She kicked her bare feet into his wet sides and drew the rein short, forcing him to obey her. The frightened horse reared and Cameron saw a crowd of people surging out of the well-lit house. She froze, wondering if she should dismount and run or continue her struggles with the animal. As she frantically considered, the reins were whipped out of her hands and she stared down into Alex's angry amber eyes. The young men approached and flocked around her.

"Jolly good riding, lad."

"Bloody fine, if you ask me!"

"What's your name?"

"How old are you, son?"

The questions came in deep voices from all around. Male hands patted her leg and stroked the horse who sweated and steamed despite the chill rain. Cameron kept her eyes firmly glued to Alex's, terrified of the noisy confusion around her. He forgot his anger, lost in the bright green eyes. He noted the clean perfection of her clear rainwashed face, drops hanging like dew on her trembling mouth, and he ached to sweep her from the stallion and taste them. The moment was shattered by a hard icy voice.

"Send the dirty brat to the kitchen before we all catch our death of colds, and Alex, get rid of this animal."

Fiona stood majestically at the open French doors. Cameron stared at her. She had never seen such a woman before. Her dress sparkled, seemed to be made of thousands of tiny splinters of glass, and yet it molded to her like a second skin, flowing with the graceful movements of her body as she approached and laid a proprietary hand upon Alex's arm.

"Darling, I'm cold and was left all alone with that giant, dirty beast," complained Fiona, as she nibbled Alex's ear.

Cameron jerked on the reins to free them from Alex's hands so she could race out the rage that swept through her, but Alex anticipated her move and threw off Fiona's grasp to hold them firm. He grabbed Cameron's bare foot and pulled her down into his arms, holding her for a moment before setting her down on her feet, still keeping a tight grip on her. Cameron was dwarfed by the men on all sides; she came no higher than the shortest man's chest. She fought to breathe, suffocated by the pressing mass around her as she was marched toward the open doors of the drawing room.

"Shall we go in out of this blasted wet?" Alex said cheerfully to his guests. Fiona followed the noisy laughing men, seething. She stood by the closed door in the warmth of the room, looking at Alex who stood with his back to the fire, imprisoning the wet, bedraggled urchin with one strong brown hand. She arched her neck and strode forward.

"Alex has such amusing notions, don't you think?" Fiona proclaimed in a brittle strident voice.

Alex felt the shiver run through Cameron's body, but the girl kept her chin up proudly, hiding her fear under a rebellious expression. Her teeth were clenched and her eyes unfocused, blotting out the numerous faces.

"Gentlemen!" said Alex loudly, waiting for them to

quieten. "And Fiona," he added cynically, causing her to bridle at the slur, "I'd like to introduce you to my—"

"Ward!" yelled Ian with a great guffaw.

Alex stopped. He had been about to say "wife," somehow wanting to see the hurt and confusion in Fiona's face. He had also wanted to humiliate Cameron. But why?

"Ward? Ward?" groaned Fiona in an excessively bored voice. "Are we to be fatigued by a doting guardian? Alex, you forgot your manners. For heaven's sake, send the filthy brat and that dirty animal to the stables to be washed. They smell."

Cameron turned like a wildcat on Fiona, and Alex, unprepared for the sudden movement, was powerless to stop her. As Cameron leaped, so did Torquil, growling at his young mistress's cry of rage. Fiona screamed, seeing the flashing green eyes and the enormous dog come toward her. If Ian Drummond hadn't stepped forward and caught the small wild body, Fiona might have been ripped and clawed apart. With a chuckle Ian held Cameron to his chest and whispered, "Cameron, she ain't worth it."

Cameron looked into his warm smiling face and breathed deeply before nodding her head. For the first time Alex felt pure unadulterated jealousy toward another man, and his eyes blazed as Ian set Cameron on her small bare feet and ruffled her ebony hair. As soon as Cameron's feet touched the floor she was off, running out the door and up the stairs to the sanctuary of her own room. Mackie, eavesdropping in the hall, followed her fleet escape on heavy old legs and, stopping for breath outside the girl's door, heard her racking sobs. She quietly entered and, sitting down on the bed, tried to pull the crying child into her arms.

Alex excused himself curtly from his guests. He

drew Ian aside and gruffly asked him to keep Fiona occupied. Ian nodded, his eyes twinkling merrily, watching Alex mount the stairs three at a time.

Cameron fought the need for Mackie's arms but this time Mackie was relentless as she pulled the girl to her and cradled her. Cameron stiffened, her tears suspended as the old woman crooned and rocked.

"Let the tears out, my pretty babe, let them out. Dinna let them sour your sweetness. Let go the bitterness."

Cameron let go and sobbed as her body relaxed against Mackie's loving comfort.

"That's the way my, bonny. That's the way."

Alex listened at the door, opening it softly and watching the old woman rock and croon, the ebony head buried in her breasts. Mackie looked at him sharply, tears pouring down her lined face. She glared fiercely and hugged the sobbing girl tighter, as though to protect her from Alex. He held his arms out, willing the old woman to give him the precious bundle, but she shook her head, not stopping her rocking or crooning, so Alex sat beside them and encircled both of them with his strong arms.

Cameron was oblivious to Alex's presence. Fifteen years of pent-up pain poured out, fifteen years denied of comforting arms had taken their toll. She cried from the depths of her soul, not feeling the other strong arms encircle her. She did not know the three of them rocked and cried together. Nor did she feel the transfer of herself to Alex.

Mackie silently left the room, praying that now the two young ones she loved would give each other peace. Alex rocked Cameron, feeling her sorrow as if it were his own.

"Hush, my pretty," he crooned uncharacteristically,

as the girl's sobs lessened. "Hush, my little love, 'twill be all right."

Alex's deep voice penetrated Cameron's consciousness, and she stiffened against him in panic for a moment, but the strong arms held her safely as the rocking of his body soothed her and she relaxed, burying her nose into the secure scent of him. Alex slowed his rocking and stared down at the dark head lying on his chest. She slept, her breathing punctuated with long sighs that echoed the violent storm that had raged inside her. His arms felt the dampness of her heavy wet cape.

"Let's take this off," he said softly, easing one arm from her to undo the clasp. Cameron sleepily protested, trying to wrap his arm around her again.

"Cameron, you're soaked to the skin, and I'll not have you sick again," he chided gently. "I'll call for a hot bath for you."

Drained of all emotion Cameron sat silently, undressing. She threw the wet jerkin and shirt to the floor and stood numbly as she shimmied her wet trews to her knees. Alex sat her down and kneeled before her, pulling the tight wet material from her legs as the door burst open and Fiona stormed in, followed by a rueful Ian. Torquil leaped up and growled menacingly at the rude intrusion, and the irate woman backed away.

For a moment everyone froze—Fiona, Cameron, Alex, Ian, and Torquil—and then Alex smiled wryly at Fiona's expression, which showed both fear of the dog and shock at Cameron's female charms bared for all to see. Ian grinned with obvious appreciation.

"Do you need some assistance with your ward, Alex?" he offered gallantly.

"Aye, you'll both remove yourselves and await dinner somewhere else," he replied, glaring at Ian. Count-

ering with a look of regret Ian shrugged and offered
his arm to the seething Fiona, who shot a look of violent hatred at Cameron before flouncing out with a
brittle laugh. Ian quit the room with a bow and a con-
spiratorial wink. Alex stood listening to their reced-
ing footsteps, taking deep breaths to calm himself before turning back to Cameron.

She was shaken by the bitter hatred that had ema-
nated from Fiona. She felt Alex's eyes and interpreted
his silent gaze as anger. Feeling vulnerable and exposed she stared back in bewilderment. The shocking
realization of her nakedness surged through her and
she covered her breasts from his eyes and edged back
across her bed. Alex reached to reassure her but she
ducked under his hand, wincing as though he was
about to strike her. Alex's anger at himself welled as
he saw her cringe like a frightened dog. He saw the
quick change and knew once more that the battle lines
were drawn as the green eyes now flashed defiantly.
He turned away, unable to face her, and savagely
opened the wardrobe, running his hands over the few
clothes that hung there.

"Where are the rest? I had more than a dozen sent
from Edinburgh."

Cameron didn't answer, not wishing to be beaten for
her tantrum when she ripped and tore them to pieces.
Alex pulled the bell cord and Mackie tottered in almost before his hand released it.

"The bath water won't be long, but the guests used
up all that was prepared," she puffed, as Alex looked
at her in surprise.

"Forget the bath. Where are Cameron's clothes?"
Mackie looked at the naked girl, defiant on the bed,
her back pressed up against the wall, and her heart
sank as her eyes filled with tears. Her small dimpled
hand waved helplessly to the door of the connecting

dressing room, and Alex angrily strode to it without a word. To his frustration it was locked. Mackie produced the key, and he stood aside as she unlocked it, staring at Cameron and nodding his head as if he understood.

"I put the new ones in there, as there was no need of such finery with no one here," explained Mackie, trying to protect Cameron.

"Aye, and to stop them from being torn to shreds, no doubt," muttered Alex, disappearing into the small room. Mackie smiled at Cameron, folding lip against lip to stop them from quivering as she noticed the hard rebellion on the girl's face. She shouldn't have left them together, she thought, berating herself for being a stupid old fool and wondering what she could do to make amends for her mistake.

Alex brought out a dark green velvet dress.

"And what are you doing running up and down the stairs playing lady's maid? Where's the girl Jeannie?" he snapped.

"In the scullery where she's better suited," retorted Mackie, her eyes sparkling with angry tears.

"That will be all, Mrs. MacDonald. See to your own duties. I shall have to play lady's maid."

Mackie hesitated but the cold steel tones of his voice convinced her she'd do nothing more than aggravate him if she stayed.

"You'll wear this. The material's thick and you'll not have to wear clothes beneath," said Alex, holding out the dress to Cameron. He tried to lighten his tone but Cameron heard sarcasm, her heart pounding as she wondered when he would leave. She scanned the room for some place to hide her bareness and, seeing a small screen, slipped off the bed, still keeping her naked breasts covered from his eyes. Alex watched her rebellious modesty with regret. He fumed at the shame and embarrassment he saw in her eyes. Why didn't she stand straight and proud in all her wild beauty as she'd done before? Alex waited for Cameron to dress behind the screen.

"Hurry up. The bell will sound for dinner soon and 'tis rude to keep our guests waiting," he said impatiently, before noticing the dress still laid upon the bed.

"You've forgotten the gown," he said, throwing it over the screen and looking over himself.

Cameron sat on the floor hugging her knees. Did he really expect her to go down to dinner with all those people? Did he really think she would sit at a table with that frighteningly beautiful woman who thought she smelled? Her reading being quite extensive and her natural instincts being sound Cameron knew the relationship that existed between Fiona and Alex, and she was torn apart inside.

"Cameron, I'd have thought you had more spine. Where's that Scottish pride of yours? Is it just hot air that you sit cowering like a little mouse?"

Cameron stared up, puzzled.

"You'd not be much help against the English so scared of a few people," he taunted, trying to kindle the dangerous flash of her green eyes.

"You're all talk, like most silly females. There's not but fifteen people downstairs and most canna sit a horse or throw a knife—and they're all Scots—yet you spout on of defying the English who are a legion." Cameron glared at him and he grinned, seeing the fire in her eyes. He threw her the dress.

"I dare you to put it on and walk down those stairs with me, straight and proud."

Cameron held the soft velvet against her as she tried to fathom which way around the gown went. Alex pushed the screen aside and took the dress from her,

stifling a groan as her lithe naked body stood between
his arms and she stepped into the dark green velvet.
He removed her straining fingers that reached to the
back to do the buttons and fastened them himself.

"Stand up straight and true," he growled, surveying
her, and Cameron wondered how he saw her, knowing
it mattered very much. She realized with startling clarity that she loved him. Why? She pushed the question
angrily from her mind as she watched breathlessly for
the approval in his amber eyes. He gazed at her
thoughtfully and then firmly sat her down. Picking up
a brush he ran it through her hair, delighting in the
soft ebony waves that rippled thickly past her shoulders. Cameron sat still, excited by his touch, wanting
to look beautiful for him—more beautiful than the
woman downstairs. But as her mind conjured up
Fiona, her joy fled and was replaced by painful panic.
How could she ever be as beautiful?

Alex stood her up and turned her around, and his
eyes lit on her pink toes peeping mischievously out
from the bottom of the thick velvet. Cameron followed
his gaze and quickly bent her legs so they disappeared
from view. Alex gave a laugh of pure joy and swung
Cameron around in his arms, much to her surprise.

"You look like, there are no words, see for yourself,"
he crowed, and then grew puzzled as he looked for the
long mirror. Cameron's face flushed under his quizzical eye, but he grinned and nodded knowingly.

"There are some habits you'll have to be broken
of," he said softly and warmly. Cameron didn't know
how to react to such a gentle reproach. She just
blushed more with shame and confusion.

"Are you ready?" he asked, offering his arm. Cameron nodded bravely and looked around for Torquil.

"Torquil?" she whispered, her eyes pleading with
Alex.

"Oh, of course. But Torquil isna dressed for dinner.
I have an idea—" and Alex disappeared once more
into the little dressing room and reappeared waving a
matching green velvet ribbon.

"Now hold still, you big beastie," he said, tying the
ribbon about the great dog's neck. "There. Now 'tis
time to go, we canna keep our guests waiting any
longer." Alex offered Cameron his arm once more
and, when she hesitated, gently kissed it and placed it
on the crease of his elbow where she let it rest.

Chapter Fifteen

Alex looked down the length of the table at Cameron
and smiled, pleased with her and with himself. She sat
straight, listening attentively to the men on either side
of her. He was very conscious of Fiona fuming on his
right, as she herself watched the enchanting girl who
did nothing to draw attention to herself and yet was
the focus of everyone's eyes.

Alex had timed their entrance perfectly. Just as the
dinner bell sounded, he and Cameron appeared at the
top of the stairs. In the hall below, the milling chattering guests had grown silent at the sight of the petite
raven-haired girl who gracefully walked at his side
with one hand on the enormous hound.

"That's no stable lad!" someone breathed.

Little did Alex know what the long descent in front of all those staring eyes had cost Cameron; she had used every bit of willpower to keep her face from showing the terror that she felt, and she was sure that any moment she would trip and fall headlong down the stairs, showing her legs and bare bottom. Carefully she placed one bare foot in front of the other, her hand gripping Alex's arm tightly, as though to use his strength. She finally reached the last step and stood feeling very small among the tall, elegantly dressed men, so she raised her small nose, pushed her shoulders back to appear taller, and entered the dining room on Alex's arm.

Panic had seized her when Alex seated her at one end of the table and she saw him walking the long distance to the other. Alex had been faced with a dilemma upon entering. Where should he seat Cameron? He longed for her at his side and yet his blood boiled when he thought of Fiona in the hostess's seat, ensconced as the mistress of his house. He made sure that Ian sat beside Cameron, knowing, despite his own jealousy, that his close friend's warmth would put the girl at ease.

Cameron stared down the length of the table and, seeing the fiery hatred flash from Fiona, she cast her eyes down at her place setting.

"Chin up, Cameron," murmured Ian, seeing her hands gripping the table's edge and covering one with his own broad warm one. Cameron took a breath and looked into his friendly, open face.

Course followed course and Alex marveled at Mackie and his staff being able to serve such a perfect meal at a moment's notice. He felt content seeing Cameron's attentive little face, so beautiful and serious in the flickering candlelight. Her unease and tension

left her as Ian's easy manner made her smile, and in
his kind, humorous voice he introduced her to the
young men around her. At first, watching them all enter and fit themselves into the seats along the vast ex-
panse between Alex and herself, she had drawn back
in fear, but with dinner nearly done she felt relaxed
and happy listening to amusing stories from Ian and
his friends around her. She forgot the fuming redhead
at Alex's side, forgot the pang when they sat together,
forgot the fright of the strange faces that stretched forever to the end of the long table. Her eager young
mind was open to the companionship denied her since
birth, and she heard from the young men her own feelings and thoughts; she beamed, realizing that they had
something in common. A lot of the talk was of horses
and Ian and Cameron agreed to rise at the crack of
dawn for a race across the downs. They were, in fact,
like children who, getting over their first shyness, tumbled over each other at finding there was nothing to
be afraid of.

After the fruit and cheeses had been set out and
picked at by the already-satisfied guests, Alex was
faced with yet another dilemma. Usually the ladies retired, leaving the men to drink, smoke, and swap off-
color stories, but there was no way he'd leave Cameron
to Fiona's biting tongue. He pushed back his chair
and tapped his wine glass with a spoon.

"Tonight I think we should forgo the convention of
letting our two beautiful ladies retire. I don't know
about you, but I'll not deprive myself of their company," he proclaimed, and was greeted by a loud chorus
of assent.

"So let us all retire together to the drawing room,"
suggested Alex, standing with the intention of collecting Cameron and leading the way.

"Follow us," Fiona cried gaily, setting herself on his

arm and leaning seductively against his tall strong body.

Cameron's happiness clouded and she wondered how on earth she could have forgotten Fiona's presence.

"You've got through the worst. The rest will be easier," whispered Ian, offering Cameron his arm. She stared up at him and then realized all the men were standing and looking at her expectantly.

"What are they all looking at me for?" she whispered back.

"For you to lead the way," answered Ian, this eyes twinkling so she took no offense.

Cameron rose hurriedly and put her hand hesitantly on Ian's arm.

Fiona entered the drawing room with her mind planning furiously. She'd not be set down by a skinny chit who somehow made her feel brassy and overblown, a bony little heathen who made her feel gigantic and clumsy. She sat at the piano, sifting through the sheet music as Ian and Cameron entered followed by the other men. Torquil ambled in behind and settled himself in front of the fire.

Alex shooed the servants out and busily poured brandy for his guests. The merry chattering was silenced by a crashing chord and in the silence Fiona started to sing a ballad.

"Do you have any musical accomplishments?" whispered Ian to Cameron, who was firmly wedged on the couch between him and another young man.

"I play the pipes."

"I'll be right back," he whispered mischievously, and tiptoed out of the room.

Fiona saw him leave as she sang, and she stopped abruptly.

"Alex? Alex, I need you to turn the pages."

Several other men leaped up to offer their services, but Fiona insisted.

"We know each other's beat so well. Our rhythms are so suited," she purred suggestively and Alex, not wishing an ugly scene, bowed and stood behind Fiona as she began the song again. She had just reached the exact same passage she was singing when Ian had left, when he reentered and stopped with exaggerated puzzlement at hearing the same phrase sung.

"This is where I went out," he whispered, as he sat down next to Cameron. A small titter rose and Fiona beat the piano and sang louder in her rage.

She sang three songs; the second two were love songs which she addressed to Alex. Her voice settled and her fingers relaxed as she caressed the keys, and her moist mouth kissed the words sweetly. There was a pause and then applause. Fiona knew she had played well and she stood triumphantly, both hands clasping Alex's arm as she acknowledged the approval.

"Now," she said, raising her hands for quiet. "Now it's the little ward's turn," she purred, smiling too sweetly at Cameron. She felt Alex stiffen under her hands. I'm right, she thought maliciously, the little stable brat can't play.

Cameron felt the blood rush to her head as the young men around urged her to play. To her dismay Ian dashed out of the room. She looked toward Alex but was unable to bear the sight of Fiona hanging on him, so she looked away.

"Here you are Cameron, compliments of Fergus," crowed Ian, bursting back into the room with a set of bagpipes. A murmur of consternation filled the room.

"We'll all be arrested," protested Fiona shrilly.

"Are you afraid the young lass can surpass you?" asked Ian wickedly.

"How can the squall of wailing pipes compare with the true artistry of the piano?" she spat furiously.

" 'Tis a long time since I heard the pipes."

"But 'tis illegal!" shouted Fiona.

"Aren't we all loyal Scots?" asked Alex quietly.

"Aye," chorused many voices.

"But the servants?" pressed Fiona.

"Let them hear," shouted Ian, opening the door wide.

Alex watched Cameron take the pipes lovingly in her small hands. She played, her thoughts back on the moors with the deer and the pheasants, the hawks and the gulls that swept over the endless roll of the land and sea. She stood beside Duncan's cairn and played a coronach for him, her sorrow keening a lonely, plaintive melody. Soon the tears poured silently down her face as the heart-rending music sobbed out her pain at the loss of her way of life. Each person listening felt a personal chord struck in himself, opening great sadness. The young men stood motionless as the pipes' lament coursed through them, sending shivers up their spines. They had spent their boyhoods in battles, sieges, and massacres that had robbed them of fathers, brothers, uncles, and grandfathers, and brought their native Scotland into English hands. Fiona was as shaken and moved as the rest, her jealousy and hatred pushed aside for a while by the music that brought back nostalgic memories of her childhood.

Cameron played, mourning her country's lost freedom as well as her own, pouring out all the deep emotions that she had no words to express.

The last soulful note trailed away and everyone stood unaware of the wetness coursing down their faces. Even the servants, clustered in groups outside the open door, had been drawn to the haunting music.

Cameron took the pipes from her mouth, suddenly aware again of all the people. She felt a moment of panic, but then her eyes lit on Fergus's lined face. She walked slowly to him, cradling the beloved instrument in her arms.

"Ye braw Scottish lassie," he murmured, his throat constricted with emotion. He drew her to him and held her close, knowing she had drained herself of all energy. Mackie, standing by her man, stared at Alex, whose still gaze was fixed on Cameron in Fergus's arms. She noted the tenderness in his amber eyes.

" 'Tis time the bairn slept, my lord," she ventured, and Alex, unable to speak, just nodded and remained staring at the closed door long after they'd left.

"Grown-up time!" sang out Fiona.

"I'm a bairn, too, I need my sleep," yawned Ian.

"Aye, anything would be a sacrilege following the pipes," said another man, as one by one they drifted out.

"Aye, I'm off to bed, too," Fiona whispered seductively to Alex, who stared at her coldly for a moment and rang the bell.

"Show Lady Fiona to her bedchamber," he ordered the footman who answered.

"I'll be waiting for you," said Fiona, pursing her lips to tempt him, but Alex had turned and was peering absently into the fire.

Mackie helped Cameron undress and tucked her into bed without a word. There seemed no need for the two of them to talk. Mackie saw the love and trust in the girl's clear eyes and fervently prayed that she'd not betray it. Cameron closed her eyes but opened them again quickly.

"Mackie? Did I do well?"

"Aye, oh, aye, you did better than well. We are all so proud of you," said Mackie, before she left the room.

Fiona waited and waited for Alex to come. She had painted her face and set the candles around the bed so the flickering lights would flatter and enhance. She wore her sheerest negligee and now lay posed on the bed, facing the door, with her breasts pushed up so they spilled tantalizingly. She waited and her leg started to cramp, so she changed to another alluring position, and still Alex didn't come. Finally she sat at her dressing table and examined herself, pulling the straps of her nightgown lower, spraying exotic perfume, brushing her hair over her shoulder so it tickled one breast. Then leaping up and grabbing an equally diaphanous peignoir she left her room.

Which was Alex's room? She cursed herself for not finding out. The only other bedchamber she knew was Cameron's, and she recalled the brazen chit standing naked, flaunting herself. Was Alex there now? Her agitation convinced her she needed a nightcap. What was the matter with her, getting so upset over a mere girl?

Pulling the peignoir about herself she walked quietly down the stairs to the drawing room, remembering that a decanter of brandy was there. The lights were out but the fire still glowed warmly. A low threatening growl came from the direction of the hearth, and she froze in her tracks. She swiveled her eyes carefully and was relieved to see Alex sitting by the fire beside the huge dog. All her silly jealous thoughts were unfounded.

"I need a nightcap."

"Help yourself," Alex answered absently.

"But that great dog—?"

"He'll not harm you."

Fiona warily walked to the sideboard and poured herself a stiff brandy.

"Will you have one with me?" she asked softly, still nervous of the dog. Alex didn't answer so Fiona poured one for him. She hesitated, wanting to cross to him, but was aware of the enormous dog who seemed to watch her every move.

Cameron was slowly slipping into sleep as the events of the evening went round and round in her mind. Suddenly she sat up. Torquil? Where was Torquil? She looked around and, realizing she last saw him sleeping before the fire downstairs, hastily slipped out of bed and crept to the door. She opened it and whistled softly. No Torquil. Listening and looking both ways she tiptoed down the corridor to the stairs. Everything was quiet. She dimly heard the clatter of pots and pans from the kitchen, but there was no rumble of male voices from below, so she quietly descended.

Cameron saw the firelight under the door, heard Torquil's warning growl, and was hesitant to knock or enter. She whistled softly. Torquil bounded to his feet and Fiona gave a piercing scream and dropped both brandy snifters. Alex leaped up and opened the door for the scratching, whining animal, and Cameron froze as Alex suddenly appeared. Torquil licked her in welcome as she stared into the warm amber eyes.

"Alex, I've cut my foot, I'm bleeding," whined Fiona. Cameron's eyes flickered past Alex to the woman who stood like a Greek goddess, the firelight dancing in her hair, the flames enhancing and flattering the voluptuous body beneath the sheer clothing. She gasped and, picking up the hem of her childish flannel gown, scampered up the stairs as fast as her legs would carry her.

Chapter Sixteen

Despite a sleepless night Cameron rose very early, hoping to be galloping across the countryside before anyone else awoke. She needed to be alone. Quickly donning trews and shirt, with boots in hand, she padded down the stairs with Torquil by her side.

She entered the warm cheerful kitchen to find Ian, already up and dressed for riding, being scolded by Mackie as he sat eating ham and eggs.

"I thought you'd forgotten our appointment," said Ian, standing and patting Torquil's shaggy head.

" 'Taint right to be eating in the kitchen, Master Ian," Mackie nagged.

"She's been going on at me since I was in knee britches, haven't you, Mackie?" laughed Ian.

"Didna seem to do one ounce of good, did it?" she grumbled good-humoredly, as she bustled to get Cameron some breakfast.

"What's this great brute's name?" asked Ian, watching Cameron pull on her boots.

"Torquil."

"Torquil and Torquod, the legendary MacLeod

twins?" mused Ian, thinking immediately of the age-old stories of those great chieftains. No one but the MacLeods ever used those names.

"MacLeod?" ejaculated Mackie. Of course, MacLeod! That's where she'd seen such startling green eyes and raven hair before. At Dunvegan, on the Isle of Skye, when she'd been in service to the MacLeods, forty years or more before.

"I dinna know about that," Cameron said, forgetting her boots and looking at him curiously. It was strange Ian should know her horse's name. "My grandfather named them, I think, else I came with them."

"Them?" inquired Ian.

Mackie stood silently holding Cameron's breakfast, not wanting to interrupt the conversation.

"Torquil and Torquod."

"You had a Torquod too? Where is he?" asked Ian, eating heartily, unaware of the undercurrent of their exchange.

"Dead," said Cameron softly, her eyes filling with tears and looking down to pull on the other boot so he didn't see.

"I'm sorry. Was he Torquil's brother?"

"He was my horse," she said, fighting for control of her aching sadness.

"Here's your food, lass," Mackie interrupted, seeing the girl's pain. She banged the plate loudly on the table, shooting a warning glance at Ian.

"What did you mean about you came with them?" he asked, not seeing Mackie's concern.

Cameron stared at him, perplexed.

"I don't know. 'Tis like a dream that my mind lights on and when I try to think of it, it goes and I canna grasp it," she struggled to explain.

Mackie found herself curious and, seeing the girl was handling herself well now, asked her, "Do you mean, lass, that you came to Cape Wrath with the animals?"

"I think I did, and yet I canna remember living any other place."

Ian stopped eating and stared at the old woman and girl.

"Lassie, why did you not ask Duncan Fraser?" probed Mackie.

"Duncan Fraser? So that's where the old warrior hid himself, is it? Cape Wrath?" he asked.

"Aye," said Mackie shortly, wanting an answer from Cameron.

"So you're Duncan Fraser's kin? You're his grand-daughter?" continued Ian.

"Not really," returned Cameron frankly.

"If your name's Cameron Fraser then surely you're kin of some sort?"

"I dinna know my name. I just know Cameron," said the girl, her troubled eyes staring at Ian.

"Eat your breakfast or you'll not be riding this morning," Mackie snapped, changing the subject. "Let her alone, Master Ian, she's all skin and bone and needs fattening up."

"She looks just right to me. I want her no different," he said.

Mackie gave him a long look as he gazed lovingly at Cameron, her head bent over her plate. So young Master Drummond fancied Cameron, did he? Well, there was nothing like a bit of competition to open a stubborn man's eyes, she thought.

Ian and Cameron galloped across the rolling downs through the misty morning air. He longed to talk to her, wanting to know all about her, but she seemed to have forgotten his presence as she flew, her hair streaming, her face alive and earnest. He had a hard time keeping up with her.

"Slow down a touch," he yelled, but she just turned her laughing face as she gave her horse his head and moved even faster. Ian reined his horse and watched her streak off through the whirling mist.

Cameron needed desperately to be alone and Ian's presence intruded on her routine. Each morning since settling into her life at Glen Aucht she'd ridden along the coast to a secluded cove where she'd torn her clothes off to swim and float in the salty waters of the firth. Alex's words about undressing herself in front of anyone else made her realize she'd have to miss her swim if Ian was by her side. She didn't understand the reasoning, but had no wish to incur Alex's wrath.

Reaching her haven she turned and looked back through the morning fog. She saw no one. She sprang nimbly from her horse and put her ear to the ground. She heard nothing. She led her mount down a steep narrow path that wound through the undergrowth.

Alex had passed a sleepless night staring into the fire as it slowly died to gray ashes. Fiona, unable to capture his attention by raging and pacing or sidling and seduction, had finally stormed off to a cold empty bed, leaving him alone.

Before the first pearly fingers of dawn had put one spot of light in the black sky, Alex was riding along the coast to clear the cobwebs and the brandy from his brain. He rode to the town of Crail, where the Firth of Forth opened into the wide North Sea, and sat his horse watching the fishing boats loom out of the fog, hearing the chorus of gulls that squabbled and swooped at each other in their fight for food. He breathed deeply, hearing in the kittiwake's scream the lonely wail of the pipes. He rode back slowly as the sun melted the mist and the wind blew, thinning the wisps that danced and floated above the water. The countryside yawned awake as farmers worked their fields and sleepy people made their way numbly to work. Alex, wishing to be alone with his thoughts, veered his horse from the road to the sandy shore where he rode along the beach until the high tide and a jutting headland made his passing impossible. He forced his mount up the steep bank and reined him in on the crest.

Below him lay a small inlet, the bushes grown high so he could not see down. He smiled, remembering as a small boy secluding himself there with Ian Drummond, away from his tagging, little sisters. They had been pirates and buccaneers, making elaborate hideouts and boats that invariably sunk beneath their weight. As Alex reminisced, he heard hoofbeats, and Ian loomed out of the thinning mist.

"I was just thinking of you," laughed Alex.

"You're up early," noted Ian.

"I'll say the same for you."

"Did you pass Cameron?" asked Ian.

"No," frowned Alex.

"Drat this mist," cursed Ian, as he scanned around.

"You couldna keep up with her? Don't fret, she'll be all right," Alex laughed, hiding a sudden rage that flared.

"The girl's a witch! Which way did you come from?" retorted Ian.

"To Crail and back."

"And you didna pass her?"

"Nay, but I rode the shore. She could have been on the coast road or cliff. Ian, do you remember when we were lads?" asked Alex, looking down at the nearly hidden, winding path.

"Aye, we were pirates then, hiding and scaring those sisters of yours. Och, that was thoughtless of me. I'm sorry."

"'Tis all right. I was thinking of them myself just

now. 'Tis strange to think them dead, and yet they'll never grow old and ugly like we will. They'll stay little golden-haired lassies forever. How cruel we were, not letting them play, teasing them and making them cry. Do you think if we'd known . . . had been able to see into the future . . ."

"We'd have been different toward them?"

"Aye."

"Nay. I'd like to think so but I doubt it. Some things are natural, like dogs fighting cats. Little sisters tagging after big brothers."

"Aye," replied Alex, and talking of their boyhood the two men rode carefully down the path.

"We've found Cameron!" yelled Ian, as her horse loomed out of the mist.

She was floating, staring up at the sky watching the mist gradually thin until the promising blue of a sunny day peeped out in patches. She loved being surrounded by the fog as she swam. She imagined herself a bird, soaring through the clouds. The gentle lap of the water against the rocks, the cries of the gulls, the indescribable sweetness of the air brought her peace. She wished there were shiny seals to watch play as there had been at Cape Wrath, and she chided herself for wanting the moon.

"Where is she?" asked Ian anxiously.

Alex saw Cameron's clothes by the water's edge and wondered how to rid himself of Ian's presence.

"Cameron?" shouted Ian, cupping his hands to his mouth.

Alex pulled Ian's arm and pointed to the strewn garments.

"Where do you think?" he asked, hoping Ian would get embarrassed and leave.

"What a splendid idea!" exclaimed Ian, unbuttoning his own jacket and flinging it off.

"What are you about?"

"Joining the lady for a swim," retorted Ian, divesting himself of his shirt.

"You'll disrobe in front of a young lady?"

"I'll keep my britches on," he replied, sitting to remove his riding boots.

"And what if the young lady had no britches on herself?" retorted Alex, picking up and waving Cameron's discarded trews.

Ian looked at Alex and laughed.

"Last night I saw all of her there was to see, as you and Fiona did also. Cameron seemed not to mind."

"Well, I mind!" shouted Alex furiously.

Ian stepped back, his face sobering.

"Alex, I know you are responsible for Cameron, being her guardian, but you surely don't think I'll hurt her? You've known me all your life. I'll not dishonor her. I love her and I think I want to marry her," he said softly.

"Well, you'll not!" stated Alex emphatically.

"Why? You have Fiona, and surely you see that the two of them under the same roof would mean sure bloodshed."

"What has that got to do with anything?" snapped Alex.

"We all assume the bans will be posted soon. In fact we were surprised when you made no announcement last night."

"Bans? Announcement?"

"You and Fiona. Isn't that why you brought her to your family home?" asked Ian with a frown.

"'Tis none of your business what I do," roared Alex, enraged at the assumption and with himself.

Ian stared quietly at Alex for a moment. Then he pulled on his boots.

"I'll thank you to keep out of my affairs," he said coldly, infuriated by Ian's silent calmness.

Ian gave a snort of ironic laughter as he buttoned his shirt.

"What is Cameron to you, Alex?"

Staring out at the sea Alex wrestled with himself and then turned quietly.

"My wife."

"Your *what?*" Ian exploded, dropping his coat.

"You heard me. Now I'll thank you to return to Glen Aucht, and I'll be even more grateful if you'd keep my secret."

Ian stooped and picked up his coat. He brushed it off, his eyes not leaving his friend's set face.

"I thought I knew you, Alex Sinclair, but it seems I don't. How could you? How could you do such a blackguarded thing? Bringing that fancy piece to your home with—"

Alex lunged at him with his arm raised but Ian stood still.

"Hit me, Alex, what will it change?" he said quietly. The two men stood face to face for a few minutes before Ian turned and mounted his horse.

"I'll tell you something. I dinna understand you, Alex. You are like my brother and I've loved you as myself. Now I also love Cameron. Dinna hurt her or you'll have cause to hate me."

Alex nodded silently.

"And another thing. If she was my wee mermaid I'd be in the water with her, playing like an otter," Ian said softly, before kicking his heels and urging his horse up the steep bank.

Alex sat on a rock and watched Cameron swimming out of the haze toward him. She was oblivious, in a world of her own, as she waded through the shallow water, singing softly and wringing the water from her hair. She stopped when she saw him, dropping her hands. For a moment she stood as straight and graceful as a surprised doe, still and glorious, her natural dignity holding her body proudly and without shame.

Then Cameron froze, her mind awhirl. She felt his eyes burning into her flesh and she shivered. With a cry she covered herself with her hands, hunching her body away from his eyes as she ran to pick up her clothes before hiding behind a bush.

Alex's brain screamed at the shattering of her dignity, and without thought he dragged her from her hiding place into the open.

Cameron hated herself for hiding like a coward and covered her embarrassment and shame with her usual defiance.

"You canna fault me this time. I was alone. 'Twas you who trespassed where I was," she challenged, still covering her breasts from his sight, wondering when his fury would erupt and thinking of Fiona's breasts at the same time. She had seen the older woman's body clearly through the sheerness of her nightclothes.

"'Tis contrary rules you be keeping, Sir Alexander Sinclair," she taunted. "Lady Fiona's allowed to be near naked in your company."

Despite the bravado Alex knew she felt shame and embarrassment. She stood tall, challenging him, and yet he noticed the small hand that nervously shielded her body from him.

"Is it good to be so large of breast?" inquired Cameron, her curiosity getting the better of her anger. Alex didn't hear, his own brain in turmoil.

"Is it a womanly thing?" pursued Cameron, thinking of Mara's pendulous breasts and Duncan's obvious appreciation of them.

"What?" barked Alex.

"Lady Fiona's breasts."

Alex muttered an oath, dropped her arm, and turned on his heel. Cameron watched him go and,

when he was out of sight, crawled back into the bushes
where she huddled, hugging her clothes, feeling very
confused and alone.

Ian Drummond, on reaching Glen Aucht, packed
his bags silently and rode off to his own small estate
that adjoined Alex's to the north. He needed time to
think things through. He had never been in love before, a few infatuations, but never anything like he
felt for Cameron. He was in pain as he whipped his
horse, cruelly wishing it was Alexander Sinclair at the
end of his reins.

Alex returned home to find his guests loudly eating
breakfast. Their voices grated on his nerves and ear-
drums, and knowing he couldn't do as he wished and
throw them out of his house, he strode by the sunlit,
cheerful room and slammed into his study. After four
whiskeys he reached a decision. Going into the breakfast room he silenced the chorus of happy greetings
and curtly informed his guests that there would be no
shooting party, as urgent business called him back to
Edinburgh. There was a rumble of protest, but he
turned on his heel and, summoning the servants to the
hall, ordered them to help his guests pack and to ready
the carriages. He then mounted the stairs and entered
Fiona's bedchamber without knocking, much to her
surprise and delight. She pushed her breakfast tray
aside and beckoned for him to join her in bed.

"Get dressed. We're leaving for Edinburgh within
the hour. I'll send a maid to you," he snapped and,
not waiting to hear her answer, he left the room.

"But we only just got here!" she exclaimed to the
empty room. Oh, well, 'tis probably for the better, she
surmised, thinking of the coldness of Alex's servants
toward her. She felt better able to cope with Alex on

her own home ground anyway, away from the green-eyed little witch.

Mackie and Fergus stood on the front steps watching the procession of carriages leave.

"I dinna ken if I'm on my head or my heels," muttered Mackie. "Food for his guests for three days, he says. And now that the larder is packed to busting, off they all go. What is with the lad? And where's the lassie?"

"She'll be fine, don't go upsetting yourself," soothed Fergus, herding his flustered wife into the house.

"She rode off with Ian Drummond as the sun rose, and I've not seen hide nor hair of her since."

"Young Drummond packed up and rid home hours back."

"I know, I know. That has me fretting. Where is Cameron?" worried Mackie. "What happened?"

"We'll find out soon enough, when the lass comes home," comforted Fergus. "And in the meantime I'd like a sit-down and a little something to drink after all this hurrying and scurrying."

"Fergus, I remembered something," said Mackie, when they had settled themselves in their parlor. "Remember how I said the lassie's coloring teased my mind?"

"Aye," growled Fergus.

"Well, early this morning young Drummond and Cameron were eating breakfast in the kitchen, and the inquisitive pup was asking our bairn all sorts of questions. Seems as though she had a horse named Torquod that died—"

"MacLeod!"

"Aye, just what I thought. And then I recalled about the wee babby."

"What wee babby?" asked Fergus, his usual non-committal face alive with interest.

"Well, 'twas forty years back, at Dunvegan. Remember how the old laird MacLeod, being a Protestant, refused to join the rising of the clans, because of them being Catholic and all?"

"Aye, aye. Go on."

"Well, remember as how young Donald defied his pa and went off with a group of young Highlanders to Spain to get help for the cause?" persisted Mackie.

"Aye."

"Well, he came home with a young foreign lass, and the talk was rife of her being nearly ready to whelp and all. Well, the old laird nearly blew a gasket, as he aimed to join his lands with MacKenzie, who had a marriageable daughter. Young Donald refused and took off to France, leaving the poor scared lass on Skye, not speaking or understanding a word of our language. She died in childbirth and the puir wee babby was born with the thickest black hair and greenest eyes you've ever seen. Laird MacLeod wouldna have a thing to do with the child."

"But that couldna have been Cameron. That babby would be past forty now. What happened to the child?"

"I dinna ken. No one was supposed to speak of it, so there was just the usual gossiping in the kitchen. 'Tis rare for a child to be *born* with green eyes, as usually they are cloudy, blue, and then change. Some said the child was a kelpie, but whatever they said, it seemed it was just a puir motherless and fatherless babby to me."

"'Twas a lad or a lass?" asked Fergus, and at Mackie's shrug, he shrugged himself. "There has to be many with green eyes and black hair, woman. Forty years ago hasna a thing to do with now."

"I know there's no sense in it, and yet why would our lass have a hound and horse with the name of the MacLeod twins?"

"When she gets home, put the question to her," replied Fergus.

"Young Drummond did, and the bairn knew nothing, not even the MacLeod name."

"There you are then," said Fergus, settling back in his chair.

"No, 'tis not like that, Mr. MacDonald. She has glimpses of things that make no sense. She said something about she came with them—to Duncan Fraser's at Cape Wrath—as though she weren't always with him. But then where did she come from? Who is she? And don't give me no talk of by-blows, because the lass knows she wasn't his kin. Fergus, the wee thing doesn't know who she is."

Fergus closed his eyes so his already-worried wife would not see his concern and fret more.

"And where is she?" clucked Mrs. MacDonald, staring out of the window.

"Where's the big beastie?" asked Fergus, and on hearing that Torquil was stretched out in front of the kitchen fire last time that Mackie had seen, he pulled his wiry frame from the comfort of his chair and made his way downstairs, followed by his apron-wringing wife.

"If it'll rest your mind, we'll send the hound to find her," said Fergus, whistling for Torquil.

At sunset there was still no sign of either girl or dog. Six grooms combed the coastline, returning after dark with no news. Mackie fretted herself sick in the kitchen, yelling and carping at the other servants while Fergus waited in the stable away from his wife's biting tongue in case Cameron's horse were to return without her.

All night they kept vigil, sending the rest of the staff to bed, both unable to even doze as their minds were tortured by imaginings of what might have happened to Cameron.

She rode up quietly as the sun was rising. She hadn't wanted to return, but there had been no place else to go. The house was still in darkness and no voices could be heard. She hoped everyone slept as she swung her cold numb body out of the saddle and into a pair of strong arms.

"Lass, you've had the missus and me fair out of our heads with worry," chided Fergus gently, as he led her into the house.

"You deserve to be skelped, you bad, wicked brat! 'Tis nigh on breakfasttime, and if you hadna missed your lunch and supper, I'd be sending you to bed without!" roared Mackie, banging a bowl of soup onto the table so it splashed. "And now look at what you've made me do! I dinna why I bother. Get eating!"

Cameron stared at the raging old woman and at Fergus's stern face. She sprang up, overturning the soup, and swept everything off the table so the crockery smashed on the floor.

"Aye, I'm wicked and bad. So now you know! D'ye ken, I'm witch's spawn and kelpie's kin and my soul is black as sin!" Fergus stepped forward to check her headlong rush out of the room.

"Dinna touch me or I'll curse you to hell!" threatened Cameron, but Fergus, undaunted, picked her up and carried her struggling young body from the room.

"Get on wie yer work, you lazy bunch of good-fernothings!" ordered Mackie of the sleepy-eyed servants who had just left the comfort of their warm beds to start the new day's toil.

Fergus put Cameron down in a chair in Alex's study.

"Spill it, lass."

Cameron sprang up and stood defiantly, but closed her mouth rebelliously.

"So you are witch's spawn, are you? And kelpie's kin, too? Upon my word!" He chuckled as he sat himself comfortably and filled his pipe. "Well, I dinna ken what that makes of me," he puzzled, lighting his pipe and puffing thoughtfully. "My soul is certainly blacker than yours, being a might older and all," he added, not looking at Cameron who stood tense, eyes flashing. "Och, aye, I suppose Mackie and I are all set for purgatory, loving witch's spawn as we do," he said, nodding knowingly.

"You dinna ken," retorted Cameron.

"Och, we've eyes, ears, and a nose, ain't we? So not being blind, deaf, or wanting in gray matter, we know what is. And if you be what you say, I must be Beelzebub hisself, or the king of England, not that there is much to choose between the two," he laughed.

"Dinna mock me!" spat Cameron. "You'll see, aye, you'll see. Mackie knows the truth of it."

"The truth of what?"

"Of what I am."

"Aye, she knows the truth of it all right. She knows you're a lost, frightened bairn whose life has turned topsy-turvy."

"I am not a child!" shouted Cameron furiously, not sure of how to deal with the leathery old man who calmly smoked and showed no anger or violence.

"We are all part child, lass, you more'n me."

"Well, Mackie knows I'm wicked and bad, spawn of evil things. Spit up by the sea at midnight, I was!"

Fergus stared past Cameron's shoulder to Mackie, who entered quietly and stood still by the door.

"Aye, Mackie knows. She said it and you heard her, too!" continued Cameron, unnerved by Fergus's silence.

"Mackie knows nothing of the sort. She loves you, and a tongue whipping is the price you pay for giving heartache. You were away, without word, for twenty-four hours, robbing her of peace of mind," explained Fergus softly.

"Twenty-four hours! Hah!" scoffed Cameron. "'Tis no time at all. At home I'd be gone much longer."

"Aye, but this is Glen Aucht, not Cape Wrath."

"Aye, but this is a prison, not Cape Wrath," returned Cameron bitterly.

"Aye, I suppose loving takes away some freedoms. There's a price to everything," admitted Fergus, puffing his pipe.

"Who needs to be loved!" she sneered.

"Every living thing on this earth," burst out Mackie, unable to remain quiet.

Cameron started and backed away from her. Her eyes narrowed and, recalling Mara's cunning attacks, she clenched her fists and prepared to defend herself.

"She thinks I mean to hurt her!" cried Mackie, the tears springing to her eyes.

"Go to Mackie, Cameron," growled Fergus. "Stand still and open your arms, Mrs. MacDonald."

Cameron stared at the loving expression on the old woman's face, seeing the tears that poured down her cheeks. She shook her dark head, trying to clear it of the need to be hugged and comforted.

"Afraid to be loved, lass?" challenged Fergus, and the green eyes flashed angrily at him.

"Aye, and so what?" she spat. "Seems from all I've seen of love, 'tis only a fool who isn't."

"Aye, there's a might of sense in that, but 'tis the fool who's blind to love's dangers and the coward that runs from it. Takes a brave, strong person to face it and accept."

Cameron felt trapped, her mind torn in two as the safety of the open arms seduced her, and her fear of being so exposed and defenseless made her want to run. I need no one. I need no one. I need no one, thumped her pulse, as her legs moved involuntarily and she found herself enfolded in Mackie's loving arms.

"But you dinna like me anymore?" she whispered.

"I dinna like fashing myself sick, but it dinna stop me loving you," sniffed Mackie, her teary eyes smiling brightly over the tousled black head into her husband's not very dry ones. "And if I dinna love you, I wouldna have fashed myself sick. Seems everything goes round and around in circles in this life."

Cameron sat in her bath as Mackie bustled about the room getting the bed ready.

"All those fancy people left?"

"Aye, thank the Lord," answered the old woman.

"All of them?"

"Every last one."

"Back to Edinburgh?"

"Aye. Now we'll have some peace again," said Mackie, and seeing the woebegone face added, "Should have thought you'd be glad."

"That Lady Fiona is very beautiful, is she not?" ventured Cameron after a pause.

"Painted trollop!" snorted Mackie. "Come on, out you get. It will be sunset before you get to bed." She wrapped a warm towel around the girl.

"Sir Alex ruts with her?"

Mrs. MacDonald nearly fell back into the bathwater at Cameron's words.

"Who's been putting such thoughts in your head?

Young girls like you should not be thinking such things," she exclaimed indignantly.

"Is it wrong?" asked Cameron. "Rutting?"

"Animals rut, not people. But come to think of it, 'tis a very good word for some people I'll be thinking of."

"People don't rut?"

"Well, they do, but 'tis not called that. And only when they're married," answered Mackie, pulling the nightgown over Cameron's head.

"What is it called then?"

Oh, my heaven, thought the flustered old woman.

"Well, now, let me see. There's a lot of things they be calling it. Loving, that's it. It be called loving."

"Loving?"

"Aye. Now into bed with you."

Little did Mackie know that her choice of words had caused her young charge great pain. The thought of Lady Fiona and Sir Alex "loving" was even worse than the "rutting" of before.

"You mean they can't if they're not married?" asked Cameron hopefully.

"Well, they can, but they shouldna, 'tis wrong," stumbled Mackie.

"Why is it wrong?"

The child's questions were like a four-year old's, every answer met with a why, thought Mackie, as she tucked the blankets and then sat on the bed.

"Why is it wrong?" Cameron repeated.

"Because loving brings babbies and life is hard, so they need a ma and a pa to help them grow straight and strong," answered Mackie, kissing the girl's soft cheek and delighting in the arms that hugged her in return.

"I had no ma and pa. Am I not straight and strong?"

"Sure you are. And you have a ma and pa if you wish it—me and Mr. MacDonald," stated Mackie, rubbing her nose and swallowing a lump in her throat.

"Oh, I wish it. Will you always be?"

"Aye, till past the grave, my bairn, till past the grave."

Chapter Seventeen

In Edinburgh Alex tried for two weeks to block his seething emotions by attending every available entertainment and every available female who crossed his path. Yet his anger at himself and his frustrations grew, and he got no release. He continued his relationship with Fiona, determined to settle back into his comfortable scheme of things before he had been burdened with Cameron. Yet each time he was with his mistress, he wordlessly used her and afterward hated her for allowing the abuse and himself for abusing her. He felt totally trapped, and sooner than reason out his torment he kept himself moving on a merry-go-round of partying, drinking, and debauchery, so each night he fell asleep exhausted and too drunk to think.

One night he attended a debutante's ball and became irritated and furious listening to the Scottish chiefs speaking with English accents, their natural brogues tempered to the more staccato tones of their southern oppressors as they flaunted their improved wealth and tried to sell their pubescent daughters to the highest bidder. At hearing one such laird refer to Scotland as northern England, he quit the formal gathering without ceremony and trod the wet, dark streets.

Who was he to feel so pompous and self-righteous? Hadn't he been brought to heel by the English? Hadn't he made the decision to abide lawfully by their rules to recover some of his family estate? Once again he blamed Cameron, not questioning the lack of logic. Somehow the little green-eyed witch had made it impossible for him to be comfortable. There seemed to be no area of his life untouched by her.

Alex fumed, determined once and for all to rid himself of his obsession with Cameron. No one would have such power over him. Totally lost in his own thoughts, he was oblivious to the poor creature that beckoned to him from a doorway. A pulling at his cape caused him to turn around abruptly.

"I's cheap, sir, just a few coppers, sir." Alex looked down at a pitiful young girl dressed in sopping rags, her thin pinched face staring up at him.

"Please, I'm clean too, sir," she whined, taking his silence as assent and unfastening her clothes.

"I may be debauched but I draw the line at doorways," he muttered, dragging her under a street lamp and staring once more into the very young face. Thinking of her youth and her profession his ire grew; somehow, although she bore not the slightest resemblance to Cameron, he saw the same innocence in the young, bewildered eyes. On an irrational impulse he hailed a passing coach and pushed the girl in.

"In here, sir?" asked the little whore, unbuttoning herself again.

"No," snapped Alex, with a mean look in his amber eyes, giving the coachman directions to Fiona's house. He then settled back as he contemplated Fiona's reaction.

Fiona heard the loud knock and stared over the bannister as the servant ushered Alex in. She frowned seeing the girl with him and stepped back as they mounted the stairs.

"Alex?" inquired Fiona, looking at the ragged, shivering waif.

"See that she's bathed," he ordered tersely.

"Why?"

"Just do as I bid," he barked. Fiona noticed his eyes were hard and bright and she was afraid. Yet she feared losing him and did as he asked.

Alone in her bedchamber with him, after the half-grown chit had been ushered out by a disapproving servant, she tried to wrap her arms about his neck, only to be pushed coldly aside. Fiona sat at her dressing table unable to bear his rejection and the strange calculating stare. He wasn't the same Alex as before their visit to Glen Aucht. She screamed inside now when he made love to her so brutally, without tenderness, but she said nothing, not wanting to chance driving him away. She closed her ears to the rumors that he indiscreetly slept with any willing female. She loved him and she would do anything to keep him.

The pitiful child was thrust into the room where she stood nervously, wrapped in a large towel. Alex strode to her and roughly pulled her covering off. Not too bad, he thought, figuring her to be about sixteen.

"Alex?" cried Fiona, a sick fear snaking through her.

"Get your clothes off," he ordered.

Fiona's face blanched and she wrapped her arms about herself and backed away, shaking her head. The pathetic little whore stood scared and confused.

"Then you'll not see me again," replied Alex tersely, picking up his cape and preparing to put it on. Fiona ran to him with tears brimming in her eyes.

"Alex, please, please have pity."

He stared down at her and smiled cynically.

"You don't wish me to leave?"

Unable to talk, Fiona shook her head.

"Then I'll not," he said coldly, and proceeded to unbutton his shirt. She looked from Alex to the naked, shivering girl, not knowing what to do, her insides churning with fear.

"You did wish me to stay?" he inquired harshly, and laughed as he drew the younger woman to him and rubbed her bare breasts against his chest.

Fiona felt a pulse ticking deep inside her. She tore at her own clothes, not wanting what she felt was hers to be given to anyone but her. Alex shouted a satanic cry of victory at her defeat and continued to play with the other woman as though she were a toy. Fiona's hands trembled as buttons refused to come undone, and her eyes refused to leave the undernourished female body that was receiving the caresses she hungered for.

Alex found the young whore stiff and unyielding in his arms. He tried to melt her, wanting her passionate so Fiona's rage and desire would be fanned. He lay her on the bed and nibbled her breasts, gently stroking her flesh, but she shivered violently. He found her lips and gave to her the very tenderness that Fiona had craved for so long. Alex felt the girl stir beneath him as her mouth opened and she hungrily returned his kisses. He covered her body with his, excited by his ability to bring her to life, and felt Fiona lay on top of him, her heavy breasts pressed against his shoulder blades. After a moment he rolled over, toppling Fiona so she lay back, her eyes glazed with passion.

Alex wanted more. He wanted to punish and manipulate as he felt he was punished and manipulated. He pressed the two naked women together. For a moment they froze, breathing hard.

"Kiss," he demanded.

Tentatively their lips met. Fiona felt torn in two; her passionate sexuality pulsed and yet she was repelled. Alex cruelly kneaded both pair of buttocks, straining their pelvises together, and Fiona felt the fire run through her at the feel of his hand and the pressure she writhed against. She wanted something to pound with, wanted a tool to thrust into the other woman. She bent her head and sucked the small breasts beneath her as she imagined she was male. She wanted the power to drive into and dominate, and she laughed hysterically as she felt the other woman respond. She kissed her brutally, bruising her lips as had been done to her, as she hammered at the pelvis that rose to meet hers. She pushed the woman's head to her own breasts and quivered deliriously as she felt a warm hungry suckling and a delicious yearning spread through her, driving her on.

Alex's face was the picture of contempt and fury as he buttoned his shirt, keeping his eyes on the writhing bodies on the bed who sought comfort and release from their own private hells. He left, laughing sardonically, knowing Fiona was oblivious to his departure.

Fiona woke the next morning, alone and feeling sick inside. What had she been reduced to? She had actually payed the pitiful little whore wanting her to be gone, not able to face the fact that her treacherous body had betrayed her. What was the matter with her? Where was her pride and dignity? She burst into tears as she realized she had lost them. She had become the very thing she despised in other women. She was spiteful, grasping, possessive. Why? She steeled herself, stopping her self-pitying sobs, rationally telling herself that she loved Alex and because of that love she'd stoop to anything to keep him.

Fiona stared at herself in the mirror. She imagined Cameron's face, and she compared herself to the young green-eyed girl, feeling very old. Where had the years gone? Why didn't the lonely days and nights speed by as rapidly? Lonely was the word she feared—to be alone as the wrinkles cracked her face into a million pieces, to be alone as her breasts lost their firmness and sagged, dragging her youth, beauty, and life with them. A nightmarish future loomed ahead and she saw herself as all the gross caricatures she'd mocked and sneered at. She saw a pathetic, painted hag paying young men for their favors so she could pretend she was still desirable.

She didn't feel any different than when she was fifteen. Life had been child's play, a game, and she had been playing a part, swaying majestically between her gaming tables. She had been a naughty little girl dressed up in her mother's clothes. What had happened changing it all to such stark and unwelcome reality?

Fiona thought back to when she first met Alex two years before. He had seemed much older than his peers, who laughed and embarrassingly displayed their callowness. He had seemed self-contained and stood out from the crowd, his handsome chiseled face assessing her frankly. Those amber eyes had smiled cynically, as though he knew her game of make-believe and found her amusing. She'd felt uncomfortable and yet excited. Their arrangement—how she hated that cold word—had been stated by Alex from the onset of their affair and she had agreed, though inwardly she screamed in protest. She had acted the role of the independent worldly woman, insisting they both have the right to take other lovers, hoping he would display some jealousy, but he didn't. She had refused to take anything material from him, knowing instinctively that he'd be impressed by that, and for two long years she had slept with no one but him, even though her whole being lurched sickeningly at the thought of him embracing others. She had played her part so well, even pretending she had other lovers, so he wouldn't think of her as possessive or grasping.

What had she done wrong? Just grown old; but apart from that she could think of nothing except a few trifling bitchy displays, but she didn't think they could be taken seriously. After all, she was only acting her part.

Fiona stared at herself, feeling oddly like a donkey with a carrot just out of reach. For two years she'd hidden her emotions and tried to gain the love she hungered for, but it always dangled just in front of her. Distraught, she blamed Cameron, not being rational enough to realize the girl had had nothing to do with Alex during the past two years.

Alex woke up with his head aching unbearably. He soaked in a hot tub as fragments of the night before tore into his already abused brain. Why was he so cruel? Why was he trying to punish Fiona? What was he becoming?

The sordid events of the previous two weeks bombarded his mind. He thought of his indiscriminant gropings and felt like a sewer rat. He thought of his hypocritical presence at the assemblies and balls of the bon ton and cursed the Scottish gentry for their bowing and scraping to the English. But he was not much better than they.

Why wouldn't his life settle back into the comfortable, uncomplicated rhythm of before? He had been happy and contented, working hard overseeing the farms and families under his protection. He had the best of both worlds, the pastoral peace of the country and the cultural benefits of the city within easy reach of each other. Why wouldn't it all flow back together? Why did everything seem jarring and discordant? Women! he irrationally surmised, furious at their power.

Alex knew he was drinking far too much as he tried to buffer himself. He had been asleep for so long, blind to anything beyond the boundaries of his estate and interests. He'd been wound numbly in a tight cocoon, buried safely under layers and layers of thick protection, and he now longed to clutch them back to himself. He was appalled at how easily he had succumbed to debauchery. His skin crawled inside and out as he recalled his crude, inhuman hostility. He longed to be able to return to Glen Aucht and throw himself into hard manual labor, but the winter was fast coming and there was nothing to be done while the ground slept and revived itself for the spring. He longed to hibernate also, but where and how could he stop his brain that struggled and leaped in his head?

He couldn't stomach what he was becoming. He vowed to shun the social whirl of both the upper class and demimonde, which left him in a strange limbo.

Alex deliberately stopped his mind from thinking of Cameron. His nights were fragmented with images of her standing straight and proud, and then bowing cowering and cringing from him. He could not return to Glen Aucht for peace and solitude, for even there was something to haunt him. He vowed not to return to Fiona or to his life of the previous two weeks, which left him nowhere and with no one.

He tried to bury himself at the university, sitting in on lectures and fervently debating with the students, absorbing and buffering himself with politics, religion, and economics.

James Watt was at the same university perfecting his condensing steam engine, and Alex was fascinated by the ingenuity of it, yet afraid of the change it foretold, as he envisioned clouds of dark vapor blocking the horizon and dimming the clear Scottish air.

Alex spent a week riding through the central lowlands from the Firth of Forth to the Clyde. How had it all happened, the dark oppressive bustle of the mills and mines? It seemed all of Scotland huddled together in one dirty, squalid mass. Tiny emaciated children crawled out of the coal shafts; women covered in sweat and grime clawed each other for jobs to feed themselves; bent, bowed men walked listlessly, their lungs choked, unable to breathe freely. For what?

Alex learned the Scottish representatives in the union parliament in London were mostly lairds out to accumulate more wealth and personal power. Those that weren't were treated with disdain by the English lords. He grew even more depressed as he realized the parallel of the death of old Scotland to his own personal dilemma. Cameron represented the wild free country and Fiona the contained, inexorable future—wild innocence and civilized worldliness. And he stood with one foot in the aching past and one in the stark new reality of the present. Politics, religion, and economics were no diversion to his problem, as everything seemed to entangle and interweave.

*   *   *

Fiona, finding herself shunned after the sordid events of her last meeting with Alex, grew desperate. She found herself waiting and waiting, each ticking second interminable. Three times she lost the battle with her self-pride and went to his townhouse, only to be told he was not home. The third time her self-control snapped, and she pushed past the housekeeper to search the three stories, ranting and raving at each servant who tried to prevent her. Not finding him, she had stormed out in an even greater rage, knowing she had debased and made a fool of herself in front of those she felt were her inferiors.

At Glen Aucht Cameron lived her own hell, trapped by the love she felt for Alex. She had no pleasure galloping across the waking countryside in the morning. She rode full of pain, unable to even look at the waters of the firth, knowing across them were Fiona and Alex, joined as one in her mind.

Mackie and Fergus noted her quiet withdrawal and loss of appetite and were concerned.

"The lass is pining for her own wild home," concluded Fergus.

" 'Taint so sure about that," answered his more astute wife. "There's things the bairn has said, little things. More than once she's mentioned about how beautiful Lady Fiona is, that painted trollop!"

"You think our lass is jealous?"

"Aye, I do, and so she should be," remarked Mackie indignantly, thinking it was about time she broke her promise to Alex and told her husband the truth.

"She's his wife," she blurted.

"Who? Lady Fiona Hurst?" ejaculated Fergus after a shocked pause.

"Nay, you daft lad, the lass. Cameron is Lady Sinclair." And she proceeded to relate all Alex had told her of the events leading up to the marriage.

"Makes a might of sense now of the lad's behavior," chortled Fergus, giving into mirth, but stopping as his wife eyed him coldly.

" 'Tis no laughing matter," she reprimanded.

"Aye, you're right. Now you think the bairn loves him?"

"Aye, and he her, but they're both cut from the same cloth and too stubborn and proud to admit it," answered Mackie.

"Can you just see Sir Alex introducing Cameron to his fancy society friends?" remarked Fergus dryly.

"Meaning what?" apostulated Mackie. "She's as good if not better than them!"

"Aye, but she looks like a stable lad," interrupted Fergus. "She ain't been taught their ways and I doubt she'd be happy among them."

"She's of their class, you can be certain of that."

"And how do you know that, woman? The puir wee thing has no idea of who she is," returned Fergus.

"One day I'm hoping all that rubbish will count for nothing."

"Dinna bite my head off. I agree with you, Mrs. MacDonald, but that doesna help with the now."

"We'll teach her the ways. Help her."

"Only if she wants, only if she asks it," replied Fergus firmly. "That spirited filly will only accept the reins and the trappings if she has a mind to."

Cameron herself had come to the same conclusion, but her problem was how to ask for help. She'd never admitted to needing anyone or anything before, and it went against her proud nature. She saw the asking as weak and despicable, a losing of her independence. She had been strong in her solitariness against the world, but that had been before Alex, when her world had been smaller and so much less complicated. She fought the love she felt, not wanting to be so bound, but lost, knowing she wanted to be what Alex would admire. She would become a lady and learn to dress and act the part and fit into his world.

A week after Alex had left with Fiona and his house guests, Mackie entered Cameron's bedchamber to find her dressed in the dark red riding habit.

"You look a treat," crowed the old woman, clasping her plump hands together.

"I feel silly," shrugged Cameron.

"That's 'cause you canna see yourself," replied Mackie, taking the girl's hand and dragging her out along the corridor to Alex's room, where there was a long mirror.

Cameron stared around the chamber, knowing where she was and therefore very curious.

"There now. Take a peek at yourself," smiled Mackie.

Cameron stared longingly around the masculine room, loving everything she saw. She stared at an oil painting over the fireplace. A man, a woman, and three children posed formally. She recognized Alex as a boy of about eight, standing straight and proud in the dress tartan of the Sinclair clan, next to a tall bearded man also in full Highland regalia, and a wistful pretty woman holding two little golden-haired girls who were little more than babies.

"'Tis the whole family together," whispered Mackie, suppressing tears. "The two lassies are Alex's sisters, Ailsa and Annabel."

"What happened to them?"

"All dead, and their gentle mother too."

"How?"

"On their way to the New World to start again.

Told them 'twas a barbarous place. Maybe it was as well they died before reaching it."

Cameron looked thoughtfully at the family portrait, dimly remembering Alex's voice pouring out his story. Had he? Or had it been a dream?

"They died on the ship?" she asked.

"Aye. We can't be chatting all day. Come and take a look at yourself," said Mackie briskly, trying to throw off her aching sadness.

"The cholera took them?"

"Aye, how did you know that? Did Master Alex tell you?"

"I don't know how I know," puzzled Cameron, walking to the long glass.

"Well, now, don't you look the fancy lady?" Mackie asked, forcefully trying to change the subject.

Cameron, confused by her knowledge, stared at her image, not answering. She recalled Alex's voice painfully telling her of his life. But when?

"See how that rich red brings out the green in your eyes? And what a graceful figure. Why, the lass in that glass is prettier than any picture," cooed Mackie.

Cameron focused her eyes on herself.

"I still feel silly."

"You have to get used to yourself. Pretend you're looking at another girl. See how bonny she is?" urged the old woman.

"You're not just saying it?"

"What do you think I am? If you looked a fool, do you think I'd let you parade around, loving you as I do?" retorted Mackie. "You come down the stairs with me and we'll see what Fergus has to say. I'll not open my mouth. You go in the kitchen first."

"You think Fergus would teach me to ride sideways?" asked Cameron.

"Aye, if that's what you want," beamed Mackie.

* * *

Every morning Fergus coached Cameron in the use of the sidesaddle until she sat comfortable and assured. She still preferred riding astride, but her objective forced her to concentrate on her education.

She ate all her meals alone in the dining room or breakfast room, and she was waited on as befitted Lady Sinclair. She hated the cold isolation, though, and thought longingly of the warm cheerful kitchen. She kept a book of etiquette beside her and pretended Alex sat at the distant end of the table, facing her as she practiced polite empty phrases.

Cameron's determination and stubbornness helped her to learn quickly, much to Mackie's delight and Fergus's disgust, as he saw her free spirit controlled and corseted.

" 'Tis a sin that such a rare sparkling gem should be turned to a common stone," he grumbled.

"She's no longer common, she's polished gentry, and you hush yourself. 'Tis what the lass wants. 'Tis time she practiced among her own kind, though. Maybe we should send word to the Dummonds."

"What is the wee thing's own kind? And what would we be doing sending word to the Drummonds? You forget your place, woman," muttered Fergus.

"Aye, that's a sticky knot, isn't it now?"

Ian Drummond could not rid his thoughts of the black-haired girl on the adjoining land, who had so taken his heart. He had no wish to return to Edinburgh, to see Fiona and Alex socializing, as he was afraid of his own anger and could see himself losing control and calling out his former friend. Many mornings he got up early to ride the banks of the firth, hoping to meet Cameron, but to no avail. Each time he returned home chiding and railing at himself. What was he doing? Cameron was another man's wife and it was none of his business how Alex treated her. But a few mornings later he'd find himself galloping through the frosty morning, the breath of his horse and himself steaming the crystal air.

It had been nearly a month since his encounter with Alex on the small beach. He stood still, staring over the fishing boats, hearing the gulls' cries echo forlornly as his eyes saw the gray haze of the distant shores. He was dimly aware of the approaching hoofbeats and, as they neared, he turned in their direction, desperately hoping it would be Cameron. Not seeing the wild little tomboy with cape flying, his heart fell. He watched the elegant sedate rider with groom, absently wondering who she could be and where she could be visiting.

"Good morning, Lord Drummond," said Cameron, hoping she was comporting herself properly by speaking first. She forced herself to be cool and aloof, curbing her joy at seeing him.

"Cameron?" stammered Ian after a minute. "What the hell have you done to yourself?" She now looked like a thousand other insipid young ladies of his acquaintance. Luckily Cameron's education had not progressed to the stage of recognizing cold snubs or she might have been hurt by the impropriety of his curse and set him down for being impertinent. Instead the old Cameron bubbled over and she laughed out loud.

"I'm becoming a lady," she giggled.

"You are already a lady, Lady Sinclair," retorted Ian.

"Who told you that?" she demanded, her joy fading.

"Alex."

Cameron sat silently, digesting the information and wondering why Alex had told him the secret. Ian watched her pale worried face for a few moments before speaking.

"Why did you marry him?" he blurted.

Cameron didn't answer.

"Did you want to?" Ian probed relentlessly.

"Not then," she said quietly.

"But now?" asked Ian after a pause.

"Now I want to be all he wants me to be."

"Why? He married you as you were, Cameron."

"But he dinna want to," explained Cameron, somehow needing to unburden herself and enlist Ian's help. After all, Alex had trusted Ian with the secret, she reasoned. All the events leading up to Alex's entrapment poured out of Cameron's mouth, the more intimate side excluded, thanks to Mackie's careful coaching. If Ian hadn't been so infatuated with the girl himself he would have roared with laughter at his old friend's predicament; as it was, he saw the pain and confusion in the green eyes.

"And now you want the marriage?" he asked softly, as she concluded.

"I want him to be proud of me, I want to be worthy of him. So I have to learn all I can so I don't shame him anymore. Could you help me?" she asked earnestly.

Ian groaned to himself, torn between wanting to do anything to alleviate her pain and yet knowing it would cause him to suffer if he did.

"Aye. I'll do anything I can."

Cameron's face lit up with delight.

"Come back with me to Glen Aucht for luncheon so I can practice my conversation," she begged enthusiastically.

"You converse beautifully already, Cameron," answered Ian.

"You'll not eat lunch with me?"

"'Tis not advisable with Alex away from home," explained Ian. "He's still in Edinburgh, is he not?"

"Aye," replied Cameron, looking crestfallen, "but why is it not advisable?"

"'Tis not the thing for a single man to dine alone with a married woman," he explained uncomfortably, longing to spend time alone with her. But he felt it was taking advantage of her ignorance.

"Why?"

"It could be misconstrued, give rise to gossip. It's socially incorrect unless there's a chaperon present," stammered Ian.

"Mackie is there."

"Being a housekeeper she'd not pass muster as a chaperon, Cameron. Should be an older woman of equal class."

"Equal class? I dinna ken, 'tis so mixed up and complicated, I doubt if I'll ever become a lady. I am too addlebrained to make head or tail of any of it. Seems before, each thing I learned had a sense to it. Now all I learn is just 'because,' no seeing rhyme or reason," she cried bitterly.

"Cameron, don't despair. I'll ride over to talk to Mackie, as I have an idea and would like to get her thoughts on it," reassured Ian.

"An idea? What?" exclaimed Cameron excitedly.

"I should like you to be the guest of my grandmother and aunt, for a week or so. There you'd be properly chaperoned, as I have to go to Glasgow for a spell. They'd be able to teach you better than I what is expected of you, if you are so eager to go through with this plan. But I have to tell you honestly, Cameron, I don't like it."

Mackie was delighted at Cameron's invitation to the Drummonds'. It was all very proper, she noted, as young Master Ian would not be home, and the request had come formally from the old lady herself. She bustled about, packing Cameron's trunk with great enthusiasm while Cameron stood there terrified.

"Why can't Ian come here?"

"Tut, tut. 'Tis not done, and 'tis also *Sir* Ian to you, Miss Cameron," reproved Mackie.

"Dinna say 'Miss Cameron,' Mackie."

"Dinna say 'dinna.' It's 'do not' or 'don't,' Miss Cameron," retorted the old woman. "Learning new ways is not easy. If it's what you want, you must set your mind. Is it what you want, child?"

Cameron had not confessed to Mackie her reasons for so fervently wanting to improve herself, as she had no idea that the old woman knew about the marriage, but she felt instinctively that both of them knew she loved Alex.

"You ken that the big beastie has to stay here? 'Tis not the thing for a young lady to go scrambling about with a giant of a hound, inconveniencing her hostess," informed Mackie.

So Cameron gritted her teeth and set out for Ian's estate to learn drawing-room etiquette and the social graces—alone.

Chapter Eighteen

Fiona made discreet inquiries as to Alex's whereabouts and was relieved to find out he was still in Edinburgh. Her fears were allayed further on discovering his new habits were free from any sexuality. It had been a very long painful month deprived of his company, but she kept herself busy making the acquaintance of several university students, hoping to find an ally to help her resume her relationship with Alex. Finally she met a young medical student by the name of Adam Munroe, whose fervent desire to be a doctor blinded him to the immorality of any measure necessary in order to achieve his own ambition. He was a cold, asexual man, preferring the dissection of cadavers to the caressing of warm, female bodies. Fiona housed him in her attic and paid his tuition in return for any information he could glean about Alex. Adam recognized his good fortune, expecially as there were no unsavory carnal strings attached, and he was able to obtain for her a list of the new circle of friends that Alex now consorted with.

It was Adam who came up with the brilliant idea of

the intellectual dinner party, as he himself wished to ingratiate himself into the closed society of scholars and professors. Fiona leaped at the idea and immediately contacted a very notable lord who owed her a considerable amount in gambling debts. She proposed wiping his slate clean in return for the use of his large house in Lieth and the use of his servants. Adam carefully compiled the invitation list of the people who could best further his career and also tempt Alex to attend. He was pleased with his plan, even though it caused Fiona to get carried away with delight and excitedly hug him. He froze with distaste and pushed her away.

"Adam, I have no naughty designs on you. Never fear," reassured Fiona, eying his thin skeletal figure with distaste. "But we must have the appearance of lovers at our dinner. We have parts to play. You will escort me and be gallant and attentive."

"In a crowded room I shall be most romantic," replied Adam, not wishing to deprive himself of his benefactor.

Alex received his invitation and, not recognizing the name Adam Munroe, put it aside disinterestedly. He had no desire for partying; in fact he had a downright repulsion to it, as the hypocrisy of sitting at sumptuously laden tables, when his newly opened eyes saw stark starvation all around, turned his stomach. But he changed his mind on learning through the university circles of the others invited, and his new-found curiosity was intrigued.

Cameron settled into the dreary Drummond household by shutting off her emotions and, like a drudging horse with blinkers, trod an unfeeling existence. Grandmother Drummond was an English woman married at fourteen to a man she considered to be a bar-

baric Scot in a savage land. For sixty years she hid her superiority and distaste behind a brittle facade of manners, but with the challenge of Cameron she rose like the phoenix from the gray ashes of her life. She had hated Duncan Fraser even more than her own rough, crude husband, as he epitomized for her all she most abhorred. Remembering his enormous kilted figure looking down at her for being of a more civilized culture, she took great delight—tinged with more than a little cutting spite—in teaching Cameron the rules of etiquette.

Mercifully, Cameron's objective had become so one-dimensional and obsessive that it blocked the violent reaction to being taught by the hated English. She sewed samplers, practiced endless scales on the spinet, poured pots of tea until her arm ached, recited empty, meaningless phrases and insipid verse, walked literally miles with tiny, dainty steps balancing heavy books upon her head, and did countless other boring things without question or complaint.

When Ian returned from Glasgow at the end of two weeks, he stared at his grandmother in shocked amazement. Where was the pale colorless shadow who had shivered in a corner as his bluff grandfather ruled with an iron fist? Where was his homely, lonely, drab maiden aunt Morag, who had camouflaged herself into the dark woodwork, torn between the two races she had sprung from? Since the death of his grandfather and father on Culloden Moor, Ian had watched over his two womenfolk, thinking he knew them. Now he stared in horror as they bloomed bossy and dictatorial, putting Cameron through her paces like a docile, broken young horse. Her eyes were dull and blank and she performed obediently, like a puppet.

Ian sat through an interminable dinner, desperately hoping for some spark of spirit from Cameron, but she sat as cold and remote as a porcelain ornament. What had he been a party to? He was determined to catch Cameron alone, hoping that without the two formidable, overwhelming women he would see her bubbling nature thaw and flow.

For two days Morag dogged Cameron's steps until Ian despaired. Finally in the late afternoon he found her in the garden reading aloud some Shakespeare sonnets.

"Cameron, put the book down and talk to me."

Cameron obediently closed the volume and looked up at him politely. Ian raged inside at her lusterless eyes and her demure, controlled pose.

"Oh, Cameron. I'd like to fly with you back to the Highlands. You are a wild flower, not a hot-house plant. I wish I could leave those dependent on me and take you away," he cried, longing to enfold her in his arms. Cameron's eyes sparkled for a split second as she saw the treeless, rugged moors and then her head lowered and her small hands clenched, the knuckles whitening.

"I'm not doing well?" she asked anxiously.

"Too well. I scarce recognized you as the same Cameron," Ian retorted savagely. "Walk with me a little," he added, taking her hand.

"Lady Morag will rail at me."

"Let her rail, I'll protect you. Come on. Run," he laughed, and they raced from the formal garden into a nearby copse. "All work and no play will make Cameron a very dull child."

"I am not a child."

"Nay, you're fast becoming an old lady, and if I'd known that, I'd never have consented to your staying here. 'Tis not worth it, Cameron."

Cameron withdrew her hand from his sharply.

"You are impertinent!" she cried, and then her new

poise and breeding cracked. "'Tis worth it. 'Tis. I'll win him from Lady Fiona! I will!"

Ian's words had hit a small sore place inside Cameron that each night ached as doubts assailed her.

"Oh, Cameron," crooned Ian, folding her in his strong arms so her clenched fists were useless. "Be yourself. If a man canna love you for yourself, he dinna deserve to love you at all. You'll make yourself over so shallow and fancy and still feel unloved."

Cameron, feeling the sense in what he said, redoubled her efforts to get free from his arms, terrified of his convincing her that all her striving had been in vain.

"You dinna ken!" she shouted, forgetting all the elocution she had painfully learned.

"Explain to me then."

"Unhand me first."

Ian released her and stood afraid that she'd flutter off like a frightened bird.

"I love him. I didna ken love before, eating into you so you canna rest or see anything else around you. I want to be free of such pain, and yet I would kill to keep it."

Cameron's words, reflecting Ian's own ache for her, hung in the still air between them.

"Aye," said Ian finally. "You must go your way and do as you must. But perhaps 'tis time to put it to the test."

Cameron paled.

"How?" she whispered.

"Edinburgh, the city. Away from the quiet of the country," stated Ian ruthlessly.

"I thought to await his return at Glen Aucht and surprise him," stammered Cameron.

"And what would that prove?" asked Ian brutally. Cameron didn't answer.

"You say you want to win him from Lady Fiona, but are you willing to share him with her? 'Tis very socially acceptable, you know. Will you be a docile wife, Cameron? Sit home sewing samplers and drinking tea while your man plays with the big city dolls? I can just see you knitting and making small talk while you breed!"

"While I breed?" repeated Cameron, puzzled.

"Aye, for that's the only reason gentlemen marry ladies—to breed like sheep!"

"To breed like sheep? To get a good strain?" asked Cameron, her face white.

Ian cursed his temper for taking the upper hand. This wasn't the conversation to be having with a fifteen-year-old girl who was striving to become a lady of society. There was only one thing to be done. He had to get the painful situation cleared up one way or the other. He'd take her to Edinburgh and force his friend to either accept or reject her as his legal wife.

"I'm taking you home to Glen Aucht tomorrow morning, and we'll leave for Edinburgh at the end of the week, taking Aunt Morag as chaperon," Ian informed her. "I'll order your trunk packed." And with that he strode from the woods, leaving her alone with her terrified thoughts.

Cameron sat dressed for travel, anxiously awaiting Ian's and his Aunt Morag's arrival. Mackie hovered nervously around the trunks, hoping there was nothing forgotten. "Fergus be a'going too, lassie. 'Tis a long time since he's been a groom. 'Twill keep his head small and in its right place," she laughed, trying to ease the set, white face. Cameron sat with a small gloved hand resting on Torquil's shaggy head.

"Well, with Fergus and Torquil to protect me I should have nothing to fear," replied Cameron, and she laughed in a false society way that curdled Fergus's blood as he entered to see to the trunks.

Mercifully, nature came to Cameron's rescue by switching off all feeling, and she was swept painlessly from Mackie's comforting arms to Edinburgh. Numbly she stepped from carriage to boat as though in a dream, her eyes blank and blind, her hands holding the ridiculous little reticule all the way to the city.

Ian now questioned his actions. He had been so determined to resolve his own dilemma by confrontation, making Alex accept the responsibility of his own wife or reject it—in which case he would shoulder it gladly—that he hadn't thought of the consequence to Cameron. What was he doing to her? he wondered, looking at her strangely impassive face and knowing that they passed sights she couldn't possibly have seen before, but they evoked no reaction whatsover.

Morag chattered endlessly, filling the silence as they crossed the choppy Firth of Forth. At forty-seven years old, it was as though the old biddy was coming out as a debutante. Poor old aunty, thought Ian. Closeted with her mother for years, she deserved to kick up her heels and enjoy herself. She was probably the only one of them who would.

Cameron was unaware of the bustling city. She stared out one window of the swaying coach, seeing nothing. Morag hung out of the other, hungrily devouring and spitting back with relish all she saw. Ian sat between wondering, as did Fergus on top with the coachman, what was going on in Cameron's mind.

Ian registered them all at a respectable hotel on Princes Street, deciding it would be infinitely better for Cameron to eat in the public dining room. If she then shied away from the noise and constraints of social life, he'd return her immediately home to Glen Aucht.

At the hotel liveried doormen handed them from the carriage, and Morag, primed to pick and hiss directions at Cameron, found to her pride and disappointment that her charge moved silently and gracefully through the milling throng.

The night of Cameron's arrival in Edinburgh coincided with Fiona's elaborate, intellectual dinner party. What a bore! thought Fiona, peeking into the smoke-filled room at twenty-odd men who conversed fervently about the economy, the union, and other subjects that she found stodgy and dreary. Her heart skipped a beat as she saw Alex's russet head bent as he listened attentively, and she wondered apprehensively what his reaction would be when she entered with the other women for dinner. She congratulated herself and Adam on their shrewdness in inviting that weird breed of Scottish intellectual who absentmindedly cared nothing for class or reputation, living as they did with their musty, dusty, abstract theories.

Fiona walked majestically into dinner on Adam's arm, delighted that he played his part gallantly. She hoped she looked breathtaking and stunning as she entered with the other couples, followed by the unaccompanied men. Fiona sat at the table strategically facing the door as she waited for Alex to enter and see her. She had lived the hope of their eyes locking, as he stood transfixed, over and over again. She planned to allow the magical moment to last a few beats before turning adoringly to Adam at her side. Her anticipation caused her to sit forward, straining her eyes and holding her breath. But she slumped back with a small hiss as Alex entered, deep in conversation, without seeing her. He sat concentrating totally on the spry old man beside him, and Fiona decided her only recourse was to be so charming and witty she'd capture all attention, including his.

Four courses were served and Alex remained oblivious to Fiona's presence, as he listened intently to the wiry old Scot and the ensuing arguments he engendered by his statements. He felt drawn to the white-haired little man who provoked interesting debates around the table as he damned the church as well as the English for the death of Scottish pride. A heated discussion arose as some men lauded the English for forcing Scotland to compete in the foreign market, which improved the economy.

"Whose economy is improved?" challenged the feisty old provocateur, at which a hubbub of conflicting answers were voiced. Alex himself heard a little truth in all, but dimly felt it was the rich who accumulated more riches. He voiced no opinion, though, preferring to listen. One pompous young student loudly praised the English for introducing culture and civility to Scotland's barbarous feudal system, whereupon the old professor's eyes sparked dangerously. Yet he kept his peace until hearing the Stuart cause spoken of in such disparaging terms as "romantic" and "self-indulgent," and then he exploded.

"Aye, we must thank our oppressors for rooting us from ignorance and teaching us to be materialistic and imperialistic!" he said cynically. "Why canna one country allow another to evolve without interference? Can one of you point out to me one civilization that has nothing to fault it? Aye, you canna. One day there will be no Scotland. She'll be devoured and digested to be part of the whole of England. Och, I'm spoiling a delicious dinner with my bitterness. What's done is done and there is no way to go back in time. There is no way for old Scotland, nor for old me, to start again as there is for you wee uns. Ha! Ha! If I had your

youth I'd be off to the New World, but being I'm a
sad old man I'll be off to the Highlands, to the furthest point north to find the old ways, spend my last
days reminiscing with Duncan about the old days."

"Cape Wrath?" ejaculated Alex.

"Aye," returned Dougal Gunn guardedly.

"Duncan Fraser?"

The old man froze, his twinkling blue eyes hardening to an icy stare before pointedly turning away and
ignoring Alex, as he threw himself back into conversation with the other young men at the table. Alex sat
puzzled for a few moments before realizing the danger
of speaking so openly about a wanted man in the presence of so many unknown people. Duncan, and a few
like him, were still being sought out by the English.
They wouldn't yet know of his death.

Alex sat silently listening to the resumption of the
heated arguments, as Dougal challenged and provoked. He idly let his eyes roam around the long table.

Fiona! What was she doing here? A coldness shot
through him, reminding him of so much he had
successfully blocked. He shook himself, forcing himself
to see her objectively. She looked well. Her face and
eyes seemed soft, not hard and demanding as they had
appeared the last times he had seen her. She smiled
warmly before turning to a young man at her side.
Alex raised his glass to her and forced himself to smile
tightly back. He didn't know how he felt and, not
wanting to know, he submerged himself in the tantalizing debate about him, letting the words flow over
and in until he successfully drowned out her presence.

Fiona read a thousand wonderful and terrifying
things into the split second their eyes had met. Part of
her leaped and rejoiced, the other half panicked.
Hadn't he seemed a little cold and detached? she
thought, and then quickly chided herself. What could

he expect? After all, they were in company and she couldn't very well be put out because he didn't leap up and come charging to her side, could she? Later, she told herself, and squirmed with excited anticipation.

After the women retired from the room, leaving the men to drink, smoke, and use any turn of phrase without fear of offending, Alex found himself ensconced in a dark secluded corner with Dougal.

"What's your name, lad? Seems I know your eyes," the old man barked sharply.

"Alexander Sinclair, Professor Gunn," replied Alex, extending his hand to the old man who pointedly ignored it as he stared suspiciously.

"You know my name?"

"Aye, I've had the good fortune to attend many of your lectures, sir."

"Sinclair, is it? Aye, I knew your father. Same name. Same eyes. I wonder, is that where the similarity ends? I hear you got some of your lands back?"

"Aye."

"And the name you so rashly mentioned?" probed Dougal.

"Duncan?"

"Aye, who is he to you?"

"He was my father's closest friend."

"Aye, I heard of Sinclair's death, but I asked what Duncan is to you, not what he was to your father," snapped Dougal in the manner of an inquisitor.

"I dinna ken your meaning, sir."

"Where do your sympathies lie, young fellow? Och, you young Scots get more English each day."

Alex knew exactly what Dougal was getting at, especially with the reference to the returning of his estate. How to answer truthfully was a dilemma. To say he had no sympathies would surely stir the cantankerous old man into a frenzy. To say he had no love for the English but chose to coexist would probably have the same effect.

"I have no love for the English," he returned stiffly.

"Aye, and no hate either, 'twould seem. You young are so passionless!" returned Dougal with contempt. Alex stared into his glass. Did he have hate? He should have plenty and yet it cost too much effort. What purpose would it serve? He had hate but it was buried, deeply shrouded with the other bitter pains that he had chosen to forget.

"What makes you think he's at Cape Wrath?"

"Duncan Fraser sent for me."

"Bite your tongue, boy, there's many who'd sell their souls for the English reward."

"They'd be too late," retorted Alex.

Dougal stared searchingly at the younger man for a few moments, his face softening to almost childlike lines.

"Dead?" he said sadly.

"Aye."

Dougal took a long swallow of spirits as he digested the news.

"How did he die?"

Alex wondered what he meant. In what manner? Accident or the like? Or how did Duncan receive death?

"Impatiently," he blurted, not sure where the word came from.

"Expand a wee bit on that."

Alex sought for a way to express himself and made some hesitant grunts in his frustration to explain.

"Take a drink and take your time," growled the older man.

"Time! That's what he said. Too much time to

think and not enough time to undo," remembered Alex.

"Not enough time to undo?" repeated Dougal.

"Aye."

"Why were you there?"

"I told you. He sent for me. Duncan and my father were like brothers," he explained.

"Aye, I recollect. I knew your father. Damn fool like Duncan hisself, giving up the ghost as if life itself had stopped. But I canna judge them as I'm about to do the same. I heard about your mother and wee sisters. 'Twas and still is painful times." The old man's eyes seemed less accusing now as he looked at Alex.

"Aye."

There was a sad moment as both men drank, lost in their own thoughts.

"I've had too much talk, food, and spirits and I'm an old weary man who needs the comfort of his bed," muttered Dougal, hailing a servant. Alex stared at him in dismay as there were many questions he'd hoped the old man could answer.

"Dinna fash yourself, lad. There's plenty you'll learn from me, tomorrow. Here's my card. Show yourself at four for tea," reassured Dougal, shaking Alex's hand.

"Until tomorrow, sir."

"Aye," nodded Dougal, turning to follow the servant, and then he turned back. "Was the wee bairn there?"

Astonished, Alex nodded and opened his mouth to let forth a stream of questions, but the old man cut off the words before they began.

"Tomorrow, lad, tomorrow. 'Tis not safe to talk here. Wait till I'm sober and rested and used to knowing my dear friend is dead."

Alex stood staring after the spry old man long after

the door had closed behind him. He was shaken from his reverie by a warm hand and a cheerful voice.

" 'Tis good to see you, Sir Alexander," said Fiona brightly.

Alex was relieved to see her face still soft and her eyes gentle.

" 'Tis good to see you, Lady Fiona," he replied.

"It's been a long time," she added conventionally, with a roguish twinkle in her eye.

"Aye, it has at that," Alex laughed, enjoying the undercurrent that ran beneath their polite small talk.

"How have you been keeping yourself?" purred Fiona.

"Chaste," he retorted. "And you?"

"I have been keeping myself in my usual style," replied Fiona, her blue eyes twinkling.

"So you were not as put out as you'd have me imagine, my lady," chuckled Alex.

"We are much the same, my lord. We like our enjoyment unencumbered by possessive strings," Fiona lied, hoping to regain his confidence.

Alex felt a stirring at the open invitation in her eyes.

"It has been a long time. Too long," he growled huskily.

"Has it?" replied Fiona. "Then perhaps we should do something about it."

"You are escorted, Lady Fiona," informed Alex, with mixed emotions.

Fiona leveled her gaze, wishing she could read his thoughts.

"I can excuse myself from him," she said softly. His eyes bore into hers for a moment before he nodded. Hurriedly she crossed to Adam Munroe, whom she hugged lovingly as she whispered for him not to return to his attic room and discreetly pressed a large sum of money into his hand.

The coach swayed along in the pouring, late October rain as Alex sullenly stared out into the darkness, wishing himself alone in his own carriage as he tried to clear his mind of the effects of alcohol. Fiona looked out of the other window, not knowing how to approach the remote, seemingly angry man.

The carriage jolted and she allowed herself to be swung against him, her hand grasping his thigh to steady herself. She let it stay there and Alex steeled himself, not willing to give her encouragement, as he kept his eyes trained on the passing night.

Fiona let her hand move slowly up his thigh, her own eyes not leaving the other window. She inched her fingers, seemingly innocently, toward his groin. Alex burned and held himself in check, determined not to be seduced by her. He sat still, ignoring her but enjoying the sensations that flared through him. Fiona felt his hardness and longed for his hands to caress her, but to her frustration he acted as though she wasn't there. She pressed him rhythmically, trying to break his control as her own passion grew. The miles flew by and Alex remained impassive as Fiona's aching reached dangerous proportions, and she wondered how he could sit so still and be so noticeably aroused.

Chapter Nineteen

Cameron sat in the hotel dining room with Ian and
Morag, unaware of the attention her rare beauty in-
spired. Morag, feeling so many eyes focused on their
table, became very animated and extravagant with her
gestures, preening and turning as she tried not to appear self-conscious. Cameron quietly picked at her
food as Ian sat embarrassed and uncomfortable with
the spectacle his aunt was making of herself. He was
most relieved when, in the midst of recounting a very
boring story in the loudest possible voice, one of Morag's dramatically flailing hands knocked a glass full of
wine into her lap, forcing them all to retire. Cameron,
in her cushioned world, left the crowded dining room
with a graceful dignity that had men staring after,
wondering who she was.

Unfortunately for Ian, Morag's ardor for a gay social
evening had not been dampened by a glass of bur-
gundy. She insisted on them waiting in the connecting
sitting room to her suite while she changed her gown,
before being taken for a night on the town.

Ian stared forlornly at his boots as Cameron gazed

blindly over the twinkling lights of Edinburgh. Where should he take them, pondered Ian unhappily, knowing if he were alone there would be many desirable haunts but none befitting an old spinster aunt and a young lady. It was too late for the theater or the opera, and any other acceptable social gathering was by invitation only. But Morag, deaf to Ian's protests, dragged them out, insisting that he point out all the sights of interest as she strode heartily, breathing deeply and loudly, Torquil at her heels.

Ian, with his raucous, ebullient aunt on one arm, and the mute beauty on the other, resigned himself to his fate as he fervently prayed they'd meet none of his acquaintances. Both women, in their different moods, were unaware of the consistent cold drizzle that misted the lamplights and beaded on their cloaks. Concerned at Cameron's withdrawal and his aunt's conspicuous behavior Ian suggested that they hail a carriage and return to the dry warmth of their hotel, but his words fell on deaf ears. A loud roll of thunder caused him to shudder and Cameron to look around, green eyes sparkling, but there were no wide spaces to roam, just narrow streets. She stared around as though just waking, oblivious to Morag's endless chatter.

"By jove, boy! Do you want us to catch our death of colds?" snapped Morag, finally aware of the teeming rain. "Get us out of this deluge at once!"

Ian looked helplessly around at the empty street and, seeing no vehicles, held both women's hands firmly.

"We'll have to make a run for it," he shouted over the storm, as he bent his head against the driving force of the rain, hoping to find shelter.

Cameron threw back her head and laughed as her cape flew behind her and the cold water splashed her face. Morag clutched Ian with one hand and held her hood tightly with the other as she galloped, groaning.

Ian managed to shelter his charges in a fairly respectable public house frequented by university students. They entered to a warm blast of stale beer and lively conversation, Morag moaning wetly and Cameron radiant and glistening.

"Begone, you great scruffy beast!" yelled the innkeeper, aiming a savage kick at Torquil.

"You'll not harm my dog!" cried Cameron.

"There's no animals allowed here, ma'am."

"Do you have a private parlor where the ladies may warm and refresh themselves?" inquired Ian hurriedly, as he saw the dangerous sparkle in Cameron's eyes.

"They be all full, sir," answered the publican, eying Torquil suspiciously, "and that animal must go."

Cameron marched to the door with her hand on Torquil's head and a loud protest went up from the students who had heard the exchange.

"Ye canna turn a dog out on a night like this, let alone a pretty lassie. Where's your heart, Joe?"

"No animals allowed," Joe insisted.

"Plenty of us here," called another voice, which was greeted with laughter and good-natured protests.

"Speak for yourself, Jocko, and make room at the fire so the pretty ladies can dry off," yelled another gallant, pushing the men that clustered around the generous blaze.

"Brew something hot, Joe, something to burn the wet chill out."

Morag, after sniffing disdainfully at the commonness of her surroundings, smiled flirtatiously as she was seated by the fire by a chivalrous young man who helped her out of her wet cape.

Cameron stood hesitantly with Torquil by the door. She was frightened and shy of the warm friendly mob, yet the cold strangeness of the city outside frightened

ler more, although the storm beckoned her. Ian led
ler gently to a vacated seat by the fire as someone
tarted to play the piano.

Torquil by her feet, Cameron nursed a hot toddy as
he students sang, and Morag, forgetting herself,
oined in, her raucous voice blending with the rough
nale tones around.

Alex looked down at the naked woman at his side
and hated himself for weakening and her for her per-
istence. Fiona lay satisfied, like a large marmalade cat
vho, full of cream, now purred contentedly with eyes
narrowed to watchful slits and soft paws that hid
harp claws.

"Where are you going?" snapped Fiona, her body
uddenly losing its softness as she tensed upon seeing
Alex pulling on his clothes.

"Home," he answered tersely.

"You'll not stay the night?" she crooned invitingly,
willing her claws to remain hidden as she stretched her
hand to stay him.

"No."

"Oh?" Fiona's eyes hardened, and she longed to tear
into his lean hard body as he stood calmly tying his
cravat.

"Why?" she asked, hating herself as the word
popped out. Alex didn't deign to answer but stared
caustically at her reflection in the mirror for a moment and resumed dressing.

"It's so cold and wet outside, and so warm and cozy
inside," she tempted, suggestively.

"I need to walk and clear my head."

"I do too. I'll walk with you," said Fiona, leaping
off the bed and starting to put on her own clothes.

Alex was at a loss. He needed desperately to be
alone and yet was feeling a trifle guilty at his use of

Fiona. He was surprised at his feeling and also loath to subject himself to one of her grasping, self-abasing scenes.

Alex paced Fiona's boudoir, noting with distaste the furnishings he'd seen countless times and yet not really noticed. Flagrant sexuality, shallow, like a sordid stage setting. Fleshy pink satin covered the curves of the cushions and bed, lit by cunningly contrived lamps that flickered hot tongues, casting sultry shadows and a vulgar glow. The heavy scent of stagnant, cloying, perfume hung over everything, and Alex had the urge to smash the windows and allow the violent storm outside to tear into the deadly vacuum. He paced, curbing his rage and repulsion, wanting to beat Fiona's adoring smile to a pulp and fling himself outside to race the wind and challenge the thunder and lightning as he'd seen Cameron do.

Sedately Alex and Fiona walked arm in arm down the stairs, her every cooing, clinging gesture irritating him. He stood deliberately on the front steps, letting the torrential rain beat down on him, feeling the cloying closeness of Fiona's smell wash from him.

"Alex, I'm getting soaked," protested Fiona.

"Then go back inside," he answered, descending to the pavement. Fiona closed her mouth firmly and hung on to his arm as he strode silently, his face upturned to the water that freed him of the sweat of his previous exertions.

Alex continued walking, oblivious to the woman clinging to his arm as she tried to keep up with his pace through muddy puddles that splashed and dirtied her stockings and gown. Fiona was out of breath, panting exhaustedly.

"Alex, stop. I have a pain in my side, a stitch," she gasped, but relentlessly he continued until she screamed shrilly and beat on him with hard sharp fists clenched in freezing wet gloves. Alex looked down, somehow surprised at her presence, and then laughed. She looked to him like a cornered rat, her face tight and pointed with cold anger, her teeth bared and rather yellow, her red hair lank and stringy, her eyes small and sharp with black lines of water running down her cheeks. If she hadn't looked so mean she might have looked pathetic, Alex mused, as he looked away from her, repelled.

The street was deserted and most house lights had been extinguished for the night. At the very end of the shiny black emptiness he saw a red glow and heard the faint strains of merriment. Fiona, seeing his eyes and feet aimed in that direction, hung back.

"Let's call a carriage and go home to a nice hot bath," she suggested.

"Find yourself a carriage and do whatever you want," he retorted, continuing toward the inviting warmth of the inn.

"It's a common man's drinking place. I'll not go there," Fiona protested, releasing his arm and stamping her foot. Alex kept going and Fiona, finding herself deserted on the dark quiet street, bit back the angry words and ran after him.

"Wait for me! Please wait?"

Despite himself, Alex slowed his pace, allowing her to catch up to him. Again the irritation at her clawing, clutching hand on his arm rose in him, and he shuddered.

"Why? Why are you doing this to me?" panted Fiona.

" 'Tis time we went our separate ways," said Alex, weighing his words carefully as he looked straight ahead at the square patterns of light reflected on the wet pavement outside the noisy tavern. Fiona forced a laugh.

"Our separate ways? Surely not this minute in the middle of a storm?" she tried to lighten the conversation, deciding to make her entry into the common public house as dignified as she could.

Without answering her Alex pushed open the tavern door.

"Is there a private parlor?" he inquired, divesting himself of his dripping cape.

Cameron looked up at the sound of his voice and Torquil bounded to his feet and pranced over to Alex, waving his long tail in ecstasy.

"Sorry, sir, they're all in use, and sorry about the animal. I told them. Didn't I tell them?" the landlord's whining voice trailed off as Alex, seeing Cameron's wide green eyes, slowly walked toward her, leaving Fiona dripping by the door.

Everything faded. All Cameron was aware of was Alex's amber eyes locked to hers. Ian stood nervously as Alex approached, his face red with consternation. How was going to explain their presence in Edinburgh, let alone in a public saloon? What right had he to get so involved? Many excuses came into his mind but none made any sense at all. Fortunately Alex was oblivious to everything except Cameron. It did not occur to him to even wonder what she was doing where she was.

"Alex!" called Fiona in a tight hard voice, but Alex did not hear.

Ian, on seeing the petulant, half-drowned woman seething with anger, groaned, realizing there were to be serious repercussions.

"Alex?" screamed Fiona, bringing Alex down to earth and to his senses.

He turned and glared at Ian, his eyes probing and demanding answers as he pointedly ignored Fiona.

"Where's the music?" shouted Morag tipsily, awaking to the heavy silence. "I want more music. Oh, look, it's Sir Alex. Ian, why did you not tell me Sir Alex was here?"

"Aunt Morag graciously offered to chaperon Cameron," explained Ian helplessly.

Cameron, her heart beating painfully, remembered her reasons for being in Edinburgh and sat up very straight in an attempt to look fashionably bored. Fiona, furious at being so rudely snubbed, strode with great hauteur to the fireplace where she disdainfully unseated a curious student who was watching the scene in awed fascination.

"I want a brandy," she ordered of the landlord, who also strained to watch the intrigues of the gentry.

"Brandy!" he told a buxom barmaid, without letting his eyes move from the still, tense tableau around his hearth.

"Brandeee!" screeched the barmaid, waving her arm behind her to the bartender as she didn't want to miss a thing.

Alex turned and surveyed his curious audience with a withering look. The landlord shoved the barmaid, as if to reprimand her for eavesdropping and absolve himself, and the students looked away in embarrassment.

"Lady Morag!" acknowledged Alex, bowing over the robust lady's hand, "I'd like to introduce you to Lady Fiona Hurst." Fiona extended her wet glove coolly to the older woman who, knowing of her reputation, looked shocked and locked her own two hands tightly in her lap.

"Play the piano!" barked Morag, ignoring Fiona, and an old ballad began as they stared silently into the fire and the landlord served them drinks.

"Would you send someone out to hail a carriage?" asked Alex, taking the offered whiskey.

"Aye, right away, sir," nodded the publican, shuffling away.

Alex's head boiled with innumerable questions that their too-public surroundings made impossible to ask, while Fiona boiled with rage at Morag Drummond's snub and Cameron's ethereal beauty that somehow seemed enhanced by the same weather that had reduced *her* to a bedraggled, unattractive state. Her tongue ached to spit out bitter words, but she clamped it down between her teeth and contented herself with flashing smiles of pure loving devotion at Alex.

Cameron sat, her eyes burning and dry, staring into the fire. Why had she come to Edinburgh? How could she hope to compete with Lady Fiona Hurst? Alex was obviously in love with the other woman's sophisticated, worldly ways, she thought sadly.

The carriage arrived and much to Morag's disappointment they were bundled into their wet capes and ushered out. Fiona's quickness earned her a seat next to Alex as they all squashed into the small dark coach. And Cameron, firmly wedged between Ian and Morag, noted the woman's delicate hand placed carelessly on Alex's knee.

"We'll take Lady Fiona home first," decided Alex.

"No, no. The child is soaked to the skin and children take colds so easily," protested Fiona sweetly, but Alex ignored her and called out her address to the coachman.

"Isn't he considerate and loving? He's always so concerned about my health," crowed Fiona, staring at Cameron, longing to peck a hole in her seemingly serene face.

Cameron was far from serene. She felt her heart was breaking, but she kept her head high and her teeth ightly biting her inner cheeks for fear loud racking sobs would scream out of her.

The carriage stopped and, out of civility, Alex was forced to accompany Fiona to her door. Cameron watched them against her will. The front door opened and, silhouetted in the warm hall light, she saw Fiona wrap her arms around Alex's neck and kiss him. Cameron looked away, unable to bear the sight, so she did not see Alex firmly and roughly remove Fiona from him.

"Until later, darling. Don't be long," Fiona called out, as Alex returned to the carriage.

"Where to now?" he asked abruptly, and Ian gave him the name of their hotel.

"Don't be long, don't be long" clip-clopped inside Cameron's head as the weary horse plodded back to Princes Street. No other sound but the horses' hooves and the rain broke the silence. Alex impersonally handed Cameron down as a doorman ushered them into the vestibule.

Cameron dismally trod the stairs beside the babbling Morag. She yearned for the cushion of numbness she had experienced earlier that day, but the blessed relief wouldn't come. Needing to be alone with her misery she waved away the maid who hovered over her and bid a civil goodnight to Morag who, removing her wet clothes, chattered incessantly to the sleepy swaying maid.

Ian stared out of the window of his room wondering how to explain to Alex why he was escorting his wife.

"Well?" Alex asked hostilely, and Ian found himself furious. What the devil did Sinclair mean by putting him in the guilty role?

"Well *what*?" he turned, his eyes flashing.

"What the hell do you mean by 'well what'?"

"Exactly what I said," retorted Ian.

"I find my ward—"

"Wife!" interrupted Ian.

"As you wish. I find my wife in Edinburgh, in a hotel under your so-called protection, and I demand an explanation."

Ian cursed himself for his correction of Cameron's relationship to Alex.

"What is it to you? Does not seem to be your concern *where* she is as long as she's not inconveniencing your philandering!" Ian blasted.

Alex felt the low blow and his own rage ignited.

"What I do and don't do is none of your concern," he countered.

"Unfortunately you are correct—socially correct, that is. But humanely you are . . ."

"I am what?" Alex's nostrils flared dangerously.

"Cruel and insensitive!" blurted Ian. "But I stand corrected. I should not have brought your wife here to be further humiliated, and I shall remedy the situation and return her to Glen Aucht in the morning, unless you'd prefer me to dispatch her right now?"

"I am quite capable of handling my own affairs," stated Alex.

"So I am well aware," quipped Ian with a sarcastic laugh.

The two men glared at each other in the tense silence, and then Alex turned abruptly on his heel and quit the room. Ian stood a moment longer staring at the roughly slammed door before sitting heavily into a chair as rage pulsated through his entire body.

Chapter Twenty

Alex stormed out of the hotel into the wet night. He walked the empty streets muttering to himself furiously. Damn Ian Drummond! The man's audacity went beyond the limits! How could a trusted friend suddenly just turn coat?

Alex's anger was further fanned by the realization that he couldn't demand satisfaction by calling Ian out, as it would make public his marriage to Cameron. He cursed himself for giving Ian the very weapon that tied his hands. Why had he confessed to his marriage? After an hour Alex's rage ebbed, leaving him drained and frustrated. Morning had not yet lightened the sky or his dark brooding thoughts.

What was he going to do? He'd not have Cameron under Ian's protection, for if the news of his marriage did leak out, and it probably would if Ian's actions were any indication of his honor, he, Alex Sinclair, would be a laughing stock—a cuckold! At the thought of Cameron in Ian's arms his anger was renewed. What was he doing walking the cold wet streets while Ian and Cameron were snug at a hotel? He'd return and take what was his. For a moment his mind planned to use Morag as a chaperon but, not wishing the braying woman under his roof, he swiftly rejected the idea. Damn it! Wasn't Cameron his wife?

Alex stopped under a street lamp. Aye, she was his wife whether she wanted to be or not, and it was about time she started acting like it. After all, hadn't she been the one responsible for his entrapment? He resumed walking briskly toward the hotel, feeling triumphant. He would collect what was his. To hell with convention of bans and public announcements and what people thought. Didn't Cameron herself deny them all?

Disregarding the hour and his disheveled appearance he strode noisily into the hotel and loudly rang the bell. The desk clerk slept, cushioning his head on the large register which Alex violently swept out from under him, causing bone to hit wood with a sharp crack.

"Hey, hey! What's a'going on?" protested the stunned clerk, leaping to his feet and prancing like a boxer with his fists prepared. But Alex was already taking the stairs three at a time.

"What's going on?" inquired another voice, as several nightgowned members of the hotel staff shuffled sleepily into the vestibule.

"Madman went up that way. Big, rough, wild man," pointed the desk clerk excitedly.

Alex burst into Cameron's room to find her bed empty. He noted her clothes hung neatly, her shoes in a line underneath, and her reticule was with her cape on a chair. He opened the door to the connecting room where Morag snored happily. There was no sign of Cameron. Cursing out loud he stormed out, pushing the cluster of curious whispering people aside as he purposefully strode to Ian's room.

Ian was asleep in a chair by the dead fire.

"Where is she?" Alex demanded, pulling the dazed man to his feet by his shirt collar.

Ian looked at him in confusion and Alex dropped him back into his chair, then stormed to the bed. He ripped back the covers.

"Where is she?"

"Who?" Ian tried to raise his heavy lids.

"Cameron."

"Probably fast asleep in her own room."

Alex gave him a sneer and wrenched open the armoire.

"She isn't in her room?" ventured Ian, trying to clear his sleepy brain.

"Dinna play the innocent with me!" he bellowed.

Ian shrugged helplessly as Alex continued to search the room.

"Where's the dog?" asked Ian, hoping to put Alex's suspicions to better use.

Alex looked at him sharply and let out his breath with a hiss. He opened the door and, ignoring the crowd of people who stood there, whistled.

"Fergus is here," informed Ian, when they heard no answering bark.

"So you're stealing my servants too! That takes the cake!" ejaculated Alex.

" 'Twas his idea, not mine," retorted Ian.

"Where is he?" demanded Alex.

"The stables."

"The stables? The man's no common groom!"

Ian resorted to a shrug, not willing to be put on the defensive.

"Where are the stables?" Alex asked roughly of the people who choked the hotel corridor.

"Sir, we must ask you to leave, as you are disturbing our guests. This is a respectable establishment," ventured a brave little man in a ridiculous nightcap, but Alex pushed by him and strode purposefully to the stairs.

Followed by the white-clothed group that mumbled reproaches and waved fists, Alex made his way out into the wet night and, seeing a small muddy lane with the evidence of horses, assumed correctly the direction to the stables.

Fergus sat on a bale of hay, cushioning Cameron's head as she slept; Torquil was curled at their feet. The old man looked up at the ruckus and smiled at the sight of his master's tall figure surrounded by an indignant mob. Looks like a bunch of geese with their feathers ruffled, he thought. Alex stood, his feet apart, too charged with rage, liquor, and adrenalin to be touched by the sleeping girl.

"Is our carriage here?" he demanded.

"Nay, we used Sir Ian's," replied Fergus softly.

"Ready it!" snapped Alex, wishing he'd had the foresight to have hired a hack.

Fergus touched his cap servilely and smiled wryly.

"This should pay for my wife's stay," barked Alex, pulling out a wad of bills.

The murmurs and threats around were replaced by gasps and a few giggles.

"Which one of you is responsible here?" demanded Alex, out of patience.

"I am, sir," stated the little man in the nightcap.

"I should like my wife's things packed and sent to my address. I am Sir Alexander Sinclair."

A few more gasps, giggles, and frantic whispers issued from the crowd.

"Aye, sir, I'll see it done. The rest of you get back to

your beds. Morning's near and there'll be time enough tomorrow for your gossiping," ordered the pompous little man. "Barley and Ross, help with the carriage."

Cameron found herself roughly snatched from the comfort of sleep. Her exhausted, emotion-drained body screamed, but the hum of voices and a strange jolting awoke her. She stared up and saw Alex's firmly set jaw and her confused mind tried to grasp the situation. She remembered leaving her room with Torquil, determined to get Fergus to help her return to Glen Aucht. She recalled him telling her that there was no way across the firth until morning, and his deep gentle voice broke down the dam against the tears that ached to be released. Her last recollection was of being rocked in Fergus's arms.

But now? She tried to get her bearings. It was still night and she was being carried by Alex. Just as she had realized that much, she was thrown like a heap of old rags into a cold place that smelled of damp leather. She pulled herself up to a sitting position and stared out of the window at the throng of improperly dressed people who giggled and whispered. Alex got in beside her and slammed the door, and the carriage started amid cheers and whistles.

Ian watched from the shelter of the lobby. He was relieved that Cameron had been found and yet worried about her safety as he seriously questioned his former friend's sanity.

Cameron sat in the jolting coach, aware of Alex's angry eyes boring into her. She didn't know what to say and so said nothing. Was it worth putting to the test all she had so painstakingly learned? she thought miserably. She raised her head haughtily, realizing that at least it would be a way of protecting her vulnerable feelings, and stared at him in an extremely bored way.

At her look of disdain, Alex momentarily forgot his rage. Who the hell did she think she was to look down her nose at him in that manner? He matched her bored look with a steely stare.

"Well, madam?"

"I beg your pardon?" replied Cameron coldly, with a brittle, almost-English accent.

"And so you should," remarked Alex.

Cameron wasn't sure how a lady would answer that, so she gave an arch look and ignored him.

"You will have the courtesy of looking at me when I am addressing you," he ordered, and Cameron's heart beat wildly.

"Oh? Were you addressing me, my lord?" she inquired politely.

Alex wanted to reach out and brutally shake her icy composure. He did not like this hard, polite exterior; he longed for her green eyes to flash rebelliously and her mouth to spit out her rage, and he was determined to goad her into the hotblooded Cameron he preferred. He insulted her with his eyes, letting them languidly linger as he appraised her.

"I see you've taken to wearing shoes, my lady," he remarked witheringly. "Do you also wear petticoats and drawers now?"

"Don't be impertinent!" snapped Cameron, imitating the dowager Drummond's quavery indignation.

Alex collapsed with laughter.

"Do that again," he begged, when he was able to speak, but mirth bubbled over again and he lay back with tears of merriment pouring down his face.

Cameron froze. All her diligent training had been futile. She wasn't well-bred and sophisticated, she was an object of ridicule. She forced her aching eyes to the darkness outside.

Fergus smiled with satisfaction hearing Alex's untrammeled laughter. He hummed merrily as he halted the horses outside Alex's townhouse. Still choked with laughter Alex leaped from the carriage and held out his hand to Cameron, but she kept him waiting as she pretended to fasten her cape, not trusting herself. She wanted to fly at him, punching and clawing the mocking face. Alex turned to Fergus and gave him a long look.

"There's much you have to explain, but it can wait for the morning," he growled, not seeing Cameron alight unaided and mount the front steps. His hand was still outstretched to assist Cameron and, annoyed, he turned to see why she was taking so long and found the carriage empty. His heart skipped a beat. My God, has she taken it into her silly head to run into this cutthroat city? He panicked before catching sight of her waiting quietly at the front door.

"That was very uncivil of you," he snapped coldly, as he opened the door.

"I beg your pardon," returned Cameron frigidly, as she stepped into the warm hallway.

The housekeeper bustled up, still in her nightgown.

"Sorry, sir, but I figured you weren't coming home, it being nearly morning and all," she said, and her eyes widened at the sight of Cameron. She had heard some stories about her master's wild ways, but he'd never brought one of his doxies to his house before.

"Go back to bed, Mrs. Wilson," ordered Alex, as he propelled Cameron toward the stairs.

"But, sir?" gasped Mrs. Wilson in a scandalized tone.

"What?" roared Alex in such a quelling voice that the flustered woman painfully entangled her fingers in the housekeys chain.

"Nothing, sir," she stammered, as they disappeared up the stairs.

Alex flung open the door of the master bedroom and, as Cameron hesitated, he firmly pushed the small of her back so she was forced to step inside. The door was slammed loudly behind her and Cameron stood still, noting the large bed with no excitement whatsoever. Now she was where she had so often fantasized being, with Alex whom she ached for with all her heart, and yet all she felt was cold fear.

Alex sat on his bed pulling off his boots and watching her with a strange smile.

"Well?" he asked softly, suddenly feeling drained and awkward.

"I want my dog," said Cameron, realizing that she didn't know where Torquil was.

"Drat that infernal animal!" he exclaimed, throwing his boots violently across the room. Cameron's knees shook at his burst of anger, and she leaned back against the door to steady herself. Alex wished she'd fight him instead of cowering.

"Oh, Cameron," he whispered sadly, aching to hold her and somehow win her confidence.

"I have not given you leave to address me by my given name," she replied distantly in a cold, clipped voice, as she desperately resorted to one of her hard-learned phrases to stop herself from flinging herself on his lap to be enclosed by his strong arms.

Alex looked at her with undisguised horror.

"I'm in no mood for fencing, madam," he said tersely, and pulled the bell chord.

Cameron stood silently, her heart beating triple time as Alex ignored her and removed his coat and shirt. A sharp knock reverberated through her spine and she stood quickly away from the door.

"Enter!" barked Alex, and a uniformed maid stood there with her mouth open, shocked at seeing Cameron alone in her master's bedchamber, the man himself near naked.

"Show the lady to a room," ordered Alex, savagely underlining the word "lady."

"Very good, sir," bobbed the maid. "Which one, sir?"

"Does not matter, any with a bed," retorted Alex impatiently.

"Very good, sir. Come this way, miss."

Alex fell into a deep, dreamless sleep as soon as his head touched the pillow.

Cameron sat alone in a strange room after suffering the impudent, suggestive remarks of the maid when she told her there was no luggage.

Fergus, renewing his acquaintance with the townhouse staff, firmly rebuffed and reprimanded both the housekeeper and the upstairs maid for their slurs on Cameron's reputation. It was a hopeless task as he was unable to divulge the secret marriage. He finally took himself off to bed in a rage when the saucy, spiteful creatures answered him back with jeering laughter. He left them even more convinced that Cameron was a whore, as without chaperon or baggage what else could she be?

Alex slept until three in the afternoon and, remembering his appointment with Dougal Gunn, shaved, dressed, and rapidly left the house with Fergus.

Cameron dozed fitfully in a chair by the cold fire. She was awakened by a footman entering without ceremony to dump her trunk in the room and walk out with a suggestive leer. She sat, still fully clothed, watching three giggling maids unpack and hang her garments. They made unsavory remarks to each other and snorted rudely behind their hands.

"Bet she had to bounce a lot to get this one," snickered one girl, holding a gown against her and swirling around.

"Had to do more than bounce, I reckon," answered another, digging a bony elbow into her friend's ribs.

"I'd like a job I could lie down on," sputtered the third, and they all blew raspberries through their fingers as mocking laughter spurted from their loose lips.

Cameron vaguely understood, recognizing the spitefulness of the barbs more than their inferences. She longed to ask them to leave but she was afraid her voice would crack uncertainly, so she remained silent until the cocky girls left.

Cameron did not know what to do. She longed to change her clothes but was loath to be caught uncovered and vulnerable by the servants who burst in without knocking.

Mrs. Wilson popped her head around the door and stared at the small, white-faced girl, still dressed in the heavy outdoor clothes. Her eyes took in the tidy bed.

"You been sitting there all night?" she snapped, assuming she didn't need to be deferential to a little trollop who looked as young as her own daughter— except her Louise was a good girl. Cameron didn't answer. Snotty little tart, Mrs. Wilson fumed. Who does she think she is? How dare she look down her nose at me?

"Humph!" she snorted, and turned to leave.

"Please? Please, is Fergus here?"

"Fergus, is it? Mr. MacDonald to you, it is. No, he ain't here. He went off with the master."

"Do you know where my dog is?"

"Murderous looking beast, if you ask me. He's out in the stables with the other animals. I ain't having no mangy, flea-ridden curs in my clean house. This is a respectable establishment, I'll have you know," carped

Mrs. Wilson. She slammed out of the room, spouting a stream of abuse as she went through the house. Cameron heard the many adjectives and epithets used to describe herself as the story and the servant's indignation at her presence grew. "Whore, harlot, Lilith, Jezebel, tart, trollop, guttersnipe—" the list was endless. Cameron's ears burned and she longed to flee with Torquil, away from the sharp voices that wouldn't stop tormenting her.

A loud hammering at the front door quieted the cruel chatter.

"Oh, they'll be sparks a'flying now," chortled a low voice, as a cluster of upstairs maids peeked through the bannister at Lady Fiona Hurst in the front hall.

Fiona had been sitting outside Alex's townhouse in an enclosed carriage, debating with herself whether to return home or demand to see Alex. All night she'd tossed and turned, hearing his voice telling her they should go their separate ways. She had seen Cameron's trunk carried into the house and her blood had boiled, knowing instinctively whose possessions were being brought in. She had to speak with Alex.

Fiona knocked and the door was opened by the housekeeper, Mrs. Wilson, who violently disapproved of Lady Fiona.

"Yes?" snapped Mrs. Wilson.

"Is Sir Alex at home?" asked Fiona sweetly, smiling at the thin, frowning face.

"No, he ain't," retorted Mrs. Wilson, ready to slam the door.

"But there is a young lady here, is there not?"

"Lady? Hah! If that's what you call a snooty young snippet with no chaperon!" exclaimed the housekeeper.

Cameron heard the footsteps ascending the stairs and approaching her door. She held her breath, somehow knowing the worst was yet to come. There was a sharp knock and the door was abruptly opened.

Fiona shut the door behind her and leaned back on it as she stared coldly at Cameron, who forced herself to sit tall and straight.

"You stupid little fool," Fiona spat, after a long pause. "Sitting here waiting to fling yourself at a full-grown man who you're nothing but an encumbrance to."

Cameron stiffened her neck. " 'Tis none of your business," she breathed, her throat painfully constricted.

" 'Tis my business. He loves me and I love him. Since he has known you, he has changed. Oh, not in his love for me but in his happiness. You cling to him like a parasite, draining him of everything as you pretend to be a helpless child, tormenting him with your cloying dependency until he doesn't know which way to turn. You drove him and his friends from Glen Aucht. You made it impossible for him to be at his country home, and now you are here driving him out of another," Fiona ranted, firmly believing everything she flung at Cameron.

"I didn't ask to leave Cape Wrath," defended the girl.

"Did he ask you to come to Edinburgh? Well, did he?" pressed Fiona.

Cameron silently shook her head.

"You made it impossible for him to stay at Glen Aucht, didn't you?"

Cameron stared at her without speaking.

"Did you know Alex had invited us all there for four days of shooting?" demanded Fiona.

Again Cameron shook her head.

"And you made sure we left after one night's stay. You drove the poor man from the peace of his own home. He came here to get rid of you, but here you sit as calm as you please. Well, it *is* my business! I have seen Alex Sinclair change from a happy contented man to a tormented and cruel monster, and you are to blame," accused Fiona, ready to do battle. To her surprise Cameron stood up quietly.

"You are right, Lady Fiona. 'Tis your business and I am to blame," Cameron acknowledged. "I see how wrong and stupid I was. Will you help me get away?"

Fiona frowned warily. What trick was the skinny chit up to now?

"Where will you go?"

"Back home to Cape Wrath, but I need a horse and some coins to exchange for food," stammered Cameron, hating herself for begging for Fiona's help.

Fiona's rage diminished and consternation took its place. As much as she hated the younger girl she didn't relish having her death on her conscience. Winter was setting in and the long trip alone to the north would be suicidal. It's a ruse to get my sympathy, Fiona decided, and her eyes narrowed.

"Have you no kin nearer?" she asked.

"I have no kin at all," replied Cameron.

"Frasers abound. Some must be of some relationship?" retorted Fiona impatiently.

"Sir Alex just called me that because I have no other name but Cameron," confessed the girl frankly.

"A bastard? You are a bastard!" Fiona screeched, her fears of Alex considering a marriage to Cameron suddenly dispelled. "You are more of an encumbrance to poor Alex than I realized," she chuckled. "Oh, how I'll tease him when we next romp together."

Cameron heard the word that Mara had spat with new meaning. She had been a stupid fool, as Fiona had stated. How could she really have expected Sir Alexander Sinclair to fall in love with a bastard? No wonder he was so infuriated and kept their marriage a secret.

"You will help me then?" she asked the still-laughing Fiona.

"Nay. I'll give you money but that's the end of it. The other things you'll have to get for yourself, but beware: They hang horse thieves," said Fiona, throwing a handful of coins onto the bed. "Leave after I have gone." And with that she whisked herself out of the room and down the stairs, calling out very cheerful good-byes to the servants.

Chapter Twenty-one

Alex tooled his horses, not saying a word to Fergus, who sat impassively beside him. He masterfully guided the steeds through the narrow busy streets until reaching the outskirts of the city, where he gave them their heads.

"What do you mean by coming here with Drummond and the girl without my orders?" he asked curtly.

"She needed a friend," stated Fergus cryptically, after a lengthy silence.

"Good God, man! Anyone would think she'd been thrown to the wolves!" ejaculated Alex.

"Aye," agreed Fergus.

"Who told you to bring her?" Alex snapped, ignoring Fergus's obvious impertinence.

"The lass."

"Who do you take orders from?" raged Alex.

"My heart, I suppose, when it comes down to it."

"Aye, but does it pay you?" retorted Alex coldly.

"Aye. One way or t'other."

Three miles passed and not a word was said.

"Fergus?" said Alex softly, the old man's silence burning into him.

"Aye?"

"Why did she want to come?" Slowing the pace of his horses Alex stared at the lined weathered face he'd known all his life. Fergus didn't answer, he just stared into the amber eyes he'd first seen tinged with cloudy blue from his mother's womb. He remembered Alex as a small toddling boy full to the brim with whys, but this was a full-grown man now asking, and he looked away knowing it would be easy to answer, yet also that it wasn't for him to say.

"You'll not tell me?"

"Nay," replied Fergus.

Alex, frustrated by the answer, urged his horses back to a bruising pace.

"I met a man by the name of Dougal Gunn last night. That's who we're going to see. He's an old friend of Duncan's and seems to know of Cameron. Do you know of him?"

"Aye," replied Fergus, his eyes not leaving the road.

"What do you know of him?"

"Good man," answered Fergus noncommittedly.

"Have to pry answers from you like winkles from their shell," snorted Alex.

"Aye."

"You are angry with me?"

"Aye."

"Why?"

" 'Taint my place, Sir Alex," replied Fergus, closing his mouth in a hard, firm line. Alex, recognizing the resolute look, respected the silence.

They arrived at Dougal Gunn's modest cottage half an hour late, but they were greeted by the spry old man as he jumped down from his own carriage, full of apologies for his own lateness.

"Fergus MacDonald!" Dougal chortled with glee, wringing his hand.

"Aye, Dougal," smiled Fergus.

Dougal stepped back and surveyed Fergus's lean leathery figure.

"You're looking good. Hah! Takes a lot to kill off us old Highlanders, don't it?"

"Aye," replied Fergus.

"See you're as talkative as ever," laughed Dougal.

"Aye."

"We fought side by side," Dougal explained to Alex, as he led them up the garden path, slapping Fergus affectionately on the back. "He never spoke unless he had something to say. It should be you teaching the young lads, Fergus. They're all too full of hot, empty words."

They entered the small house and Fergus and Alex had to stoop through the low doorframe.

"Goodie? Goodie?" called out Dougal, and a tiny round woman trotted into the room.

"What'll you have? Tea? Hate the miserable stuff myself. Or something stronger?"

Alex opted for whiskey and Fergus declined altogether by shaking his head and following the little round woman to the kitchen.

"Where are you going, Fergus MacDonald?" asked Dougal.

"That way," answered Fergus, disappearing.

"Great old man," said Dougal, looking after him. "Have you known him long?"

"All my life," answered Alex, wondering which old man was older. He was impatient to get to the business of Cameron, but he bided his time staring around at the warm, cluttered room, noting the piles of scribbled pages and books that balanced precariously on every available surface.

"Sit down, sit down. I'm not one for formalities." chirped Dougal. "Now, where were we? Ha, whiskey wasn't it?"

"Aye."

"Here you are, then," said Dougal, pouring a very generous amount, which Alex took apprehensively as he remembered he'd not eaten since the previous night.

"Now, where were we? Ha! Right. Here's tae us!" he toasted, and looked through the glass speculatively. "You've eyes the same color as the whiskey, lad. Deceptive. Sometimes warming, yet can cut to the heart," he chuckled, and took a healthy swig. "Aah! Hits the spot."

Alex politely sipped his drink, wondering how to approach the subject.

"Duncan Fraser, sir?" he ventured.

"Aye, terrible blow to hear he's gone. They'll be none of us left soon. We were all so young and now mostly old or gone," mused the old man, taking another gulp of his drink.

"You mentioned a child?" coached Alex.

"Did I, now? Must have been in my cups."

Alex stared at Dougal in amazement.

"I dinna think you were drunk, sir. You clearly mentioned a child."

"I've a running mouth when the whiskey's in me," chortled Dougal, refusing to meet Alex's eyes.

"A child with raven-black hair, bright green eyes, having a horse and hound named for the MacLeod twins?" pursued Alex, determined to get some reaction from the stubborn old man. He was gratified to see the gnarled hands tighten on the whiskey glass as if to snap it, and yet Dougal did not look at him or answer. The silence was long and heavy, metered out by three old unsynchronized clocks.

"Such spirit. Och, aye, such glorious spirit, did my heart good to see such spirit. If only there were more like them, our Scotland could rise like the phoenix out of the ashes," reminisced Dougal.

"Them?" puzzled Alex. The old man came sharply to reality, pursing his lips tightly as though he didn't trust his own mouth.

Alex felt anger and frustration rise up in him. What was happening? Obviously Dougal Gunn did not trust him. He leaned back in his chair, sipping his drink in silence and feeling the old man's eyes sharply raking him. He forced himself to appear calm as he idly scanned the small room.

"Fergus MacDonald? Fergus, get your old bones in here!" roared Dougal.

After a pause Fergus entered.

"Aye?"

"I need your counsel. Sit you down and have a wee drop," he directed, pouring a glass.

"What do you know of this lad?" he asked Fergus, when he'd found an unencumbered place to squeeze himself.

Fergus pursed his lips in contemplation as he looked at Alex.

"Still got some growing to do," he concluded.

"Don't we all?" chortled Dougal.

"Aye. Some more than others," replied Fergus.

"Times are a'changing," lamented Dougal.

"Aye."

"Remember 'the fifteen'?"

"Aye."

Oh, no! groaned Alex! The two old men were now going to reminisce about their past battles against the English.

"Dinna groan, laddie," snapped Dougal, pouncing on the barely perceptible sound. "Open your head and listen.'Twas 1718 when I went to Spain with Duncan and Donald MacLeod. Strange country, Spain. I was there for four months and it dinna rain once. Can you believe that? We went for help from the Spanish to get James, the old pretender, on the throne of Scotland where he belonged. Well, Donald MacLeod ups and marries hisself to a senorita, and when all came to naught in 1719, he ups and hides hisself away from his father's wrath at Dunvegan, on Skye. The MacLeods had planned his marrying a MacKenzie, thinking to increase their boundaries, and in he walks with his senorita. You listening, lad?"

Alex was frankly totally disinterested in the MacLeods and their past problems.

"What has that to do with now?" he asked impatiently.

"If you're not of the patience to find out, I'll save my breath," snapped Dougal.

There was silence as the old man poured himself more whiskey and took a large sip.

"Now, Donald MacLeod was a strange lad. Oh, away from his family on the battlefield he was braw—he could not only defy his father but his whole Hanoverian clan by fighting the English—but near his sire he turned to a

wee shivering bairn, pissing his trews and stammering
something fierce. 'Twas sad to see. Did you know him,
Fergus?"

"Aye," answered Fergus with a frown. "Mrs. Mac-
Donald come from Skye—MacLeod land."

"How is your dear woman?" inquired Dougal, much
to Alex's frustration. Fergus smiled and nodded.

"Good. Ha! We're itching young Sinclair's pants
something awful, ain't we now?" remarked Dougal,
and both old men laughed.

Alex forced himself to relax, reminding himself that
old men's ramblings had to be endured.

"Well, now, where was I? Ha, right. MacLeod weren't
a very strong man. Oh, he was full of himself and
good in a battle against the English, but against his
father he couldna defend hisself. I think he wanted to
be dragged home with his tail between his legs, else
why did he hide hisself on Skye, eh?" asked Dougal.

Alex shrugged. How was he supposed to know the answer?

"Skye is MacLeod land, lad. Of all of Scotland to
hide hisself, he hid in his own garden so to speak.

"Och, aye, that Donald MacLeod was a paradox all
right. Well, his old man, on hearing all the talk of his
heir marrying a Spanish papist, come a'thundering
from Lewes to Skye, and puir Donald fled on a fishing boat to France. But his wee wife was too far gone
with child, and not carrying too well, being scarce fourteen years old and not full-grown. Well, he left her behind, hoping the lass would have a boy and old
MacLeod would weaken at the sight of a grandson. But,
it weren't meant to be. The bairn was a girl and he
wanted nothing to do with her. Maybe 'twas all for the
good that the little senorita died giving life. She spoke
not a word of our tongue. Imagine yourself alone in a
strange country with no one to converse with, still a

child, and pregnant to boot, you'd be more'n a wee bit sad, now, wouldna you?"

"But this was 1719?" questioned Alex. The child certainly could not have been Cameron.

"Dinna ruffle yer brain; it'll constipate yer gray matter," growled Dougal. "I'll tell what has to be told in my own way. Seeing as how the MacLeods wouldna recognize the wee bairn as kin, Duncan and I decided to take the babby to Spain, to her poor dead mother's people. 'Twas more'n forty years ago and we were immortal lads, I can tell you. Forty years! Och, how time gets a'gobbled up, don't it Fergus?"

"Aye."

Dougal and Fergus nodded sadly, thinking of their departed youth as they sipped at their whiskey. Alex forced himself to be patient.

"Well, the Spanish were no better than the rest of the so-called civilized world and wanted no part of the puir wee un, feeling the mixing of blood and religion was a sin unless territories were joined or gained. That's a stupid sadness, ain't it, now?"

"Aye," murmured Fergus.

"So Duncan Fraser and I decided to become fathers to the child, both of us deciding against ever marrying. We payed a good woman to tend her, and when she was of an age of reason, about eight or nine, put her in a convent in France. We visited her when we could, and she grew to be a bonny lass. We were young men and didn't know no better, still having a might of growing to do ourselves. A might of thinking would have done us more good. Being good Catholics and Highlanders we felt a convent in France the best place for our little ward, away from the strife of Scotland, where religion was changed according to who was ruling. Duncan and I had killed to remain true Catholics. We were fervent because the English told us not to be.

We were fervent because the Protestant lowlanders and Hanoverians told us not to be, because we were what our fathers had been before us and before that and before that." Dougal stopped and took a long drink to calm himself.

"Do you ken? We weren't Catholic because we chose to be?"

"I don't quite understand."

"A man should decide for himself, not just settle, accepting what was chosen for him. We made a mistake with our wee Dolores. That's what we named her. Like dour lass, means sadness. Well, nature took her course and Dolores grew up and took out of that convent bursting with life after being incarcerated in that stifling, stilted place." Dougal stopped sadly for a moment.

"Do you know what happens, lad, when you wrap a living spirit up too tight?" he asked.

"You can break it," murmured Alex, thinking of Cameron.

"Aye, you can stifle it so even when you unwrap it, it stays wrapped with all the emotions and life trapped inside. Or it can explode as you unwrap it. Do you ken? Same with people and countries."

"Aye," nodded Alex, staring into the old eyes that beseeched his understanding.

"Well, our wee Dorores exploded. Bang! One minute a subdued little novice, and the next the most outrageous experienced woman of the world. We heard tales of her various conquests in every court on the continent, from Frederick II's of Prussia to his arch enemy's, René Louis de Voyer de Paulmy, le Marquis d'Argenson, but we dinna see her again until 1744. We were in France organizing the invasion to get the bonnie prince on the throne, and who comes in on our Charlie's arm, but none other than our wild Dolores.

She dinna look well, and Duncan and I felt very dolorous for our Dolores, scarce twenty-five and looking much more. After the forty-five and our hopes were ground into Culloden Moor, our bodies were not young anymore, and we knew we were mortal. That's the end of youth. You can be as old as Methuselah and still be young if you can retain your immortality. Have you seen the old faces of the very young bairns in the pits? They've lost their immortality and been robbed of their youth." Dougal's voice trailed away, lost in sadness again for departed youth.

"What of Duncan's wild child?" asked Fergus, to Alex's surprise, as he noticed the usually noncommittal face was alive with earnest interest.

"Wild, free bairns! Och, Duncan was right and I was wrong, but at least I got to tell him that," mused Dougal.

"Bairns?" ejaculated Alex.

"How was he right?" probed Fergus at the same instant. Dougal shook his head angrily. He banged his glass, muttering to himself before composing himself.

"Duncan claimed 'twas best to raise the bairn free, without reins, and I, being the teacher, naturally disagreed."

"But you said 'bairns'?" repeated Alex firmly. Dougal turned his back on the young man and addressed Fergus.

"'Tis strange and uncomfortable to me, Fergus, realizing I can spill my life, hopes, and sorrows and they all fit into a small amount of time and space. Yet they echo in that vast infinity inside myself."

"Aye, I ken," growled Fergus, his own face mirroring the aching he saw in Dougal's.

"Well, back to it. After Culloden, Duncan and I hid in France for two years, and when the hue and cry had died down a bit we returned to Scotland to go our separate ways. He to exile himself at Cape Wrath, me to keep fighting—or so I fooled myself at the time—by keeping Scotland alive in the minds of the young, even though we were oppressed and repressed by the English. Och, but many times in the last twelve years I went up to Cape Wrath, needing a rest from the apathetic youth around."

Alex sat forward impatiently as the old man stopped and drank more whiskey. Alex was afraid he'd soon be too drunk to make sense.

"Duncan lived in that great heap of cold stones with that crazy, grasping Mara woman. Irish she must have been, wailing away like a banshee. Hated the black-haired wild child, she did."

"But where was the child from?" urged Alex, feeling great pain at the old man's circuitous rambling.

"Hold yer horses, I'm a'getting there. 'Twas just before we left France, We'd searched high and low for our Dolores, and then we received a message from the sisters at the convent that she was dying. The puir lass was dead before we arrived, but she was a mother, having given birth two years before."

"In 1746? Same year as Culloden?" questioned Alex eagerly, remembering Cameron's assertion of the year she was born.

"Aye. Well, Duncan swore that the church, that had caused our Dolores to rage, should not bind her offspring. We stole the wee un away from the nuns and he hid him on the island of North Rona."

"What a sad spot for a bairn, nothing but barren rock for seals and gulls," remarked Fergus.

"Him?" exclaimed Alex.

"If yer'd stop your interruptions and let me speak! Now, where was I?" snapped Dougal.

"North Rona," prompted Fergus.

"Aye, that's where he hid him."

"Why?" asked Alex.

"He was afraid of harm coming to the child."

"From some French nuns?" laughed Alex.

"Drat my undisciplined tongue!" raged Dougal, and he waved his hands in frustration. "Och, how do I know why he hid them! You know how it is with old men stuck alone with painful memories. We get old and embittered with strange fancies. I dinna ken why he hid them—him!"

He said "them" again, mused Alex, but knowing he'd just aggravate the old man further, he changed tacks.

"Why name the child Cameron?" he questioned.

"A name's a name! What would you have him name the lad?"

"Cameron is a lass, Dougal," remarked Fergus.

"Nay, not so. Wore the kilt, did my eyes good to see, and rode that great stallion like the young warrior he was," argued Dougal.

"Why the horse and hound named for the MacLeod twins?" pursued Fergus.

"Duncan's weird humor, no doubt. Probably had the wicked thought to send the lad to tease his relatives in Lewes or enlist his help if things came to pass," answered Dougal.

"What things?" queried Alex.

"There it goes running away from me again!" shouted Dougal, smacking himself hard across the lips. "How should I know what things? Och, sometimes I thought Duncan Fraser had gone mad! Acting like the walls had eyes and ears, and 'tis no wonder. That place would rob any of sanity. You should have seen it!"

"I did. Duncan called me to Cape Wrath as he lay dying to make me guardian of the lass, Cameron."

"And 'tis a lass, you say?"

"Aye, Dougal, a right bonnie lass," nodded Fergus.

"Why, that conniving old fox! He dinna even trust me, his oldest, closest friend," snorted Dougal.

"But why name the child Cameron?" repeated Alex. " 'Tis a clan name and surely not arbitrary?"

"Is it any less arbitrary than Mary, Jeannie, or Jane? or Aye, Bee, or Cee? or One, Two, or Three? Isna one name as good as another? Why? Why? Why?" railed Dougal.

"But Mary Cameron or Jeannie Cameron would have made more sense than just Cameron," hammered Alex.

"I dinna ken, I dinna ken. Cameron . . . Cam O' Rona . . . come from Rona? Farfetched, but no more so than the reason you're called what you are," struggled the old man.

"Unless Cameron is her father's name?" added Alex. Dougal crashed his glass on the table with such violence it smashed.

"You'll never ask that! Never ever ask that! 'Tis the past and you'll trust me without question, you ken? 'Tis a matter of life and death. I repeat, *life and death*! Let the past rest in peace with Duncan or there'll be blood on your hands, and it won't be just the blood of the bairns, but 'twill be Scotland's."

Dougal lay back spent in his chair among his books. His eyes seemed to stare sadly back through history. Alex noted how the old could appear so young, with smooth pink cheeks and fluffy-white, baby-fine hair.

"How old was Cameron when Duncan brought her from North Rona to Cape Wrath?" he asked gently.

"The age of reason. About eight. Where is the bairn?"

"With me in Edinburgh."

"Must seem strange after the freedom of the moors."

"Aye," Fergus tersely spat.

"Maybe I wasna wrong after all. Duncan's way was

only right if the child remained wild and free, like Scotland herself, and there's no way to be so in this day and age, I'm thinking."

"I'll bring her to see you," smiled Alex.

"Nay, I'll remember. I'd not like to see a proud young spirit harnessed. 'Tis the past. Just keep the bairns safe, as there are many who'd wish them dead. Now go and give me peace." And with that, Dougal closed his eyes and waved them out.

Chapter Twenty-two

Cameron knew she had to leave Alex's home and protection as quickly as possible. Everything that Fiona had flung at her dovetailed into all she'd felt and experienced, leaving her no doubt as to the truth of it. She'd be dependent on no one. Her innate pride and dignity had suffered greatly, and she grew angry and winced, seeing herself as she imagined she appeared. She had become everything she detested. Oh, why hadn't she been left alone to ride freely on the moors, where she hurt no one and had been impervious to hurt herself? Even as her mind raged, she felt a sharp pang, knowing part of her—beyond her control—had been bound to Alex. She'd rid herself of it, she vowed. No one would bind her spirit and take her freedom again.

She sat summoning up the courage to open the door and brave the servants. She planned to walk down the stairs with as much dignity as she could muster, but how could she with her hands clutching the coins that Fiona had thrown so disdainfully at her? Her eyes scanned the room, frantically seeking something to wrap the coins in so they didn't go spilling and clinking as she made her escape. She quietly removed a pillowcase and put the money in, tying it firmly so the coins did not clank together. That accomplished, she stared around and realized all her possessions were there. Her mind was so frantic she couldn't think or see straight. She forced herself to breathe steadily to calm herself and then systematically rummaged through her armoire and trunks. She found her riding boots and quickly changed out of the low shoes she'd worn since dinner the night before. She had to find something more appropriate than the creased evening gown she was wearing. The red riding habit. That's right, she'd say she was going riding. She leaned against the door as she changed, so that anyone trying to get in would have to push hard, giving her warning.

Finally dressed she rummaged through the bottom of her trunk and found her saddlebag. She sat still, fingering the bloodstains, thinking sadly of her horse Torquod. The bag bulged and looking in it she found her kilt and plaid, dirk and book. Many memories flooded her mind and she saw Alex's amber eyes. He *had* kept her few precious treasures safe for her. Why? Cameron held back the painful aching that filled her and resolutely stuffed her pillowcase of coins into the saddlebag and stood. She hardened her face and stared at herself in the looking glass. Satisfied with the set of her jaw and her look of quelling disdain she purposefully opened the door.

Cameron saw no one as she descended the stairs with her head held straight and proud. She heard furtive giggles and whispers, but she kept her eyes directed straight in front of her, not turning until she reached the hallway. Where were the stables, she wondered frantically. Noticing a bell cord, she pulled it, forcing herself to look bored and aristocratic as she waited.

"Well?" The skinny housekeeper stood with her hands on her hips.

"Where are the stables?"

"Master says you was to stay put till his return," snarled the woman.

"I am going to see my dog."

"Looks to me like you're all dollied up to go riding," accused the housekeeper.

"That is none of your business, my good woman," snapped Cameron.

"Don't you put on no fancy airs with me, you trollop!"

"I beg your pardon!"

"Who do you think you are, coming here dirtying up a respectable house?" spat Mrs. Wilson.

"How dare you speak to me like that! I am Lady Sinclair."

"You're what?"

"Lady Sinclair."

"Go on!" crowed the bitter woman, "and I'm the parson's nose, if I'm to believe that."

"Very well. We shall see what my husband has to say about this on his return," threatened Cameron, sitting down calmly despite her terror.

Mrs. Wilson looked less sure of herself. Her nervous bony hands wrung her apron and smoothed it out a few times.

"Stables are out back," hissed the housekeeper.

Cameron stood, wondering how to reach them.

"If you're having me on and you ain't her ladyship, I'll get you," snarled the white-lipped woman, whose mind raced with her dilemma. If the girl was the master's wife, then the fat was really in the fire. Standing there looking so hoity-toity she could very well be; then again she could just be one of those actresses. Either way it seemed better to let the chit have her way. If she rode off she wouldn't be there to tell any stories.

"This way," she said curtly, leading Cameron down a dark passage and into the large kitchen where the clatter and chatter stopped abruptly.

"Keep your noses out!" barked the housekeeper, as curious eyes looked up at them.

"Over there, your ladyship," directed the woman facetiously, pointing across a cobbled courtyard and slamming the kitchen door, leaving Cameron alone outside.

Cameron forced herself to walk slowly, conscious of the prying eyes staring at her from the windows. She whistled, and Torquil whined pitifully. He was tied up on a very short length of rope so he could not even stand. Her blood boiled; the tender feelings she had felt for Alex at seeing her precious things were safe turned to rage. How dare he? Torquil had never been so bound before. That's all Alex Sinclair wanted, to rob living, free spirits of their precious freedom, she ranted, as she worked at the hard, tight knot that imprisoned her hound. She knelt in the mud as she caressed him, and he whined and licked her face as she freed him.

Fortunately no one was in the stables, so Cameron quickly searched around and found a leather jerkin, shirt, and britches, which she stuffed into her saddle-bag. Her experienced eye scanned the horses until she found a large, strong-looking black stallion who reminded her of Torquod. She pushed the thought from her mind and judged him the one to endure the ravages of the rough trip that lay ahead.

Cameron, realizing that she would have to ride sidesaddle through Edinburgh unless she wanted to attract attention, readied the horse, planning to change her clothes and ride bareback as soon as she reached open country.

Cameron mounted the skittish animal and, whistling for Torquil, rode sedately through the courtyard, aware she was being watched. She planned to head straight north, taking directions from the sun. It was late afternoon and the narrow streets were thronged with vendors, people, and carriages. She wove her way, unaware of the attention she attracted, as she was too preoccupied trying to calm the great horse who reared and pranced nervously, unused to the traffic. The winding streets seemed to go on forever, all looking the same, and Cameron wondered if she was riding around in circles. The maze of streets and alleys confused her as she threaded her way, and just as she was about to really become discouraged, the houses thinned and she saw the firth in the distance.

She rode the west bank, hoping she could ford the river, and as the sun was setting she crossed the bridge, ignoring the many invitations of the young men who, seeing an unaccompanied young lady, took it into their minds that they should escort her. The men frightened Cameron as they reached out and pulled at her clothes. Torquil, sensing her fear, growled menacingly, his teeth bared.

Cameron despaired of ever reaching open country. It seemed she was swept along by a multitude of noisy people on foot and in carriages. Her arms ached from keeping her terrified horse in control, and more than

once her heart lurched in fear for Torquil as less
patient travelers speeded and cut across their path
not caring who they crashed into. She had skirted
Dunfermline and, faced with three roads branching
north, had chosen the middle fork. It was dark now
and her eyes searched for a shelter where she might
stop and change her clothes so she could ride more
comfortably.

Alex handed the reins over to Fergus as they rode
home, and he leaned back, deep in thought. So Cameron was the daughter of one Dolores, herself a product of a union between a Spaniard and the rebel son of
a MacLeod laird. What did he know of Donald
MacLeod? Once it would have been easy to find out, but
with the disbanding of the clans and the changing of
alliances it was a much more difficult task.

"You know of Donald MacLeod?"

"Aye, died in France," grunted Fergus, deep in his
own thoughts. The brooding silence resumed.

Dolores had been mistress to countless men, including, it seemed, Bonnie Prince Charlie himself. Countless men on the continent of Europe at that time could
have sired Cameron, including some Jacobite by the
name of Cameron. And yet, why had Dougal got so furious when Alex had asked that question, screaming
and ranting about life and death? How many times
had the old man's tongue slipped and said "bairns"
and "they"?

"You ken there's a Rona on MacLeod land, of
Skye?" said Fergus, breaking into Alex's jumbled
thoughts.

"No. What are you thinking of?"

"Old Dougal did say *North* Rona, didn't he?" queried Fergus.

"Aye, a few times. Why?"

"Puzzling up my mind. The girl Dolores, born on Skye, there being one Rona there and another fifty miles off Cape Wrath, there being a horse and hound named for the MacLeod twins?" struggled Fergus.

"Go on."

"I canna quite grasp it, but there seems to be a puzzle of twos."

"Aye, and Dougal slipping up all the time and saying 'them' and telling me to keep the *bairns* safe."

"Aye, things seem in pairs. Two Ronas, the animals named for the MacLeod twins. Maybe coincidence. I canna make head or tail of it," growled Fergus, ruefully shaking his head.

"So enraged, he was, when I questioned who sired Cameron."

"Is it of importance to you?" asked Fergus cryptically.

"What?" replied Alex, bewildered at the old man's sudden change of mood.

"Hah! 'Tis not the social thing in your circle," returned Fergus with an ironic twist.

"What are you about?"

"Is it why you'll not acknowledge the lass as your wife? Because her blood lines aren't set down according to fashionable convention?"

"So Mackie wagged her tongue! Are there no secrets kept?"

"Just between you and the lass," retorted Fergus, adding, as Alex lapsed into a brooding silence, "Is who sired Cameron of importance to you?"

"Nay, 'twill be a mite awkward socially, but it doesna matter a farthing to me."

"She's a proud, spirited piece of old Scotland."

"Aye, and she's mine," crowed Alex.

"I wouldna count on that braw lass belonging to

any but herself. And there's a mighty lot of patching and mending to be done between you, it seems."

"Aye," murmured Alex, and he fell back silently into brooding once again as he remembered their last encounters. How should he go about undoing the hurts and misconceptions? How was he to loosen the constrictions he'd wrapped around Cameron's spirit? What right had he to expect a return of the love he felt for her? He damned himself to hell and back as he realized the countless cruelties and insensitivities he'd tied her with. If he were Cameron, he'd put as much distance between them as he could, he thought savagely, and at the thought panic surged through him.

"Can't they go faster?" he roared, tugging the reins from Fergus's hands.

Fergus sensed a foreboding in his own bones even before Alex's spurt of impatience.

Alex cursed the crowded streets that made their progress painfully slow as they inched their way through Edinburgh. Finally, unable to curb his frustration, he threw the reins back to Fergus and leaped down.

"I'll get there faster on foot," he yelled, before disappearing among the throngs of people.

Fergus knew in his heart that Cameron had fled. How? He pondered, and knew she seemed a part of him. And knowing she had been reared amid the wild things of nature, also knew she would return to what she knew best. He feared for her survival as he realized she was no longer wild, nor yet tamed, but stood uncertainly between the two. He bided his time as the horses slowly made their way home, his own frustrations and fears shaking deep in his belly. Poor old Mackie would be fretting herself silly, he thought. If *he* felt so grim, what would she be feeling with her Gaelic second sight?

* * *

Alex reached his townhouse out of breath and, not wanting to search his pockets for his key with his nervous hands, he hammered impatiently at the door. The housekeeper opened the door, her mouth agape, but Alex rudely pushed her aside and took the stairs four at a time.

Mrs. Wilson stood, her mouth still open, as she heard him throw open doors, and he appeared at the top of the stairs.

"Where is she?" he roared.

"I told her she was to stay put. I dinna like these carryings on. Twenty years I've been here and never in all my born days have I—"

"Where is she?" bellowed Alex, striding toward her.

"Who's to know what sort of trollop she was, coming here putting on airs, looking down her snotty young nose at me and with no chaperon?" whined the woman, backing away.

"Where's my wife?" thundered Alex, seizing the skinny woman in rage.

Mrs. Wilson's eyes bulged and her neck knotted like a chicken's.

"Where's my wife, you foul-mouthed woman?" he demanded, shaking her violently.

Constricted by his murderous grasp and her intense fear, the woman could only emit strange, strangled squawks. Alex dropped her in disgust and she fell to the floor. He turned to the white-faced maids who peered through the bannisters and kitchen door.

"It weren't me, sir, please, sir, it were Alice and Annie. I told them not to, really I did, sir, but I'm new here and then the lady come . . ." wailed a very small scullery maid, thinking Alex's eyes singled her out.

He stared at the terrified girl and fought to calm himself.

"Come in here," he ordered, and propelled the weeping child into his study and slammed the door.

"Cross me heart it were them, sir, and she says not to light the fire nor take nothing up 'cause we ain't catering to no baggage, she said. I felt sorry for her, I really did, but cross me heart and hope to die, sir, I weren't one of them what done it."

Alex poured a shot of whiskey and handed it to the hysterical child.

"Stop the bawling and calm yourself," he snapped, unable to make head or tail of her words.

"I canna drink that, sir. Me dad would kill me," she sobbed.

"Then stop the wailing or I'll pour it down your gullet and kill you myself. Now, who said not to light the fire?"

"Housekeeper, sir," hiccuped the maid, trying hard to control herself.

"From the beginning," said Alex softly, holding his impatience in check so he didn't scare the girl even more.

"Well, sir, I come on at five to clean the flues and all that, you know?"

"Yes, go on."

"Well, I heard them all talking. I wasn't listening sir, but they was talking so loud, I couldn't help but overhear, sir." She stopped, watching his face anxiously.

"Please hurry, I haven't all day," he barked, and then cursed himself as he saw he'd increased the girl's agitation so tears poured down her tiny face.

"I'm ever so sorry, sir, I canna stop crying, sir. They dinna know 'twas your wife, sir. Really they dinna, 'cause if they had, sir, they'd have lit the fire as it were really chilly, sir, and they'd have given her some victuals and drink, sir," she trailed off in a loud wail.

Alex was now able to understand the treatment that Cameron had been subjected to in his house.

"What lady came?" he roared, trying to make himself heard over her noise.

"What, sir?" The girl stopped her bawling and stared at him bewildered.

"You said a lady came?" he repeated in a clipped voice.

"Oh, oh, oh yes, sir."

"What lady?"

"I dinna know her name, sir, but she come before—about a fortnight ago, sir. Was the same one, sir."

Alex looked puzzled. He wasn't in the habit of entertaining females at his own home. What lady was this girl raving about? The girl watched his bewildered expression anxiously.

"She made a big fuss, sir. Was ever so cross 'cause you weren't here, sir. Give Mrs. Wilson a real big shove, sir." prompted the small maid.

"What did she look like?"

"Ever so pretty, sir. Red hair, tall, had—er . . ." The thin hands nervously made gestures around her own little breasts to indicate voluptuousness.

Fiona? What the hell had she been doing here?

"What happened then?" he demanded.

"She searched the house, sir. She come right in where I was scrubbing, dirtied my clean floor, she did, sir."

"What then?"

"When she couldn't find you, she left, sir."

"So she did not speak to my wife?" Alex breathed a sigh of relief.

"Oh, we dinna know you had a wife then, sir. Oh, you mean today, sir?"

"Of course I mean today, you stupid child!"

"She went up, and then come down and left, sir."

"Who?" screamed Alex in pain.

"I dinna know her name, sir," sobbed the girl.

"Who went up and came down and left?"

"The one that come, sir," wailed the maid.

"With red hair?"

The waif nodded.

"The lady with red hair went up?"

She nodded.

"The stairs?"

She nodded.

"To speak to my wife?"

"She went into the room, sir, but I dinna know if they spoke. I don't listen in, sir."

"But she went into my wife's room?"

The girl nodded.

"Did my wife leave with her?"

"No, sir, 'twas later, sir. I dinna see her go but some others did. Said she rode off as cocky as you please on one of your lordship's new horses, sir. Oh, with the great beast too, sir."

"What was she wearing?"

"I dinna see her, sir."

There was a rapping at the door.

"Should I get the door, sir?"

Alex nodded and the sniffling girl admitted Fergus.

"That's all for now, girl," said Alex, waving her out, whereupon the young maid started to bawl loudly.

"For godsakes, what now?" demanded Alex.

"They'll get me, sir, for telling, sir. I'm scared, sir."

"Sit over there and stop that infernal racket," he growled, depositing her in a chair in the corner, not wanting another bruised child on his conscience.

"Thanks, sir."

"How old are you, anyway?"

"Eleven, sir," whispered the girl.

"Eleven? My God, there's child labor even under my own roof! Fergus, she's gone."

"Aye, on the new horse you bought," growled Fergus.

"I bought it for her, to replace her Torquod. Strange . . . she dinna know and yet she took him," said Alex, and laughed hollowly.

"He's not properly gentled yet. High-strung and un-used to the busy town," worried Fergus.

"Then he and Cameron will be good company for each other," retorted Alex savagely. "See that bairn gets to her own home safely," he added, dismissing Fergus.

Fergus beckoned the girl and, putting a comforting arm around her, led her to the door.

"Fergus?"

"Aye?" said Fergus, turning at the door.

"You think she returned to Glen Aucht?"

Fergus shook his head.

"When did she leave?"

"They estimate about four," replied Fergus, ushering the weeping maid out.

Alex sat alone, brooding. Cameron had been gone more than four hours. He tried to get his thoughts in order. How was he to find her? Had she run back to Ian Drummond? What could Fiona have possibly said to Cameron? He was shaken from his thoughts a few minutes later by Fergus entering with a tray of food.

"Better to think on a full stomach."

"No, I'm to find Drummond and Fiona to see what they know," retorted Alex.

"I've learned more, so you sit and eat and I'll tell," muttered Fergus, as Alex eyed the food with distaste.

"She wore the fancy red riding habit, took nothing else, but that bitter woman out there says she stole a pillow slip."

"Fergus, were all her things packed or just a few?" The old man stared at him puzzled. "I checked her room and there were three trunks there. Did Mackie pack all her things?"

"Aye, every last one of them. You know women and their hopings?" admitted Fergus ruefully.

"Even the few things that Cameron arrived with?"

"I dinna ken the wee un had anything except the clothes on her back and the hound."

"I gave Mackie an old saddlebag, told her to keep it safe," explained Alex.

"Then if I know my woman, she packed it. She sort of looked on it all as a hope chest—trousseau, so to speak."

Alex gave Fergus a long hard look.

"What are you telling me?" Alex demanded.

Fergus eyed him thoughtfully and pulled on his lip with his long fingers.

"Dinna be vexed with Mrs. MacDonald. She loves you both as the bairns she never had. She felt the girl's place was with her legal husband."

"So she packed everything?"

"Aye."

Alex left Fergus sitting there as he burst out of his study and bounded up the stairs.

"She took what you thought of?" inquired Fergus, when Alex returned a few moments later.

"Aye. I know where she's headed."

"Cape Wrath?"

"Aye."

"She'll not get far riding sidesaddle," remarked Fergus, shaking his head. "The puir wee thing tried her damnedest and rode like a trooper, but never really got her wee bum comfylike."

"Sidesaddle or not she's bound for Cape Wrath," said Alex.

"And she'll not make it alive with winter setting in," replied Fergus. "Has she food? Money? She's all dressed up in fancy clothes that are no protection against the weather—or the hands of lechers. She's lost herself and her pride, tied up and strangling in corsets, bodices, eloqution, and etiquette. All to be a lady, and what the hell is a lady?"

Alex was stunned at the storm of words that poured out of Fergus's mouth.

"What?" he ejaculated.

"Let me finish my piece, whether it's my place or not! I have to say it before I bust. I held my tongue watching that proud, unspoilt lass torture herself as she forced herself into a mold, trying to be what you wanted her to be. A lady! An icy, coldblooded, polite lady!" roared Fergus.

"I dinna want her to be that," protested Alex.

"Then why did you beat her? Why did you shame her? Why did you flaunt your fancy strumpet in front of her? Why did you bind her up in layers of clothes so she couldna feel her own body?"

Alex stared into Fergus's furious eyes. Why had he hurt her so?

"I dinna ken myself. 'Twas like beating myself," he said slowly. "I hurt but I dinna ken why. I reached out to her and she ran from me. I saw her pride stolen until she cowered like a frightened animal, and I hated her because I couldn't raise my arm to comfort without her cringing. It tore into me, and such fury choked me that I thought I'd die from the pounding of my blood, and I wanted to beat her again."

"Why did you beat her?" repeated Fergus, hiding his emotions at the younger man's pain.

"I dinna ken, I tell you!"

"Why did you beat her? For if you won't know, you

just sit with your misery and leave the finding of her to me," stated Fergus coldly.

"Why did I beat her? Because I loved her against my own reasoning."

"Aye, lad. It's about time you understood yourself. I'll go pack your things. 'Tis a long hard road to Cape Wrath, and no point in leaving till first light. Get your rest," smiled Fergus, collecting the empty tray and leaving Alex alone with his new thoughts.

Chapter Twenty-three

As the night grew darker, so did the bustling crowd of fellow travelers thin, and Cameron breathed deeply, enjoying the fresh chill of the air and the nostalgic sight of the moon and stars. She rode, savoring her freedom as she stared overhead at the familiar sky, easing her tension. Though fatigued and aching Cameron felt free for the first time since Duncan had died.

Across a moonlit field she spied a barn; slowly and carefully they trod the rutted ground, approaching the shelter. Finding hay inside she fed the horse and changed from her ladylike garb to the ragged clothes of a saddle lad. It was difficult, as in the enclosed pitch-blackness she had to rely on feel to distinguish which of her borrowed garments were which. She threw off the red velvet riding suit with gusto and giggled as she was sure she thrust a leg into the arm of a sleeve. The combination of tiredness and frayed nerves caused her giggle to expand to a whooping laugh which started a not-too-distant dog to bark. She quietened quickly at Torquil's answering growl and hurriedly pulled on the stableboy's trews, hoping she donned them the right way around.

Cameron froze as she heard a voice muttering angrily, and the sounds of an eager, straining dog approached. She silently unbuckled the saddle from her horse, trying to calm Torquil, whose hair raised as deep, menacing rumbles reverberated through him. She mounted the bare back of the stallion and, with her hand on the latch of the door, waited, tensed, to escape.

The approaching farmer kicked the excited dog, who nearly tore his arm out of its socket in his eagerness to reach the barn. With a curse he released his animal, put his lantern down, and aimed his gun at the wooden door.

"All right, you thievin' rats! Crawl outa there!"

Cameron sat astride her horse, hearing the farmer's gruff voice and the dog frantically scratching and whining outside. She took a deep breath, pushed open the door, and kicked her heels into her horse's sides. There was a flash of light and an explosion as she charged, and Cameron, bent over the galloping steed's neck, prayed that Torquil was at her side.

The farmer fell back with astonishment as his gun fired and two large black shapes leaped out, seeming to fly.

Down the empty moonlit road galloped the trio, the

horse's hooves shattering the night's silence. Cameron, fearing for Torquil, slowed down after a mile or so and whistled softly. The moon had been swallowed by clouds, and darkness was thick around them. Straining her eyes she whistled again and was reassured by an answering panting whine.

"We'll go slower now, 'tis too dark to see," she whispered to her hound, and felt a sharp pain run through her shoulder. Her hand felt wet and sticky, the leather rein slippery in her grasp. She gave up the uselessness of trying to see, and urged the horse into a trot, determined to put as much distance as she could between them and the irate man.

All night she rode, slowly but steadily, keeping to the road for fear the horse would stumble and hurt himself crossing the rutted fields. The back of her shoulder now throbbed with pain, but she shut it out of her mind and concentrated on the rhythm of the animal beneath her.

Leaving Alex to rest Fergus packed and, satisfying himself that he'd forgotten nothing needed for the grueling journey to Cape Wrath, slipped from the house to comb the streets for anyone who might have seen Cameron. He lucked upon a small tavern where several people remembered the spectacle of the very small, unattended girl on a very large, skittish stallion and, following their directions as to where she was headed, he trudged the winding streets until he concluded she was heading due north.

He returned to find Alex dressed for his journey and impatient to go, even though it was midnight and as black as pitch outside. He had found it impossible to sleep, even though he needed all his wits about him. He'd close his eyes only to see Cameron alone on the

open road, and he cursed Fergus's reference to lecherous hands, that having been the furthest worry from
his mind until it was mentioned.

"She made quite a spectacle of herself on that great
rearing brute, traveled north and many remember
seeing her," informed Fergus.

"Seems no matter what Cameron is trying to do, she
makes a spectacle of herself," murmured Alex, recalling her trudging behind him with her skirts held high
up her bare thighs, surrounded by ogling young men.

"Seems she's headed for Lieth."

"Lieth? You think she's going to cross by boat to
Glen Aucht?" asked Alex.

"Nay. That horse wouldna take kindly to the noise
and strangeness; neither would the lass for that matter.
I think she'll follow the firth to the bridge."

"I wonder where she is now?" worried Alex.

"Asleep in some ditch somewhere, dirtying up her
fancy clothes, no doubt. Too dark to travel. Moon's
covered, ain't a drop of light. That's why 'twould be
fool to go galloping off now. You'll not be able to see
your hand in front of your face. Could pass right by
the bairn."

Cameron huddled in the ditch, wishing she'd
brought her heavy wool cape. She huddled close to
Torquil for warmth, wishing the ache in her shoulder
would cease. Finally she slept, waking suddenly to the
growl that reverberated through the hound she cushioned her head on. She lay still, hearing the sound of
voices, and opened her eyes, blinking in the bright
sunlight. She sat up and a sharp pain shot through
her. Coming toward them down the road was a band
of men, pointing at her horse that cropped the grass at
the side of the road. Sensing danger she untied him

and threw herself onto his bare back, despite the agony it caused. Drumming her heels into his sides she urged him into a frantic gallop, and they sped, with Torquil alongside, away from the men who shouted and ran toward them.

She looked back and nearly fainted at the surge of pain that made her neck stiff and her head throb. She saw the dark crusted blood on her hand, now mixed with fresh bright red that still trickled. She forced the fear from her mind as they traveled a mile or more at a bruising pace. Turning slowly and carefully in an effort not to jar her injury, she saw the road behind was clear of people, but still panic flared through her. Which way was she headed? She had fled from the men without thought. She looked to the morning sky and to her relief saw she was headed north.

Looking behind her again she saw that Torquil straggled back, out of wind. She waited for him to catch up. He was old and should have been curled in front of a warm hearth, thought Cameron. There was no way he could keep up, so she decided to get him up with her on the horse's tall back. To each side of her was open farmland, no woods to cover their resting. She carefully scanned around and, seeing no one, dismounted at a wooden stile and tied the horse.

"Whoa, Torquod," she crooned, as the great horse shied. She attempted to lift the heavy dog that weighed as much as, if not more than, herself. The pain to her wounded shoulder was unbearable, and she sobbed with that plus her frustration at the prancing stallion.

"Help me, Torquod," she panted, not realizing the name she called him.

As if the horse understood her voice and Torquil's

soft barks, he eased his flanks flush to the stile and
the old hound struggled up as Cameron lifted.

Poor Torquil lay across the horse in a very undigni-
fied position as Cameron held him firmly and rode
behind. It was very awkward as the large dog
squirmed to gain his balance and slipped this way and
that. Cameron's arms ached with the burden of holding him and the reins of the skittish horse. They could
travel faster walking, she finally decided, reining to a
halt and allowing the grateful hound to lumber off.

Alex left before dawn, after giving instructions to
Fergus to close the townhouse, releasing all the servants from his employment except the eleven-year-old
maid who would be given the option to work at Glen
Aucht if she wanted to.

He was out of Edinburgh and past Lieth by the
time the sun rose and briskly traveling the shore road
toward the Forth Bridge. His eyes combed the hedgerows and fields on each side. Reaching the bridge he
learned from the street merchants that Cameron had
crossed at sunset the night before. They chattered excitedly about the ferocious hound that had protected
the wee lass from the clutching of would-be lechers
and Alex, with a curse, urged his horse even faster,
leaving them still recounting their tale. Outside Dunfermline the road branched three ways, and all his inquiries were met with blank stares and shaking heads.
Cameron would not have taken the east fork, he reasoned, but she could have taken the straight north or
northwest. As far as he knew the girl was not ac-
quainted with maps, so what would he have done if he
were her? He chose the road straight north and, urging
his horse on, scanned the ditches and fields along the
way.

Spotting a small barn with a clustered group of excited farm workers talking, he rode to them and asked if any had seen a young lady on a black horse with a large dog. There was a moment of silence as the men all looked at one.

"Well, old Jackie here swears he were attacked by two giant beasties last night. Tell the gentleman, Jackie," chuckled a man.

"Aye, we found a wee lad with horse and hound sleeping in a ditch up yonder, but old Jackie here swears it wasna them."

" 'Tis God's truth," insisted the furious Jackie. "Bigger than life itself they was. Flew out on giant black wings they did." He pointed frantically at the barn.

Alex dismounted and looked in the barn, finding discarded clothes and saddle. Without doubt they were Cameron's.

"They headed straight?" he asked, pointing north along the road.

"Headed straight up into the sky," ranted the farmer. "I took a shot at them, hit them dead center and they dinna falter, just kept flying, flying, flying, their great wings rushing and humming."

"You *shot* at them?" gasped Alex in horror.

"Aye, couldna have missed them. They flew straight at me, then up, up, up, up to the moon," he raved, pointing at the heavens as Alex looked at the ground. The other men watched Alex a moment and then, understanding what he was doing, searched the earth also.

"Over here," shouted one, "there's blood here."

Alex stared at the dark spots, his heart beating wildly. Without a word he mounted and rode off, following the trail of blood until it ended. He scanned the ditches on each side of the road, but his eyes saw no crushed grasses or place to hide. Three miles further he spotted more blood, this time seeming fresher and, doubling back a few yards, he found the place where Cameron had spent the night.

Why hadn't he asked the farmers when they had spotted them, he railed, and then reasoned it had to have been that morning on their way to work, possibly at seven o'clock or thereabouts. She was but two hours ahead of him, he realized excitedly, and she couldn't travel as swiftly as he because of the old hound. Which one of them had been shot? His blood ran cold as he searched the hedgerows and ditches.

Cameron rode north, straight across the road that led to Kinross due east. She recognized the signpost and the name of the town, and shuddered as she remembered trudging behind Alex with her skirts held high so she didn't tangle in them and fall. It seemed so long ago, almost in a different life. It had been mid-August when Duncan had died, and now it was just about November, she calculated, bewildered at how vague and dreamlike everything seemed since leaving Cape Wrath. Ahead of her on each side of the road she saw mountains rise with trees for cover. Her heart sang and she urged her horse faster as Torquil, sensing her spurt of joy, found new life and pranced puppylike beside them. She left the open road and struck west into the wooded hills. To her dismay the trees thinned quickly and she found herself in the busy outskirts of Stirling, but to her amazement no one stared, shouted, or was the least curious about her. Still she didn't dare stop to buy food, remembering how Alex had warned her not to talk.

The wound in Cameron's shoulder had festered, swelling the flesh across her back and down her right forearm, making it impossible to hunt or fish. Hunger gnawed into her, but as the poison spread through her system, it made her nauseous, so the mere thought of food was repugnant. For two days she traveled bearing straight north again, not understanding why the lowlands went on seemingly forever, and town upon town of frightening, busy people came into view instead of the rugged Highlands she was seeking. Finally on the outskirts of Perth she struck off west, loath to ride through the ugly gray mass of houses that conjured up painful memories of an ironic marriage.

As Cameron reached the welcome sight of high land, she knew she was in serious trouble. Her right arm was now swollen to the wrist and her body burned with fever, blinding her eyes. She forced herself to hang on to consciousness and her horse by knotting her aching hand in his mane as the scenery spun at a dizzying rate. She headed west past Crieff and toward Comrie, not knowing if the direction was right or wrong, as she tried to hold on to her sanity. All she knew was that she had to get away from people, and shelter herself in the rugged tangle of nature that soared above her.

Alex frowned when he reached the Kinross crossroads, knowing that ahead woods covered the slopes on each side of the road. Realizing the cover was thicker on the east, he struck out in that direction and, after not finding sight nor sign of her after two frustrating hours, cursed his own stupidity.

"How on earth would Cameron know the thickness or extent of a forest, not having a map or being familiar with the area?" he roared aloud, frightening a flock of crows that seemed to mock him raucously.

Alex traveled for two days, bearing west after Stirling, passed Callandar, and rode into the mountains. He was discouraged. Nobody had seen hide nor hair of the "lad" with a giant hound. What if the loyal beast had been the one shot? he wondered. What if it were Cameron who'd been shot? As he pushed the terrifying thought from his mind, more horrific possibilities flooded his brain. What if she'd been robbed of the horse? What if she'd sold the horse? As far as he knew she had no money but the one coin from her knife-throwing prowess. What if she'd somehow found the big redheaded man, Ben, and was traveling with him from fair to fair? Thinking of the other possibilities—being forced into prostitution or onto one of the boats that plucked the luckless poor off the streets for bondage in the colonies—he almost wished she was with Ben. Consumed with worry, he urged his tired mount toward the town of Lochearnhead.

Alex arrived at the town and registered at an inn, where he soaked in a hot bath before a blazing fire, wondering whether he should turn back or cross east toward Perth. What if the girl lay dead or dying? She could be anywhere in the rugged Grampians. Why, when she had only been two hours ahead of him two days before, had he not found her? The openness of the lowlands was where he should have caught up with her; now the soaring mountains tangled with forests made his search almost impossible.

He lay in bed, trying to sleep but tortured by nightmares; he rose and paced his room. He'd asked everyone he'd seen in the town of Lochearnhead if they'd seen Cameron, describing her hair, eyes, and possible dress. But all had shaken their heads in a very negative manner. It would be difficult not to notice a stranger in these parts, thought Alex. The fast-approaching winter had driven the sportsmen back to their warmer townhouses, leaving a few hardy Scots to fish the loch.

Early the next morning Alex waited at the stable for his horse to be saddled.

"Giant wolf, bigger than a horse," insisted a lad, raking out a stall.

"With fire burning out its eyes, no doubt," mocked an old man.

"Aye. Cross my heart. I dinna see it but my pa did. This side of Comrie on the Crieff Road," stammered the boy.

"And how much did your pa have in him?" chuckled another man mending a bridle.

"Some, I reckon, but I heard it howling myself. So did my ma. Set our blood cold, it did."

"We know your pa. He's pickled his brain," laughed the men.

"But I heard it meself," protested the lad.

"Fanciful lad, ain't he?" chortled the old man, as Alex mounted and rode off.

The road to Crieff circled the loch, that seemed cut out of the steep, forested mountains. The still water reflecting the blue of the sky was set deeply, embedded in the soaring green like a sapphire nestled in velvet. Alex was blind to the breathtaking beauty; to him it appeared cruel and unfathomable, a merciless maze that could swallow and devour Cameron forever.

He rode thinking of the lad's tale of the giant wolf. There were no wolves in Scotland, the last said to have been killed eighteen years before in Inverness County. Yet who was to tell? There could have been a few still surviving, but not so far south, especially so early in winter. Probably the lad's imagination fanned by his drunken father's hallucinations, thought Alex, and yet for some reason he wanted to believe the story. Perhaps they'd not seen a giant wolf but a giant hound, named Torquil.

Alex whistled and two young does raised their heads from drinking and bounded away into the forest. Hearing nothing he chided himself for his foolishness. The lad probably heard an abandoned dog, left when the sportsmen returned to the city after the hunting season had ended. Cameron couldn't possibly have traveled so far. It was over thirty miles from Edinburgh as the crow flies, longer by road. She, or one of them, was wounded, and the dog was old, so there was no way they could have traveled as rapidly as he, Alex reasoned.

Where was she? What should he do? His search seemed hopeless. Should he turn back? Make his way to Cape Wrath hoping by some miracle she reached her destination? What if Fergus had been misinformed, and Cameron was that very moment elegantly sipping tea with Ian Drummond in an Edinburgh teashop? Or reading by the fireside in the kitchen at Glen Aucht? Alex had never felt so totally helpless and impotent. He dismounted and walked down to the water's edge, where he stood numbly staring at the still, deep loch that reflected the scenic beauty all around. He picked up a rock and smashed the still mirror, fragmenting the images that seemed to mock him.

A terrible aching void welled up, consuming him, and Alex bellowed out his pain and frustration as he had done as a baby, not caring that the sound of grief was much harsher from the heart of a full-gown man. He cried; consumed by his keening, his sorrow reverberating across the still waters and gradually diminishing to low echoes. Spent he sat dully, his breathing noisy and rapid, not hearing the answering howls. He bent and submerged his hot face in the clear, icy water, angrily splashing the signs of his grief away. Alex didn't hear the mournful baying until it stopped, and then the silence startled him. He stood listening, wondering what he had heard.

"Echo?" he experimented, and the word vibrated through the still air across the water, bouncing off the high land in diminishing tones. He listened carefully, hearing the faint mocking of his last syllable extended longer than he would have expected.

"Cameron!" he yelled between cupped hands, and listened.

" 'meron . . . eron . . . ron . . . ron . . . ron," came the echo, and was joined with "ooo . . . oooo . . . oooo . . . ooooo."

Alex's heart beat faster as he realized the echo could not have changed itself. A dog's howl had joined his calling. But where? The water and mountains played with sound so it was impossible to fathom its source. He turned his back to the loch and shouted, his voice sounding flat. The dog howled again. Still, Alex was unsure of the direction as the water picked up and threw back the sound for the mountains to toy with.

Alex was nearly positive the dog was on the same side of the loch as he. He led his horse back to the road, mounted, and called again, his eyes trying to probe the thick wooded slopes. He turned back toward Lochearnhead, desperately trying to pinpoint the origin of the answering howl. For four frustrating hours he rode this way and that, back and forth, without getting any closer. Sweating and intent, calling and feeling sudden bursts of joy thinking the howling nearer, only to be confused by his own ears that strained so hard they distorted sound, he traversed the five-mile stretch of the loch three times, wending his way in and out of the trees. But still he got no closer to the animal that consistently answered his call.

Should he get help? Was it indeed Torquil answering his call? He sat to rest, burying his face in his folded arms. He felt he was so near and in his heart nearly positive that it was Torquil calling him to the aid of his young mistress. Again the mournful sound echoed. Think logically, Alex commanded himself. She didn't come through Callandar and Lochearnhead, so from where did she come? Obviously through Gleneagles and Crieff. If so, she was somewhere in the mountains that reared north above him. The stable lad had said his father was on his way to Comrie, which was two miles east of the loch toward Crieff, but when he'd ridden in that direction the howls had faded. Somewhere up in the impenetrable slopes, of the five miles that ringed the loch's north shore, was the source of the mournful cries. Riding and listening, Alex narrowed the five miles to a half mile. His ears detected a faint increase in volume but he couldn't be sure, as they were strained to near deafness. He took a chance and urged his horse into the forest, knowing he could go backward and forward along the road all day and be no nearer.

He picked his way carefully through the fir trees, stopping to call and listen intently. The answering howl came back as before, now muffled by the thick branches overhead. All afternoon Alex chased the sound, going forward, doubling back, and striking off in different directions. He worried about the approaching darkness as he rode, it seemed, in circles through the maze of trees.

He came to a small clearing and to his surprise looked down to find he had climbed quite high. Below him rippled the sparkling waters of the loch. He rested his tense, throbbing head. What if he tracked down the sound and found just a strange dog? He was shaken from his thoughts by the haunting sound, seeming louder than ever before. The sound teased him, spinning through the tree trunks, getting louder and then softer as he twisted this way and that. Suddenly, when he felt he could go no further, as an iron band wrapped his head in a throbbing squeeze, he saw a narrow path threading through the forest and, on an impulse, spurred his horse with new life.

"Cameron?" he yelled, and his excitement grew as the answering call came steadily louder and louder. The small, well-trodden path snaked across the slope and broke free into a glen just big enough to hold a small hunting lodge, outhouses, and a field. At the door of a small barn sat Torquil, his head raised, howling, to the sky.

Cameron lay at his feet and Alex froze, thinking she was dead. He stood before bending, afraid to touch her still face. Before his hand touched, he felt the heat that burned her and breathed with relief. Quickly he removed his cape and wrapped her warmly.

"Cameron? Cameron? Can you hear me?" he whispered, but the girl did not react. He picked her up and carried her into the barn, resting her on some hay.

"Stay, Torquil," he ordered the dog unnecessarily, and strode out to the hunting lodge.

The door was locked. He felt around in the obvious places for a key and, not finding one, tried to open the door with brute force to no avail. Swearing, he tried the windows, but they were all shuttered from the inside. At the back of the house he found a cellar door, which yielded to his determined strength and, praying it led to the floors above, he entered and felt his way in the darkness. His hands blindly groped shelves of bottles and jars, rough stone walls, but no stairs. He stood for a moment, letting his eyes accustom themselves to the dimness, and he spotted the regular squares of a ladder hanging tidily on the far wall. He scanned above until he made out a rectangular shape among the dark blotches on the high ceiling. Propping

the ladder carefully he climbed up and found the
hatch firmly bolted from above, and no amount of
pounding or thrusting caused it to give an inch.
Searching the cellar for a tool to pry it with, his hands
felt along the dusty shelves, and he grasped a ring with
dangling keys. Unhooking them, he strode outside and
impatiently tried them one by one in the front door.
Finally one of the great many turned and the sturdy
door opened.

Part Three
Winter

A voice so thrilling ne'er was heard
In springtime from the cuckoo bird,
Breaking the silence of the seas
Amongst the farthest Hebrides.

Will no one tell me what she sings?—
Perhaps the plaintive numbers flow
For old, unhappy, far-off things,
And battles long ago:
Or is it some more humble lay,
Familiar matter of today?
Some natural sorrow, loss, or pain
That has been, and may be again?

—Wordsworth.

Chapter Twenty-four

The hunting lodge was a far cry from the humble little stone house of their first journey. This abode obviously belonged to a wealthy sportsman, having not only a well-stocked cellar below but two floors of rooms above—ample space for servants and guests.

Alex soon had a fire blazing in what he assumed to be the master bedchamber, and Cameron slept fitfully on the enormous bed. He noted the crusted blood on her hand and arm as she tried to throw the covers off in her delirium, but he forced himself to take one step at a time, remembering the lung inflammation he'd nursed her through before. The first thing to do was get the chill from the house so he could safely undress her and see the extent of her injury.

The kitchen was large and well equipped with two fireplaces for cooking, plus pots and pans of every size and description. Alex lit a fire and, picking up two buckets, went outside to find water. The sun was setting and it reflected on a small stream that bubbled down from the mountain behind and cut through the small green pasture. Cameron's black horse grazed by the bank, his glossy coat glowing with the redness of the sky.

The water heating and the oil lamps lit, Alex turned his attention to the girl. Her skin was hot and dry, yet to his relief her breathing didn't rattle and rail. He tried to ease the coverings from her but she woke screaming as the pain tore through her. She fought him, her fingers clutching the woolen material, making their removal impossible. Gentleness won't get me anywhere, thought Alex, and, curbing his aching tenderness, he firmly pried away her fingers and uncovered her. Cameron's eyes opened, glazed and frantic, not recognizing him. She shivered violently in the thin filthy rags of the stableboy, the blood stiff and dark all down her arm.

Alex stared in horror at the festering wound, the surrounding flesh swollen to almost twice its size. Was the bullet still lodged in her shoulder? Was it a bullet or grapeshot? He forced his mind to reason calmly, as fear clutched him with panicky hands. The shape of the wound indicated a bullet, as the entry was small and round. Whatever was lodged in her had to be taken out, but how? Alex racked his brain and recalled the searing pain of a hot knife digging into his calf, but his wound had been clean and free of infection, and Cameron's was poisoning her body, the swelling spread across her back to her neck, and down her right arm to the wrist. He forced his brain to recall all he had ever learned about doctoring, and he remembered treating a horse for an abscess with hot poultices before lancing it. Not knowing what else to do he tore up towels and soaked them in boiling water. He prayed that nature would be merciful and keep Cameron unconscious and oblivious as he laid the first steaming compress on her already-tortured shoulder. He thrust his dirk into the

fire and sustained himself with a healthy swallow of
his unknown host's brandy. Thank the Lord for the
well-stocked house, he thought, as he rummaged
through chests to find clean linens and blankets. Cameron stirred as he removed the cooling cloths and
arched her body in agony as he replaced them with
hot ones. She writhed, trying to rid herself of the burning pain, and Alex had to hold her firmly, knowing
that he was causing her unbearable pain, but also
knowing he had to if she was to survive.

For three hours he worked trying to soften the hard,
angry wound as Cameron screamed and struggled,
fainted and reawakened to the painful nightmare.
Both of them were wet with perspiration and agony,
but Cameron succumbed to the agony and then sank
into dark oblivion.

Alex dipped the red hot knife into a mug of brandy
and his blood ran cold at the angry hissing. How could
he stab into Cameron's flesh? He steeled himself and
prepared to cut, but she regained consciousness and resumed her battle. Once again his temerity was causing
her more suffering. He bit the inside of his cheek and
pinned her strongly with his legs, kneeling across her
body so she could not move. Her desperate muffled cries
tore into him.

"Cameron, I have to, I have to," he sobbed and, taking a breath, he plunged the hot knife into the angry
wound. He felt her body, under his, rise and sink
limply back into darkness.

Alex watched her sleep. He was spent. He felt as if
his own energy had drained away with the poison he'd
brutally squeezed out of Cameron. He had luckily
found the bullet, but it had taken more than an hour
to pry it out of her. He had done all he could do,

pouring brandy into the wound and replacing the hot compresses. He had also poured brandy into Cameron's mouth, hoping to give her some relief from the tremendous pain. He stood up, forcing his limp limbs into action as he remembered that his poor saddled horse still waited by the small barn where he had found Cameron. He was loath to leave the sleeping girl even for a minute. She still lay in the filthy rags, her face streaked with grime, sweat, and tears. He couldn't submit her aching body to any more agony. He re-covered her with blankets, wanting the dry fever to break, and quietly left the room to stable both horses for the night.

He came back through the kitchen door with his and her saddlebags. He dropped them to the floor, hearing her screams and Torquil's frantic whines. Cameron stood in the middle of the room, babbling and raving as she clawed at the wet bandages, trying to rip them off her. Alex caught her as she fainted and carried her back to the bed, noticing the blood pouring profusely through the dressings and down her arm.

What should he do? Tie her to the bed? Rebandage? Alex spent a busy night as Cameron's delirium grew. He applied the steaming compresses and replaced the heavy blankets which she repeatedly kicked off her. Every muscle in his body ached and he wondered at her strength that, after fainting for five minutes, could renew itself so vigorously.

As the sky lightened, Alex fell asleep, lying half across her to keep the covers pinned down firmly. He could not fight his exhaustion any longer. But it seemed his eyes had just closed when Cameron's struggles began anew. He sat, dazed and haggard, blankly watching the babbling, screaming girl, knowing each movement she made caused excruciating pain, but not knowing how to stop her without increasing her struggles. He banked the fire and covered her with even more blankets, desperately trying to break her fever. By midafternoon he noticed the beads of perspiration on her upper lip and brow. Her struggles diminished and she relaxed into a deep, peaceful sleep.

Alex longed to close his eyes and join her in the arms of Morpheus, but he knew there was work to be done that couldn't wait. He forced himself outside into the chill air, freeing the horses so they could romp together in the pasture. He submerged his throbbing head in the icy stream, trying to clear his senses and face the day, which was already half over. He stared around at the peaceful glen, breathing in the sharp air before returning to the lodge to check on Cameron.

She still slept and Alex, not wanting to be out of earshot, explored their new abode. It was doubtful that the real owner would return before spring, so Alex decided he would take over as master in his absence. What better place to come to terms with Cameron? Soon the heavy snows would cut them off completely from the outside world, making her escape impossible. They would be forced to confront each other without interference from anyone. Alex's heart sang and he whistled merrily as he explored the house from top to bottom. The cellar yielded, among other things, wine, preserves of all kinds, tubs of tallow and oil, and various grains. There were rifles and traps for hunting, warm clothing, blankets, a larder stacked with various bins and jars. What else could they need? There was fresh water outside, plenty of food for the horses, wood for the fires. The place was perfect. Alex laughed out loud, excited by the prospect of what lay ahead when Cameron recovered. *Would* Cameron recover? The question clawed at his heart and he realized he'd been so intent on his fantasies of the future that he hadn't checked on Cameron for an hour or more.

Cameron still lay sleeping. He felt her head. It was hot and damp, her untidy tangled hair falling in wet tendrils around her flushed face. He curbed an impulse to kiss her and put another log on the fire.

Alex explored outside the house and found a small, overgrown vegetable patch. Among the thistles and dandelions he unearthed some kale, turnips, carrots, and potatoes and humming happily, returned to the lodge. Seeing Cameron was still asleep, he busied himself in the kitchen making broth. He'd never cooked anything except fish and game over an open fire, and he enjoyed his domesticity as he chopped the vegetables. He put three large pots of water to boil and then rifled the chests in the bedroom for towels, soap, and nightshirts, and so armed took down the heavy copper bath that hung on the scullery wall. He placed it in front of the fire and looked doubtfully at Cameron. He was eager to get on with life but no, he would wait, he thought. Let her sleep, protected from her pain, as long as she could. He wanted to start afresh, just the two of them, exploring each other and learning all there was to know, but he curbed his impatience. He dragged the bath back into the kitchen and filled it with hot water; then he stripped and sank his weary body into the comforting warmth.

Alex was happy; he lay smelling the mild fragrance of his own creation bubbling on the wood stove, and he gazed with starry eyes around the well-ordered kitchen, delighting in all he saw; even the table bleached white and smooth from years of diligent scrubbing seemed just perfect to him. He'd never really stopped to think of a kitchen table before, he mused merrily, and he burst into song as he scrubbed himself, lathering the soap into great fleecy mounds. Torquil joined in the chorus of his rousing song and stuck his nose in the bubbles of the bath.

Cameron slowly emerged from the thick layers of sleep hearing laughter and singing. She turned her head, puzzled, and a searing pain shot through her. Moving just her eyes she looked around. Where was she? She smelled food cooking, felt warmth, and heard a crackling fire. Where was she? Who was singing? She pursed her lips and whistled for Torquil, but she found that even moving her lips jolted the terrible pain.

Alex saw Torquil bound out of the room.

"Not in the middle of the chorus, old boy, 'tis rude," he laughed, and then realizing where the dog was going, he quickly stepped out of the bath. Wrapping a towel about him he followed.

Cameron heard Alex's deep voice and the padding of Torquil's big paws.

"Torquil?" she whispered, unable to turn her head to see him, and Torquil placed his cold wet nose on her hand.

"So sleeping beauty has decided to wake, has she, Torquil?" said Alex's warm strong voice, and Cameron's heart beat painfully fast as his face appeared above her. She stared up at him in bewilderment. His wet hair dripped down on her but she didn't blink, just gazed steadily with a little frown. It couldn't be real; she had to be dreaming. She wrenched her eyes away and the pain shot through her. She cried aloud and closed her eyes tightly. Where was she? The pain was real but nothing else seemed to be. She recalled being lost in the woods and finding a house, but there had been no one there; the door had been locked. She was going to sleep on the hay in the barn; that was the last thing she remembered. She opened her eyes and Alex's face was gone. She saw the ceiling but there were no rafters as in a barn. She tried to inch her head around but the searing pain caused her to gasp.

"Dinna move, you'll open the wound again," warned Alex, watching her intently.

"Are you really there?" Cameron whispered.

"Aye, I'm really here."

"Where?"

"Here—" and Alex's face loomed above her.

"Where are we?"

"Seems you stumbled on a hunting lodge in your travels. You've a good eye. 'Tis a right bonnie place."

Cameron closed her eyes again. She was too tired to try to fathom anything out.

Alex waited for the green eyes to look at him again, but they remained closed. And, feeling disappointed, he tiptoed back to the kitchen to see to his cooking. Dressed in warm, clean, borrowed clothes he sipped his broth and was very dismayed. It tasted like hot water. He looked around the kitchen, opening jars and tasting until he found dried herbs and salt which he added liberally. In the pantry he located flour, lard, and honey and debated trying his hand at scones, but he put it off for another day, as he hadn't the least notion of how to go about concocting them. He munched contentedly on stale bread and cheese from his saddlebag, waiting for Cameron to wake up. He was very well organized. He congratulated himself as the bath water heated, and the sheets, towels, nightgown, soap, brush, and clean blankets were piled in readiness. He smiled at his domesticity and thought that he'd never felt so joyous and complete before.

A watched pot never boils, Alex chided himself as he sat poised, waiting for Cameron to open her eyes. Here he sat impatiently waiting for her to wake, when sleep was the best healer of all. He should be busy. He threw his worries aside and strode outside to stable the horses. The two animals grazed peacefully in the setting sun, the surrounding forest making a natural enclosure to prevent them from straying. He sat and leaned against a tree, gazing at the spectacular scenery with appreciation. What a perfect spot, a Garden of Eden. One would have to search the length and breadth of Scotland and maybe still not find such an ideal setting to spend a season alone with Cameron. As he sat musing, a small goat pranced into the clearing to nibble the grass. Alex watched the spirited kid for a few moments without realizing he was looking at food, their next meal. He rose quietly to fetch the gun he'd spied in the house, berating himself for his lack of foresight in not checking to see if it was in working order. The young goat froze at Alex's movement and then leaped away into the thick forest.

Alex spent the evening cleaning and priming the guns he found. He sat by the fire near Cameron, hoping she'd wake, but she didn't.

It was morning. Alex wakened sitting in the chair by the dying fire. He stretched his stiff cold body and looked over at Cameron who slept peacefully. The sky lightened behind the thick fir trees as he led the horses out of the barn, watching their breath mist the sharp morning air as they galloped joyfully across the clearing. It was a wonderful day, a fresh new day, Alex rejoiced, as he awakened his face with the icy tingle of the stream. It felt like the first morning of creation; it was a good time to start anew.

Cameron awoke as pain flared through her. She opened her eyes to see Alex bending over her, his face grim and determined. What was he doing? Why was he hurting her? Alex was being as gentle as he could as he tried to change the bandages, but to Cameron, in her agony, he was a torturer. Once again Alex berated himself for being so timorous, and firmly cut away the dressing.

Cameron forced herself to hold onto her conscious state and willed herself not to succumb to the waves of faintness that flooded her. Her battle spirit rose and a stream of offensive epithets flew out of her mouth instead of the pitiful howls she longed to release.

"That's the way, lassie, spit them out at me," he challenged, as he turned her over in one quick movement so her face pressed against the mattress and muffled her words. Alex examined the wound objectively. The incredible ordeal of having to cut into her flesh had somehow bonded him to her, making her flesh his flesh. The wound was still angry but less so than before, and Alex noted to his relief that the red lines that radiated from the swelling had diminished.

"Keep up your swearing, Cameron," he ordered grimly, as he prepared to place a steamy compress. Her body rose in shock and her feet drummed against the mattress, but the muffled curses weren't uttered. Damn! If I didn't forget her rebellious ways, thought Alex, remembering his contrary bride was apt to do the exact opposite of what he asked.

"That's a good lass, you mustna swear," he praised, preparing to squeeze more poison from her swollen shoulder. Cameron raised such a clamor that Alex smiled despite his pain at the agony he was inflicting. Satisfied, he rebandaged the wound.

"Now dinna take a deep breath," he cautioned, hoping she'd do the opposite as he turned her over in one movement. Cameron stared at him hostilely, her face wet with sweat, the dirt running down in rivulets.

"You're mending well, Cameron," he said gruffly, as his heart leaped with joy seeing the green flashing eyes. It had been too long, and he'd sorely missed the wild spirit that sparkled. He smiled at her, and then frowned.

"But you are dreadful dirty, lass."

Cameron still glared at him as the searing pain receded to a deep throbbing. She licked her dry, cracked lips.

"Water," she whispered hoarsely, hating herself for asking anything from the brute.

"Aye, and you need to wash too. You'll feel better with the dirt off you."

Cameron heard him leave the room and clatter pots and pans before his heavy footsteps returned. She wished she could move her head as her eyeballs ached from twisting them in her futile effort to see what was going on. All she could look at was the ceiling.

Alex returned and sat on the bed but jumped up quickly when she cried out in pain. He cursed his stupidity, realizing his weight on the mattress had jarred the girl's injury. He stood above her, looking down.

"Sorry, lass. Now you'll be in for a spot more discomfort, but when you're washed off with clean linens under you, you'll be a lot more comfortable."

"Leave me be," whispered Cameron, hating her own helplessness.

"Nay. I won't. Who knows what other scrapes and sores are festering under those filthy rags," said Alex firmly.

"I will not let you," hissed Cameron, through gritted teeth.

"You are in no condition to stop me, and fighting me will just hurt you more," he stated, leaving her sight. Cameron heard him in another room, whistling. He came back, put something down, and left again. She lay there, frustrated, unable to see what he was

doing as he walked in and out muttering to himself.
Finally he stood over her looking very purposeful.

"Now, I'll try to be as gentle as I can. I'll cut the
clothes from you and move you as little as possible."
He smiled reassuringly. "Let's clean off that sticky little face first."

Cameron closed her eyes tightly as Alex gently
washed her face with a piece of warm flannel. She felt
herself relaxing as he smoothed up into her hairline,
and she fought the feeling, hating him, as he carefully
removed her clothes. He cut up the sides and across
the shoulders of her shirt, lifting it off instead of painfully tugging it out from under her. He debated pulling off her trews but realized that would jar and put
pressure on her shoulder. He carefully cut down the
outside of each leg.

Cameron gritted her teeth as she felt herself exposed
bit by bit. She refused to open her eyes, certain that if
she did she would see his face mocking her helplessness. Alex had no recourse but to pull off her riding
boots. He sat carefully on the bed so his weight
wouldn't jolt her and, easing himself so he knelt astride
her legs, he tried to painlessly remove the tight leather.
Cameron felt the warmth of him on her thighs, and his
efforts pulled her aching shoulder against the mattress.
She arched her back in agony, making it worse. Alex
swore and wrenched the offending boots off in two
strong movements as Cameron bit her lips to stop from
howling.

He looked down at the naked girl and saw the perspiration beading her face, her cheek ticking as she
clenched her jaw against the waves of pain. His own
face was gray knowing what she endured. Alex gently
sponged Cameron with warm water and fragrant soap
as the violent pain once more receded. He saw and
loved each inch from her neck to her small toes. Her

face was set angrily, her nostrils flared with pain, or so
he thought. Cameron felt humiliation and hated him
for subjecting her to such degradation. She tensed,
fighting the delicate fragrance of the soap and the
warm gentleness of the hands that touched her. Was
not a single part of her to be left untouched? she
railed, as Alex's hands circled and stroked. Despite
herself, Cameron relaxed.

Alex looked down at her. She looked so very vulnerable and fragile that he was overwhelmed with fear.
His emotions for her rose achingly in him and he was
frightened that she was not real, not mortal, that she
could disappear, be extinguished like a candle. He
wanted to wrap her in his arms and never let her go.

Alex was relieved to find no other injuries or abrasions on Cameron's body. He washed her back, then
rinsed her off, covered her with a warm blanket, and
turned to make the bed with clean fresh linens. He
threw the ragged remains of the stable lad's clothes
into the fire.

Cameron seethed, face down on a blanket in front of
the fire and unable to move her head, at Alex's inhu-
manity. Blinded, unable to speak or breathe properly,
smothered, not able to move her head either way, she
drummed her feet frantically, not caring that it caused
her wound to flare.

Alex surveyed his handiwork. Not as neat as most
beds he had seen, but not bad either for a first attempt. At Cameron's muffled curses and drumming
feet he turned, irritated at her inability to appreciate
his efforts on her behalf.

"I'm thinking it would hurt more to dress you in a
nightshirt, so you'll not mind sleeping as nature in-
tended you to, would you?"

At Cameron's muffled stream of abuse and the resumption of her kicking he laughed.

"Of course you wouldn't mind. You're more at home naked than clothed," he said, as he bit his lip and bent.

Cameron howled in agony as Alex picked her up, and she rolled down his strong arms, coming to rest against his chest facing him, her body taut, caught in an excruciating paroxysm of pain. She was blind to the tears that started in Alex's eyes as he carried her to the bed. He stood a moment before lowering her rigid body onto the fresh linen.

"I canna help it, my love," he murmured, his own body howling with her agony. But her screams drowned out his words.

Chapter Twenty-five

Cameron woke and stared at the ceiling that she knew so well, having memorized every tiny crack and stain. She tentatively moved her neck backward and forward. The pain was there but not as sharp and crippling as before. She slowly swung her legs around to the edge of the bed and, taking a deep breath, threw her body up into a sitting position. The room spun, the floor heaved, and pain shot through her. She fought the waves of cold, nauseating faintness. Torquil, watching, whined his concern and padded toward her.

Alex watched from his mattress on the floor, willing himself to lie still, knowing that by thwarting her attempts to get up she'd fight him and only hurt herself more. She was in such a weakened state, he reasoned, she'd soon give up. He pretended to sleep.

Cameron's face was startlingly pale as she fought the cold, clammy sweat that covered her. She clung to the mattress, afraid to let go despite the excruciating agony that throbbed through her shoulder and down to her hand. She breathed deeply and looked around the room, stopping sharply at the sight of Alex's prone form. Satisfied that he slept, she took stock of her surroundings, appraising each item as it came into focus. It was a warm, comfortable room, very masculine, she concluded, as she pressed her calves against the edge of the bed to steady herself before standing. Alex watched through half-closed lids and marveled at her grim determination, knowing what it must cost her to move her head, let alone sit and stand.

Naked, Cameron slowly walked out of the room followed by Torquil. Alex watched her painfully slow progress, noting she still could not move her head. He wondered fearfully if he'd cut tendons when he probed into her shoulder for the bullet. As soon as Cameron was out of sight, Alex bounded to his feet to follow, frightened that she might injure herself further. The pale girl leaned against the doorjamb staring into the kitchen, turning her whole body and head as one, as she examined each corner. Through all the rooms on the ground floor Alex silently followed the stiff, naked girl who awkwardly and painfully tried to come to terms with her strange surroundings. She returned to the kitchen and opened the door that led outside. Alex longed to see her face as she stared out over the breathtaking vista. Did she see the beauty? What did she feel? He watched her bare back, as she stood framed in the open doorway, for some sign.

She stood still in the cold morning air without shivering but Alex, seeing her breath mist, was concerned, yet he didn't want to intrude on or shatter her private moment. He quietly returned to the bedchamber and banked the fire noisily to let her know he was awake. He expected her to call to him or to return to her bed, but she did neither. Cameron stood looking over the peaceful glen and the tears burned down her cold cheeks. She knew with sudden clarity that she couldn't stay, as a fear grew inside that she would be lost forever if she did.

She felt a prisoner as never before, not just because her movements were limited, making running and riding impossible, but because somehow she was tied inside as though her very inner freedom was in danger. Her mind railed at Alex, who she felt spun the web. What was he doing there? All that energy and pain she'd used to leave him far behind her in thought and reality had been for nothing. Why wasn't he back with his Lady Fiona instead of playing the diligent guardian? He just needs to master and control, she concluded.

Alex watched her standing in the open doorway. He walked toward her, his boots firmly sounding on the paved kitchen floor, yet she made no move she had heard him. He draped a blanket across her bare shoulders carefully and, reaching around her, closed the door.

Cameron faced the closed door, the mountains blocked from her sight by hard wood. She stood still, seething, and despite the pain shrugged the blanket off her and flung open the door.

"You're chilled, Cameron. I won't allow you to make yourself sicker," he said gently.

"You won't allow?" challenged Cameron.

"Aye. Now get back to bed or near the fire."

"No!" retorted Cameron, wishing she could turn on him, but her injury made it impossible.

Alex stood in front of her, closing the door firmly.

"Cameron, I dinna want to hurt you," he growled, draping the blanket around her again.

"Hah!" she sneered, tossing the blanket to the floor. How she wished she could raise her eyes to his instead of having to stare at his stomach. She turned away from him and her fury increased at her inability to make a dignified exit. She tried to spin on her heel, but having to swivel her body and head in the same movement made it impossible. Alex, watching, laughed softly, thinking she looked like an injured kitten, her green eyes flashing as she tried to be arrogant, though stark naked and listing stiffly to one side. Cameron's rage blossomed at his snort of mirth. She halted abruptly at the kitchen table, her fists clenched at the edge. She longed to hurl everything within reach to smash his mocking face but she was powerless to do anything more than keep herself upright. She closed her eyes feeling the murderous pounding of her blood, as her breath hissed frantically and her white-rimmed nostrils flared.

Alex, too, felt powerless. He knew she was standing on her own two feet by pure willpower and determination, and that his impulse to pick her up and carry her would somehow hurt her more than just physically.

She waited until her frustrating rage ebbed to a bitter hard knot in her stomach, then she took a deep breath, preparing to walk the few steps to the door. It seemed so far, but at last her hand touched the frame and she clung to it, feeling Alex's eyes burning into her back.

Alex watched with consternation. His own breath

released with relief as she reached her objective. Should he help her now? What was it that he feared? That she might resist him and open the healing wound? Did he want to spare her that pain? Or was it her striving for dignity that had made him laugh? He remembered Fergus's words about Cameron being neither tamed nor wild but standing on unsure ground in between the two. He suffered, seeing her slow progress as she painfully made her way back to the bedchamber.

Cameron saw the welcoming bed and her only thought was to get there unaided. The distance seemed so vast, with nothing on the way to cling to. She steadied herself against a washstand, sensing Alex's presence and, summoning every fiber of her being to give her strength, she launched herself into the seemingly yawning space. Alex held his breath, his hands unknowingly were outstretched and fingers splayed. Cameron, unable to look down, felt the edge of the bed crack her shins and she slowly swiveled, pressing the backs of her calves against it as she lowered herself, keeping her head and neck stiff. She hung suspended, every muscle screaming, expecting to sit on the soft mattress, sinking lower and lower until she sat with a thump and a scream of agony.

Alex gently lifted her legs onto the bed and covered her up. He looked down at her unconscious face and wondered at himself. Why had he just stood there watching her put herself through that unnecessary torture? His joy at the new morning disappeared and he stormed outside toward the horses that stomped in the barn, impatient to be free. He opened the door and they pranced out, swishing their tails and kicking up their heels. Noticing with irritation that their coats were dull, he spent the morning grooming them and getting himself back into his former good mood. Savagely he brushed and combed out his frustrations until he delighted in the feel of their glossy coats.

When he became hungry, Alex heated his broth, adding some dried meat he found in his saddlebag, and to his surprise found it palatable. He offered some to Torquil who, after one sniff, turned up his nose in disdain.

"All right, old dog, go catch your own dinner," he laughed, opening the kitchen door for the huge hound to bound out.

Cameron awoke in the late afternoon and drowsily saw Alex through sleepy eyes as he tended the fire. She wondered dreamily if she were back in the tiny, stone house in the northern Highlands; she had lain the very same way then, watching his broad back and tousled, tawny hair bent over the same chore. It was like a sandwich with a bitter middle, she thought, as remembrances of all that had happened since flooded through her brain, dominated by the image of Fiona's beautiful, laughing face.

Alex turned and, seeing her wide green eyes staring at him, smiled.

"Time you ate," he murmured.

And Cameron hardened her heart that leaped at the sound of his voice. Alex left the room and reappeared with a bowl of his own broth. He carried it proudly and frowned at her sneering look.

"You're just like the dog, turning up your nose at my cooking."

"I'm not hungry."

"You will eat," smiled Alex, as he piled pillows against the wall at the head of the bed. "Now, if you can wiggle your bottom up the bed, you'll be able to sit comfortably, or should I lift you?" he said carefully, giving her the choice but knowing which she'd accept from her mutinous expression.

Cameron accepted neither as the thought of wiggling her sore back up the mattress was too much to consider. She gritted her teeth and gave a tremendous push with her uninjured arm, swinging her body up and sideways.

Alex swore as he saw the fresh blood welling through the bandages, but Cameron's eyes never left his face as she stared triumphantly, despite the excruciating pain that knifed through her. Alex nodded wryly.

"You need to go another two feet north," he indicated dryly, pointing at the pillows.

Leaning on her good arm, Cameron shot him a look of pure unadulterated hate. He knew she had drained all her energy, and he reveled in the knowledge, she raged inwardly. There was a tense moment as their staring eyes locked, and Alex wondered what he could do to help without undermining her. It would be easy to pick her up and settle her back. But easy for whom? Obviously just for him, he thought. He picked up the pillows and moved them down so they wedged under her back, but Cameron stubbornly refused to relax against them. Nothing I do is right by her, sighed Alex to himself, as he looked with concern at the blood that now poured down her arm.

"All right, Cameron, you win," he said, forcing a laugh, and he left the room to get fresh bandages and hot water. Cameron sighed with relief and lay back on the pillows. She had just relaxed when he reentered and wordlessly started cutting the dressing off her arm. She had been tricked, she raged silently, submitting to his administrations. Alex slid his hand behind her head, forcing her to sit, leaning her body against his as he examined her injury. To his relief it was clean and less swollen, the infection nearly gone. It would be a week or so before she was really able to use the arm, he estimated, and he worried again of the further damage he might have done by his inexperienced operation.

Cameron's nose was pressed against his chest and the clean scent of his body assailed her senses. She steeled herself, forcing Fiona's face into her mind as she silently allowed him to dress the wound.

"'Tis healing well, but you mustna use it, as you're not letting it mend," growled Alex, laying her back against the pillows. It was time she wore the nightshirt, he thought, aroused by her nearness.

Freshly bandaged and propped against the pillows, Alex handed her the bowl of broth.

"I'll put it in a cup if it'll be easier," he offered, but received no reply. "Surely 'tis not the same old game of being mute, is it? Now listen to me because I'm fast running out of patience. I am ten times stronger than you in your present condition, d'you ken? If you refuse to answer me I'll assume you need assistance and will oblige. You ken?"

There was a pause as Cameron deliberated. Unable to nod she grit her teeth.

"Yes," she hissed.

"Good," snapped Alex. "Now, would you prefer a cup?"

"Yes."

"Good," answered Alex, and he left to return with a cup of broth which he placed in Cameron's left hand. He then sat on the end of the bed and watched her, willing her to drink.

Cameron sat mesmerized by his deep, amber eyes, momentarily forgetting her anger. Suddenly she gave a small cry and threw the cup across the bed at him, hitting his chest, the contents spraying. Her eyes widened, shocked by her action. She had felt no fury when she hit out. She had suddenly felt exposed, vulnerable, and sought to protect herself.

A dangerous tic beat in Alex's cheek, and he walked out angrily slamming the door behind him. He strode out to the stream to cool his temper and returned in better spirits an hour later to find Cameron kneeling on the floor by the bed, trying to sponge out the broth stains. She heard him enter but, unable to move quickly, pretended not to as she continued her ineffectual scrubbing. Alex's temper rekindled, and he picked her up firmly and deposited her on the bed. He silently turned and grabbed a nightshirt which he wrung in his hands.

"I've given great thought to this so listen. Until your shoulder is knit, you will do as I say without question. You'll have to put up with my ways, d'you ken? When you are healed, and I'll be the judge of that, you'll have your say." The speech he had prepared had sounded more eloquent and masterful at the stream; saying it now to the white-faced girl he felt like a bully.

"Cameron, you make me feel like a brute, but I canna and will not put up with this any longer. Now, I'll get more broth and you'll drink it," he said tersely.

Cameron listened to him rattling pots and swearing in the kitchen, as his words echoed in her ears. He never wanted to put up with her at all, she thought miserably. She sipped her soup as Alex stared broodingly into the fire.

This was not the way he had envisoned their relationship at all. This wasn't at all what he'd romanced about. She was meant to lie passively and adoringly as he nursed her. When would the war between them end? Maybe loving her was his mistake. He should be distant and objective, forget his emotions, insure her recovery; until then all else had to wait. Let her hate him and think he's an ogre, he decided; when she was well they'd remedy it together.

A week went by slowly and silently as Alex firmly tended her; bandaging; handing her food; leaving her alone to wash and have her privacy; emptying the basin and the chamber pot as if he were an impersonal servant; he slept in the small adjoining dressing room, her presence and seeming fear of him making it impossible to spend the nights in the same room. He kept his days full, mostly working outside in the fresh air, setting traps, hunting, fishing, and chopping wood. He was proud of his ability to support them both. He found that by taking each hour at a time he relaxed more, brooded less, and fell asleep quickly at night, feeling positive and sure of himself.

But Cameron was bored. She steeled herself against Alex's cheerful whistling and singing as her mind planned an escape. She noted his detachment and impersonal attitude toward her, and it confirmed her worst fears. She would be a burden to no one, she swore, exercising her arm vigorously. It now moved quite easily with just an occasional twinge, but she kept the knowledge from Alex as she stored the resentment over each thing he did for her. Each bowl of food or water that he served or emptied became a sign of her own dependency and weakness. Each clean bandage and sheet became another link in the chain that mockingly bound her with him. Each time he left the house she lay waiting for his footsteps to fade before jumping out of the bed to search out and add more to the collection of provisions that she stored away in an upstairs dresser drawer. Soon she would have her freedom and pride, she vowed, as she folded warm clothes and tucked them away. Soon she would be free.

Alex missed certain things like his sharpest skinning knife, but he thought nothing of it until one day, well into the second week, he saw Cameron pass an upstairs window. He stole quietly into the house and heard the patter of small bare feet, then found her sitting up in bed, slightly out of breath, with flushed cheeks. He had wondered why she didn't seem anxious to be up and about, knowing full well she was nearly recovered, but had put the worry aside, telling himself she'd be up as soon as she was ready. Now something nagged at his brain. She was up to something. But what? He decided she had been an invalid long enough.

Cameron lay awake that night brooding over her narrow escape. She felt he knew more than he'd said; she had seen his eyes narrow with speculation as she sat trying to even her breathing from the fast run down the stairs.

Cameron sat up and listened, knowing Alex had gone to bed hours before. Lighting a candle from the fire she tiptoed into the hall, wishing she'd had the foresight to hide her provisions somewhere closer at hand. Slowly and quietly she inched up the creaky stairs.

Alex was awake pondering how to once again free Cameron's spirit. He sat up suddenly, hearing a soft rustle and a creaking noise. He strained his ears and from upstairs heard the protesting squeak of wood rubbing against wood, as though a warped drawer was being opened. He swung his legs out of bed and tiptoed to where Cameron slept. Seeing by the glow of the fire that her bed was empty, he tiptoed to the stairs and listened.

Alex quietly opened the door of the upstairs room as Cameron, dressed in an enormous pair of men's britches, was attempting to roll up the legs so she could walk without tripping. She was so intent on

what she was doing that she was not aware of Alex
leaning nonchalantly against the wall, watching her
with amused interest. Torquil thumped his heavy tail
with relief at Alex's presence and Cameron, turning to
hush the dog, saw two large bare feet beside him. She
looked dismally up the nightshirted length of him to
his smiling face.

"Glad to see you're feeling so much better," he
grinned.

"I have to go home," stated Cameron boldly, bending to roll up the leg of her trews again.

"You are home, Cameron," replied Alex softly.

Cameron tingled at the warmth of his voice, but
kept her head bowed. Forcing her shaking hands to be
calm she unfolded a large piece of cloth and, taking
the rest of her provisions from the bottom drawer,
carefully wrapped them up.

"I was wondering where that dirk had gone. 'Twas
the sharpest for cutting meat. I've been quite lost without it," he remarked casually.

Cameron took a deep breath and stood up.

"Please," she said in a small brave voice that fought
to be steady, "you'll not stop me."

"Aye. I'll stop you."

Cameron pleaded with her eyes but, seeing no
change in his benign expression, strode determinedly
to the door.

"Aye, I'll stop you if those breeks don't first," he
chuckled, looking at the unrolled trouser leg. "They'll
trip you and you'll fall down the stairs breaking your
stiff neck," he added, scooping her into his arms. Cameron dropped her bundle and dealt him a ringing
crack across his face. She fought her desire to be in his
arms as she rained blow upon blow at his face and
head. Alex carried her down the stairs, smiling grimly,
as he had to admit she packed a rather mean punch.

He dumped her unceremoniously on her bed, but no sooner had she landed than she was up again, tripping on the ridiculously large clothes, her fists swinging as her wild temper raged out of control. Alex stepped back out of range, his face already stiff from her bruising treatment.

Cameron's blood roared. She didn't know why she fought, she just had to, had to keep him away from her or she was lost. Leaping off the bed, hampered by the clumsy clothes, she pulled up the dangling sleeves as she reached for something to throw at him. Little sobbing noises burst from her tight lips as she hurled a bowl and a cup. Alex nimbly avoided the missiles, no longer smiling. She was out of hand. He didn't want to be violent with her, but he was damned if he'd allow her to smash the house or himself.

"That's enough!" he roared, but Cameron lashed out at him, unable to stem the furious tide that had taken her over completely.

Alex threw her onto the bed and, pinning her down, tied her long dangling sleeves together, imprisoning her hands. Cameron lay, her face constricted with rage, kicking out at him savagely.

"Calm down!" he roared, but Cameron couldn't hear him over her own compulsive screams. Alex left the room, returning with a bucket of cold water which he threw over her. Cameron gasped as the icy water hit her, and choked as it went into her nose and mouth.

Alex stood watching her body, calm as the coughing ceased, until she lay still, her arms bound together, her green eyes empty of fury but full of fear. He approached her but stopped short when he saw panic flare and she whimpered and shied away from him.

"Cameron, I'm not going to hurt you. I don't ever want to hurt you again," he said softly. "I promise I'll take you back to Cape Wrath, but not now, maybe in the spring when the snow has melted."

Alex slowly neared the bed and sat on the edge. "Are you hearing me?" he asked, hurt by her eyes that stared at him with hatred. Cameron was backed to the wall, forcing her terrified body to sit proudly, to hide her fear of him.

"Do you hear me?" Alex repeated.

Cameron nodded. He didn't know what to do. Cameron was afraid of him despite the brave rebellion in her expression. Each tiny movement he made caused her to wince for a split second before showing her bravado.

"Oh, Cameron, don't be so scared of me, give me your arms and I'll free them," he pleaded.

"I'm not afraid of you or anybody else," she hissed, extending her imprisoned arms and Alex, not wanting to alarm her more, stretched his hands toward her, keeping his body still. The bulky knot was hard to untie and, seeing her shiver, he drew her to him, feeling the tension in her shaking body. He undid the buttons and pulled the shirt over her head. With a groan Alex folded her to him and felt the frantic beating of her heart close to his. He rocked her, trying to comfort and reassure, but she remained tense and shaking.

Cameron shivered from his nearness as she fought her treacherous desire of his arms around her, forcing her muscles to stiffen and her arms to remain firmly at her sides lest they return his embrace. He lifted her and carried her to a comfortable chair by the fire, covering her with a dry blanket and telling himself that it was not the time to give in to his stirring emotions. The bed was drenched and he berated himself for his drastic measure, not fully comprehending the reasons for Cameron's violent tremors as he tended the fire so it blazed hotly.

Cameron sat alone and confused as Alex clattered around the kitchen. The rising panic had receded from her brain, leaving her feeling lost and unprotected. How often had she longed to be held by his strong arms? Why must she be tortured and tempted that way? Was she like a child to him? He had said more than once that a guardian was like a father, but she wasn't a child, she was a woman, an independent woman who didn't want to so achingly yearn for such comfort. How could she prove it to him? Why did she want to prove it to him? She even recoiled from the word *woman*, somehow feeling it was traitorous to Duncan's memory. She had to prove her womanhood so she'd be allowed her freedom—the freedom entitled to an adult—and yet the thought of being free from Alex tore her insides into little pieces.

He returned with a warm flannel nightgown and the copper bath.

"Your bath will be drawn in just a moment, Lady Sinclair," he grinned bowing, as he tried to lighten the tension between them.

Cameron looked sharply into his smiling face. How could he tease her so? It was all a cruel game to him, this playing the servant to make her laugh, as if she were a disgruntled child. But two can play the same game, she raged.

Alex filled the bath with steaming water.

"Your bath, my lady," he proclaimed.

My lady! seethed Cameron. I'll give him my lady, and she threw back the blanket pretending she was his Lady Fiona Hurst, with rounded voluptuous breasts and hips. How would Fiona take off her britches? she wondered as she improvised.

Alex's mouth dropped open in astonishment. What

was she up to now? The small, bedraggled waif stood up languidly stretching, wiggled suggestively out of the enormous baggy britches and sauntered to the bath.

Just as Cameron felt she was being very successful, Alex roared with laughter, glad she was able to enter his game. She sat down in the hot water with a splash and froze with her head averted. Alex realized too late that once again he'd been insensitive.

"Oh, Cameron, I'm sorry," he apologized, trying to curb his mirth and kneeling beside her to gently touch her cheek. Cameron brought her fists down heavily in the water, drenching him, but Alex, noting the angry gleam in her eyes, grabbed her wrists, soaking himself even more.

"No, no more, Cameron. No more fighting. I was wrong. I shouldna have laughed, but it was seeing you trying to be something you are not—" he pleaded desperately, hoping she would understand, but she made no motion or change of mutinous expression.

Cameron was furious hearing his words "trying to be something you are not." She had tried with every fiber of her being to be a lady and, once again, she'd been ridiculed. Why didn't he let her go back to the moors to be the savage he obviously thought she was?

Alex stood and handed her the soap.

"Wash your hair," he said tersely, and immediately chided himself, seeing her jaw set even more rebelliously. Why did he say that? He had longed to bathe her himself, but fearing to drive her even further from him, the silly command had just burst out.

"Let me do it?" he offered, taking the soap from her motionless hands.

Alex washed Cameron's hair, as she sat motionless like a cold, marble statue. Her deliberate passivity hurt him, and he felt like a hired servant. His anger rose and he decided he would enjoy himself despite her obvious hostility. He closed his eyes as he traced her neck and jawline, letting his soapy hands linger and play with her firm breasts.

Cameron closed her own eyes and, despite her resolve, relaxed into the pleasurable sensations. She felt a stirring deep inside herself as her desire rose. Why not? she thought, as her breath quickened.

Alex was aware of her rising passion as his hands passed over her hardened nipples.

"Stand up," he murmured huskily, and Cameron knelt facing him as he soaped down her stomach, his hands stroking her silky flesh. Delighting in his velvet touch, she froze, her eyes suddenly flying open in panic as she remembered his incredible anger when she had felt the same way before. Alex stared in surprise at the naked alarm in the green eyes.

"What's the matter, Cameron?"

"I'll wash myself," she gasped.

Alex nodded silently and handed her the soap before leaving the room.

What was wrong? he wondered, as he paced the kitchen floor and drank whiskey.

"Oh, well, 'tis an hour at a time," he reminded himself out loud. He poured himself another drink and, on an afterthought, poured one for Cameron.

Cameron hastily pulled the flannel gown over her head as Alex entered the room with two glasses.

"Here, it'll warm your insides," he said, handing her a glass and draping a dry towel over her shoulders. Cameron took the glass and silently sat by the fire, goading herself to hate him as she sipped the drink, allowing the towel to just fall to the floor. She knew how to pick up a towel and dry herself! She wasn't the helpless baby he seemed to think she was.

"I'd appreciate some help. I'm not too proficient at

bed-making," remarked Alex, pulling the wet covers from the sopping mattress.

Cameron looked at him with surprise.

"That's not what I've heard tell," she retorted wickedly.

Alex lifted a quizzical eyebrow at her.

"Oh? Well, let's see if you're any better than I, shall we?" he growled provocatively. "The sheets and blankets are in that chest."

Cameron put down her glass, after draining it recklessly, and fetched what was needed.

"The mattress is soaked so we'd best turn it over. That's right, we'll pull it toward us and when I say 'now' we lift it up," he explained.

Together they turned the mattress and made the bed with fresh linens. That's progress, thought Alex, seeing Cameron curled back in the chair by the fire. He picked up her discarded towel and, sitting on the arm of her chair, gently toweled her hair. She made no move to help but didn't pull away from him.

"Here, have some more, it'll warm you," said Alex, handing her his glass. "Then let's get to sleep. We'll get no work done tomorrow, staying up all night." He pulled Cameron to her feet so she stood close without touching him.

Cameron tingled with the whiskey and the closeness of his body. The tiny space between them vibrated with excitement. She fought the impulse to press herself to him but, afraid he would push her away, quickly scrambled into the bed. Alex stood a moment watching her, put another log on the fire, blew out the oil lamp, and got into the bed with her.

Cameron froze. "What are you doing?" she asked, moving away from him until she bumped into the wall.

"Going to sleep, unless you have other plans," came the low answer.

"But 'tis wrong."

Alex sat up.

"Who said so?" he asked roughly.

"You did."

"You are my wife and your bed is my bed. Besides, I'll not sleep in that small, uncomfortable bed and have you run away. I want you where I can keep my eye on you," he retorted and lay down, determinedly turning his back on her, all too conscious of her small desirable body.

Cameron, her own back pressed against the cold wall, fought to stay awake but fell into a deep sleep just as morning lightened the sky.

Chapter Twenty-six

She woke to the brightness of the sun filling the room. She blinked and stretched, feeling warm and content, then froze as she remembered the night before. She turned her head to the pillow beside her, expecting to see the tawny, unruly hair or the warm amber eyes that laughed at her but when he wasn't there, she lay with the conflicting emotions of relief and disappointment. Part of her ached to just curl into his safe warmth until he returned to Fiona. It would be so easy, not having to struggle and fight and yet, in the end, what would she be left with? She had too much to lose. She remembered a baby hawk she had nursed who, when she set him free, had been torn to pieces by the other birds, as he couldn't defend himself in the wilds. She felt the same would happen to her. She had learned enough about the civilized gentry to know that a bastard couldn't hope to be loved by a lord, just rutted with producing another bastard, and so on and so on, in circles. Hadn't Mackie said 'Life was circles'? She sat staring at the bath from the night before, promising herself that she would be strong, no matter what the temptation.

She padded to the window and sucked in her breath at the nostalgic sight of snow. That's why the room was so bright, she thought, and remembered wistfully her glee as a child at waking to the sun's reflection on the icy crystals. It wasn't a thick snowfall, just patches of sparkling white and sprinkles delicately powdering the deep green of the firs.

She longed to go out and smell the air, remembering the exciting exhilaration of its crispness. She tugged at the flannel nightgown and wiggled her bare feet, wondering what she could wear.

"Good morning."

Cameron turned. How long had he been there? She nodded stiffly to him noting his face was ruddy and glowing and there was snow on his boots.

"Want to go out?"

Cameron plucked at her nightgown with a grimace and rocked back on her heels to show her toes. Alex left her with a grin and a gesture that seemed to say "Don't move, I'll be right back." He returned with an armload of clothes which he threw onto the bed with a great flourish.

"Take your pick," he offered, and left.

Cameron tried on every article, but they were each too big, falling down even when she rolled, tucked, and tied.

"Find any that fit?" called Alex from the kitchen, wondering why she was taking so long. Not hearing an answer but a lot of sighs of angry vexation, he peeked into the room to find Cameron near tears in an over-sized shirt with what he assumed were britches around her ankles.

Once again Cameron found herself in the humiliating position of a helpless child, standing on a kitchen chair holding up the waist, while Alex cut the legs of a pair of oversized trews.

"Dinna wiggle or I'll be cutting more than the cloth," he muttered.

Finally Cameron was dressed. The waist of the trousers came under her armpits and was secured by a leather belt that Alex had also shortened. He surveyed his handiwork, suppressing his amusement, as he was very conscious of Cameron's flashing eyes watching for even one indiscretion. He felt she looked cuddly and adorable, but he was too wise to remark on it, knowing she'd manage to take offense.

"Well, what are you waiting for?"

"Permission!" retorted Cameron sarcastically.

Alex opened the kitchen door with an exasperated sigh. Cameron resented his action. She stood unable to move toward the door. Why couldn't he have just let her go? Why did he have to mock her by opening the door for her like that? She couldn't walk by him to get outside no matter how much she wanted to.

She'd go out the front door, decided Cameron, turning on her heel without a word to Alex, who still stood holding the kitchen door open, a look of confusion on his face. She heard it slammed shut as she tugged at the heavy front door, finding to her dismay it was both locked and bolted. She stood still, feeling shamed and foolish, unable to turn around for fear Alex stood watching. Hearing nothing, and hoping he'd left the house when he'd slammed the kitchen door angrily, she turned and saw him leaning back against the wall, staring at her with a familiar, narrow-eyed gaze, and she filled with rage. No matter how she strove for independence, he always managed to trip and thwart her in some sly, undefinable way.

Alex recognized the dangerous gleam in her eye and, still nursing bruises from the night before, decided to beat a hasty retreat. Picking up the water buckets at his feet he strode out of the house to the stream.

Cameron shook with impotent rage. She felt trapped, unable to go out or stay in. She forced her mind to slow down and reason. He didn't want her to go out, that was why he'd done what he'd done. What had he done? She couldn't quite put her finger on that. Throwing logic aside she decided to go outside to spite him.

She stood watching Alex for a while, deliberating whether to just walk off and explore or to give in to her rage. The need for revenge triumphed as she saw him deep in thought and unaware of her. He intruded on her constantly, now she would do the same to him. Quickly and quietly she worked behind a hillock, making a pile of hard, icy snowballs.

Alex sat puzzling Cameron's behavior as he idly played with the paper-thin ice that coated the shallow puddles in the bank of the stream. His tranquility was shattered by a stinging blow to his cheek, and the icy wetness of snow melting down his collar shocked his warm body. He sprang up angrily as several more firmly packed snowballs hit him.

After the first initial shock Alex got into the spirit of the game, not realizing that to Cameron it was deadly serious. He discovered where she was hiding, and as she ducked back after throwing, he hid himself, searching for snow with which to retaliate. Where had she scraped together so much? he wondered, finding the thin powder nearly impossible to hold.

Alex circled around the glen, under cover of the forest, until he reached the back of the lodge behind her. He found deep snow that had spilled off the roof, and he scooped and shaped, keeping his eyes on her back. He gently lobbed them at her, catching her off guard.

She turned, surprised, and seeing his laughing face, felt her fury resurge. Once again he'd made a fool of her, sneaking up behind, and to add insult to injury he threw the snowballs softly as though she were some silly frilly baby. She picked up a hard ball, pressing it to pure ice, and threw it with all her strength, determined to smash the jeering smile off his face.

Alex realized belatedly that Cameron meant business, as the blood flowed down his cheek. He advanced on her, ready for battle. She tried to stop him, throwing more, her arm getting wilder as he came closer without flinching. Keeping her eyes on him she felt behind her for more ammunition, but her cold hands found nothing. She turned quickly to look and realized she'd used up her supply. She leaped to her feet to run but was caught by rough hands that dug into her shoulders causing her nearly healed injury to throb.

Alex held her in front of him, her feet off the ground, her eyes level with his. She hung suspended, unaware of her own pain or the blood on his face as his angry eyes held hers prisoner.

"Goddammit! I am sick to death of your games," he rasped, his voice constricted by suppressed rage. "You want violence then you shall have it . . . but this time my way!" He stalked toward the house, flipping her over his shoulder as he held her legs in a painful grip.

"You want violence, I'll teach you a more mature way," he roared, standing her on the bed and ripping off the clothes that he had lovingly and patiently fitted to her earlier. He grabbed her by the back of the neck and pulled her face even closer to his. The pain jolted Cameron to her senses and she began to fight.

"That's the way," he jeered savagely, as he stopped the flood of abuse that poured out of her with his mouth, toppling her backward onto the bed, where he imprisoned her with the weight of his body.

Alex ground his mouth to hers, forcing her tightly closed lips to admit his tongue. Cameron grew still, unable to breathe as his nose pressed painfully into hers. She tried to jerk her head to the side and could not move, so she bit down and tasted the salt of his blood in her mouth. Alex did not relent, the pain only spurring his already soaring fury. His pulses roared, all his pains and frustrations joined as he ruthlessly ground his body against hers. Cameron fought back as her own rage and desires surged at her inability to move her aching body against him.

Alex released her lips and looked down into her flashing eyes, noting through the haze of his own desire that her eyes too were veiled with her own passion. He laughed mirthlessly and, supporting himself on his arms, he softened the movement of his own hips to tantalize her further, then aware she just wanted to thrust against him, he stopped all movement and smiled demonically as she tried to urge him to continue. He held himself away from her and laughed as she arched to meet him. He would not make it easy for her; he wanted to punish. Cameron's own fury and passion ignited as she understood his cruel teasing. She clawed at his mocking face hovering over her, but he ruthlessly pinned her arms over her head with one strong hand and knelt with one leg on each side of her as he undid the buckle of his belt. Cameron froze for a moment and her eyes widened in fear. Was he going to beat her? She renewed her struggles, kicking her legs frantically so Alex abandoned any hopes of removing his own confining clothes. His fury and lust were now one. He had two burning desires, one to punish, one to love, and they were fused. He ground his mouth back to hers, still keeping her arms imprisoned with one hand while the other teased her, slowly circling and avoiding the very places she ached to be touched.

Alex wanted Cameron to feel as helpless and impotent as she made him feel. Under his hand the girl writhed and moaned as her hungry young body was unable to touch any part of him. She drummed her feet with frustration, preferring his hot anger to the cold fury that made him withhold himself from her. He rolled on his side, pulling, pulling her with him and finally Cameron felt the most wanted pressure thrust against her. She wriggled against the taut material of his breeches and rubbed her breasts against the leather of his jerkin, furious at not being able to feel his warm bared flesh.

They lay side by side, their lips locked, their tongues dueling as their bodies writhed in frenzy, each wanting to be the raper. Alex softened his mouth and his excitement pulsated at her strong, probing tongue that moved to the beat of her thrusts. He wanted to tear off his clothes and mount her, but somewhere in his madness the faint voice of reason surfaced and he bided his time, enjoying the prolonged anticipation.

Cameron felt like the conqueror and ran her hands down his back, under his shirt and trews, delighting in her mastery of his muscular body. She grasped his hard, lean buttocks and pressed them to her, hating the feel of the rough wool against her soft skin. Alex groaned as her hands slid across his bare flesh, exploring and rubbing rhythmically. She pulled open his jerkin and shirt and rubbed her breasts against his, as she raked his sides trying to find the release she had before. Alex pulled his hips back, allowing her searching hands room to caress him. He held his breath as Cameron's hand slowed and felt his pulsing hardness. She wanted to hold him but also to rub against it. Her fingers frantically fumbled with his buttons and Alex leaned back as, with agonizing slowness, she released his impatient manhood from the confining cloth. He raised his hips as she tugged his tight britches down, watching her through half-open lids as she breathed heavily, nostrils flaring. Cameron had bared Alex to his knees, and she lay against his warm flesh, wriggling her bottom and thrusting her hips against him. Waves and waves of incredible feelings pounded through her until she arched stiffly, straining against him as she climaxed.

Alex sat up and tore off his boots and clothes. She'd had her way, now it was his turn. As she lay half dazed, still feeling the ticking deep inside of her, she opened her eyes in alarm as she felt her legs abruptly parted. Naked, Alex knelt above her, and she stared in fascination as he gently touched her still pulsing flesh with his straining hardness. Alex resisted entering her with the giant thrust that would satisfy him, knowing the pain it would cause her. He teased her with slow movements until her hips rose to meet his. Then he entered her just a little, controlling the climax that threatened to explode at the feel of her warm, tight softness. He felt her open to him and then, unable to control himself, he drove into her, barely heeding her cries as the frustrations of the past weeks detonated and he lost all sense of time and place.

Cameron lay still beneath him; after the first searing pain she found her excitement renewed and was strangely disappointed when his strong thrusts ceased. That moment, when he'd stopped deep inside her, his hands pressing her buttocks to him and she had felt the spasms, had been wonderful, but now she was left dissatisfied.

Alex rolled off her, swung his legs over the side of the bed, and sat. He did not know what to say to her, as he assumed once again that he had violated her free spirit in an unforgivable way. He must have hurt her, he thought, as he silently pulled on his clothes without turning. He didn't want to see her hurt, angry face.

Cameron watched Alex dress and all the joy and excitement she felt turned to fear. What had she done wrong now? she thought miserably. He stood looking down at her sadly, noting the hand pressed between her legs.

"I'm sorry," he muttered, embarrassed. "Did I hurt you?" he asked, as his eyes strayed to the traces of blood on the sheet. Cameron shook her head and followed the direction of his eyes.

"I'm sorry about your face," she stammered, misunderstanding the source.

Alex sat beside her and looked down at her hand.

"Does it hurt?"

Cameron looked at him in confusion and stared down at where he indicated, feeling a quiver of anticipation. She looked into his face but didn't answer as she debated what to say. They sat with their eyes locked and Cameron squirmed as she felt his large, warm hand cover hers, then caress the tenderness between her thighs. Alex recognized her hungry look and laughed softly, as he gently pushed her back, still gazing into her eyes. He felt very virile and debated whether to enter and retake her, but he knew she'd be raw and sore for days if he did, frustrating them both.

"You've just lost your maidenhead," he said softly. "You must be patient."

Cameron pleaded silently with her eyes.

"I'll ease your hunger if you'll ease mine," Alex growled mischievously.

Cameron nodded eagerly.

"You promise to bake some bread and scones?"

Cameron's green eyes widened for a moment in astonishment before she smiled and nodded.

Alex kissed her gently, but Cameron impatiently jerked her hips.

"You've a sweet mouth, Cameron," he murmured, his mouth leaving hers reluctantly and continuing down to her straining nipples that stood stiff and quivering. Cameron tensed in anticipation as she felt his warm breath tickle her navel.

"You promise about the baking?" he muttered, as Cameron drummed her feet with impatience.

"Aye," she breathed.

"All right," said Alex, sliding his hands under her bottom and lifting her hips.

Cameron held her breath with wonder as his soft, hungry mouth covered her aching. She opened her eyes in wonderment to see his tawny head bent between her raised legs, and she thrust toward him, wishing she had something to drive into him as he had done to her.

Cameron lay glassy-eyed and sated, but Alex's own passion flared as he stroked her softly.

"I've now a hunger myself," he said ruefully, staring at his bulging breeks. Cameron smiled and gently traced the hardness, laughing as it rose to meet her hand. She pushed him back on the bed.

"I'll ease your hunger if you help me with the baking?" she teased mischievously.

Alex nodded and Cameron kissed him tenderly.

"You've a sweet mouth," she imitated.

"Aye, should be," retorted Alex wickedly, as she copied his actions, her mouth tracing and nipping down his long, lean body. She unbuttoned and pulled down his britches as he raised his hips to help.

"You promise to help with the baking?" she asked thoughtfully, her face cushioned on his belly as she blew tantalizingly on his rearing impatience.

"Aye, aye . . . I do . . . Anything," he groaned, feeling the unbearable teasing of her warm breath circling, but never quite touching.

"Promise?"

"Aye, aye, I do."

"All right."

Chapter Twenty-seven

Alex and Cameron were awakened by Torquil's persistent barking. Seeing the room was pitch black and the fire out, Alex swore. He had no idea of the time, except that the sun had evidently set hours ago. He leaped out of the bed and tripped against the bath, cursing loudly. Cameron rose and felt her way to the kitchen, where the fire still cast some light. She lit two candles and opened the back door to Torquil, who bounded in shaking the snow off his shaggy coat. Then, seeing Alex occupied with the pails of dirty bath water, Cameron grabbed a blanket and oil lamp and went into the night to tend the horses.

The snow was falling thickly and she had trouble seeing the black horses in the dark. She listened and heard impatient snorts and pawings near the barn. With difficulty she opened the door against the wind, allowing the cold horses to enter.

"What the hell are you doing?" roared Alex, as he helped her to swing the heavy door shut. "Get back in the warm, you've no clothes on."

"More than you," retorted Cameron, pulling the

blanket around her and shining her lamp on Alex's naked body jumping up and down.

Grabbing her hand Alex raced back to the lodge, where they sat toasting their frozen feet in front of the kitchen fire. Dressed warmly in an odd assortment of clothes, Alex set about relighting the bedroom fire as Cameron explored and examined all the treasures in the kitchen.

"Is there no meat?" she inquired of Alex, as he carried in the empty bathtub and hung it on its hook.

"Some hare and a wee bit of fish. 'Tis downstairs in the cold so it wouldna turn."

"Downstairs?" frowned Cameron.

Alex showed her the trap door and with a lantern they descended, Alex leading the way and keeping a tight hold on Cameron, who didn't seem to mind. He smiled broadly as they reached the bottom and he held her and kissed her.

"No time for that; There's work to be done," said Cameron firmly, pushing him away and examining the neat rows of jars.

"Blackberries, bearberries, pickled onions," she exclaimed.

"Can you cook?"

"That's for you to find out," retorted Cameron, selecting jars.

"Put them in here," volunteered Alex, holding out a basket.

"Where's the meat?"

"'Tis barely half a hare and 'tis very tough," apologized Alex.

Armed with an assortment of different things Cameron looked around the large kitchen.

"We need to light the other fire," she announced, pointing at an enclosed range. "Well, that is, if you want your baking done."

Alex sat contented by the fire, smelling the delicious
aromas as Cameron hummed and rushed around. She
was happier than she'd ever been. She knew how t
cook, as Mara often refused. The servants came an
went with such regularity that often there were week
when there weren't any, and Duncan Fraser had de
manded good food if nothing else. With little to wor'
with, Cameron made a pie of the hare, onions, and a
few shriveled potatoes she found. She clucked softly a
no milk or egg to make the crust shiny and brown. Sh
rubbed her nose with a floury hand as she concen
trated on her blackberry tart, making up for the lim
ited ingredients by artistically weaving a lattice of past
ry over the preserved berries.

Alex contained his curiosity, realizing Cameron
would probably prefer his appreciation at her fin
ished products. His heart sang as he recalled the deli
cious day, and his nose breathed in the fragrant aro
mas.

Cameron was not pleased at her finished product
She stared unhappily at her hare pie that was slightly
scorched on one side. Duncan would have yelled fu
riously at the sight of it, but Alex was delighted and
his saliva ran freely.

"'Tis the most beautiful pie I've ever seen," he de
clared, puzzled at Cameron's disgruntled frown.

"'Tis disgraceful," retorted Cameron, her floury
nose wrinkling with dismay. "Are you blind? 'Ti
burnt, and strange-looking. See here and here?" she
cried, pointing out all the imperfections.

Alex folded her in his arms, but she tensed furiously
so he quickly released her.

Not having eaten all day they both ate hungrily
Even Cameron forgot her scorched crust as they fin
ished every morsel. Alex congratulated himself a
Cameron bustled about. She brought the blackberry

attice pie to the table tentatively. It could look better, she thought, but she was pleased with herself neverthe-ess. Tomorrow she would hunt for wild roots and erbs before the snows covered them all.

Alex looked at her flushed pleased face and praised he pie, hoping he was saying the right thing. This ime when he enfolded her in his arms, she snuggled p to him, knowing she deserved praise.

Alex pushed back his chair after the last vestige of ie was gone and, remembering the well-stocked cellar, escended through the trap door with a wink. Cam-ron now noticed the incredible pile of dirty plates. He had not bothered to wash one, she observed, and vondered what he would have used if the lodge hadn't een so well equipped. She laughed to herself, remem-ering the ones she had thrown, as she looked for soap.

Alex's head appeared through the floor and he held loft a dusty bottle.

"Cognac," he crowed with glee.

"Dirty platters," indicated Cameron dryly.

Together they cleaned the kitchen. At first Alex ad been surly, irritated at her dampening remark, ut as they worked together, he relaxed and enjoyed imself.

Their rest earned, they sipped cognac at the kitchen able. Alex was about to suggest they go back to bed vhen Cameron leaped up and disappeared into the antry. She was excited about the house and, unable o resist any longer, she climbed up to the shelves to liscover tea, herbs, spices, beef jerky, oatmeal, honey, nd a host of other welcome produce.

Alex felt abandoned and robbed of her presence.

"Is there a quill and paper?" Cameron called out.

"You can write?" answered Alex in astonishment. Cameron stalked out ferociously, looking ridiculous with the floury nose and odd assortment of clothes.

"Of course I can write," she spat, furious at his laughter. Why did he always have to make her feel silly and stupid?

"Oh, Cameron, sit down," said Alex, feeling they should be able to talk about her getting angry at the least little thing.

"Then stand if you've a mind to," he added, seeing her stand defiantly, her face set more rebelliously.

Cameron shook with rage and yet could not reason why. It seemed each time she let down her guard she got hurt. Her mind wrestled trying to find the words for her feeling. It was as though each time she forgot her incompleteness, there was a subtle reminder that made her feel clumsy and ignorant, and she knew she did not belong with him anywhere. Even her desires had changed. Cape Wrath now seemed cold and inhospitable without his presence in her imaginings. She knew the crumbling castle would echo lonesomely, and her beloved moors would be bleak and mournful with her longing. She stared at Alex in horror, as she realized her promise to herself—to be strong no matter the temptation—made just that very morning, had been broken, shattered into a thousand pieces. She looked to her feet as though she stood on quicksand, feeling unsure and lost as her whole world tipped and disoriented her. What was the matter with her? Why couldn't she be as she had been before she met him?

Alex watched her face change from furious defiance to sheer terror. She looked so lost and confused he longed to be able to hear her thoughts. Cameron saw his tenderness and, mistaking it for pity, screamed:

"Aye. I can write and read, calculate and juggle figures, cook and wash, ride and hunt, swim and fish, but I will not be a lady."

She ran from the kitchen and hid herself in the small dressing room that Alex had occupied. She

eeded to be alone in the darkness to steel herself
gainst the futile tears that ached to spill, as she con-
inced herself that she didn't want to be a lady, push-
ig aside the nagging conscience that told her she
ould never be one.

Alex poured himself another brandy and brooded.
Vhat was so terrible about asking if she could write?
Ie knew many women who couldn't, including Fiona.
Ie missed Cameron's presence, but he forced himself
o sit an hour or more before blowing out the lamp
nd going to bed. He entered the fire-lit bedchamber
nd saw a shape on the mattress so, assuming she slept,
e threw a log noisily into the hearth, hoping to wake
er seemingly by accident. There was no movement, so
e sat heavily, and at no protest or recoil, reached out.
Alex's hand sank into the cold pillow. He patted the
vhole of the bed and, finding it empty, cursed as he
an up the stairs to search the other rooms. Checking
is anxious rage he stopped and whistled for Torquil,
vho padded up tiredly and stuck a wet nose in his
and. Then she hadn't flown the nest, he sighed with
elief, sitting on the cold stairs, absently toying with
he hound's floppy ears.

"Whcre's your mistress?" he whispered, and the dog
tared at him as if to say he was mad, before wearily
valking off. Alex followed him to the little dressing
oom and there, curled asleep, was Cameron. He lifted
is lantern and stared down at her floury cheeks
treaked with tears.

Carefully, so as not to wake her, he picked her up
nd carried her to the larger bed, where he covered her
p. He slid into the cold sheets beside her, cradling
er so she fit into the curve of his body.

Cameron had been awakened by the sound of a log
eing thrown onto the fire, but she kept her eyes
ightly closed, hoping he didn't feel or hear her quick-

ening pulse as he held her cradled to his heart. After the storm of tears had raged, despite her resolve, she had lain wondering how to regain control of herself. Regain not just control of her emotions but of her very being. What had happened to her? Where was the strong, self-reliant, proud person of a few short months before? The images of herself in Edinburgh flashed through her mind and she cringed, hating the weak, groveling creature she saw. She vowed never to allow herself to be so again, and she wept anew at the stark realization she could also never be the wild, carefree child of Cape Wrath either.

Cameron lay curled in the warmth of Alex's body, wide awake, forcing her body not to move or respond to his closeness. He seemed content just to have her within the circle of his arms, his breathing even, as if he slept soundly. Cameron felt a hardness press against the bottom of her spine, and for a moment her traitorous body flared with excitement, but her mind refused the temptation and she turned from him as if in sleep, leaving the safe circle of his arms.

Next morning Alex awoke with empty arms and sat up sharply in fear, but sank back with relief at hearing a clatter from the kitchen. He stretched as he wondered what to expect from his unpredictable bride that day. It was time they really talked and he puzzled how to, as she seemed to take offense at the strangest things. Words were a bane. If only he could somehow win her trust and show her that he loved her. One minute at a time, he reminded himself, as he got out of bed and dressed.

He entered the kitchen, not knowing what to expect but feeling prepared for anything. Cameron had swept and polished the room so it sparkled. Large pots of water boiled, and he frowned thinking she shouldn't be lifting such heaviness, but he clamped down on his tongue. If Cameron saw him, she didn't acknowledge his presence. She had been up and working since before sunrise and the steady unfeeling rhythm satisfied her. She had led the horses out and raked the steamy manure from the shed. She had found the little vegetable plot and scraped away the snow and unearthed potatoes and carrots from under their bed of hay. She had cleaned and put to order the cellar and the kitchen, and now she was at work on the pantry.

Alex sat at the table piqued at her exclusion of him as she bustled in and out. He was glad to see her active and occupied, and yet he felt no part of her, he thought sadly. He had felt the same way before when loving her. He had delighted in her freedom and passion, but had felt a small, cold nagging which he hadn't been able to define. Now he realized that she kept some part of her insulated, out of reach, held back from him. He puzzled at his new reasoning. On one hand she abandoned herself without coyness and embarrassment, unlike any other woman he had ever known, and yet it was not enough. What was it he wanted? With a shock he knew it was for her to claim him as her own. He wanted her jealousy, her possessiveness, he wanted all the things he had ever despised in his other women.

He was sharply brought back to reality by Cameron slamming a hot pan from the oven onto the table. He looked up, bewildered, but Cameron's flushed face turned, avoiding his eyes. He sat dejectedly, seeing the curling steam circle above the hot scones. Cameron marched back and loudly banged down a jar of jam and a knife. Alex sat back and watched, amused by her determined effort to get his attention.

Cameron felt awkward, his presence broke into her protective numb rhythm, breaking her stride. She found her usually sure hands fumbling and clumsy.

She grasped the heavy teapot and thumped it next to the jam, causing liquid to spurt out of the spout. Alex stood and reached for a cloth.

"I'll mop it up myself," snapped Cameron, ignoring the proffered rag and fetching another. She briskly wiped up the puddle and banged down a mug.

"There's the scones I promised in payment."

Alex didn't know how to respond, as she turned her back on him and busied herself at the sink.

"I thought the bargain was that I help?" he said softly. Cameron didn't turn. How seductive and tempting his voice was, she thought, and she forced her hands to clatter the pans loudly.

"You found tea?" Alex tried at polite conversation as he poured himself a cup.

"Will you have some?" he added, when she didn't answer.

"I've had," replied Cameron curtly, as she left the room armed with a broom.

Alex sat hearing her busy, angry sweepings. Well, at least she was beating the floors and mats and not him, he thought cynically. He stared at the scones, feeling no hunger in the tension, and stood and left the house abruptly. The snow was deeper now, covering most of the glen except for the tips of the grasses on the tufty hillocks. The horses stood, steaming the chill air with their hot snorts, their glossy black coats stark against the white blanket. Alex, finding all his jobs done for him, sharpened an ax and spent the morning chopping logs, trying to still his mind that raced and wrestled. Cameron heard the steady sound of the ax slicing through the still air as she scrubbed, polished, washed, and hung the bed sheets to dry in front of the kitchen fires.

Angry at her subservient domesticity and finding nothing substantial to cook with, Cameron examined the guns that Alex had cleaned and primed. Excitedly she dressed in her cut-down clothing and riding boots and, whistling for Torquil, left the house, making sure Alex didn't see her, feeling sure he'd insist on accompanying her. She strode with the gun over her shoulder, looking for deer tracks, as Torquil bounded ahead sniffing eagerly.

Alex stopped his chopping at about noon and returned to the hunting lodge with an armload of logs, having stacked the rest neatly to dry in one of the sheds. He kicked at the back door with his boot.

"Cameron? Cameron? Open the door," he yelled, and at no answer swore loudly as he leaned balancing his heavy burden, groping for the latch. He entered and found himself blinded and entangled by wet linen.

"Cameron!" he roared, hopelessly trapped and hampered by the heavy logs that he couldn't drop for fear of breaking his own feet. He took a deep breath to calm himself, smelling the soap and lye that flattened, damply, on his face. He dropped the logs as he forced his legs apart and swore at the bruising of his shins and toes. He tore the sheets from him, stamping them to the floor, where they lay muddy and mixed with the dirty logs. He furiously kicked them aside, abusing himself even more.

"Cameron," he bellowed, and hearing no answer searched the rooms. He sat angrily drinking cold tea and noticed her jacket no longer hung where he had left it, one of the two guns was missing, and Torquil didn't answer his whistle. He looked out of the back door at the footprints that converged, noting where his struck off to the barn and where a double set led around to the opposite side of the house. He followed Cameron's and Torquil's to the edge of the forest and saw to his dismay the thick dry pine needles where their trail ended. There was no way to track as the snow had been obstructed by the thick overhanging branches. As he scanned around he heard a sharp crack shatter the still air, and he quickly strode toward the sound. He saw nothing but the maze of trees and remembered his frustrating search for Cameron as Torquil's howl had reechoed, bouncing off the surrounding mountains. Alex whistled for the large hound and was relieved at the answering joyful bark from nearby.

He found Cameron standing triumphantly next to the body of a yearling deer. She turned and stared at him, her green eyes gleaming and her small face flushed. Alex felt irritation and, not sharing her joyful triumph, glowered back coldly.

Cameron's victorious feeling turned to puzzled pain at Alex's cold fury. She flared her nostrils and glared defiantly at him before turning back to her prize. How was she going to get the deer back to the lodge? She wished she had had the foresight to bring a knife to disembowel and cut up the meat. Alex made no move as Cameron decided to carry the heavy carcass across her shoulders, as she'd seen her grandfather do. How to get it up and across her shoulders was a problem. Finding the feat impossible she attempted to drag it and was slightly rewarded as it slid an inch or two. Shaking with rage and frustration, and very conscious of Alex's cynical eyes watching her futile operation, she tugged and pulled with all her might, sobbing with her exertion.

Why couldn't the stubborn girl ask for help? thought Alex savagely. He was damned if he was going to move a muscle on her behalf without her request for assistance, remembering each time she had attacked him before as she thought he deliberately insulted her.

Cameron, exhausted, sat down suddenly, her back to

Alex. Once again he had managed to put her in an embarrassing, awkward position. It didn't occur to her that she would have had the problem of moving the deer whether he was there or not. She sat staring at the deer, thinking desperately how to regain her dignity and pride. Making a sudden decision she stood and stalked off, holding her head up and pushing her shoulders back.

"Cameron," shouted Alex angrily, but Cameron kept walking, her steps even. She'd not give him the satisfaction of running.

"Cameron, come here," ordered Alex, but she kept the same insolent pace, not caring which direction she headed.

"I said, come here," roared Alex, also loath to lower himself by running after her. Torquil whined at his feet, torn between staying with Alex or following his young mistress.

"Torquil, go with the sulky child so she doesn't lose herself," he commanded loudly, for Cameron's benefit. Cameron was furious and wished she hadn't left the gun by the carcass of the deer.

Alex watched the girl and the dog until the trees swallowed them up. Would she try to run away? It would be sheer suicide if she did. He comforted himself with the thought that the great hound would lead him to her if she was gone too long, as he heaved the heavy carcass across his shoulders and returned to the lodge. He entered and nearly broke his back as he tripped on the scattered logs and wet muddy sheets.

Cameron walked off her anger, knowing it would be impossible to set off for Cape Wrath without food, a horse, or other provisions, especially now that winter had really set in. It also seemed impossible for her to return to the lodge. How could she face his mocking laughter? Did he expect her to swallow her pride and walk in humbly? She would sooner die. Why was she always caught in these painful, impossible situations? She sat under a large pine tree and brooded, the resinous smell taking her back to another such place, and she stood angrily as the sensuous memories flooded in. She was cold and longed for the warm kitchen, as did Torquil, who shivered and whined at her feet, but her stubborn pride kept her outside in the woods where she walked furiously to keep her blood circulating.

In the kitchen Alex disemboweled the deer, saving the offal for Torquil and throwing the rest of the entrails into the woods. He scanned around anxiously for Cameron and, seeing nothing, returned to his task of butchering the venison, reassuring himself she'd return when she was cold enough. He worked for a couple of hours skinning and carving, not wanting to examine his anger. He took his rage out on the poor animal that was mercifully dead and unfeeling, killed by Cameron; not realizing therein lay the source of his fury. He had only been able to trap small game and fish, enough for a day or two at a time. He had felt manly and able to provide; now with one shot she had reduced his efforts, making them seem petty and trivial. He left a large haunch to roast on a spit over the fire and hung the rest in the cold cellar.

Alex estimated Cameron had been out for more than three hours, as he sat drinking cold tea and eating scones. He was damned if he would go out and drag her in, knowing that there would be a violent tantrum if he did.

Cameron sat shivering, wondering what to do. She would not return dragging her tail and wounded pride; it would be better if Alex dragged her back and she could pretend reluctance. So much had changed in her. At Cape Wrath she had hidden out for days at a time from Mara's rage, not feeling the cold or the hunger that now growled inside. She'd hidden in the caves along the beaches and watched the seals and birds, feeling complete and content. Now she felt like a useless lump with nothing to do but suffer and wait. For what?

Two more hours passed painfully slowly, the sky darkened, and Torquil shivered violently.

"Go back," chattered Cameron, her teeth compulsively hammering against each other.

Torquil rose stiffly and wagged his tail, expecting her to follow. He eagerly ran a few paces only to return to her, whining puzzlement at her stillness.

"Go get him," hissed Cameron through stiff, frozen lips. She was determined to freeze to death sooner than give Alex the satisfaction of her humiliation.

Alex watched the darkening sky with consternation, as he led the horses into the shed for the night. He scanned around and, seeing nothing, whistled for Torquil. The enormous dog pricked up his ears and barked expectantly at Cameron.

"Go on," she said angrily.

At Alex's second whistle the great dog bounded away toward the hunting lodge. Alex, on hearing the answering bark to his first whistle, knew Cameron was not far and was safe. As Torquil bounded up he had a vague idea of Cameron's game. He patted the icy coat and his anger surged at Cameron's insensitivity to the old dog. He determined not to fetch her as he led the old hound into the warmth of the kitchen and closed the door firmly. He toweled the matted, icy fur, giving a sinewy foreleg of the deer for him to gnaw in front of the fire, as the shaggy coat thawed and dripped by the warmth. But Torquil refused to relax and eat; he whined anxiously looking at the door. Alex swore as he struggled into his jacket. He knew Cameron's stubborn nature. She'd sit and freeze before she'd admit defeat. What about his pride? It wasn't so great that it meant having a death on his conscience.

"Come on then, old dog. Let's get her so we can both have some peace of mind, though I doubt if her turbulent presence will give us any sort of peace," he muttered, opening the kitchen door.

Alex found her as he expected, not far from the house. She sat hugging her knees with a rebellious look on her face.

"I dinna care if you freeze yourself, that's your own concern, but I expected more from you than to let your faithful old hound freeze his bone marrow for your stupid pride!" he said harshly.

Cameron felt the stinging truth of his words and froze inside as well as out.

"Get up and get inside," he barked.

Cameron stayed where she was. Shame flooded through her and her heart was heavy for the punishment she had inflicted on Torquil. Each thing she loved she somehow hurt. She longed to wrap her arms around his shaggy neck, but she was not sure if her locked arms could move.

Alex mistook her immobility for defiance.

"No more games," he roared, wrenching her to her feet and pushing her roughly, so she fell forward on her face.

"Walk!" he shouted, feeling no pity, and he jerked her upright by the scruff of her clothes.

Once inside the warm kitchen he let go and ignored her as she slumped to the floor. He tended the meat. Cameron leaned against the door feeling the pain of the warm blood trying to circulate in her cold extremities. Her eyes took in her clean washing, dirty on the floor among muddy logs, and rage covered her shame and humiliation. She sat unmoving as Alex filled the copper bath with hot water.

"Get in," he ordered.

Alex's rage exploded as she made no move or sign she had heard. He picked her up roughly and threw her fully clothed into the hot water. Cameron screamed as the boiling liquid contacted her frozen flesh, and she leaped up, but Alex relentlessly sat her down again. He noticed her face screamed with pain and not rage, and feeling the scalding sting of the water, he swore and hauled her out.

"Goddammit! You deserve to be boiled alive; and dinna blame me if you are. You test a man so he doesna know what in hell he's doing!" he thundered, furious at his own carelessness, as he poured cold water in the bath and dumped her back in.

Cameron sat fully clothed in the bath. Now what was she expected to do? Undress? Step out with dignity just to be thrown back in? She sat burning with rage as the warmth of the water painfully eased into her cold stiffness.

Alex had no idea what he expected of her, so he carved himself a large hunk of venison, poured an equally large glass of whiskey, and sat trying to gnaw through the tough meat nonchalantly, nearly breaking his jaw.

Cameron rose, the water pouring off her, and the wet heavy clothes weighing her down. She stood a moment watching Alex chew complacently before stepping out in her sodden boots and, bending, deliberately tipped the copper tub so a flood of water poured over Alex's feet and swirled around the logs and muddy sheets. Alex resisted the temptation to react, forcing himself to continue chewing the leathery meat calmly. Cameron reached for the nearest weapon to shatter his cool composure. Her hand grasped a jar of blackberry jam.

"Don't be childish," Alex warned coldly, goading

Cameron beyond endurance. Giving a scream of pure, unadulterated rage she dashed the jar at his feet where the sticky dollops splattered. Alex sprang up, his own fury matching hers, blind to the simple fact that this time she had not aimed to injure. Her sureness of arm could have split open his skull if she so desired. He struck her across the face, jerking her head back sharply, crying out as he connected and hugging her to him. Cameron pushed him away and stared with hatred, her lip swelling and bleeding, before striding out of the room, her boots swishing.

Alex sat shaking at the kitchen table, his head buried in his hands. Why couldn't he hate her as she so obviously hated him? What was this demon that possessed him, ensnaring him until he was powerless and impotent in its grasp? How comfortable and uncomplicated his life had been before Cameron. It had been safe and harmonious; now the rhythm was uneven and unpredictable. Everything had changed, been jostled and soured—his relationship with Fiona, his homes, his servants, even his own eyes and ears saw things more sharply and with a jarring clarity. Why did he need this disturbance? His fury grew at finding no rhyme or reason and with the knowledge that Cameron was in his blood, somehow imprisoning him.

Cameron angrily tore off her wet clothes and threw them violently around the room she had so painstakingly cleaned that morning. Her stomach growled with hunger at the smell of the roasting meat, and her irritation at his ignorance fanned her fury. Didn't he even know to hang venison, or at least stew it when it was freshly killed? Her deer, her prize, he had taken over and appropriated. She muttered and railed furiously, knowing she would not, could not, enter the kitchen. She pulled on her flannel nightgown and sat hugging her knees in front of the bedroom fire.

Alex surveyed the mess of logs, sheets, muddy water, and jam. He was damned if he would clean it up, and damned if he'd let the poor, old, exhausted dog cut a pad on the shards of broken glass. He stormed into the bedchamber.

"Clean up your mess before your dog is even more injured by your thoughtless behavior," he raged.

" 'Tis not just my mess; you stole my meat, trampled my clean washing," retorted Cameron.

"Aye, and the logs. I'll see to my part," he acknowledged, leaving the room to start stacking the logs by the kitchen hearth. Cameron sat without moving for a few moments, furious that he had somehow managed to take the wind out of her sails, leaving her no recourse but to do as he said. She slowly walked into the kitchen.

"Put your boots on or you'll cut your feet," growled Alex.

"You wet them," snapped Cameron coldly, taking rags and dabbing at the sticky mess. She knelt in the muddy puddles on the floor and tried to scoop up the sticky jam that prickled with splinters of glass. It was a frustrating, messy job and, in pushing her hair out of her eyes, she managed to transfer the irritating substance from her gluey fingers to her face and hair. With a brush and hot water she scrubbed away her violent feelings until she was satisfied. She surveyed her handiwork, the whole of her nearly covered by the muddy, sticky mess. Even her fingers and toes were glued together. Alex watched her as he tried to ineffectually remove the dirt and jam from the sheets. If the MacDonalds could see him now, he thought wryly, would they think this was wedded bliss? He, Lord Alexander Sinclair, doing laundry like an old washerwoman.

Cameron wearily mopped the water from the floor. She never wanted to see blackberry jam again. It was everywhere, stiffening her face, sticking sharply to the fine hairs on her arms and legs, gluing the nightgown to her knees, and oozing between her bare toes.

" 'Tis best to leave this soaking in the water overnight," sighed Alex, despairing of ever cleaning the stubborn stains on the sheets, and drying his hands. Cameron leaned on the mop, drained by her emotions, the long ordeal in the cold, and the hard manual labor. Alex, purged of his fury by their working side by side in the same room, smiled affectionately at her.

"Hungry?"

Cameron nodded, too exhausted to resume the battle, and Alex filled a plate with venison and two mugs with whiskey and set them on the table. He looked at Cameron who still stood leaning on her mop, staring at her fingers that she opened and shut, seeing her glued skin picked up and stretched before popping apart.

"You are a sticky mess, aren't you?" he said kindly, and to Cameron's horror she felt tears ache and well at the warmth of his voice. Alex noticed but felt impotent, afraid to offer any comfort.

"Soak them with the sheets a moment," he offered softly.

Cameron sniffed resolutely, dashed the tears from her eyes with the back of her hand, and nodded.

Too tired to eat, she sipped the whiskey and tried to keep her heavy lids from closing. Alex noticed and wondered how he could help her without offending, knowing she must be totally drained of energy. He decided to wait until she slept and then carry her to bed.

Cameron rose abruptly, forcing her weary body to move. She had to rid herself of the pinching jam before she went out of her mind with screaming irritation. She reached for the copper tub that she had hung up as she cleaned the kitchen floor, and it fell with a crash, bruising her foot. She sat on the floor nursing her injured toes and Alex, unable to sit idly by, leaped up and crouched beside her, rubbing the bruised, sticky foot. Cameron was too tired to protest; she leaned against his warmth and went to sleep. Alex removed his jacket and pillowed it beneath her head as he filled the bath.

Cameron felt herself gently shaken awake; her sleepy hands helped him undo the buttons of her nightgown, as her legs sagged, and she moaned to just curl up and sleep. Alex undressed her, like a baby, and lifted her into the warm water, after making very sure that the temperature was not too hot. Cameron fell back to sleep with her sticky head resting on the uncomfortable rim of the bath. Alex looked at her bruised, swollen lip and hated himself, as he carefully washed her relaxed face. She murmured sleepy protests as he washed the whole of her. Everything was too much effort, so she passively submitted to his tender ministrations. Alex delighted in his chore, as he examined each part of her, marveling in her petite perfection. Balancing a towel across his chest, he bent and lifted her up into his arms, cradling and wrapping her cozily. He sat on a kitchen chair, supporting her with one arm, while he dried her hair. Was this the closest he would ever get to Cameron? Was his relationship with her destined to be violence? Would he only be able to hold her when she was drained and not caring? He was not satisfied. He wanted her in all ways, not the extremes of her raging and hating, or spent and sleeping.

Alex carried Cameron to bed and was gratified at her sleepy arms that clung to him when he tried to release her. He let her have her way and lay beside her as she burrowed into his warmth. Cameron slept as Alex lay deliberating beside her. He stared down at her damp, glossy head cuddled into his chest and knew that her unaware state trusted and needed him. Why was the battle line drawn and her guard up when she was alert and awake? He was determined that they should talk, and also determined that he'd not be used. If he stayed and slept so close to her, he knew their bodies would join by morning without anything else being resolved. Alex dragged himself from the warm comfort of the bed, and Cameron, deep in sleep, did not protest his leaving.

Alex put the cooked meat into the cellar and sat drinking whiskey at the kitchen table as he rehearsed what he would say to Cameron. He was aware that he loved her and wanted to be with her, but not with the hateful violence that existed. One or both of them would be dead by spring if things continued the way they were going. He felt a cold fear knowing that as much as he loved her, she might hate him, but comforted himself remembering her sleeping arms clinging to him. He fell asleep on the kitchen table with his folded arms pillowing his head.

Chapter Twenty-eight

Another week went by and Alex found no opportunity to open the much-needed discussion between them. Cameron seemed calm and detached. They ate, cooked, did the work together, and yet were miles apart. He felt himself wanting something, anything, to spark some communication. Even violence was preferable to the orderly neatness of their days.

The morning after throwing the jam Cameron had wakened and found Alex sleeping at the kitchen table. She had felt great tenderness seeing his tawny, unruly hair, but she had resisted the temptation to twine her fingers through it, turning instead to clatter pots loudly to wake him. She had recalled dimly his bathing her and a sharp pain dug into her gut as she realized he preferred to sleep at the hard kitchen table than by her side. Each night since, she had retired first and each morning awoke, relieved and disappointed, to find herself alone, as he preferred to sleep elsewhere. He was rejecting her and she found to her horror that it made her more bound to him. Each day she was aware of a burning need. She had to sit on her irritation as a strange pressure grew inside and she felt she would explode.

By the end of a week neither talked at all. There was no need, as each behaved mechanically, neither offending except in the very fact of not giving any offense. Alex bathed openly in front of the kitchen fire, and Cameron busied herself, ignoring him as if were a stray mutt searching out fleas. Cameron bathed openly and he reacted as dispassionately as she. Both of them were wound tightly, not knowing it about the other, each needing a release but neither willing to be the first. The very air was strained to near snapping, and even Torquil gazed apprehensively from one to the other, as though holding his breath, wondering when the explosion was to occur. The last two nights of that week Alex paced the second floor as Cameron paced the first floor, each hearing each other's tense footsteps, but both too stubborn to face each other.

The spring was coiled so tightly that both faces were set and rigid.

"Pass the salt," snapped Alex.

Cameron silently spun it roughly down the table so it hit his wine glass and slopped his drink.

"God damn it, I canna take any more of this!" exploded Alex, meaning the incredible tension.

Cameron sprang up, taking offense at his insinuation that she purposely and often spilt his wine.

"Then don't!" she spat, spinning her platter so it knocked the wine bottle off the table to shatter on the floor.

Alex uncurled his lithe body and sprang at her. He grasped her shoulders and kissed her brutally. He opened his eyes in surprise, his lips still on hers. What was he doing?

Cameron closed her eyes and returned his kisses hungrily, writhing her starved body against him, feel-

ing his arousal. But Alex fought his blinding desire
and pushed her back, still keeping a firm hold on her
shoulders.

"We have to talk," he growled huskily.

Cameron swallowed hard. "I'll be your mistress till
the spring. I'll ask no more of you than that," she
whispered, edging her body closer.

"Nay! I want a wife!" roared Alex, releasing her and
storming across the kitchen, his blood chilled by her
words.

Cameron's own blood froze at his brutal rejection.
He was rightfully angry with her. He wanted his freedom for a wife of his own choosing and was trapped
into a marriage with her.

"I'm sorry," she said helplessly.

"What are you sorry for?" thundered Alex.

"That you want a wife and because of my ignorance
you are not free to choose one," stammered Cameron.

"You are my wife!"

"Aye, and I'm sorry," she said, not knowing how to
right the terrible wrong. "I've read in books that the
kings divorced. There was a fat king, Henry, on the
English throne—"

"Aye, and he cut their heads off to be free. But I
don't want to be free. You are my wife. I want no
other," bellowed Alex, interrupting her.

Cameron stood dumbfounded. What sort of cruel
trick was he setting her up for now?

"A bastard?" she screamed.

"Dinna swear at me. I'm wound so tight I dinna
trust myself not to rape or kill you!"

"I wasna swearing, unless I'm a curse!" yelled Cameron. "I'm a bastard!"

"Stop with that word!" raged Alex, approaching
her, his eyes laced with icy fury.

"Why?" challenged Cameron.

"Because I don't care for it! I dinna like it!"

"*I am a bastard*," she cried, matching his roars, "whether you like it or not! And I don't care if you don't care for it. I don't care if you don't like it, 'cause that what I am, whether *I* like it or not!"

Alex stared at her white, pain-filled face, hearing her words.

"I am a bastard, Sir Alexander Sinclair—a bastard— a bastard! And you hate it, don't care for it, don't like it, do you?" she raged, pounding on his chest with her fists, unaware of the tears that raced down her cheeks. "How can a gentleman be married to a bastard? How can a bastard be married to a gentleman? How can a gentleman love a bastard? Tell me? *Tell me?* I have no name. I canna be a fancy lady, even if I wanted to be. Well, I don't want to be. I am a bastard and proud of it. Much rather be a proud bastard than one of your simpering, corseted, painted ladies!"

Alex shook her softly.

"Cameron, I love you," he said gently, but the girl ranted on, not hearing him.

"Cameron!" he shouted, drowning out her screams so she fell silent, waiting for the blows to strike her.

"Hit me. I dinna care no more," she said defiantly.

"Listen to me, you silly, bastard child. I love you and you are my wife, bastard or not. Do you hear me? I love you."

Cameron stood dazed, wondering why he didn't use his fists instead of his mouth to hurt her. She preferred being beaten to this.

"I love you, Cameron. Do you hear me?" repeated Alex, staring into her wary eyes, pleading with them to believe him.

"I'm no bastard child, I'm a bastard woman," replied Cameron lamely, playing for time to get her confused thoughts in order.

"Aye, you're a woman, a whole armful of woman," said Alex, tenderly enfolding her in his arms.

Cameron leaned her hot cheek against his strong chest.

"But Lady Fiona?" she remarked fearfully.

"F . . . to hell with Lady Fiona," shouted Alex, stopping his tongue from using a very inappropriate curse with which to reassure Cameron. "I don't care about her. I just care about you, you silly child. I mean woman."

"I'm not silly."

"Nay, you're not silly," he said, holding her away from him and searching her face.

"I've loved you since our little stone house. I am the silly one, the stupid one. You see, I was too wooden-headed to know. It made me do cruel things to you. I love you. Do you hear me?"

Cameron nodded, the tears spilling down her face.

"And what of you? Here I stand baring my soul and what of you? Do you love me?"

Cameron stared at him silently, terrified to commit herself.

"I am afraid," she murmured.

"Of what?" asked Alex, his heart clutched with not hearing that his love was returned. "Of me?"

"Aye. What if you're just saying those things and they are not true, and I tell you what I feel? 'Tis then like I'll want to die," sobbed Cameron, trying to find the right words to express herself.

"What do you feel?" urged Alex.

"I love you but I dinna know why. I dinna want to. I tried not to. But I canna help it," cried Cameron, throwing herself forward to hide her face in his chest.

"Oh, Cameron, Cameron," crooned Alex, tears pouring down his own face as he held her tightly to him, his arms wanting to squeeze her into himself so they'd never be parted.

They stood locked, rocking for a while.

"All this time fighting and hurting; we need spanking, both of us," he sighed, and Cameron giggled tearfully.

"What's so funny?"

"I'd like to skelp you like you did me. 'Twould pay you back," sniffed Cameron wickedly, as she wiped her wet face on his shirt.

"Maybe I'll let you. There's paying back due both ways, if I recollect rightly," he growled.

"Nay, 'tis not true. I didna sit for a week," protested Cameron jokingly, and she looked up to see his eyes full of pain.

"Have I said wrong?" she asked fearfully, afraid of his anger in her vulnerable state.

"Nay, love. I did wrong and I dinna know how to make it up to you," answered Alex hoarsely, wondering how he could have ever beaten her when he could have made love to her so easily.

" 'Twas my fault. I did everything wrong, running away, tearing all the pretty things you bought for me to wear. I'm sorry," she said haltingly, feeling uncomfortable and awkward. "Canna we forget?"

"Aye," laughed Alex, swinging her into his arms, quickly dispelling the somber mood. " 'Tis time for bed, wife, enough of this idle talking, has been over a week and I'm very hungry for you. How's your appetite?"

"Not very big," confessed Cameron, suddenly feeling very shy.

"I'll see if I canna whet it a bit," answered Alex, feeling a little rejected that her ardor did not match his, as he deposited her on the bed and turned to tend the fire.

Cameron watched him, feeling very afraid. She was not aroused and she wished to curl to sleep closely in his arms. It was so much easier to come together angrily or sleepily, she thought.

Alex watched her face and puzzled at the tight, nervous expression. He was eager to make love and wondered why her usually passionate sexuality was not aroused. His elation at finding his love returned was slowly souring. What was the matter? Why did she sit still clothed with her arms wrapped so tightly around her knees? It was the first time they were coming together without rage. It was the first time they were coming together with love. Alex realized he felt like a new bridegroom on a wedding night. He had never before made love with love or wanting love returned.

Alex strode out to the kitchen and collected the bottle of cognac as his own nervousness grew. He felt callow and shy as he sat on the bed next to Cameron and handed her a drink.

"Let me love you, Cameron?"

She drained her glass in two gulps, swallowing the coughs that rose in her from the burning courage, and handed him back the glass. Did she want to be a woman? It seemed an awesome responsibility, especially when she felt so small and vulnerable, somehow wishing to hide herself in the protective comfort of his arms like a child. She smiled at him tremulously, and with a groan he drew her to his chest, rocking her comfortingly for a minute before reaching for her mouth and kissing her gently.

Cameron kissed him back, their lips barely touching, just tickling the nerve endings. She became conscious of her breasts pressing against his and she tentatively opened her mouth under his and softly sucked the tip of his tongue.

Alex held himself back, understanding that there

was a lot at stake in how they made love. She needed gentling, caressing, wooing, and he would try to curb his urgency.

Cameron was content with the peaceful sensations of being held. Her mouth delighted in his as her hands explored his sculptured face, unruly hair, and ears. Alex contented himself with running his hands up and down the firm curve of her back, biding his time, waiting for her quickening.

She opened her mouth wider and, as she felt the firm thrusting, opened the front of her nightgown to allow his hand access to her aching breasts. As Alex played with her tight nipples, sending shivers through her, Cameron tentatively unbuttoned his clothes and experimented by sucking his smaller breasts. Alex had never felt it before and he tensed, recoiling from the idea before relaxing and feeling the sensation, which wasn't unpleasant. Cameron sucked and kneaded against him, nibbling and biting, until he gently pushed her back and fastened his mouth to her own soft breasts.

Cameron felt her own hunger start to pulsate. She was irritated by her nightgown wrapped uncomfortably around her neck and tried to remove it without causing Alex to stop his pleasuring. He released her and sat up to remove his own clothes. Cameron's desire ebbed and she became conscious of her fear and vulnerability. She was open and exposed, naked and cold. She buried herself under the covers of the bed like a small animal trying to hibernate, finding the darkness and anonymity strangely comforting.

Feeling robbed of the sight of her body, Alex slid under the covers and lay beside her. She was stiff and still as he gently traced her form in the darkness, but gradually she relaxed and stretched like a feline, enjoying his caresses, just content to be petted, not feeling an urgent desire.

Alex continued to stroke her gently, still exploring. Fired by his familiarity with the whole of her body Cameron turned onto her back, spreading and writhing wantonly for him. He crowed with pride at his bride so anxious beside him, and gently he parted her legs and placed himself on her, touching without thrusting, allowing her impatient movements to propel him to his destination as he knelt, watching her. His fascination and excitement at seeing them so joined consumed him. Cameron wiggled herself nearer to deepen the penetration, her back arching to press her breasts to his warmth, and Alex drove steadily and strongly.

Cameron delighted in the feel of his strength atop and inside her. She strained against him as wave upon wave of sensation culminated and left but a languid, gentle ticking. But still Alex thrust steadily, and she looked up to see his face above her, his neck ridged with the tendons that strained, his face with a grim smile of determination as though he was in a world of his own. She watched him and felt frightened and estranged. Alex wanted to hold back his climax as long as he could, knowing Cameron had reached her peak as he had felt her incredible contractions encompassing him firmly, but now he soared inexorably to his own heights of ecstasy.

Cameron's eyes met Alex's burning gaze, and the feeling of separateness that had begun to creep up on her as he pushed himself to his limit suddenly disappeared. He smiled and Cameron's whole being thawed, awoke, and he strained to her with all his might.

She felt his hardness soften within her and felt a sadness at the slipping away. She clasped him closer into her protective arms. Sensing his vulnerability she now felt stronger. He needed the comfort of her arms and she held him to her breasts to stave the moment of their uncoupling.

Later, watching the firelight play on each other's nakedness, Cameron felt a sharp fear at her exposed love for him.

"Afraid?" asked Alex, catching the brief flicker that darted across her green eyes. He watched her silently, recognizing the pride which fought her need to confess. "Everyone's afraid, Cameron. Everyone in the whole world knows fear—the pope, the English Parliament, kings, beggars, Duncan Fraser, our Bonnie Prince Charlie," he said softly.

"Are you afraid?"

"Aye. I'm more afraid of you not loving me than of any English soldier or the like," confessed Alex.

"Aye, that's what has me frightened. I feel open, with no cover to hide or protect me, loving you as I do."

"I feel the same. I have no armor. I'm open and very vulnerable," continued Alex, watching her hand caress his soft, nestled manhood.

"It doesna matter to you who I am?"

"Only if it matters to you, Cameron. Duncan was right in his thoughts of religion. The sins of the fathers or the mothers dinna matter," he told her, wrapping her in his arms, overcome by the aching tenderness he felt.

"What does that mean?" murmured Cameron, content to lie against his warmth.

"It means that you've opened my eyes to many things, my love. Things I never bothered to think about before. Not just religion but many, many different things in life that I'll share with you—but not now, as you tempt me too much."

Cameron tugged herself away from his lips that nuzzled her neck.

"It really doesna matter to you what I am?"

"Nay," he growled, pulling her back to him, and Cameron forgot that it did matter to her, as they loved each other through the night and slept half of the following day away.

Chapter Twenty-nine

Cameron awoke the next day and watched him anxiously as he slept. She was afraid as she had never been before. She stared at his hard, chiseled features relaxed in sleep as she tried to sort out her nagging fears. There was a deep void that gaped inside her, but she skirted the edge, afraid to be sucked into the panicky yawning, as she thought on her lack of worldliness and sophistication. Now as they were, cut off from the outside, she could cope, but what would happen when the snows melted and the spring arrived? How could she expect him to want her with all the other people to choose from? She had tried to be like the women he was used to and failed dismally. Would he be content to stay alone with her in the wildnerness?

Alex opened his sleepy eyes to see Cameron's worried frown and pulled her to him. She lay nestled into his warmth as he dozed contentedly with his arms wrapping her snugly.

"'Tis too early to be furrowing your little head with worries," he murmured against her hair as she fidgeted.

"There's so much I dinna know. What if you tire of me?" Cameron burst out, feeling confined by his arms.

"Oh, I'll teach you all there is to know about the art of love. I'll be your only teacher, and if I find you with another I'll skin your bare hide," he growled, keeping tight hold on her silky, squirming body.

"There's other things besides," protested Cameron.

"First things first," insisted Alex.

Cameron was successfully seduced into forgetting her worries, as she thrilled to his strength and possessiveness.

The weeks passed in wonder as they delighted in each other, Cameron still rebelling at times, but more to tease and test him playfully. Alex still got curt and authoritarian, making Cameron's blood tingle deliciously. They were two carefree, loving people, unaware and uncaring of the world outside, each being all they lived and breathed for.

Alex hung over her as she baked and cooked, and at Cameron's insistence tried his hand at scones and pies. She sat muffled against the cold watching him cut wood, and at his insistence matched him stroke for stroke. Each and every job from the hunting of meat to the cleaning of the house was shared, even the washing of each other, which never progressed very far as there were more exciting sharings to be found squeezed together in a copper bathtub.

Cameron pushed aside her grim foreboding, refusing to think of the spring and the end of their idyllic existence. She blocked it from her mind, erased it from her vocabulary, and merged her whole being with Alex. Cameron had much more to learn about love than the sexual arts, as Alex soon discovered. He reminded himself of her childhood, reared in the unloving, cold atmosphere of Duncan's bitter fanaticism and Mara's spiteful jealousy. She was too quick to strike out when she was frightened or offended. He couldn't shout at her, gently criticize, or get slightly irritated without her attacking, almost as if she thought he withdrew his love.

One night lying by the fire together, sated by their lovemaking, he watched her as she lay curled and relaxed in the curve of him. Who was this little wildcat he was mated to? One minute she was soft and pliant, almost purring, as now, but the next, she was spitting and clawing to defend herself, as if her very life depended on it. He imagined himself exposed to Mara's maniacal fury day after day. The little he'd seen of the woman convinced him that Cameron had exaggerated nothing in the conversations they had had. He had diplomatically probed Cameron about her childhood, and she had frankly described her strange existence as if everyone was reared the same way. Her head had been filled by Duncan with fears and warnings from a very young age, not just of the English but of her fellow Scots from the south, who had betrayed the cause. She was a mass of doctrine and opinions, all with a grain of truth, but all learned parrotlike from Duncan's fervent mouth and slanted by his incredible disillusionment.

To Alex's frustration Cameron remembered very little of her life before Cape Wrath, just knowing vaguely she'd been somewhere else.

"Ever hear of the Island of North Rona?" he probed.

Cameron started and stared at him with her face

very white. The word made her feel afraid and yet her panicked brain did not know why. The word *Rona* hurt and she fought to stay sane and not be swept into the dark, fearful abyss inside herself.

"No," she answered sharply, and left him suddenly to curl herself under the covers of the bed.

Alex watched the small shape under the blankets and let her alone, knowing only too well what the warning flash in her eyes prophesied if he touched her. He found if he let her be, within a few hours the thunderclouds would pass, but if he attempted to comfort or question, he had a raging storm on his hands. When the tempest in her had wrung itself dry, she became cowering and frightened, fearful she was no longer lovable.

He brooded by the fire for an hour before quietly slipping into the bed beside her. He considered holding her but, not knowing her state of mind, turned his back to her in sleep.

Alex awoke as her flailing arms struck him.

"To be sick—to be sick—to be sick," cried Cameron, in the throes of a nightmare.

Alex lit a lamp and watched her rock from side to side.

"To be sick—to be sick," she clearly annunciated, as her body rolled as though on a boat.

"Tor . . . tor . . . tor," she moaned, holding her arms out.

Torquil sprang from his place by the hearth and licked her face.

"Torquil," she sighed, embracing him, and her body relaxed and she lay still.

Alex thought the dream had passed and was about to blow out the lantern when he heard the voice of a very young child that made his blood chill.

"Grand . . . father. Grand . . . father," Cameron

pronounced carefully, over and over again, like cate-
chism. She repeated it and repeated it, getting faster
and faster as the word jumbled up, until she sobbed.

"I Cam O' Rona . . . back to Rona, please back to
Rona. Rona. Rona. Rona," she wept, as Torquil
whined and lapped her salty tears.

Alex, unable to bear her misery, held her and
rocked her gently.

"To be sick—to be sick—Rona—Rona," she screamed,
thrashing wildly.

Alex stopped his rocking but still held her and her
body relaxed in sleep. Torquil returned to his place
on the hearth and lay looking woefully at his young
mistress, with his large head on his paws.

Alex held the sleeping girl, his head echoing with
her childish voice. How old had she been? Seven?
Eight? Dougal Gunn had mentioned that Duncan had
hidden the child on the Island of Rona. Rona? Cam
O' Rona? *Camerona* rang in his brain.

He was about to place her gently back under the
covers, when she clutched him.

"Jumeau? Jumeau? Ou est mon jumeau?" she lisped.

Alex looked down into her wide green eyes with astonishment.

"Qu'est-ce que tu a dis?" he experimented.

But Cameron's eyes drooped shut and she relaxed in
sleep. *Jumeau?* What did that mean? He was frustrated that their strange conversation ended so abruptly. She spoke in French like a child of two or three.
Where is my *jumeau?* she had said. What the hell was
a *jumeau?*

The following day Cameron was as happy as a mead-
owlark in a blue midsummer sky and Alex didn't
want to cloud her sunny disposition by mentioning
her nightmare. They spent the day scraping the deer

hides that they had collected, as Cameron showed him how to cure the leather, and after a snowball fight they warmed each other making love.

"Cameron?" asked Alex gently, as she lay relaxed and content in his arms.

"Um?" she grunted, half asleep.

"What is *jumeau*?" he ventured.

Cameron stiffened in his arms. He looked down to see her flesh goose bumped, and she shivered. She stared up at him, her green eyes wide and her face very pale, without answering. Alex took a breath.

"Hier soir tu a dis 'ou est mon jumeau?' Cameron, qu'est-ce que jumeau? que vent-tu a dire?" he asked haltingly, unsure of his French.

"Jumelle Jumeau Jumelle Jumeau, le miroir de moi, l'autre demi de moi, jumelle jumeau," chanted Cameron, like a tiny child singing a nursery rhyme, her face masklike and impassive, staring straight at him without seeing, as she rocked.

Alex tried to fathom her words. The mirror of herself? The other half of herself? Was it just a song she recalled from childhood? It couldn't be. He remembered the plaintive young voice of the night before asking for her *jumeau*. *Jumeau*? *Jumelle*? Mirror? Twin! *Jumeau* was obviously the masculine.

"Cameron, you have a brother?" he asked excitedly. Cameron's childlike rocking and chanting increased and she rolled backward and forward as she had done the night before.

"I'm going to be sick. I have to be sick."

"Cameron, 'tis the past. Spit it out, so it can rest in peace and be buried," shouted Alex, trying to shake her out of the clutches of her past terrors.

Cameron sat up suddenly, as though startled awake, and stared at him.

"*Jumeau*? Rona? Tell me," he urged.

"I canna. I dinna ken. Mustna ask, 'tis but a dream, just a dream, Duncan said. Mustna ask," she stated firmly, her heart beating wildly as she heard Duncan's voice echoing from the dark recesses of her mind. "You mustna ever speak of him, 'twill mean his death and yours."

Alex struggled with himself, seeing by the grim determination in her eyes that the subject was closed, and yet he was full of curiosity.

"You said it dinna matter what I was," said Cameron, seeing his eyes pleading with her.

"'Tis not that, 'tis the demons of the past that tear you up at night. 'Tis best to rid oneself of them," explained Alex.

"One silly dream 'tis all."

Alex sat looking after her as she angrily pulled on her clothes and left the bedroom without looking at him.

The remainder of that day she was quiet and detached, her natural exuberance held in check as she watched him furtively to see if he was angry with her.

That night she cuddled into him like a penitent child, and her wild zest for the sensuous soon dispelled her cloudy mood. The next day she merrily worked and played, having successfully locked the past where it belonged, deep inside her.

Cameron's fear of his anger caused Alex great pain. Most of the time they were relaxed, happy lovers, but he felt constrained and constricted, not able to be as free with his emotions as she. He was determined to confront her, but confused as to how.

They sat eating supper. Cameron was proud of the laden table. It looked like the banquet fit for royalty that she had read about in Duncan's books. She hummed merrily, not noticing Alex's silent preoccupation as he toyed with his food. She had finished her

meat pie and was cutting another wedge when she
stopped abruptly.

"Is there something wrong with the pie?" she asked
anxiously.

"Nay," replied Alex absently, without looking at
her.

Cameron felt a spark of fear run through her. What
had she done wrong? He was not happy. He looked
cold and angry.

"There's plenty else if it's not to your liking," she
offered.

"'Tis fine," snapped Alex.

Cameron stared at him with her face white and eyes
wide.

"That's it," stated Alex, staring at her obvious terror.

"What's it?"

"Look at you, cowering and quivering like a frightened rabbit," pointed Alex. Cameron set her face rebelliously.

"Cameron, you get angry with me, sulky and quiet,
wrapped up in your own thoughts. You spit and claw
and I know it doesna mean that you've stopped loving
me," explained Alex as gently as he could. "Or does
it?"

"Dinna be foolish," cried Cameron.

"Then why will you not let me be the same?"

"Can I stop you?" replied Cameron flippantly, to
cover her discomfort.

"Aye, you do. Bind me up so I tippytoe. I canna be
free for fear of your fear," he tried to explain.

Cameron froze with terror. She was binding him?
He wanted to be free of her?

"'Tis like being free," strove Alex, trying to find the
elusive right words to express himself without offend-

ng her. "Loving and just being together, freely given, ight?"

Cameron nodded, not understanding anything he was saying except he had tired of her and wanted his reedom. She braced herself against the wall trying to over her terror.

"Well, I feel bound not able to just do, or just be, or use words as freely as you do for fear you'll be hurt. Do you ken?"

Cameron shook her pounding head.

"You have the freedom to rail, scream, and be angry with me when you feel the need, but you steal my free-dom to do the same." Alex was frustrated in his inabil-ty to articulate what he felt.

Cameron's icy fear now thawed at her intense rage at his accusation that she stole his freedom.

Alex recognized the flashing eyes and stiffening body as she prepared to attack him.

"Like right now, Cameron. You are all armed to hit out at me. I canna speak my mind without you feeling I dinna love you. I love you even when I want to wring your stiff, stubborn neck! Listen and learn and stop shutting me up with your fear."

"I have no fear!" spat Cameron, as she stormed out of the room and slammed the door. She sat upstairs in one of the cold, impersonal rooms as his words rang in her head. She didn't understand anything except she wasn't perfect. Alex saw her as a coward stealing his freedom and binding him with her weakness—as Fiona had stated. If she did all that, how could he pos-sibly love her?

Alex sat watching their glorious supper congeal to an unappetizing mass. He was furious with himself and Cameron. If she didn't tie and trip up his tongue in fear of offending her, he felt he would have been able to express himself better. He sat for an hour or more not willing to back down. He had taken the first step, he'd not run to her to soothe her ruffled feelings. Let her think on it awhile. He loudly unset the table and put the food away, hoping she'd hear and come to help.

Cameron sat dismally in the upstairs room unable to hear or think of anything but Alex's disapproval and obvious hatred of her. She was empty and devoid of all feelings, caught in a dark, cold vacuum, totally desolate.

Alex determinedly got into bed and tried to sleep. He tossed and turned in the empty bed and finally sat up swearing. He found her sitting upstairs, wide-eyed and awake.

"Cameron, come to bed, 'tis late," he said, after sitting beside her for a few moments, hoping she'd say something first.

She didn't answer and so they just sat in the dark, cold room.

"I shouldna have ruined a wonderful meal. The words dinna come out the way I meant them," he conceded.

Cameron still didn't answer and Alex grew angry.

"'Tis all right for you to shut me out, sit and not answer me, but if I were to do the same. Hah! You can walk out of the room and slam the door. Oh, that is fine, but let me do the same. Hah! Have I no feelings?" he roared, turning her roughly to face him.

"Answer me! Do I have feelings?" he repeated.

White-faced, Cameron nodded, not hearing him, but very conscious of his rage. She fought to be free but Alex held her firmly.

"No, you'll not run from me, Cameron. You'll stay and face my anger, 'tis part of my love. You expect me to face yours."

What was her anger in comparison to his? He was

twice her size and could be much louder and more brutal, thought Cameron, as she forced herself to meet his eyes without flinching.

"What would you feel if the next time you railed at me, I ran and hid?" persevered Alex.

Cameron shrugged.

"Answer me, goddamn it!"

Cameron didn't know what to answer. Her eyes flickered with panic and she struggled to be free again.

"No, Cameron, you'll stay and talk to me."

Her nostrils flared and she pressed her lips together firmly.

"Aye, now you're getting furious yourself," he snorted.

"Let go of me," raged Cameron.

"Finally you deign to speak. Well, 'tis about time. Go on, get mad, spit and claw and I'll take it. 'Twill not kill me or stop me loving you."

Cameron was still beneath his hands. How she hated the position she was in. She saw herself as a weak parasite, clinging and cloying frantically to his strength. Where was her own? Why did she feel that she couldn't stand up and face life and the world without him? Why had she been so sapped and drained?

Alex took her bowed head and cessation of temper as capitulation. He held her close, convinced that she had finally started to understand.

"'Tis important, Cameron," he said, as he carried her unresisting body down the stairs to bed. "'Tis important to understand. If we had a bairn and the wee un did naughty pranks and made us angry, would it mean we no longer loved him? Or what if the bairn was angry with you, would you think he didn't love you anymore?"

"'Twould not be the same."

"How would it differ?" asked Alex, covering them both and looking down at her.

"If we had a bairn, if we had a bairn . . ." murmured Cameron, more awed by the thought of her giving birth than what Alex was trying to explain.

"Aye? If we had a bairn, what?" he prompted patiently.

"What would we call him?"

"I sincerely hope we'll not have that problem for a time," answered Alex, resigning himself that the lesson had to be continued another time.

"Problem?" whispered Cameron.

"Aye, I don't relish the thought of a bairn just yet," yawned Alex, feeling Cameron was not more than one herself and needed time to grow.

"'Tis because I'm a bastard?"

"Dinna fash yourself more tonight, Cameron, 'tis late. Of course 'tis not because of that. We've our whole life to have babbies, I just want you all to myself for a while," he said, pulling her close to him.

"There could be a wee un growing in me right now, couldn't there?"

Alex froze. Of course he knew the facts of life, but it had not been anything he had ever worried about before. He had slept with many women and never given a thought to the possible consequences.

Cameron slept fitfully in his arms and Alex was wide awake, worrying. How many of his offspring probably walked and crawled the earth? How did Fiona avoid pregnancy? He was aware of Cameron's cycle, having intimately nursed her during it, but it was not a subject one discussed openly. He lay racking his brains, trying to remember when last she bled. It had been the first few days when she had lain delirious and unable to move. How long ago had that been? He had no idea of the time or date, and trying to estimate addled his tired brain. Had it been six weeks? Was it December? Nearly Christmas? Which made him think of another baby, and on that thought he drifted off to sleep.

Chapter Thirty

Alex resolved not to worry about anything until it happened, as talking seemed to build small problems out of proportion and made matters worse than they really were. Matters were really wonderful. He was happy and fulfilled, which was all that counted. They never spoke of a possible pregnancy or Cameron's fear of his anger. Alex secretly resolved the next time she got out of sorts and railed at him, he would give her a dose of her own medicine by reacting as she did.

Cameron tucked her belief—that he didn't want a child by her—away with all her other nagging doubts and tried to erase them from her memory as she determined to be perfect, giving Alex no reason to reject her.

The weeks sped by in exploring and hunting in the surrounding mountains, making love in many different places, including the snow, where they nearly froze off their exposed parts, and on a very prickly carpet of pine needles. Their days were deliriously happy and full of work, play, and love, and they fell asleep sated each night in each other's arms.

The closer and more joyous their days were, the more terrifying became Cameron's nights. More and more often she awoke and lay silently sweating as dark, ominous, nameless clawings clutched inside her. She kept still, unable to sleep but also unable to wake Alex, as there were no words to explain.

She lay rigid in the darkness, willing away the million picky things that ate into her head. She was all too aware of Alex's reticence to truly talk to her. They spoke of many things, but nothing that had meaning. Had she really robbed him of freedom to speak his mind? Had she bound and tied his tongue, or was she too ignorant for him to really converse with? He never mentioned the future; was there to be one? The winter could not last forever.

One evening they lay across the bed reading aloud from some books they had found in a trunk in an upstairs room. The books were a disappointment after the first teasing hour. Alex read some poetry in a stentorian voice, sending Cameron into hysterical giggles. When it was her turn to read, she demanded silence and waited until he looked seriously attentive before reading recipes, but she was unable to finish, as she collapsed laughing at his appreciative expression. He then comically shouted for her undivided attention, telling her he had truly found a masterpiece of literature. She listened carefully as he read a list of accounts and threw pillows at him when he refused to stop.

"I have a book," she said, scrambling off the bed. "I've always had it, anyway for as long as I can remember." She leaped on top of him, clutching the small, leather-bound book from her saddlebag.

"I wager you canna read it," she said, placing it open on his face.

Alex rolled over onto his stomach and turned the pages. It was handwritten and faded.

"Well, aren't you going to read it?" she challenged.

"What language is it?"

"Come, come, my lord, you mean to tell me you canna read?" giggled Cameron.

Alex moved the lamp nearer.

"A civilized, educated gentleman like you canna read a wee book?" she teased. "I'll give a hint. 'Tis not Gaelic."

"Nor German nor Greek neither," remarked Alex. "How do you know 'tis not Gaelic?"

"Because I could read it myself if it were."

"You mean you yerself canna read it!" laughed Alex triumphantly, and pounced on her, wrestling and tickling until she cried for mercy.

"'Tis Latin!" said Alex suddenly, looking down at her happy, glowing face. Cameron's body froze beneath him.

"You can read it?" she exclaimed, fear knifing through her. "No! No! You mustna! Give it back, I shouldna shown it! 'Twas wrong, give it to me!"

Alex stared in amazement at Cameron's sudden change of mood.

"You mustna read it, d'ya ken? 'Tis better your eyes be put out," she pleaded, struggling to be free, her face mirroring her intense terror.

"All right, all right, no need to go into such a taking. I'll not read it," he comforted, rolling away from her and watching as she scrambled across the bed. She clutched the book to her wildly, looking this way and that for a place to hide it. Her face was drained of all color and her limbs trembled.

"Cameron, trust me," begged Alex gently, "share

your secret, let me help you find some peace from the past."

"Nay! I canna. I canna! You mustna ask, dinna tell. Promise you'll not tell I showed the book."

"Tell who?" asked Alex softly.

Cameron's brow furrowed in bewilderment. "Tell who?" she repeated.

"Aye."

Cameron stood stock still.

"There's no one to tell, Cameron. Duncan's dead," urged Alex.

Cameron nodded slowly and then her eyes widened in panic. "Maybe he can reach beyond the grave itself? Aye, he'll get me from the grave."

"Cameron, even if he could, which I doubt, he'd not harm you. He loved you," soothed Alex.

"You dinna ken! 'Tis life or death. You'll not read it or tell a living soul, swear!" she ranted.

"I swear," promised Alex, secretly determined to translate Cameron's book at the first opportunity. "Now come to bed."

"I need to be alone!" And with that Cameron fled from the room clutching her book.

Alex sat on the bed staring into the fire as he heard her scurrying around upstairs, opening and shutting drawers. He surmised she was hiding her worn leather book so he'd not find it.

Cameron sat in a dark upstairs bedroom, her thoughts in turmoil. She had shown her book. How could she have done such an evil thing? The guilt and agony filled every inch of her. How many times had Duncan warned her? And yet without thought she had shown it to Alex. She tried to calm her racing mind and think logically. What did she remember? Nothing but terrifying bits and pieces. Words like *Rona* and *brother* conjured up violence and darkness, Alex's voice speak-

ing in a strange tongue that plunged her immediately
into a nightmare of insanity.

"That is a chair. That is a wash basin and jug," she
stated, trying to ground her rising panic with mundane
realities. But even the furniture took on threatening
shapes, throwing shadows that seemed to reach out to
claw at her like hands from the grave. She fled downstairs to Alex, unable to be alone.

The next day Cameron was anxious and tense, starting nervously at the least sound. As night came she
stayed close to Alex, following him from room to room
and looking fearfully into each dark corner. Alex
sought to comfort and reassure her.

"Tomorrow we should cut down a tree and bring it
in for Christmas."

"Christmas?" puzzled Cameron.

"Aye. I estimate it's coming or just gone, but either
way you had better be very, very good or Saint Nicho-
las will creep down the chimney and put coal in your
boots."

Cameron looked even more puzzled.

"What are you talking about?"

"Christmas, you silly wench," laughed Alex, softly
rubbing her wrinkled little nose.

Cameron pushed his hand away and sat up angrily.

"I am not silly!"

"What's the matter?"

"Stop teasing me with riddles of trees and coal and
saint whatever-you-said," she raged.

"I wasna teasing. I was merely speaking of Christmas," he explained gently, "as I think it's about that
time."

"About what time?"

"Christmas."

"Dinna keep saying it. Christmas! Christmas!" yelled Cameron.

"You dinna ken Christmas?" asked Alex in astonishment.

"You dinna ken Christmas? You dinna ken Christmas?" she taunted angrily, pushing herself from the bed.

"You'll not run from me, Cameron. You'll not sulk away like a spoilt child," he said firmly, catching her arm.

"Let me go!"

"Nay! If you dinna ken Christmas just ask and I'll tell."

Cameron renewed her battle to free herself.

"You can write? Aye, the ignorant bastard can write, can she? Does she ken Christmas? Nay, the ignorant bastard dinna ken Christmas. She dinna ken Christmas, she dinna ken Christmas, the silly, ignorant bastard . . ."

Alex pulled her under him, confining her kicking body with his weight and stopping the furious words with his mouth. Cameron bit his lip and he bit her back.

"Christmas is," he said firmly, staring down at her rebellious face as he pinned her arms over her head, "when the Christ child was born in Bethlehem."

Alex saw from her eyes as she looked away that she had no idea what he was talking about.

"The Christ child was the start of the Christian religion," he continued.

Cameron's face turned to him and she looked disgusted.

"Religion," she sneered, "'tis the cause of all wars."

"Aye, it has caused many wars."

"'Tis evil; binds men's souls," spat Cameron vehemently, deflated that Alex had agreed.

"Not in itself."

" 'Tis corrupt and evil, used by kings and popes to make the powerful rich and the weak poor. 'Tis a terrible, terrible sickness is religion. Can be used to kill whole countries, not just smashing bodies but the very soul," she spouted, remembering Duncan's words. "'Tis an opiate to dull man's spirit so he becomes like the sheep."

Alex stared at her, recalling Dougal's words about Duncan's disillusionment with the Catholic Church. What should he expect Cameron to know of joyous festivals? He laughed at his own stupidity, as he imagined the incongruity of a decorated Christmas tree among the cold gray stones of Cape Wrath. Did he expect Duncan and crazy Mara to celebrate the virgin birth?

Cameron heard his laugh. How dare he ridicule and mock her words! She renewed her struggles but Alex held her tightly.

"I was not laughing at you, Cameron. It was my own ignorance I found amusing," he said softly.

"Oh, to a high-born laird ignorance is amusing, is it?" jeered Cameron.

"Nay, ignorance is never amusing, but should I beat myself instead? Surely to be able to laugh at one's own ignorance is a step on the road to knowledge?"

"How can a gentleman who is civilized be ignorant?" taunted Cameron.

"Very easily, and you of all people shouldn't have to ask me that question! What has my ignorance and stupidity done to you? Look how it has wounded you."

Cameron lay still and looked at him with bewilderment.

"Me?"

"Aye, you," he answered, staring into her eyes.

"But 'twas mine, my ignorance."

"Nay, 'twas mine. I was blind and arrogant, insensitive and cruel. I was ignorant."

"Nay, you were just ignorant of my ignorance," said Cameron slowly.

"But you are not ignorant, Cameron."

"Oh, I can read and write, but there is so much I dinna ken that everyone else already knows. That is why, why—" her voice broke and her eyes filled with tears.

"Why what?" probed Alex, releasing her hands and smoothing back her hair.

"Why, why I canna, we canna be together when the snows melt." And the sobs consumed her as she fought to be free to run to hide her sorrow, but Alex held her firmly.

"Look at me, Cameron," he begged.

"Dinna shame me more. Dinna shame me. Let me go," she screamed.

"Shame you more?" he repeated.

"You break me down and then mock my weakness. I canna bear it."

"What shame? What weakness? What mockery?" he asked, totally bewildered.

Cameron fought him and the flood of hot angry tears.

"Is this shame? Is this your weakness?" he asked, touching a finger to her wet cheeks.

"Dinna mock me more," pleaded Cameron. "You change me to a sniveling, weak babby, and I'm not like that. I am strong, I dinna need anyone. You hear me? I am not this person you see. I lost myself. I dinna ken who I am, but this is not me. You make me weak and shamed. Oh, Mara would laugh, oh, how she would laugh."

Alex stared at Cameron, whose sobs had changed to hysterical laughter. He imagined her as a tiny child having to hide sorrow and fear away. His heart ached with her pain, and his own sorrow for the lonely, lost child welled.

Cameron stared in horror at the tears pouring down Alex's face. What had she done?"

"I'm sorry. I'm sorry," she cried. She had never seen a strong man cry before, and the enormous guilt for it ate into her.

"Everyone cries," said Alex huskily. "I held my own tears back for many years thinking it was unmanly. Even disrespected my own father for his grief. I saw Duncan Fraser hisself with the tears rolling down his face as he watched you ride that last storm of his life." Alex rolled over and they looked at each other, both faces wet.

"Remember the night you played the pipes at Glen Aucht?" Cameron sniffed and nodded. "There wasna a dry eye in the whole house."

Cameron stiffened in fear. Maybe she really was witch's spawn and kelpie's kin, able to weaken all those strong men. Alex noted her tension.

"There is no shame in tears, Cameron. You think I'm less because I cried?"

"Nay, 'twas not your fault. 'Twas mine," protested Cameron.

"Oh, Cameron, Cameron," he crooned, rocking her tightly in his arms. "You know what Mackie always said to me when I was a wee un? She said tears were like sweet nectar from the flowers of the soul which, if kept in, could sour and ferment, pickling your innards. I remember a time she said such to you. 'Twas the night you played the pipes, remember?"

Cameron nodded and recalled the safe arms and pent-up storm within her.

"What did she say?" prompted Alex.

"Dinna let them sour my sweetness," she said slowly.

"But I dinna want to be sweet," she added vehemently.

Alex laughed. "Nay, I would not want you too sweet, 'twould set my teeth aching."

Cameron relaxed against him, her mind still whirling. "Now, Cameron, you were telling me why we wouldna be able to be together in the spring?"

She stiffened as the near-forgotten terror flooded back.

"Because I canna and I dinna want to be a fine lady."

"You are my lady," answered Alex, holding her closer, but Cameron put her two hands against his chest and pushed herself away so she looked directly into his eyes.

"Nay. You must listen, 'Tis difficult enough to try and say. I canna be a lady. I canna—"

"Oh, Cameron—" interrupted Alex.

"Nay! Please, please listen," she pleaded desperately. Alex relaxed his hold and looked at her earnest face. "I canna be. I think of myself back in Edinburgh and a terrible coldness goes through me. I want to be with you wherever you are, but I know I would shame you. No, dinna say a word! You must let me finish!" she shouted, as she saw him open his mouth to protest.

"I would shame you and shame myself too. Sometimes I know I'm very weak and would do anything to stay with you, and then I see myself and it isn't me. I'm all disappeared in fine clothes and fancy words. I canna recognize myself by sight or sound, and inside I'm all cold stone and not feeling. Do you ken? I would hate my own self and also hate you for making me something I'm not. And you'd hate me, seeing me next to the other ladies."

Alex stared at her a long time after she had finished, not sure of what to say. Cameron's heart froze in the endless silence and she rolled away, determined this time to be alone. But Alex held her wrist.

"You know what I've said is true, so let me go. You have no pretty words to answer," she cried.

"Right, I have no pretty words in answer. But 'tis my turn now to speak, so be still and let me have my say," he said firmly, holding her head so she couldn't avoid his gaze. "Nay, there are no pretty words. Life is painful, and maybe all that there is worthwhile is loving, and we have that. 'Tis something I have just now learned. I dinna ken what will happen tomorrow or the next day, in a week, a month, a year, or ten. All I do know—really, truly do know—is I want you with me, by my side, as my lady, my wife, wherever we happen to be—"

"But just wait—" interrupted Cameron.

"Quiet! Stop your running tongue. 'Tis my turn," Alex roared. "You are my wife and that is a fact I have no wish to change. There will be difficulties for you and some for me. There'll be frightening things for both, but we'll face them when we reach them, together, sharing. Aye, maybe we'll have to change ourselves a wee bit and ask for help. Did you hear that, Cameron? *Ask*? I'm not a fortune-teller and canna read into your mind, and unless you learn to trust me and tell me what you need, I'll do the wrong thing not knowing, and you'll be hurt. I dinna want ever to hurt you, but life is strange and we hurt each other, and we'll continue to do so if we canna share or ask."

His voice trailed lamely, and he did not know if he'd made any sense.

Cameron remained silent, not knowing how she felt about his words. Part of her yearned to hear him say they needed nothing but each other and that they would stay together, secluded from the rest of the world, maybe here or maybe at Cape Wrath.

"We'll live in Edinburgh?" she asked fearfully.

"Aye, and at Glen Aucht, and maybe this summer visit Cape Wrath," he said lightly.

"But I canna live in Edinburgh," whispered Cameron, appalled at the idea.

"Aye, you can and you will. But not all the time. Cameron, there is so much for you to see. Theater, libraries, the university, the opera, the ballet—"

"And Lady Fiona," spat Cameron.

Alex's own guilty anger made him want to strike out at Cameron.

"Aye, and Lady Fiona," he retorted cruelly, and then groaned at the pain on her face. "You see how we try to hurt each other? I love you, Cameron, not her. Trust me."

"You'll still bed her like you do me?" pursued Cameron. But her mind had jumped to another thought entirely. "Trust me," he'd said. Had she already trusted too much?

"'Tis not seemly to ask such things. I have no wish to bed the woman; you are more than enough for me."

"Why is it not seemly to ask? Didn't you just tell me to ask?" she replied, trying to follow his conversation, her mind whirling.

"Aye, I did, but just keep such questions for my ears only," he smiled. "Now, wife, if you want to insure my fidelity and keep me from bedding those fancy painted ladies, you'd better start now, because I'm tired of words and hungry for action."

Cameron looked at him with speculation. She had a knot of anger inside that she couldn't release, a terrifying fear and guilt gnawing in her belly. She needed some time to think but was afraid of offending Alex.

"I've some cooking to do, so you'd better find another bed," she teased, covering her need to somehow push him away.

"Cameron—"

"Nay," she laughed falsely, escaping his arms and leaping off the bed.

"Cameron?"

She stood in the hall, frowning. In her mind's eye she could see Duncan's face, and she heard his haunting, warning words. And when his angry image faded, it was replaced by a triumphant Fiona, laughing at her. She ran up the stairs, her hands over her ears, trying to stop the mocking laughter and the echo of her grandfather's voice.

"I'll not go mad! I'll not," she hissed as once again the dark shadows reached to claw her. "I'll not be a timorous coward. I have to be strong and need no one." How many times had Duncan warned her to trust no one? But hadn't Alex himself asked her to trust him? Was it a trick to get her to tell secrets? What secrets? her mind puzzled. She knew nothing and yet he mustn't get any closer or something terrible would happen—the things Duncan had warned her of throughout her whole childhood.

Alex called out again. She wanted to play games and he wanted to make love to her. He felt they had somehow attained their greatest intimacy in sharing their thoughts. He felt so close and tender toward her, but she seemed to want to gambol like an energetic young colt. He lay there trying to get himself in the spirit of her play.

Alex quietly got out of bed and stole to the kitchen.

"Cameron?" he growled, as he crept into the pantry. Finding it empty he tiptoed out to the hall and listened.

Meanwhile Cameron sat in an upstairs bedroom with a large dressing table full of pots of perfume, paint and powder. She hurriedly and messily daubed her face, doused herself with scent, and puffed the powder. She searched frantically for something appropriate to wear and found a lascivious lavender robe. Quickly she climbed into it and surveyed herself in the mirror, hardening her face as she tried to make her small breasts bulge over the bodice. Finding it an impossibility, she posed on the bed and leaned forward, opening the lurid gown to the waist. She heard the stairs creak and shivered with anticipation.

"Cameron?" called Alex, in a very enticing voice. She heard him opening the door of the adjacent room and she stifled a nervous giggle. Alex heard the tell-tale sound and rapped sharply on the door.

"Yes?" quavered Cameron.

Alex popped his head into the room.

"My God! What have we got here?" he ejaculated, staring at Cameron who posed on the bed.

"Lady Fiona Hurst at your service," imitated Cameron.

Alex was not amused. His face turned to thunder, but Cameron was laughing too hard to notice.

"Cameron?" he said threateningly.

"Oh, no formalities, please, just call me Fiona," said Cameron imperiously. "You have my permission to address me by my given name."

Alex grabbed her with very rough hands, but Cameron howled with laughter.

"Don't be impertinent, sir. One lump or two? You'll wrinkle my ball gown. How do you do? Lovely weather we're having, isn't it? How is your gout?"

Alex shook her until her teeth rattled and the brittle stream of polite inanities ceased. Shaken by his own violence he stopped and stared at her. Her rouge was smeared, making her mouth an open wound, two round blobs marked each cheek, and the powder was stuck to her nose and eyelashes.

"Is that how you handle Lady Fiona?" inquired Cameron. Alex slapped her hard across the buttocks.

"Oh? Is *that* how you handle her?" repeated Cameron without flinching, pretending awe.

Alex flung her down flat on the bed and strode out slamming the door.

She lay still, feeling no triumph at accomplishing what she had set out to do. She felt absolutely desolate. Her eyes flickered around the dark room, noting the enormous threatening shadows that danced from the wavering candle. Nameless, imcomprehensible terrors flooded her mind and clutched at her heart. Anything was better than being alone with her imagination of unearthly things, even Alex's fury. She steeled herself against his wrath, trying to quell the urge to run to him like a frightened rabbit.

Alex was sitting at the kitchen table drinking whiskey when Cameron came quietly down the stairs. She had waited a long time and, assuming he had gone to bed, dared to descend. She stood in the doorway as she saw him; his head was bowed and she resisted the urge to sneak away. Alex looked up at her coldly. The red paint still smeared her powdered white face, her green eyes were bright and very large as she faced him bravely.

Alex's rage renewed. He hated artifice. He saw her pure clean beauty marred and cheapened, the image of her degradation, and joined with the guilt he felt at being somehow responsible.

"So you want to play the whore?" he taunted, as he drained his fifth glass of spirits.

Cameron shook her head.

"I have need of a harlot," he declared, walking to her and ripping off the lurid lavender gown.

Cameron stood naked and shivering as he stalked around her, pinching and poking.

"Skinny and not yet grown, but you'll do," he decided, picking her up roughly and sitting her on the kitchen table. Cameron sat mute and wide-eyed as he unbuttoned his britches. He yanked her to him, pulling her hips forward so the hard edge of the table cut into the small of her back, her feet suspended off the floor, and thrust into her with no ceremony. She cried out at the dry, painful friction, but Alex didn't relent; he hammered into her, raping her coldly and impersonally, using her to soothe his battered conscience.

After the initial pain Cameron desperately tried to hug him to her, but he kept his upper body apart from hers, and she clung to the table edge for fear of falling off. She took a breath and let go, trying to wrap her arms about his neck to kiss him, but he threw her back roughly and pulled away.

"I dinna kiss whores. 'Tis not love I need!" he slammed some coins down on the table next to her. Turning aside he poured another drink, furious with himself for not being able to go through with his intentions, but the sight of her trying to cling to him had made it impossible. Angrily he left the room.

He lay morosely on the bed, staring up at the ceiling, when Cameron charged in.

"Well? How do you like playing the whore?" he asked dismally.

"Fine, if you'd finish what you started," retorted Cameron.

Alex rolled onto his stomach and laughed.

"But I dinna pay a whore for *her* pleasure, just my own."

"Then here's coins. I'll pay for mine," she shouted, tossing his coins on the bed.

"I'm wrung dry, Cameron. Go wash your face," yawned Alex, draining his glass.

"No, 'tis your turn to play whore."

"A man canna be a whore."

"Why?"

"Why? Why? Why?" he groaned tiredly. He was upset and confused and just wanted to sleep.

"Aye, why?" insisted Cameron, jumping astride his waist.

"Go wash that rubbish off your face."

"No," said Cameron, bending and kissing him. Alex rolled over and gripped her arms to throw her from him but weakened, and he opened to the warmth of her mouth. He did nothing to encourage her, though, just lay available as she rubbed herself longingly against his exhausted passive body.

He knew he'd imbibed too much whiskey and knew how furious she would be to find that, for all her sensuous sinuous sidlings, he remained soft and sleeping. He moved over as her pelvic bone dug painfully into him and hindered his rest, but she slyly insinuated herself into the curve of his body, tucking herself snuggly so her small bottom pressed against his abdomen. Alex wrapped her tightly in his arms.

"Now settle down and let me sleep," he murmured. Cameron lay obediently still, waiting for the steady deep breathing that signaled he slept, and then very gently she circled her bottom against him. Feeling an answering stirring her excitement mounted and she pressed harder until he groaned with resignation and lay on his back, giving her access.

Cameron played with Alex, her pleasure increasing at her mastery. She fit herself to him and rode astride, resisting his efforts to unseat her to gain the upper position. She rode until her race was done, then rolled off, leaving him aroused—and frustrated—as she curled up for sleep.

Alex smiled ruefully in the darkness at her deft ability to turn the tables, as he willed the whole of him to relax.

Chapter Thirty-one

Cameron wished the protective blanket of snow would stay forever, guarding her from all that loomed so terrifyingly in the future, and buffering her from the panics of the past.

"You promised to take me to Cape Wrath in the spring if I wanted. You promised and I want," she begged.

"Aye, but first we must go home to Glen Aucht. I've many things to settle and Fergus and Mackie must be fretting themselves ill," returned Alex gently.

"But you promised," repeated Cameron, understanding his reasoning, but her apprehension and fear were uppermost in her mind.

"In the summertime we will. You must be patient," he chided.

"I have to find who I am."

"You are my wife, my Cameron, my love. Isn't that enough for you? It isn't what we're called, it's who we are in here," said Alex, putting her hand on his heart.

Cameron pulled herself from him and stared out of the window at the snow that melted and shrank at the first touches of spring.

"Cameron, if knowing who you are is so important to you, maybe your—" he stopped, apprehensive of her reaction.

"My what?"

"Your wee book of Latin holds the key."

Cameron's face drained of all color, but she didn't speak.

"If you'd let me try to read it, try and translate what's written there, maybe you'll know who your parents are." Alex waited for a response, wondering if he should take the chance and tell her all he'd found out already about her mother Dolores and yet, how was he to explain her mother's wild ways? Cameron seemed so hurt by her own illegitimacy, knowing her mother's character would only confirm the worst feelings she had about herself. He couldn't tell her. He just didn't want to lose her.

Cameron silently shook her head, trying to clear it of the ominous pulse that beat.

"Trust me, Cameron," pleaded Alex.

Trust no one. Trust no one, thundered in the girl's ears. Trust no one, 'tis someone else's life you hold. 'Tis Scotland's very future you hold. *Trust no one.* Duncan's words pounded with Cameron's painfully thudding heart. Unknowingly she mouthed the words, at first silently and then aloud, caught in a strange limbo between past and present.

"Trust no one. Trust no one. 'Tis someone else's life you hold," she intoned.

"Your brother's life?"

Cameron stopped suddenly and stared into Alex's amber eyes as if just waking.

"I have no brother," she stated sharply.

"You told me you had," pursued Alex.

"When?"

"In sleep, in French."

" 'Twas a silly dream. I don't speak French," responded Cameron, as her confused mind tried frantically to grasp reality.

"You spoke French, Cameron. A sleeping mind does not have the ability to speak another language perfectly unless the waking mind has it."

"I canna speak French. I canna," ranted the girl. "If I could, surely I would know it. If I had a brother, surely I'd know that too. You're trying to trick me and trap me so I'll show you the book. But you'll not get it!"

"Why would I want to trick you? All I want is to help you find out who you are."

"You'll not want to know, 'twill just say what I know already, that I'm witch's spawn and kelpie's kin, spit out of the sea at midnight by the light of the full moon."

"If it says that, I'll still be enchanted by your spell, Cameron," returned Alex gently, as his mind wondered if the reference to the sea at midnight was the voyage from France to Scotland or from North Rona to Cape Wrath.

"I could be spawned by a thief, even a murderer."

"Nay."

"Aye, you forget I killed a man. You saw. You were there!" she challenged, as somehow even the horror of the dreadful day that Torquod died with the mangled man beneath his powerful hooves was a more real and comforting memory than the shadowy, unnamable glimpses of before that time.

"Cameron, that was self-defense, not murder. 'Twas kill or be killed," reassured Alex. "I dinna care who spawned you, I love you as you are."

"What if I never find out who I am?"

"If you dinna find yourself by then, we're surely in for trouble. 'Tis what we make of ourselves," he said huskily, daring to draw her to him and holding her close.

Cameron heard the strong, steady beating of his heart. Trouble? What trouble were they in for? What did he mean? She buried her face into the warmth of his chest.

"Cameron, I dinna care who spawned you. I dinna care. You are you and I'm content," he crooned, feeling her rapidly racing heart. He bent to kiss her.

Alex looked down at Cameron, asleep in his arms, and carefully edged from the bed so as not to wake her. He was determined to find her book. Methodically he had combed the whole house and the out buildings and found nothing. He stood a moment watching the firelight flicker across Cameron's face. Where had she hid it? The words she had intoned of trusting no one were surely Duncan's. What a heavy responsibility to lay on a child. No wonder she couldn't remember. He was certain Cameron had some kind of amnesia, a condition he had heard and read about. From her reaction to his questions, she didn't remember that she spoke French or had a brother. What better way was there to insure keeping secrets than for the mind to forget them? Dougal had mentioned bairns, Cameron had mentioned *jumeau*—male twin. How old had the pair of them been when they were separated? What had that separation cost the two young children who had shared a mother's womb? From Dougal's words it seemed that the two had been together on the barren rock of North Rona, so the separation must have been at what he had called the age of reason, eight years old. How *un*reasonable and inhuman, thought Alex. Should he attempt to unlock Cameron's mind? But what if nature, by shrouding it, was keeping her sanity? What would be the consequences of forcing her to remember? He could lose her, and that he was not prepared to do. As he sat, his eyes rested on Cameron's bloodstained saddlebag. Impulsively he felt inside it and smiled. His green-eyed little witch was a cunning survivor, having the audacity to hide the precious book right under his nose.

Night after night when Cameron slept, Alex poured over her book, cursing himself for not having paid more attention to his Latin tutor. Not only was his Latin limited, but the writing was tiny and the ink faded on the yellowing paper. He surmised that Dolores had written the book, as it started out as a letter to her children. By hit and a lot of missed words Alex was able to make out the gist of the first few pages, and the incredible sadness of Dolores's message shook him. She knew she was dying, leaving her most precious possessions, her children, alone. She herself had had a lonely childhood without family love and warmth, not knowing her parentage until she had been sixteen, and she was determined that her children should not so suffer. Alex laughed at the irony of life constantly repeating itself. The sins of the parents certainly were revisited and revisited.

Impatiently Alex studied the little book, forcing himself to progress from start to finish instead of skipping through as his bewilderment grew. There seemed to be nothing in the book to warrant Duncan's dire warnings to Cameron. It went into detail of Dolores's own search for her identity, yet when was she going to reveal it? Page after page of feelings, guilts, self-recriminations, hopes, and dreams were set down. Oh, that he had such a legacy from his own father, to really know and feel his own parent as a human being instead of the god or fallen idol, he thought.

Each day the strain of too little sleep and his preoccupation with all he'd managed to translate caused Alex to appear distant and aloof. Cameron was afraid, not able to confront him for fear he'd withdraw further. With the spring approaching maybe he was preparing her for the separation that had to be. She forced her mind to a blank, not able to deal with any emotion for fear she'd break into millions of screaming little pieces and not become whole again.

Alex was unaware of Cameron's detachment. The burden of the book was all his waking mind could deal with, and he automatically worked on the daily chores with Cameron, as his mind wondered what he would discover that night while she slept.

Alex had translated most of the book. He sat at the kitchen table, determined that that night would see an end to it. At last he made out a family tree. The Bermeo family from a town of the same name in Spain. Maria Teresa Oliveira de Bermeo married Donald Alistair MacLeod in Bilboa in 1718. A child Dolores was born in 1719 on the Isle of Skye. But to Alex's frustration the family tree ended there, showing no offspring of Dolores. He turned the page, hoping, and was disappointed to find that her close, tiny writing filled every inch of the next two pages. In frustration he turned to the end of the book, only to find more of the same. He sat with it open to the very last page, which was refreshingly blank, meaning his fatigued brain did not have to continue the chore of translating, and yet he was disappointed at not finding another family tree or the extension of the Bermeos'. Resignedly he grasped the back cover to flip back to the last part he'd read.

The cover was not flat and smooth; something was un
der it. Excitedly Alex slid a sharp knife under the
leather covering and carefully drew out a folded piece
of paper. A sudden noise startled him and he just had
time to close the book and hide his discovery in his
pocket before Cameron appeared sleepily at the door.
He sat watching her face wake into fear and fury as
she saw her book on the table in front of him. She
flew at him, reaching for the knife at the same time.

"You promised! You promised!" she screamed. "You
lied to me!"

Alex sprang back as Cameron stood, knife in hand,
her face wild. What could he say? She was right, he
had broken his promise to her and been caught red
handed.

"Put the knife down, Cameron, before you do some
thing you'll regret," he said tersely, furious with him
self for not keeping track of the time. It was morning;
he'd been sitting with the confounded book all night,
so determined to finish it.

"I've done a lot I regret already, including trusting
you! Duncan was right!" she raged, advancing with the
knife. Alex stood his ground, loath to step back from
her. Would she really use it on him? The Cameron of
Cape Wrath would have had no compunction at all,
but what of the Cameron of now? he wondered, re
membering the knife-throwing contest when she had
been unable to throw the last knife. Had it been fear
of hitting him that had stayed her hand?

Both of them were motionless. Cameron stood, her
right arm raised to throw it, and yet she didn't. The
tension was unbearable; neither spoke nor moved a
muscle. Alex steeled himself as he tried to fathom
what was going on in her mind.

Cameron's mind was a blank. She forgot her hand

was raised to injure, as she saw in her mind the lewdly painted woman at the fair in Durness. "Your mother's a whore. Your mother's a whore." Mara's words came lashing into her brain. "A painted whore. A painted, fallen woman."

"My mother is a painted whore like the woman on the wall at the fair," she said, as if in a dream, her arm still raised with the knife.

Alex looked at her in astonishment.

"Nay, not so. Your mother was a loving woman, Cameron. She wrote you that wee book, a book of feelings that she shares with you and your brother."

The knife hit the floor a fraction of an inch from Alex's bare foot and quivered with the impact.

"I wish my mother or father had left me such a legacy, Cameron," went on Alex, ignoring the lethal weapon and not moving his foot.

Cameron stared at him, white-faced, her green eyes wide. Her arm fell limply to her side.

"What's her name?" she asked softly.

"Dolores."

"Dolores?"

"Aye, 'tis a Spanish name."

"Spanish?"

"Aye."

"I'm Spanish?"

"The book doesna say. But your mother was born on the Isle of Skye. She was half Scot."

"And my father?"

"Doesna say."

"Does it say where she is?" whispered Cameron. "Does it say where I can find her?"

"Your mother is dead," breathed Alex.

"No! She canna be, she canna!"

Alex stood helplessly, seeing the naked pain flare through the green eyes.

"She couldna have died and left me!"

"She dinna want to," comforted Alex, feeling very inadequate.

"She is dead. My mother is dead," stated Cameron numbly, and silent tears welled as the spark of hope was extinguished. She breathed deeply, drawing on the inner strength that had seen her through so much already, and picked up her book. She stared blindly at the cover for a moment, fighting to control her sorrow.

"And what are you not telling me?"

"What?"

"There's something you read here that you're not telling me!" she accused coldly.

"There's your mother's love for you, her growing up, what she learned of life."

"And?"

"And what?"

"If that's all, then why was the book to be hid from all eyes? Why did Duncan say it meant life and death? He was neither a fool nor fanciful. He did or said nothing without reason."

"Aye, that's a puzzle. I'll read you the book and you will have to reason that out for yourself," replied Alex, the folded paper he'd found in the back cover burning a hole in his pocket.

"You'll not!"

Alex watched in amazement as Cameron threw the book into the kitchen fire. He leaped forward to save it, but Cameron picked up the poker and pushed it deeply into the flames. They watched silently as it blazed and then died among the embers.

Cameron stared at her book being consumed. She wanted to grab it back. *Why* had she done that?

"Why did you do that?" asked Alex.

Cameron shook her head, the tears spilling down her cheeks.

"I thought I hated her. Now I'll never know what she wrote to me. I wanted to hurt her."

Alex stepped nearer to comfort, but Cameron angrily wiped the tears from her eyes and glared at him.

"Cameron, I'm sorry. I read the book to help you, and now I've hurt you more."

"Aye, what right did you have?" she spat.

"None, except loving you."

Cameron stood staring at his face, which was full of infinite sadness. She felt so alone. She forced her eyes back to the fire, trying to decipher which of the glowing embers was the remains of her book.

" 'Tis like I killed my own mother, isn't it? And I dinna ken why. There have been mothers in books I've read, wonderful mothers. Sometimes I'd pretend I really had one to love me—to brush my hair and tell me stories and the like. I suppose you think that's weak and fanciful?"

"Nay."

"I was just a wee bairn then," Cameron interrupted defensively.

"Each needs to be loved," answered Alex gently.

Cameron fought the aching tears as she fixed her burning eyes on the fire.

"I wanted a mother, but I knew it was wrong. I wanted to be held so close, but I knew she was a painted witch as Mara said. So while she held me she could change from a mother to an unearthly creature, and the hands that held me would become claws with the nails of the hawk."

"Your mother was no witch, Cameron."

"I had a dream," she interrupted, without looking at him. "I think it was a dream, for things back then are so shadowy that I canna be sure. I was standing on the very top of a pointed mountain. It was dark and yet I could see a figure walking away from me. I cried and screamed, 'Mama, come back. Please, Mama, come back,' but she didn't even turn around, just kept going down the slope away from me. I kept calling 'Mama, come back!' She walked down to the valley, getting smaller and smaller, but as she reached the flat she turned, and the moon shone full on her face till it got as big as the sun, and green like festering water. Her eyes burned red in her head and she had snakes instead of hair. She laughed an ugly evil sound that bounced and echoed in the mountains so they shook. I dinna care. I wanted my mother. 'Mama, come back! Mama, please love me!' I screamed, but she went on laughing, and she had little pointy teeth like the bat, but I loved her, for she was my own mother."

"Cameron, that was Mara's spiteful tongue muddling your child-mind in sleep. For nights on end I've read your book and feel I know your mother better than I ever knew my own. She was a mother to be proud of, for she loved you. If it had been possible, she would have held you, told you stories, brushed your hair, and more."

"Aye, and I've killed her without knowing her or loving her. Why, when I want her so much? 'Twas like I was afraid of the past, of what I'd find. I want to live and yet the past drags me back. I canna remember so many things that I should recall. There are just dark, fearsome shadows that when I think on them the ground is not firm, it moves and cracks as though it will swallow me up like a grave."

Alex made himself stand still, although he yearned to hold her close, brush her hair, and tell her stories. He held his breath, knowing that within the next few minutes their futures would be determined. By breaking his promise and reading her book he'd given her the power of the decision. He didn't resent her for it, he just knew it had to be. In the long silence he realized that Dolores's words had been for him too. He had learned so much from the outpourings of her soul. For him there had always been a separateness between male and female, as though each was of a different species, and yet the honest, heartfelt emotion expressed in the tiny, neat handwriting had crossed the barrier of sexual gender. He now understood what had made his father the man he was. Without the ability to love and the courage to admit it man or woman was really nothing.

The silence ticked on. Cameron wished that Alex would just sweep her into his strong arms. She felt drained, squeezed dry of emotion. The enormity of throwing her book into the fire took her breath away, appalled her, and yet there was a relief, as though a burden had been lifted.

"The past days you've acted like you were tired of me," Cameron said haltingly.

"Nay, my love. I'll be honest with you now. I've been up nearly every night deciphering your book, and tying my brain in knots trying to reason why Duncan Fraser thought it so damaging to you or—" he faltered.

"My twin," Cameron added quietly.

"You remember?"

"Nay, just glimpses, riding somewhere, swimming, and making Mara so angry, but she couldn't catch us. Then everything changed. It's like there was a storm. Mara was still there, but *he* wasn't. I lived somewhere else and wasna allowed to speak our secret way that Mara couldna ken."

"Our secret way?"

"My mind lights on it, but I canna grasp no more," replied Cameron forlornly.

Alex stared into the fire wondering how he could approach her. He felt as vulnerable as she looked, but somehow the fear of her possible rejection of him made mincemeat of his pride.

"Does it matter?" asked Cameron, in a small voice, not wanting the darkness of the past in her mind, just wanting the safety of the presence of his strong arms.

Alex looked at her questioningly. He saw the pleading in her green eyes.

"All that matters is that you'll not leave me," he said with difficulty, emotion knotting his throat. "Cameron, I love you, and although I've given you little reason to trust me, please believe me." He dared open his arms and, to his great joy, Cameron rushed in and clung to him tightly.

Later, as they lay in each other's arms, Alex smiled down at Cameron, who traced his golden eyebrows.

"Why so worried, my love?" he asked, concerned at her earnest expression.

"Can we forget the book, for now?"

"Aye," agreed Alex, holding her tight.

"One day when I feel stronger, will you tell me what my mother wrote to me?"

"Aye," murmured Alex, rejoicing in her adaptability.

"But for now can we be as we were before? Just be together not thinking of the past?" asked Cameron, adding to herself "and not thinking of the future either."

"Aye."

Alex slept, and Cameron, in his arms, stayed awake for hours. She wanted desperately to block out everything but the present. She clung to the strong golden man as though her whole life depended on him, uncaring that her promises to be strong and independent were broken. She clung to Alex as though to keep from drowning in the dark, turbulent sea of her past and the fear of the future.

Chapter Thirty-two

For two days Alex was unable to read the folded paper he'd found hidden in the cover of Cameron's book, not having a minute to himself. He was cutting wood, delighting in a sensuous feeling of well-being as he sweated with his exertion in the chill early-morning air. He stopped to tug a hankerchief from his pocket to wipe his face, and the scrap of parchment flew out, making an imperceptible brushing noise as it skittered across the crisp snow. He sat on a log staring at the yellow square that just missed blending into the white all around it. It had been so important—it still was—but his relationship to Cameron had taken priority, blocking it from his mind. His eyes remained riveted on the neat shape that probably contained the key to Cameron's mystery as he thought back over the past two days. There had been no conflict between them, and his relief that she had somehow chosen to stay with him despite the breaking of her trust had made him force a nagging anxiety away. He now dared to brood on what the discomfort was. Cameron had been loving and compliant, more affectionate and eager to please than she'd ever been—and yet something was very wrong. What? Something was missing. It was her wild, rebellious spirit. But was not that just what he wanted? Aye, he wanted her trust, not her docility. Alex was confused. What did he really want Cameron to be? Everything, he decided. He wanted her spirit and her passivity. Was that possible? Did not one cancel out the other?

He shivered and realized he'd been sitting, coatless, lost in thought for a great while. His eyes had not left the small square of paper. He was almost afraid to pick it up. On one hand he rejoiced, felt stronger and more masculine with Cameron curled into him for comfort, but was that trust? What did the scrap of paper mean to them? What if it contained information to hurt her, to drive them apart, put their relationship back to the beginning again? It was the past and maybe it should be buried, remain unread. It was Cameron's, so maybe it should be handed to her unread by him.

As though an unseen force was holding him back, Alex reached down with difficulty and grasped the folded paper.

"Alex? Alex?" Cameron's clear voice cut through the still, clean air, and the paper was once again thrust deeply into his pocket before he turned and opened his arms wide to the raven-haired girl who raced across the crunchy snow.

"You left me all alone!" she gasped, her cheeks rosy from sleep and the chill wind. "I woke up alone. You weren't there!"

"You were afraid?"

Cameron didn't answer, she just burrowed into his hard muscular body, feeling safe as the strong arms held her tightly.

"Why were you afraid?" Alex repeated, tipping up the face she hid from him. Cameron didn't answer. She stared into his amber eyes knowing that without his presence she felt incomplete, crippled, somehow unable to be a whole person. She thrust the knowing from her.

"I'll not leave you, Cameron. Trust me," pleaded Alex, and seeing shame and confusion in the bright green eyes, he lightened his tone and changed the subject.

"I've been up since before dawn and have a hunger for a big, hot meal. I'll race you to the kitchen." And with that Cameron turned to run but stopped suddenly. Alex noted her hesitation and galloped past her.

"The loser cooks and does the washing of the pots," he challenged, pretending to run like a fat old man as Cameron swiftly passed him, laughing.

Alex had not a moment alone to read the paper that lay so heavily in his pocket and on his conscience. That night he lay staring at Cameron's small hand that, even in sleep, held on to him so desperately. Why wasn't he content? He had longed for her dependency and now that he had it, it clawed into him somehow. In fact it terrified him. The thought brought back bitter memories of his own father's cloying dependency. With a loud oath Alex sat up, loosening Cameron's hands, but she didn't wake. She murmured softly and turned to the wall, her breathing even.

He'd not sneak anymore, he vowed, noisily getting out of bed and striding across the room to his clothes. He pulled them on, humming as he did so, hoping to rouse her, but Cameron slept undisturbed. 'Twas almost unnatural, thought Alex, as he realized that the past nights since the burning of the book she was in bed before sundown, seducing him earnestly, as though to block out the approaching darkness, and falling into a deep, deep slumber that lasted until the sun was high in the sky.

He thrust his hand deeply into his pocket and pulled out the paper, as he stared at Cameron in contemplation before crossing to the bed and sitting heavily so her light frame rebounded on the mattress. She didn't stir so he shook her.

"Cameron? Cameron?"

"No! I don't want to be awake. I don't want to wake up!" she cried, and burrowed into his legs.

Alex stared down ruefully at the glossy ebony head and the slim white arms that encircled his knees. She was sound asleep again. He lay her back against the pillows, covered her, and left the room.

He sat at the kitchen table and poured himself a liberal glass of whiskey as he stared at the small scrap of yellowing parchment. Such a small thing and yet what could it portend? He took a long drink and then slowly unfolded it, spreading it out before him. His eyes refused to focus, not wanting to see. Through the blur was a pattern, the familiar pattern of a chart. Three family trees side by side. He brought the left side of the paper into focus, scanning down the branches of the Bermeo family until they joined to that of the MacLeods and showed the birth of Dolores. He stared at the name of the man written beside, that joined the third family tree. Charles. Not allowing his eyes to stray up to the name at the top he kept his gaze fixed to the offspring of the two. No names, just sexual gender: boy and girl. And the year 1746. Alex knew the surname of the third family; he didn't have to look above to confirm. How blind and stupid he'd been! Of course, it had to be! All the clues had been there, so why hadn't he wanted to see it? Even Dougal had mentioned the name. Charles Stuart, Bonnie Prince Charlie, pretender to the throne of Scotland. Why else would Duncan Fraser go to such trouble to hide a pair of children? Certainly not out of sentimentality for the death of Dolores, his own young ward. Everything now made sense, every dire warning of life and death, the secrecy, the intrigue, even the talk of witchcraft to keep people away. How could he have been so blind? Alex sat stunned at his inability to have put together so obvious a puzzle. Had Fergus guessed? Surely he had, but he had chosen not to share the knowledge. Now he was faced with the dilemma of what to do. Cameron and her twin brother, wherever he was, were Royal Stuarts. What had been Duncan Fraser's plan? Surely not to raise the Highland chiefs for another uprising against the English? That would come to naught, as there was no support left; Scotland was drained, and yet the old warrior was embittered and fanatical, living alone with the memories of past glory, so it was definitely possible. Alex looked down at the chart to the date marking the twins' birth. How sad that it didn't show names or the day of birth. But it did list the place: Olaron-Ste. Maria, Gascony. Probably the convent where Dolores had spent her lonely childhood and equally lonely death. Maybe there was a record in that tiny town high in the Pyrenees near the French-Spanish border? Yet, what would be the point in looking? What pain and possible dangers would surface by dredging into the past?

Alex carefully folded the document and hid it in his saddlebag. He stared down at Cameron, curled into a small ball under the covers. That petite, beautiful woman was Royal Stuart. He shuddered, thinking of the consequences of anyone ever finding out. She could become a political pawn to fanatic Scottish loyalists who refused to see reality, or be used as an example by the ruthless English to put the same down. He sat back at the kitchen table, his body aching with fatigue and yet his brain too excited to relax in sleep.

What should he do? It was inconceivable to even think of telling Cameron, and yet the thought of having to keep such a secret from her distressed him greatly. It had to be so, he concluded. Everyone had some sort of cross to bear in life, and keeping the name of Cameron's father from her was to be his. She must never know. What of the brother? Somewhere, there was a fifteen-year-old boy, a Stuart prince. What of him? Alex justified his decision to let the past lie by reasoning that as Cameron now had him, she had no need of a brother whom she'd been without for seven or eight years. Besides, even Duncan had felt them safer apart, as maybe there were people that could connect the name Stuart to twins.

Cameron lay, her eyes closed, the covers over her head. Why had Alex rudely shaken her from her protective blanket of sleep? Why had he left her? She dozed in a limbo of neither waking nor sleeping, unable to get up and go to him, and yet unable to fall into the unthinking nothingness of slumber. She drew her knees up closer to her breasts and hugged them, holding herself together as she fought a vast, aching desolation. A shining young face flashed into her mind, a face so like her own, topped with an unruly crown of shining black hair. Wide-set, bright green eyes seemed to look into her very soul, the mouth grinning warmly with love.

"Jumeau! Jumeau!" screamed Cameron, as the beloved face faded and she sat up wildly, searching.

Alex heard her cry and raced into the bedchamber.

"Jumeau reviens! Reviens!"

Alex took her in his arms. Cameron froze and stared up in bewilderment at his face, pushing her hands against his chest to see him better. She looked around the room remembering where she was.

"I had a dream," she said slowly.

"Aye, it's gone now, my love."

"He's gone—my jumeau," faltered Cameron, her eyes dark and haunted with sadness.

"It is the past. 'Tis gone, Cameron. We must live in the present."

Cameron nodded miserably. "He's gone. He's all I ever had and he's gone."

"You have me now, Cameron."

"I remembered his name—Jumeau," she said, trying to smile through her tears. Alex was touched and couldn't correct her by saying that *jumeau* was not a name, just the French word for twin. "I wish, I wish . . ."

"You wish what?" prompted Alex gently.

"That I had my brother as well as you," she blurted out, and then hid her face in Alex's chest and clung to him tightly. Alex fought with the need to tell Cameron he'd search the ends of the earth to find her twin. He thrust the thought from his mind as he bit down on his tongue and rocked her comfortingly. Cameron was his and he'd protect her. They would stride forward to a bright new future without a backward look.

Chapter Thirty-three

Alex noted the signs of the impending spring with mixed feelings. On the one hand he felt a surge of rejoicing at the new life springing forth and was eager to step out and face the world with Cameron. On the other hand he remembered the clashing discordancy he had felt before. Would it be possible with Cameron by his side to achieve the smooth harmony he'd known before she tumbled so turbulently into his life? Maybe he could again enjoy all the things that had palled and become distasteful; maybe he could become content, he reasoned, as it was only his unadmitted love for her that had soured all he looked upon. He grew excited at the prospect of introducing Cameron to so many things she had not experienced, hoping that through her eyes he too would see them differently, in a new light.

He carefully mapped out their future life together in his mind, determined that once they settled back at Glen Aucht into a steady, comfortable rhythm, all her fears and terrors would fall away, and her wild, untamed zest for life would return. He smiled as he thought of the spring planting, rising early to work with the farmers, gardeners, and gamekeepers; the humdrum soothing of the seasons full of hard work—plowing, sowing, birthing—through the buzzing laziness of summertime to the sweaty, prickly harvest into the sharp, cool tang of the autumn when their play was well-earned and they would depart for Edinburgh to enjoy the wonders of culture. He refused to let his mind dwell on his discontent at the hypocrisy, poverty, politics, or any of the other things he had seen with such brutal clarity. Cameron's presence, like a breath of fresh sweet air, would sweep off the tarnish and he'd see everything once more in a favorable light.

"'Tis time we thought about leaving," announced Alex, as they tramped across the shrinking, crackling patches of snow.

Cameron looked up at him sharply and Alex thought she had never looked more beautiful. Her cheeks were pinked from the cold, her black glossy hair rioted in the wind, and her deep green eyes lit with emotion.

Cameron turned away and stared unseeing at the mountains that peaked to the clouds in the distance.

"When?" she asked without looking at him, her breath steaming the still air.

"A week," he answered, knowing they needed time to adjust to the idea of leaving and to put their borrowed house in order.

"I wish we could just stay here for ever and ever."

"'Tis time to start living in the real world," said Alex, putting an arm around her and staring over the vista.

"This . . . all this isn't the real world?"

"Aye, 'tis a part of it, but just a wee part. Cameron,

we've been so much luckier than most. We've had a five-month honeymoon."

"Honeymoon?" asked Cameron, turning to him.

"Aye, honeymoon. 'Tis a time newly wedded people shut themselves away from the eyes of the world to learn about each other. Most get but a week or so, some none, but we are setting out with more than most ever dream of," he explained, kissing her lightly on the nose.

They walked slowly to the lodge, lost in their own thoughts. Cameron felt a fierce aching and her teary eyes burned in the sharp cold wind. Everything around her was so startlingly clean and fresh, and the thought of Edinburgh grimy and squalid. She held Alex's hand firmly, clutching at his strength to stop from falling into a dark pit of panic as she teetered on its edge.

Alex returned her pressure and smiled reassuringly at her.

"'Twill be a great adventure, Cameron. We've much to do, learn, see, and feel before we die. 'Tis a journey together through life," he stated enthusiastically.

"Aye," she responded, still unconvinced.

"Cheer up. Let's not have our last week clouded with your frowns. 'Tis nearly spring—time to wake up and live," he chanted merrily.

"Our last week," repeated Cameron dully.

It tolled with such an ominous sound. Was it to be their last week of happiness?

"Cameron, will you spoil our last week together?" he chided gently.

"Our last week together?"

"You know what I mean. 'Tis the last week in our enchanted lodge, so dinna spoil it. Let's look ahead to all the surprises of the future," he pleaded, looking into her frightened, upturned face.

"Hold me very, very tight," she whispered.

Alex held her to him, wrapping his arms protectively around her. She trusted him, trusted his strength. He felt incredibly strong. They had come a long way together already, he thought happily, pushing an uncomfortable, ominous feeling aside.

Cameron clung tightly, breathing his fragrance, trying to submerge her whole being with him. If only she could somehow give herself up for him, everything would be safe and secure. But hadn't she already done that? she wondered, the sudden realization making the ground seem to shudder beneath her feet.

They tidied and cleaned the hunting lodge, Alex singing contentedly and Cameron working mechanically to stop the dark thoughts from clouding the horizon. She didn't want to see the horizon. She refused to let her mind probe any further than the particular minute. She forced herself to smile and bravely join the chorus of his songs, but no matter how she tried to rein her galloping fears, they strained and escaped until her heart thudded out of control. At such times she longed to mount her horse and race with the storm inside herself but, unable to move, she just stood still until Alex, seeing, wrapped her in his arms and held her tightly.

The days of that week seemed too short to Cameron. She tried to savor each second but they elusively ticked by.

The morning before they were due to depart, Cameron crept from their bed before sunrise and sat outside, staring at the changing shades of the mountains as morning lightened the sky. Alex had said they were but thirty miles from the smoky city of Edinburgh, yet looking over the vista before her and not seeing any signs of human life, it seemed impossible. She fervently wished that the rest of the world didn't exist.

But it did, and she knew she had to become a part of it if she chose to stay with Alex. What if she didn't choose to? She would cease to exist, she thought.

Alex had also said it was the start of their life together, and Cameron felt a deep grief as she knew that it meant the death of her own life as she had known it. She sat silently mourning, her whole body keening for the past.

Alex watched her from the kitchen door, reluctant to shatter the solitude she seemed to need. He felt shut out and lonely; he wanted to be her whole life, her be-all and end-all. He was eager for her every thought and was frustrated knowing it was impossible. He had felt a sadness at the loss of her wild sparkle, but he was more than grateful for the way she now turned to him for comfort. He gloried in the strength he felt when she stood in the circle of his arms, so small, lost, and afraid. He reassured himself that her zest and free spirit would return once they settled into the rhythm of their life.

Alex sat beside Cameron without touching her and stared over the breathtaking majestic view.

"Part of me has to die and it hurts me," cried Cameron.

"What?"

Alex looked at her with consternation as she stared straight ahead at the wild rugged country with tears pouring down her cheeks.

"No, Cameron, no. Nothing has to die," he protested, pulling her to him and cradling her like a baby.

Cameron wanted to push him away and run, but she kept herself still. What would she be without him?

"Nothing has to die," he repeated firmly, as a cold fear flashed through him. What had she said after throwing her book into the fire? Something about kill-ing her own mother? Now she was speaking of something else having to die. 'Twas right, his mind seethed, the ties to the past must be severed. But at what cost? A part of her dying? What had she said in French? *'L'autre demi de moi'?* The other half of myself. Was he demanding that she cut out and kill a part of herself? He forcibly rejected the thought, not able to bear the responsibility, as his mind strove to be rational and logical. They'd been closed up too long in their enchanted hideaway, he was getting too fanciful. Cameron just needed more time to adjust, as her descent into the busy world would be much more difficult than his. He chided himself, realizing that a postponement could just heighten her fearful anticipation.

"I think we should leave today," he said gently.

Cameron jerked herself from his arms and sat stiffly.

"No, 'tis all right. 'Tis our last day. I want it. Please, Alex, I need it."

He stared into her pleading face and felt weak and helpless.

"'Tis just hurting you unnecessarily to wait. There's nothing to harm you down there, 'tis just the waiting building up the fear in you."

"Please, dinna steal our last day?" she begged.

Alex nodded sadly.

"'Twill be the best—the very best, the happiest and most wonderful day and night ever in the whole of time," declared Cameron earnestly, trying to smile through the tears that still flooded down her face. "You'll see, you'll see. I promise!" she cried, as she raced down the glen and flung herself on her horse to ride him wildly around and around, as though it were the last free day of her childhood.

Alex watched her and was filled with the most incredible sadness. Every part of him ached with a hollow agony. What did she mean about a part of her having to die? What did she feel was to be killed? Was he to be the slayer?

Cameron was desperately determined that their last day and night should be the most perfect ever, that they ever had or would have again. Alex forced himself to smile, although he felt he watched a frantic death dance. Should he tell her who she was? Should he let her go? Was she like a wild animal that would die in captivity? He wanted to possess her, but in so doing would he smother and kill?

He tried as desperately as Cameron to enter into her determination that their day and night be the most wonderful and happiest ever. It passed slowly, tensely; their laughter sounded artificial, their every movement confined and forced as a result of their trying too hard to be free. Together they composed a note of explanation to the owner of the lodge but everything they did or said was so strained that, unbeknownst to each other, they both wanted to scream and shatter the painful gaiety. It all culminated that night when their lovemaking failed dismally.

Alex tried to relax, knowing how important their coming together was, and Cameron desperately sought to make her body pretend the excitement she didn't feel, not wanting to fail him. They both felt their last act of love in their honeymoon lodge symbolized the promise of their commitment. Each sought to prove to the other.

Alex and Cameron lay awake, each in a private hell, neither wishing to be the first to speak of the failure of their communion, each secretly hoping the other would eventually sleep.

Cameron lay with her back to Alex, feeling cold and alone. She wanted to cuddle herself into his warmth for comfort, but thought he would then feel obligated to demonstrate his love more fully, and she was already feeling frightened and guilty at his inability. Had she destroyed him in some way?

Alex lay on his back, staring up at the dark ceiling. All he wanted was to hold her soft warmth to him and reassure her. Of what? All he knew was that he loved her. He struggled with himself, wanting to be with her despite the cost to himself or her. He wanted her secure and unavailable to anyone else. He wanted her completely and utterly. Would she become a brittle empty shell, a lifeless Cameron? What was he to do?

"Cameron?" he called softly, half hoping she slept.

Cameron heard him and stiffened.

"Yes?" she whispered.

"Cameron, this is very hard for me to say, but you are free if that's what you so desire."

Alex held his breath, hating himself for giving her the choice, knowing that if she chose to be free of him, his life would be nothing more than an endless trail of gray days.

Cameron froze. He didn't want her. Now that winter was over he wanted to be free to return to his own world—free and unencumbered. She'd lost him *and* her ability to survive alone.

Alex suffered in the long silence, thinking she sought the words to claim her freedom. He wanted to shatter the straining stillness with words. But what should he say? Was there anything to say?

"Cameron, for godsake answer me."

"What should I say?" she whispered.

"What you feel."

"Even if I knew what I felt, would it matter? You want your freedom, I canna change that."

"I want my freedom? You are my freedom. I love you. I want to be with you."

"I can never be free of you!" she cried.

Alex heard the words he longed to hear, but the icy bitterness in her voice cut through his heart like a knife.

"Cameron?"

"Aye, I am nothing! I am empty! I have nothing in me but to hang on to you or I'll die!"

Alex stared at her face that was devoid of expression, every feeling masked. He didn't know what to say.

"Fergus said loving was hard and one had to give up some things, but he didna say all things."

"Cameron, I don't ask for that, do I?"

"In your way, you do," replied Cameron dully. "I canna find who I am anymore, but I suppose in a different way I didn't know who I was before, so it doesna matter."

"But it does matter," retorted Alex. "In what way do I ask you to give up so much?"

Cameron shrugged and curled up, hiding her face from him.

"No! You'll not hide from me in sleep. That's running like a coward, Cameron," he shouted, pulling her up.

"Aye, so I'm a coward. Leave me and go your own way," she said listlessly.

"I don't want to go my own way! I want to be with you and want you to want to be with me. Cameron, why won't you trust me?" his voice ached with frustration. She stared at him, seeing him as though from afar, before replying in a very distant voice.

"I am willing to go your way. I am willing to use your strength, your name, your life, your home. Is that not trust? I've tried my best, but I don't know how to show you more."

Alex stared at her in amazement. That's how it

should be. That was the way of the world. That was expected of a wife. But as his mind raged he realized that once again she was trying to obey his wishes to the letter, and once again he had expected her to be aware of social conventions when her rearing on Cape Wrath made that impossible. Even as his mind touched on the previous realization, it veered off in another direction, as he found himself not liking the convention, for it made Cameron into one of the cloying, grasping women he abhorred.

She waited for him to answer, feeling the tension crackle the silence. It was as though she were poised on a precipice and any second would go hurtling into a vast bottomless abyss to spin forever through a hollow aching void.

"Cameron?" whispered Alex, not sure if she slept. Hearing the sharp intake of her breath he went on. "You said before that you could never be free of me. Well, I can never be free of you either. You seem to hold all that I am also. Do you hear?"

"If I hold so much as you say, then why don't you trust me?" Cameron did not know where the thought or the words came from.

"But I do trust you!" exclaimed Alex quickly.

"Do you?" murmured Cameron defeatedly.

Alex lay flat on his back watching the flames' reflections play on the ceiling. Guilt and irritation gnawed at him as Cameron's unexpected question struck a sore nerve. Half of him raged that it was impertinent and disrespectful of her to ask such a thing—yet hadn't she the right to expect the same of him as he from her? That thought surprised him, and he realized how far he had traveled from the private bitter man of scarcely nine months before who'd gone to Cape Wrath.

"Oh, Cameron, Cameron, you've a deft way of turning the tables on me, my love," he laughed, enfolding her in his arms. Cameron, bewildered at the sudden change of mood, lay passively staring into his amber eyes. She felt her dread thaw as he chuckled deeply.

"Aye, we'll find that wild brother of yours and then you both can lead me a merry dance." He grinned into her wide puzzled eyes.

"What?"

"You dinna want to?" he asked.

Cameron shook her head to clear it and pushed back from him. "'Twas not in my mind just now. 'Tis not what we were talking of. Out of the blue sky you say it. But how? When? Where? What do you know? And why, Alexander, do you say so now?"

"Which first?" puzzled Alex, surprised at himself for making such a rash promise and yet knowing it was right. He'd not mention the name Stuart to her; he'd tell her all he knew, leaving out that dangerous piece of knowledge.

Cameron was spellbound as he recounted briefly what he had heard from Dougal Gunn, of Dolores dying and Duncan taking the two of them, Cameron and her brother, and hiding them on the island of North Rona.

"With Mara, 'tis true, and when the fishing boats came too near we'd play games to scare them off," added Cameron. Alex held his breath as, haltingly at first, Cameron remembered.

"Mara said as how we were cursed, and soon we saw 'twas true, as no one dared to come near the island. When some did, their ships broke up upon the rocks. Fearsome, wonderful storms would rage and Jumeau and I would race our horses around and around. Mara said 'twas because of our power. Then—then—"

"Dougal Gunn said when you were eight, or there-

abouts, Duncan brought you to live with him at Cape
Wrath?" prompted Alex, daring to take the chance as
he realized he preferred a whole woman to the fearful
extension of him she'd become in the past weeks.

"A boat came, not the usual one with Grandfather,
but another. Jumeau and I watched it coming and we
rode around, but the storm would not come and stop
it. They took Jumeau."

"Who?"

Cameron furrowed her brow, remembering the day
clearly as though it had been just the day before.

"A big braw man with a beard and a head of red
hair like a bush, and an old woman like a witch.
Grandfather was with them. I started to cry and he
was angry. He screamed at Mara, saying she did nothing right. I hid from their fury, knowing it was the
tears that made them angry. When I came back the
strange boat was gone, taking Jumeau, and a time later
Grandfather came back on the usual boat to take me
and Mara to Cape Wrath. He said if I wanted to see
Jumeau again I mustna speak of him or he'd die. He
changed my name to Cameron—before it was Jumelle.
'Tis all I remember." Cameron lay back and stared
pensively at the ceiling.

"What do you feel?" asked Alex anxiously.

"'Tis strange. No shadows but such sadness. I dinna
feel like I thought I would. 'Tis like a great weight has
been lifted, a heavy cloth that was suffocating me, gone.
My name is Jumelle!" she exclaimed.

Alex, feeling it was not the time to explain that *jumelle* was solely the word for female twin, quietly told
her that he knew not much more, but that Fergus had
puzzled about the two places called Rona, the other
being off Skye where her mother, Dolores, had been
born.

"You think Jumeau is there?" exclaimed Cameron.

"I dinna ken but, Cameron, be realistic, there's no real way of knowing where he's at, or if he still lives," he said soberly.

"He still lives!" declared Cameron emphatically.

"Because you want it so much to be so?" questioned Alex softly, rejoicing at the lively spirit in her face, and yet afraid that her hope was in vain.

"But we must go to this other Rona quickly," demanded Cameron, bouncing exuberantly on the bed.

"Whoa, my love," cautioned Alex, not wishing to extinguish the spark that he had longed to see reignited. "We have commitments first—at Glen Aucht. You'd not have Mackie and Fergus fretting, thinking we're dead and gone, now would you? Mackie is from Skye, MacLeod land like your kin, though I doubt they would acknowledge you so." He proceeded to tell her about her grandmother Maria, who died birthing Dolores. "So you see, my love, you must be patient," he ended. He was almost afraid to look at her, expecting to see her vivacity dampened by disappointment. He was elated to see her smiling at him in a serenely breathtaking way, her face above him as she leaned on one arm over his prone body, gazing into his eyes.

"You've given me back myself," she stated quietly, her face glowing with a new maturity. Alex felt a pang of fear.

"But we've not found him yet," he murmured.

"We will, but 'tis not that. 'Tis something I canna quite fathom myself. 'Twill sound foolish, but I'll dare say it. 'Tis as though you're not afraid of me anymore. There, sounds even sillier when said out loud. As if you could ever be afraid of me," she laughed.

Alex enfolded her tightly in his arms. Little did Cameron know how wise she was. Why else had he reined her so tightly to tame her? He pushed the thought away and devoted all his mind and body to the act at hand.

They set out as the sun was rising. Mounted on their horses they paused a moment to stare across the mountain, both trying to imprint it forever in their memories. Cameron looked behind them at the lodge that stood empty and forlorn in the small secluded glen. She reluctantly forced her head to face forward as the last glimpse of her haven was lost among the trees. She kept her eyes firmly on the back of Alex's head, blind to the tiny sprouts that thrust so strongly from the awakening earth. Torquil led the small procession, running excitedly ahead to smell and enjoy the springtime. Alex turned and smiled reassuringly at Cameron, wishing the path was wider so they could ride side by side.

At the clearing on the mountain side he reined his horse and, taking her hand, pointed down at the still loch beneath them. He smiled as he felt her small cold fingers clutch his. He rejoiced, remembering her former inability to accept comfort.

"Afraid?" he asked.

Cameron nodded silently and Alex wanted to cheer exultantly at her open admission.

"'Tis a great adventure we're setting out on," he reminded her.

"Aye," she replied, as she forced her shoulders back and raised her head.

"You're my braw lass," said Alex gruffly, knowing her arrogant stance covered a thousand fears. "Trust me?" he added, squeezing her hand tightly.

Cameron nodded, too full of emotion to speak. Alex leaned over and kissed her cheek before urging his horse down the steep mountain. He hoped he'd prove worthy of her trust in the many miles that stretched before them.

Cameron's own head was busy with thoughts of a similar nature, as she hoped she proved worthy of him. She had already traveled a great distance from Cape Wrath and wasn't sure how far from the wild solitary child she really was. She was fifteen years old, or there abouts, and a married woman. It was hard to believe. She clasped Alex's hand tightly as they rode side by side on the road to Crieff, aware in that one simple action to Alex she had surmounted a large obstacle. She held on to him tightly, still feeling that if she let go she might be lost, but knowing she would survive.

Cameron tugged on Alex's hand and stared into his face anxiously.

"Alex?"

"Aye, my love?"

"Do you trust me?"

"Aye, with my very life."

He leaned over and they kissed, Cameron clinging desperately to his lips.

"It will be a good life. I will be a good wife, the very best wife," she promised earnestly.

"Not too good, I hope," he chuckled.

"I'll race you!" challenged Cameron, spurring her horse to a gallop and streaking ahead of him toward the unknown new life that awaited.

Alex watched her go and smiled ruefully before raising a loud cry of triumph and chasing after her. He would have quite a time catching up and keeping abreast of her.

Torquil sighed resignedly in the new spring air as he heaved his tired, old autumn bones after them.

Alex and Cameron left the wilderness and rode down from the Highlands to rejoin life in the busy central lowlands of Scotland.

It was the spring of 1762 and before them lay a world that would change more rapidly in their lifetime than ever before in the history of man. Already the industrial revolution labored inexorably toward the births that would change the face of the earth.

Cameron's search for who and what she was would be reflected all around; the Scottish would lay down their swords and enlightenment would flower from the pens of Burns, Fergusson, Hume, MacDonald, and a host of others as they fought for their heritage against English assimilation. The New World would challenge the old, blossoming into the American Revolution; and the French would rise and storm, demanding equality, dignity, and freedom.